DESCENT: JOURNEY

Terrinoth: an ancient realm o

and faded legacies, of magic and monsters, heroes,
and tyrants. Its cities were ruined and their secrets
lost as terrifying dragons, undead armies, and demon-
possessed hordes ravaged the land. Over centuries, the
realm slipped into gloom…

Now, the world is reawakening – the Baronies of
Daqan rebuild their domains, wizards master lapsed
arts, and champions test their mettle. Banding together
to explore the dangerous caves, ancient ruins, dark
dungeons, and cursed forests of Terrinoth, they
unearth priceless treasures and terrible foes.

Yet time is running out, for in the shadows a
malevolent force has grown, preparing to spread evil
across the world. Now, when the land needs them
most, is the moment for its heroes to rise.

BY THE SAME AUTHOR

WARHAMMER: GOTREK & FELIX
City of the Damned
Kinslayer
Slayer
Slayer of the End Times

THE HORUS HERESY PRIMARCHS
Ferrus Manus: The Gorgon of Medusa
Lion El'Jonson: Lord of the First

WARHAMMER 40,000
Echoes of the Long War
The Last Son of Dorn
The Eye of Medusa
The Voice of Mars

WARHAMMER AGE OF SIGMAR
Realmslayer
Hamilcar: Champion of the Gods
The Court of the Blind King

DESCENT
JOURNEYS IN THE DARK™

The SHIELD
of DAQAN

DAVID GUYMER

ACONYTE

First published by Aconyte Books in 2021

ISBN 978 1 83908 029 6

Ebook ISBN 978 1 83908 030 2

Cover art by Jeff Chen.

Map by Francesca Baerald.

Distributed in North America by Simon & Schuster Inc, New York, USA

Printed in the United States of America

9 8 7 6 5 4 3 2 1

ACONYTE BOOKS

An imprint of Asmodee Entertainment Ltd

Mercury House, Shipstones Business Centre

North Gate, Nottingham NG7 7FN, UK

aconytebooks.com // twitter.com/aconytebooks

PART
ONE

CHAPTER ONE
Trenloe the Strong
The Crimson Downs, South East Kell

Steel glinted on the hills. Trenloe shaded his eyes. The sun struck at them, low and red from across the winding snake of the Lothan River to the east. Trenloe and his mercenaries, the Companions, had spent years building his name across the southern baronies but this was his first experience of Terrinoth's harder north-eastern edge. It was beautiful and humbling in equal measure.

"Call me blind, but those don't look like Fredric's men."

"There are many things I might call you, were I of the mind, but not blind." Dremmin squinted. The dwarf's eyes were exceptionally keen at any time of day, but particularly in the small hours when a human might find theirs tricked by the dawn light. "They're fewer in number than a Daqan patrol," she said. "Even if we've crossed accidentally into Frest, which our guide assures us we've not, they're flying no colors that I can see from here."

"How many in all?"

"A score or less. All on horseback."

"Fewer than us then."

"There'll be more tucked away in the fell, don't you worry about that."

The Companions had crossed into the barony of Kell less than a week ago, hired by an agent of the Lady of Hernfar to reinforce the garrison at Nordgard Castle, but they had been so long on the road from their base in Artrast that summer had turned into autumn and Trenloe's breath misted on the air. They were good warriors, motivated by right as much as by gold, but sixty tried and footsore mercenaries who had not yet been paid were not much of an army. At least not one he would want to lead into battle.

"*Should* we be worried?"

The dwarf's taba leaf-stained lips parted for a grin made up of cracked and yellowing teeth. "The Greyfox may call herself the Bandit Queen of Kell, but her army is made up of hungry peasants, farmers and a handful of deserters.'

South of Dhernas, he would have been lucky to find anyone, outside Trenloe's specific circles, who had even heard of the Greyfox. Cross into Kell however and there was so much said about her it was impossible to know what, if any of it, was true.

It was said that she could command the trees of the Whispering Forest and shape the hills of the Downs to her will, and that this explained why the armies of Kell had never managed to track her down. She was one of the Fae, some said, and the old spirits protected their own. It was said that she could turn gold and silver into bread, that she could alter her shape and communed with the beasts of the field and the wilderness to plot the overthrow of humanity in Kell. Some claimed without a shred of proof that she was the great-great granddaughter of the long dead and near-mythical founder of modern Terrinoth, King Daqan, while in the next valley over they would swear that she was an agent of the Uthuk Y'llan from the east, sent into Kell to destroy them all.

But on the questions that were of most interest to Trenloe the rumors had surprisingly little to say.

Who *was* the Greyfox actually? What did she look like? What did she want? What was her real name?

Would she surrender the Downs, or would she force Trenloe to fight her for it?

"They say the Greyfox can take animal shape and creep into their camps at night."

Dremmin chuckled. "I'll bet they do."

Trenloe watched as the glimmer on the hillside disappeared into one of the innumerable creases in the heath. The hills were low and rounded, like the waves on the Kingless Coast, swathed in heathers, hair grass and coarse bracken. The locals called it the Crimson Downs. Presumably for the color.

He thought it more a deep purple than a red, but Dremmin would often chide him for seeing the world as better than others seemed to see it. "I wasn't expecting to see more bandits this far east. We must be practically in the Borderlands by now. I thought we had less than a day's ride ahead of us."

"That's what the townsfolk told me back at Gwellan."

"They must have been mistaken. Or you must have been drunk."

"Don't get sour with me, lad. This country's as foreign to me as it is to you."

Trenloe shook his head. "Just thinking aloud."

He had known Dremmin for years. He had served under her in the Trastan army for a year before the dwarf had persuaded him to strike out with her on their own. But he didn't really *know* her. He didn't know what she had been doing that far south of Thelgrim. He could only guess at her age. But then who but a dwarf could say they really knew a dwarf? And perhaps not even then. All Trenloe could say for sure about her was what he could see. Her face was craggy, with a proud cliff of brow under a winged helmet of boiled leather. She wore a long hauberk of leather scales with steel plates sewn in that stretched down past her knees. As bookkeeper and quartermaster of the Companions of Trenloe (or *sergeant of the gold* as she preferred her title to be) she was indisputably very wealthy, and could have afforded a harness of Forge-made steel if she had wanted it. Perhaps even a suit of runebound plate such as the greatest knights and the lords of the baronies might be fortunate enough to possess. Trenloe had once asked her why she didn't, to which the dwarf had grunted that she was "saving." For what she refused to say, and Trenloe suspected he would never know.

Mounted on her shaggy highland pony, the dwarf tracked her gaze across the Crimson Downs.

"Nothing like home, is it?"

"Nothing like home," Trenloe agreed.

"I hate it when you do that, you know."

"Do what?"

"Repeat back what I've just said as though it makes you sound wise."

Trenloe grinned and leant closer, allowing his words to drawl. "Make myself sound wise?"

"I never know if you're pulling my leg or if you're actually as dumb as you look."

Trenloe's harness of half plate shook with his laughter.

For a while longer they sat in silence, watching the Downs for signs of movement. "This isn't good land for farming," Trenloe said, in reply to the dwarf's earlier observation. "The growing season's too short. The nights are too long and too cold." He nodded towards the glittering line of the river. "Not to mention the threat of having your crop burned by Uthuk raiders from the Borderlands."

"A bit different to looking across your border into Lorimor or the Aymhelin, isn't it?"

"Land like this is for grazing."

"I forget you were a farmer before we met."

"Son of a farmer."

"Same thing. It's hard to imagine Trenloe the Strong milking a goat."

Trenloe didn't reply.

He wasn't sure what he was meant to say to that.

"Come on," he said, after he had thought about it a bit more. "If the Greyfox is out there then it looks as though she's content to stay there for now. We need to move. Particularly if we're further from Hernfar than you thought."

"Than I was *told*."

Trenloe wheeled his horse around.

He'd seen the big warhorses of the baronial knights at work, huge animals that could carry a grown man in full armor and lived for battle. He'd even had the opportunity to buy one once, but he loved the middle-aged Trastan farmhorse he still rode and Rusticar, as he was called, generally gave every indication of returning the feeling. He may have been slow, but he was the only animal Trenloe had ever come across big enough to carry *him*.

The Companions of Trenloe were in the midst of breaking camp. Accustomed as they were to the easier climes of the southern baronies, they did so rather slowly. Corporal Bethan walked the camp in full battle harness and cloak, playing "The Rise of the Free" on her zither and liberally administering kicks to those still in their bedrolls. Quicker about themselves were the wagons full of refugees they had managed to pick up on leaving Gwellan. The town was of a size that suggested it had once been a trade destination in its own right, but the deprivation there now had been almost physically painful to witness. Everyone said it was the last settlement before Hernfar, and the Companions had stopped there for provisions. Trenloe had paid treble what the goods were worth, but still felt guilty about taking what little they had.

The least he could do was offer escort to any who wanted to make the journey with them to the castle at Hernfar.

And it seemed a great many of them did.

The Darklands were apparently less threatening than the Greyfox, and Nordgard Castle more appealing than the grim reputation that the island had in Trast.

The caravan wound around a bend in what Bethan would sometimes jokingly describe as "the Road." A few leather-clad Companion horsemen trotted alongside, complaining about the small hour, the food and the cold weather.

"The townsfolk look nervous," said Trenloe.

"Comes from being nervous folk," Dremmin countered, reaching into her pack for a pipe.

"They know this land better than we do. If they're nervous then maybe there's a reason for us to be."

"That sounds suspiciously like one of your old father's sayings."

Trenloe nodded. "'Listen to those as know,' he says."

"Aye," Dremmin sniffed. "I thought so."

Trenloe watched as the line of wagons inched their way along the road.

"We'll not make it to Hernfar until next year at this rate," said Dremmin.

Trenloe spurred Rusticar into a walk, which was close to his fullest gait. "Let's see what the hold-up is."

"Aye,' said Dremmin, sucking aggressively on her pipe and goading her pony to follow. "Let's."

CHAPTER TWO
Kurt
North of Gwellan, South East Kell

Kurt ran up the hill. Dry bracken crunched under the thin soles of his boots. Cotton grass puffed into seed off the shins of his trousers. His slice of the Crimson Downs was a parcel of jumbled heathland and bare rock running from the borders of the Whispering Forest to the foot of the two hills, Old Gray and the Ram, and the gap between them. His modest steading stood in the cleft as far from the Forest as could be. The hunched back of Old Gray sheltered it against storms from the east. A freshwater trickle from somewhere encircled it on three sides and turned a small wheel. Kurt's feelings towards the place were complicated. He loved it because it held onto the memories that Kurt refused to. But for its meanness, its cold, its thin scrag of chalky topsoil, for its short days and its deep lonely nights he hated it utterly. It cost him more in taxes and other dues to his lord than it could earn him with wool and cheeses. He had eaten better in the army. Even at the end.

At the hill's crest, he slowed.

He crouched on one knee amongst the short grass, nocked an arrow to his flatbow. The sun was rising slowly over the row of hills to the east, scratching the lowland downs with shadow. Whoops and screams carried eagerly on the fierce, cold wind. Plumes of smoke dotted the vista. The thunder of hoofbeats trembled through the ground under his knee.

The bandits were coming out of the Whispering Forest. The realization appalled him. Only the Greyfox could have been so bold as to tame those haunted bowers, or to turn those who followed her wild enough to be accepted by the spirits of the old wood.

A group of riders was descending the slope of the neighboring hillock. Kurt's training took over, pushing the small niggle of fear deep into his chest. He breathed himself wide, drawing the bowstring back, past the tooth he had broken in a fight when he was young, past his ear and taut.

He sighted along the length of the shaft.

Kurt let out his breath and loosed.

The arrow leapt from the string with a _twang_, and he grunted in satisfaction as it thumped into the rider's shoulder. The brigand pitched from his horse with a wail and fell into the bracken. Kurt nocked another, drew, and loosed. That was how they taught it in the army. It was all about the rhythm. It stopped you from thinking too much about the fact you were killing a man. The arrow punched through thick leather plates and into a second horseman's belly. The bandit fell from his saddle with a cry, but one foot became caught in the stirrup and his horse dragged him on down the sward, before veering back towards the forest.

"Go tell your friends!" Kurt yelled after him. "This is Kurt Stavener's land and the Greyfox can't have it."

The rest of the horsemen swerved and broke. Kurt allowed himself a relieved breath, but kept his eye on them as they disappeared into the heath, running in the direction of Larion's Steading. He let them go gladly. Larion could spend her own arrows. He turned back. The bandit with the shoulder wound was still writhing in the bushes.

"Boxer. Whisper."

At his command the two dogs tore off down the hill.

They were shepherd dogs, trained to chase rather than kill. But of course, the brigand wasn't to know that. Kurt smiled to himself as the wounded man picked himself up and hobble-ran screaming back into the heath.

He nocked another arrow.

At the sound of a horse charging up the hill behind him, he swung his aim around, only to then ease back on the string and turn the arrowhead towards the ground.

His youngest son, Elben, fifteen years old that last summer, struggled to rein in the black, sixteen hands-tall charger that Kurt had "borrowed" from his former garrison at Bastion Tarn. The boy looked ridiculously tiny in the high saddle, like a confused gnome still dressed in his nightclothes.

"Get down from there," said Kurt; love, fear, and old army habits lowering his voice to an unexpected snarl. "That horse is too big for you."

Elben looked hurt. "But you asked me to bring him."

"I asked you to *bring* him. I didn't tell you to *ride* him. Get down."

The boy was about to argue, but just then Boxer and Whisper came bounding back from the heath. They yapped excitedly, sitting a few feet away from Kurt and beating the ground with their tails. Boxer licked his lips and barked.

Elben dismounted.

Kurt scratched Boxer's ears, praised Whisper for being good and quiet, then took the reins from his son and climbed with some difficulty up onto the great horse's back. He swayed a moment while he found his balance. He was a competent rider rather than a happy one, but his land was too hilly and broken for him to cover it on foot.

"I could come with you," said Elben, and gestured towards his father's flatbow. "I can shoot."

Allowing himself this one moment of appeasement, Kurt leant down and handed the boy his bow. Like the horse, it looked ludicrously overlarge in his hands, but he glowed. Kurt smiled briefly, because there was more pain there than pleasure.

He wished there was some other skill he could share with his sons.

Anything but this.

"Go back now," he said, fighting to get the combative animal to turn. "Take the dogs and help your older brother defend the house. There shouldn't be too many coming this way now. I'll be back soon. *Yah!*" With that, he kicked the horse into a thunderous canter that carried him over the top of the hill and down.

The sun sank from view behind the rise, the stooped shadow of Old Gray falling across his eyes. He looked around, the tufts of heather still damp in their late little pool of twilight. With relief, he spied a couple of grizzled sheep cropping at a bit of sedge sprouting from a cleft in the side of a boulder without a care in the world. Somehow getting his great horse to walk, he chivvied the stupid animals on ahead of him.

Kurt owned forty head, scattered over his bit of land, and their milk, wool and meat were all he had. There was normally little danger to them there except for the forest itself, and no one who had grown up in its shadow would deny the fey of the wood an animal or two from their flocks. Raiders from the Ru seldom drove this far west from the Lothan, and the bandits had never been so bold as to strike out of the forest and threaten his flock.

Until now.

Atop the next rise he spotted another dozen, strung along

the outcropping in search of grass. Leading the reluctant horse in slow circles of the hilltop, he herded them up with the others. With just over a quarter of his flock accounted for, he scanned the low hills and surrounding moorland for stragglers.

A clash of what sounded like steel sounded from the direction of his home. Followed by a scream. His heart gripped tight inside his chest and he twisted in the saddle towards the sound. Even then, he hesitated.

Forced to choose between aiding his sons or eating this winter he found he did not know what to do.

Another shout rang from the other side of the hill.

He shook his head, cursing what poverty and hunger had done to his mind, and turned his horse homeward, kicking it in the ribs to which it responded with an answering neigh that might have been to snort "*finally*" and leapt hard into a gallop.

Circling the rises and keeping to the lower dells, Kurt thundered by a roundabout route to the cleft where Old Gray and the Ram stood on one another's toes. Where Kurt and Katrin Stavener had once built their home. He charged headlong into the yard, exactly as he would have been taught *not* to ride into an unscouted enemy position had he served Baron Fredric as a cavalryman rather than a yeoman archer. Fortunately his mount was a warhorse, and thoroughly bored of chasing sheep over the downs.

He knew exactly what to do.

Iron shoes clattering on the rocky ground, he went straight into the brigands where they were thickest and scattered them. He knocked one aside on its barrel chest, trampled another under its hooves. The animal's nostrils flared as Kurt reined it back. It stamped impatiently, eager to run down broken men. He drew his sword. It was a battered, bent and thoroughly unspectacular two feet of browned steel. He dismounted quickly. His old shield,

wood with a steel rim, hung from a hook on his horse's saddle. He
took it down and slid his left wrist through the straps.

"Off with you," he barked at the horse. The horse snorted and
stamped and went nowhere. "You've been too long around my
boys. On your own head be it then."

He advanced on the house.

Eight or nine brigands had broken off and were running,
panicked by the initial charge, falsely assuming that because no
solitary rider would be so stupid as to single-handedly charge
so many on that kind of ground, that they must have run into
a cavalry unit dispatched from some non-existent garrison at
Gwellan. Even with that stroke of good fortune, Kurt could see six
more still trying to break in the front door. Another was climbing,
using the water wheel and the house front to reach the sloped
roof where Elben sat loosing arrows. Not from Kurt's big flatbow,
thank Kellos and his golden fire, but the short hobby bow that
Kurt had reluctantly made for him to practice.

Half of the six at the door turned.

One against three were not odds that Kurt favored.

He went in quick, denying them the time to figure out amongst
themselves how best to use their advantage, anchoring his left side
to the stream. One of Elben's arrows sprouted from the neck of
the middle fighter and he crumpled. The distraction was enough
for Kurt to drive his sword into the belly of a second. *Twist and
pull.* The army had drilled the mantra into him so hard that he
could hear his old drillmaster screaming it when he attacked his
sausages at breakfast. He twisted his sword and he pulled. The
third swung his axe, high and wide and strong. Kurt beat the
blow aside on his shield and shouldered the brigand two steps
back. The fighter backed off a few more of his own, suddenly far
less keen than he had been two seconds and two friends earlier.
Kurt hoped he might be sensible and run, but from the corner of

his eye he saw the other three giving up on the door and turning around to see what was going on.

He liked one against four even less.

He was backpedaling quickly towards his horse, shield up, when the front door burst wide and Sarb leapt out.

A bigger youth than Elben was going to be when the younger boy hit nineteen, he probably would have been bulkier than Kurt by now if there had been more food on his plate over the last few years. As it was he had grown sinewy and tall, more alike to his father in appearance and in character than either of them would have preferred, right the way to the prematurely receding fringe. He was carrying a Kellar infantry spear, six and a half feet long, with a wide shaft and a heavy enough blade to put down a Charg'r demon hound if you caught it right, and he drove it into the nearest brigand's back.

Twist and pull, Kurt instinctively thought.

But of course, Sarb hadn't served as Kurt had. There was no real army on the Downs any more and even if there had been, Kurt would have tied the boy down before letting him go. He just pulled, and the long blade became stuck.

Just then, Boxer and Whisper came bounding through the open door, falling on a second man before he could take advantage and bearing him between them to the ground. Elben then put an arrow into the leather pauldron of the third and at that point the last two men standing and the one halfway up the wall had seen more than enough. They ran. The axeman that Kurt had been facing off climbed up onto a horse and galloped for the hills.

Kurt felt a strong urge to send him on his way with some sharp words ringing in his ears, but he was afraid that if he used his breath for that he might very well faint. He was too old for hand-to-hand. Ten years too old if it was a day. He dropped his sword. His shield would have gone too had it been strapped any less snugly to his hanging wrist.

"Are you two… both… all right?"

Elben leant forward from his perch above the eaves and peered down at the man he had shot through the neck. The color fell from his face. It cut Kurt more deeply than any poison-tipped Uthuk arrow ever had that his sons had needed to see this.

"Y- Yes," the boy managed.

Sarb didn't answer. Instead, he wrenched his spear from the dead bandit's back and hurried with it down the front path, splashing across the narrow stream after the escaping brigands.

"Quickly, Father," he said. "Get the horse. If we hurry, we can catch them."

"And do what?"

Sarb rounded on him, foot stamping in the water in frustration. His knuckles whitened around his spear. "I don't know. *Punish* them."

"Your blood's up," said Kurt quietly, calmly, the same voice he might use to talk Boxer or Whisper out of throwing themselves into something stupid when they were agitated. But inside, he railed just as hotly that both of his sons had been driven to become killers before they had been able to finish being boys. "You feel as though you could take on the Greyfox herself right now. Am I right? Well believe me, it's not a feeling that'll last when you've one of her arrows stuck in you." He glanced pointedly around him, the yard strewn with bodies. Boxer barked excitedly. "It only takes one."

"But –"

"No *buts*. Wash yourself off out here and then get back in the house."

"What about Aunt Larion's steading?" Elben called down weakly from the rooftop.

Sarb was nodding. "Who do you think looked after this place when you weren't here?"

Kurt grimaced. Sarb always knew how to make his words hurt. "Larion will have to look after herself this time."

"But Father–" Elben began, before Kurt silenced him with a tired glare.

"What about the animals?" said Sarb, his voice hard and his face cold. "Are you just going to leave them out there for the Greyfox?"

Kurt said nothing.

There were too many. It would take an army or a hero to fend off the bandit queen's attack, and Kurt certainly wasn't a hero. There was nothing for an old soldier to do but hold fast, sit it out and see what the damage was come morning.

"And if she's taken everything?" said Sarb.

Kurt turned to him and scowled. "*Inside* I said."

CHAPTER THREE
Trenloe the Strong
The Crimson Downs, South East Kell

Rusticar clumped heavily along the stony verge, bypassing the stalled line of wagons that filled the old road. At the head of the line, Trenloe reined in. The horse snorted, pawing at the scraggy bushes that grew thick along the roadside and raising his head in a loose jangle of tack as if that half minute of effort warranted a treat. Trenloe pushed his questing nose away, giving the amiable old beast a pat.

One of the refugee wagons from Gwellan had lost a wheel and was sitting on its axle in the middle of the road. A handful of vehicles had pulled up ahead of it, their drivers leaning out to peer anxiously back. A great many more were halted behind. A number of locals in prickly woolen homespun had spilled out of their vehicles to help or to harangue, a palpable sense of urgency and fear making even the most casually intended word bite. A man and a woman were already stumbling down the side of the fell to collect the lost wheel.

"Bring up horses," called a skeletally thin woman, her face smothered in the flaps of a woolen hat. "Haul 'em off the road and let the rest of us through."

"No," argued another. "We need to keep together."

"Aye, this is the work of the Greyfox."

"She's a true sorceress, they say. Bremen's wagon was just fine yesterday."

"This lot will be the death of us," said Dremmin, her rugged pony nosing up behind Rusticar. "If that wagon was fine at any time in the last hundred years then I'm Bran and Ordan's heir. We'll lose more of them before we get to Hernfar Isle, mark you." She chewed pointedly on the stem of her pipe. "If we ever get there."

"Were we supposed to just leave Gwellan without them?"

Dremmin took the pipe from her mouth. "Do you want me to answer that?"

With a smile, Trenloe dismounted.

As partners he and Dremmin could not have been more different, but Trenloe had not had the acumen to build the Companions up from one unlikely pairing into the force for good they had become. Money sat uneasily in his pockets, and had a tendency to slip all too readily through his fingers where he saw others with greater need. A sellsword of his reputation could always earn more. Unfortunately. In return, he kept Dremmin honest.

At least, he liked to believe that he did as well at it as anybody could.

The small crowd filling the road drew out of his way. Agitated as they were, Trenloe was still the biggest thing on the road after the horses.

"Trenloe!" an old woman in a quilted gray dress and a shawl called out from the rear of the stricken wagon. She raised her hand and waved to him. "Trenloe!"

Trenloe did not know what, exactly, the woman had been back in Gwellan, but here on the road she had become a sort of unappointed spokeswoman for the mercenaries' new civilian contingent. Dremmin thought her an officious, know-it-all busybody, and, so far as Trenloe could gather, the old woman seemed to dislike Dremmin along largely similar lines. They were both fighting for the wellbeing of their own, and for some reason occasionally needed Trenloe to point out that what benefitted one of them more often than not benefitted them both.

He, for one, felt immediately better for seeing her on hand.

"Maeve is here," he said.

"Oh good," said Dremmin, sourly. "Maeve is here."

"Come on," said Trenloe. "Let's see what we can do to help."

Dremmin dismounted with a heavy thump and they both walked towards the wagon.

"We have to get this wagon fixed and moving," said Maeve, looking over the busted axle with pursed lips and a sour eye. "Or failing that get it off the road and quick. We daren't linger too long on the open road with the Greyfox about. I saw her pack prowling the hills over there."

"Good eyes for an old human," said Dremmin.

Trenloe produced a strained smile, not wanting to add fuel to another bickering match between the pair.

Maeve scowled at them both. "Women with poorer senses don't get to grow old. Not this near the eastern border to the Ru."

"I don't think you're in any immediate danger," said Trenloe, with a glance at Dremmin who nodded her agreement. "Not while we're here."

"I don't know... I worry the sight of so many well-armed warriors in her country will only attract the Greyfox's interest. The sooner we're across the ford at Hernfar Isle the better. Then, maybe, we'll feel safe."

"How far are we from Nordgard castle?"

"No more'n a day or two."

Trenloe turned to Dremmin, eyebrows climbing towards his bald head. "We really are that close. When we saw the riders on the hill I thought someone had to be mistaken."

Maeve shook her head sadly. "The Greyfox commands more men than the baron these days."

"Impossible, surely! Fredric's armies are famous in the south. There are none better armed but the knights of Archault they say, and none larger in all of Terrinoth."

"Might've been true. Once. But we've seen some hard years in case you've not noticed. Sickness in the flocks and famine. Some call it sorcery, sent over the river from the Darklands. Others blame it on the Greyfox. I don't know, but now we have her banditry as well. The baron released most of his soldiers to work their own lands, supposedly to raise crops that are needed in the city and to better protect the countryside from outlaws, but..." She shrugged.

"A mistake," Dremmin grunted.

Maeve frowned, agreeing, but not wanting to give the dwarf the satisfaction of hearing her say it.

Trenloe offered no opinion.

He left the management of the Companions to Dremmin and he knew even less about running a country. Baron Fredric was a respected figure in Artrast and surely knew the needs of this country best.

"Dame Ragthorn of Hernfar wouldn't have sent agents as far afield as Trast looking for mercenaries if she had every sword-hand she needed," said Dremmin. "Kell's loss is our gain, though it irks me that we seem to be cheaper to hire than the barony's own soldiers." She grinned at Trenloe. "We should be charging more."

"Something you can argue over later," said Maeve, nodding pointedly towards the listed wagon. "Once you get there."

"Don't *tempt* us into riding on around and leaving you here," said Dremmin.

"That's enough," said Trenloe, finally running out of patience. "We aren't leaving anyone."

As he spoke, the pair who had gone to fetch the lost wheel were returning with it. Trenloe was heartened to note that one of the Companions had run down to help them drag it back to the road and into place. A half dozen of Gwellan's strongest men ranked up along the wagon's side, grunting and cursing to heave the thing a half inch off the ground. Trenloe watched them with a frown. There was not a single man or woman amongst the Gwellan folk who looked properly nourished, or fit for physical work. Spent already, they let the wagon drop back onto its axle. A few amongst them started shouting for chisels and hammers to start pulling the wagon apart, others for more hands to start throwing out the wagon's cargo. "No," argued the gaunt woman from before. "Get some horses up there and pull from the other side." The wagon's driver, a thin, frantic man named Bremen, argued with all of them.

Dremmin sighed. "We're going to be here until dinner."

Trenloe gave her a companionable pat on the top of the head, which made the dwarf scowl but which, as usual, stopped her from complaining for a while. "You worry about dinner. I'll handle this."

Leaving Dremmin and a confused-looking Maeve, Trenloe walked a slow circle around the hobbled wagon. He looked for where the ground it lay upon was soft and where it was hard, where it was uneven and where it was flat. Satisfied with his survey, he joined the group of men on its broken side. Broader of back than any two of them together he dislodged three, leaving just one man to either side, both of whom he then dismissed with a smile and a nod.

He squatted down, the steel hinges of his armor grinding, and slid his fingers under the wagon's bed.

"Ready?" he called over his shoulder to the three with the wheel.

The two locals nodded uncertainly.

The Companion behind them grinned. She knew what was coming.

"You can't be serious," Maeve called. "That wagon weighs as much as my house."

"They don't call him Trenloe the Strong for his wit or his looks," said Dremmin. "Now shut up and let him lift."

Trenloe flexed. His shoulders tightened, bulging until his harness creaked. His biceps swelled to the size of roc alerion eggs. And then he lifted, taking the weight across his shoulders with a grunt of effort. The axle came slightly off the road.

Breathing out, he let it back down.

The axle dug into the dirt, and Trenloe backed off from it, rolling the strain from his shoulders and massaging his neck.

By now, Trenloe had drawn a considerable crowd and his first attempt drew a chorus of good-natured "ooooohs" from the watching Companions.

"We don't have time for your circus," said Maeve.

Trenloe wiped his hands on his armor and then sank back to his haunches, slid his hands back under the wagon, and set himself again. He grinned back over his shoulder. "Ready?"

"Ready, captain," said the Companion holding the wheel.

Trenloe let a long breath out.

Took another long breath in.

With a sudden roar he threw himself against the wagon's side and lifted. The muscles of his upper body swelled taut. The hinges of his half-plate squealed. The crowd of onlookers fell suddenly silent as he raised himself up off his haunches, transferring the enormous weight of the wagon from his arms to his thighs.

"Wheel!" he growled through clenched teeth. "Now!"

The woman and the two men ran in, slotting the wheel over the exposed axle and fixing it into place. Then they hurried back, and with a final grunt and a tremor of effort Trenloe lowered the wagon gently to the ground. The people erupted with cheers as the wagon sat neatly across its four wheels, the Companions soon leading them in chants of "Tren-*loe*, Tren-*loe*."

Trenloe beat his fist against his breastplate and whooped, basking in their adoration.

Maeve gawped.

"You never knew your mother, did you?" said Dremmin.

"She left my father when I was small," Trenloe panted. It was a deep hurt, that one, but through time and familiarity it had become an ache that he could almost ignore. "Why?"

Dremmin shrugged. "Just wondering if there might be a bit of giant blood in you."

Trenloe laughed and waved the caravan onward. As they started to roll past, he turned another look towards the surrounding hills. He thought he saw something there. A wink of iron. Before a cloud smothered the sun and whatever it had been disappeared back into the heath.

He raised a hand and threw whatever it might have been a wave.

He hoped the Greyfox had been watching that.

CHAPTER FOUR
Fredric
Castle Kellar, North Kell

From the keep it was possible to imagine that there was nothing amiss.

The tangle of workshops, houses and inns that made up the sprawling garrison town was still bustling, the stink of cooking fat and manure as ripe as it ever was. The birds still sang from about the turrets and spires. The cold wind off the Dunwarr still roared, frightening the purple and gold banners into flapping dances. It was that east wind, or so the proverb went, that kept the land hard and its people cold.

To the south, the Whispering Forest was an ocean of sibilant greenery that stretched from horizon to horizon, to the borders of Dhernas, Pelgate, and Frest. Away to the east, no more than a twinkling thread from Kellar's highest towers, the Lothan River sparkled. The Dunwarr Mountains, beyond it, were a hazy wall capped with snow, the dividing barrier between barbarism and civility.

To the north and west were the Howling Giant Hills, frigid barrens where isolated villages worshipped Nordros, God of Cold and Death and King of Winter, and did not yet know that the First Darkness had receded. Kellar's mighty foundations had been hacked out of the range's southern foothills in millennia long past. The last confederation of northern chiefs to defy Arcus Penacor and the unification of the west had done so from its sculpted earthworks and palisade walls.

There was more of the Charg'r than Talindon blood in the men of the far north and east. According to the great history, the *Legendum Magicaria*, the nomads of the Charg'r were the first of peoples and had settled widely across Kell, crossing the ford at Hernfar, before the coming of more civilized folk from the west.

At this, however, true Kellar would scoff and took no offense.

They had been the first to feel the Locust Swarm, the Dragon Horde, and the march of the Undying One. And they had weathered them all.

The barony was too unpopulous and its inhabitants too poor to have chartered a Free City of its own, and so Kellar suffered no rival for its wealth or talent. Its walls had been extended many times. They had been thickened. They had been raised. The strength had been stiffened with massively castellated towers.

From there, it was possible to imagine that there was nothing amiss at all.

"Could we please take this council indoors." Beren Salter, the lady-chamberlain, hugged herself and shivered. "We are not all such hot-blooded young men."

The other two members of Fredric's council, neither one of them exactly a younger man, chuckled wryly. Grandmarshal Trevin Highgarde, Captain of the Knights of the Yeron and Warden of Kellar, was a big man with a proud moustache, glitteringly clad in golden armor and a snapping cloak. General Urban Brant, Lord-Commander of the Armies of Kell, was bent a little lower and wore his hair a little grayer. Being common born, he had no right to heraldry of his own or the title that Fredric felt his talents warranted, and was garbed considerably more appropriately in a thickly quilted coat with golden epaulets sewn into the sleeves.

"It is important for me to be seen," said Fredric, but not without sympathy for his oldest counsellor. He was wearing an enameled breastplate with floral patterns etched in gold and silver. Beneath it was an arming doublet of purple quilt and gold stitching that offered excellent padding and protection from an attack, but not so much from the cold. Prominent at his throat was a golden buckle bearing the heraldic Owl of Kell, pinning in place a long red cloak that bit and snapped at the fell wind from the east. He looked out across the battlements, onto the town. "The people need to see that I see them, that I understand what is happening in my barony and that I suffer it with them."

It had become his custom to take counsel on the walls so dressed. Of late, his servants would become alarmed if he attended breakfast in anything less than full plate and helm.

He was not sure if seeing their baron in such raiment, as though war were not merely on their horizon but actually on their doorstep, was a source of encouragement or woe for his people. But the armor, and the weapons he bore with it, had belonged to his father, and his grandfather, and his great-grandfather, and Fredric felt more alike to those great men simply by wearing them.

He wished that there was more of Reginal or Roland Dragonslayer in him. Then, perhaps, the famine that had blighted Kell might have been prevented, or at least a solution found. And the Greyfox, the so-called Bandit Queen, and those others like her in the north, would never have been allowed to gain such sway. His forefathers would have done something. If only he knew what, then Frederic would have gladly done the same. Even if it meant emulating his most cherished ancestor and hero, Roland,

and taking the family harness to his grave. All his interventions seemed to have accomplished so far was to make things worse.

"And what *is* happening in your barony?" asked Urban. "Because if his lordship does know, then he is better informed than I. I hear precious little any more from anywhere further than a day's ride from the gates of Kellar. Even the High Road to Dhernas brings little news. Banditry, I am told, though that is far from my greatest fear while the watchtowers sit empty to the east."

"This is an old argument, Urban." The decision to reduce the size of the army and abandon a number of the smaller border forts had been a hard one. Fredric wished he could say he was certain it was the right one, but he found it difficult to be certain of much these days. The threat of mass starvation had moved him to release as many soldiers as he could to their fields, only for the diminished army to embolden the likes of the Greyfox. What unintended consequence could he expect next? "What would you have me do?"

"Rebuild your army. Let me ride from here tonight with four captains, a hundred men apiece, and an order to conscript every man and woman between the ages of twelve and fifty. We'll take it to the four corners of your barony and raise an army that will clear the roads and hound the outlaws from their holes and drive every last one of them into the Whispering Forest." His rough-shaven face took on a sneer. "Let the dragon-kin and the fae deal with them as they always have."

Trevin peered over the high rim of his shining gorget. His lips were hidden, but his eyes smirked.

"Something funny, Highgarde?" asked Urban.

"Yes," said the grandmarshal.

Urban scowled.

"Enough," Frederic sighed.

It was enough that his people were burning and pillaging one another's homesteads without the lord-commander of his armies and oathsworn protector sniping at one another. Both men were frustrated, Fredric knew, but more than that they simply did not like one another. There was no reason for it as far as Fredric was aware. Sometimes men just didn't. It probably did not help that that Trevin could irritate a placid mule with a one-word witticism or a raised eyebrow.

Urban turned to Fredric. "Do you smell that, my lord?"

Fredric shook his head. "Smell what?"

"You can't see it from here, but..." The soldier sniffed. "Smoke. It lingers in the air, even here."

"You're imagining things," said Salter.

"Am I?" said Urban, and turned back to Fredric. "Am I? It's more than just mountain ice on the wind from the east, these days. When did either of you last take a horse east of Orrush Khatak? Or take the Forest Road to the Crimson Downs and the ford at Hernfar? Your barony burns." He gestured angrily over the walls. "Do you think it is enough for them to know that you stand here watching it?"

"You have said enough." Trevin stepped forward. His gargantuan suit of full plate was bedecked in the chivalric wings and enameled feathers of his order. The two pages that shadowed him always with the wing-hilted greatsword, *Unkindness*, dropped to their knees and presented the blade in readiness should its master be called on to duel. "You push too far."

Fredric raised his hand and turned away from them both.

It did not help to be reminded that Urban wanted only to best serve Kell, as Fredric did, or even that he was almost certainly right on every count and Fredric wrong. Fredric was not a child. He could bow to good counsel where it was offered and admit where he had strayed. But the lord-commander was the master of

Kell's armies. That was his sole concern. Fredric had to balance so many and it was exhausting to body, spirit, and mind. There were no easy answers to be had. If there were, then all would have been able to agree to them, and they would not still be arguing about it.

"It is all right, Trevin. I can handle the harsh words of my general. Let us say I were to raise this grand army you ask me for, general, and it were to achieve everything you claim it would, what then? When the crops continue to fail and the livestock to perish, what then? Will my soldiers starve quietly in their garrisons with the weapons and training we have given them? No. They would turn brigand themselves and be right to, because I would have failed them, and you will find that you have vanquished one foe in order to create and arm a greater one. And what will we do then, general? This is not Greyhaven or Nerekhall. We cannot just make new armies until we run out of foes."

Urban made a low growl-sound. "Forgive me, Baron, if I was too bold. I speak only as I see it. I meant no offence."

"Credit me at least with thicker skin than that."

Fredric drew away from the battlement, wincing at a sudden spasm in his lower back. He arched and crunched his spine.

"My lord is getting old," said Trevin.

Fredric shot him a look. It bounced off the knight's smile like arrows off rocks.

"You don't know what old is," Salter muttered.

Fredric laughed, surprised by how good it felt. He promised himself that he would find the time to do it more often. "Too many hours spent over faded maps and penning letters to erstwhile allies that are destined to be ignored. That is all." He glanced over his shoulder, staring at a distant horizon from high walls. "Walk with me a while. The stroll will do me good. My father always preached the virtues of a long walk when it came to solving life's problems."

Salter sighed, complaining loudly of older bones and stiffer joints, but dutifully fell into line and followed as Fredric and the others filed along the battlements and down a long flight of granite steps. Urban walked ahead of her. Trevin Highgarde and his pages followed directly in Fredric's footsteps, never more than a long stride from *Unkindness* or his baron in accordance with his oaths. At the bottom of the steps was a courtyard.

There, upwards of a hundred soldiers brightly liveried in purples and golds practiced maneuvers. Each was armed with an infantry spear and a round shield emblazoned with the Owl of Kell, and identically armored in breastplate, kettle helm, vambrace for the spear arm and light greaves for the shins. It was as little protection as was necessary for them to be effective, but more than the line troops of most baronies could expect. Somewhere within the endless turning, marching and wheeling blocks of infantry a trumpeter was sounding out complicated tattoos that had the formations flowering into schiltrons, compacting into squares, or bristling with spears. Fredric thought it beautiful. Like watching a court masterpiece from the time of the Elder Kings come alive for his eyes and move.

The maneuvers went on uninterrupted even as Fredric and his entourage crossed the drill yard and found another set of steps winding upwards.

They passed several more soldiers moving back and forth between posts lugging heavy flatbows, or carting shield and spear. They bowed to Fredric and Trevin, apparently too wary of General Brant who would occasionally grunt something disparaging about the angle of their spear or the polish of their helm, before continuing on.

At the top, the party came to a battlement, built wide as it was very high and in little danger of conventional assault, projecting from the side wall of one of the keep's middle towers. From there a group of twenty or so could, in some comfort, look down on the easternmost of the walled baileys that encircled Kellar Keep, between it and the first and largest curtain wall. The view was the same as it had been in the courtyard beforehand, only on an increased scale. Several hundred soldiers drilled and engaged one another in mock battles. Knights of three different chivalric orders sworn to the Barony of Kell exercised their horses while rune golems, brutal-looking constructs of rock armor and engraved magicks, slumbered in open sheds, awaiting the arcane phrases that would rouse them to battle. Other baronies stored their golems away, concealed them in remote strongholds as an insurance against dire need. But for the Kellar the Uthuk Y'llan were no distant threat.

The armies of Kell had been diminished, but to Fredric's eyes they were the martial pride of Terrinoth still.

Fredric started towards the rampart edge, thinking to lean over and watch his soldiers, only for the flicker of warning in his belly to make him think better of it and step back. He wrapped his arms around his chest and rested his shoulders against the tower's wall. To his left was a Loriman ballista mounted on a wooden turntable. It could have been one of the very machines that had cut dragons from the cold skies of the east eight hundred years before. Revered relics of a time still recent in the folk memory of Kell, when the barony had last stood firm against Terrinoth's enemies. Each of the siege engine's limbs was longer than Fredric could stand with his arms fully spread. The inclined track into which a crew of three would load bolts was longer than he was tall. The woodwork was so thoroughly oiled that it gleamed, loosely covered in a weatherproof sheet that flapped in the cold mountain wind. His council huddled around him. The pages bearing *Unkindness* shivered on the stairs.

"Kellar is well garrisoned," said Urban, unnecessarily given the evidence of their eyes and ears. "We have provisions enough to feed it for a long time. There is little enough incoming from the countryside these days, but that is not the great loss to the granaries that it might have. Kell's principal produce has always been hard men."

"And harder mutton," said Trevin.

Salter grunted her agreement.

Urban went on. "Traders from Dhernas, and even from Frostgate on occasion, do still come to replenish our stores, albeit under heavy protection from soldiers I can ill-afford to spare when the eastern watches stand empty." He walked to the door in the tower's side and opened it, checked inside to be sure that it was empty, then closed it and turned back. "I have heard rumors – from Outland Scouts and Citadel Knights on errantry here in Kell, and from those mercenaries still abroad in the south and east – of Uthuk Y'llan moving in great number along the Ru side of the Lothan. I have even heard tell of a battle, though I know not who fought it nor its outcome."

At that, the wind blowing through Fredric's coat seemed to turn chill.

The Uthuk were the great menace from the east, although more of a legend than a reality for all that they occasionally still crossed the Lothan to raid the outlying farms and even conducted trade of a sort through the lawless bandit state of Last Haven. They had not pushed as far even as Kellar in fourteen hundred years and there had been other threats to the baronies that had arisen and been pushed back since. But the Uthuk had been the first, and the greatest, people who appeased the demons of the Ynfernael planes with blood rituals and human sacrifice. They put the fear of damnation into children and old men alike, and the merest rumor of an incursion made Fredric's hand itch for his shield and his sword.

To his surprise, Trevin was nodding. "I have had similar reports." The grandmarshal gave his baron a remorseful look. "Not all knights wear armor, and I cannot shield you with all my swords here in Kellar."

"You're forgiven," said Fredric. "But it is my understanding that an army cannot cross the Lothan except at the fords of Hernfar. Not unless it chooses to cross over the Dunwarr and come at us through Forthyn Barony."

"It's the only good crossing for an army. But that's not to say small bands or agents couldn't get across while the forts are unmanned and the mountains unwatched."

"I find myself unexpectedly in agreement," said Trevin. "You have been fair to this barony and your father was well loved. The people here are straightforward. They expect no comfort and ask for little from you. They are not soft like the folk of Allerfeldt or Cailn, that a little hardship would bring them to rebellion, or give a handful of glorified cutpurse gangs control over so much land so quickly. No, I suspect the hand of the Uthuk in this, direct or otherwise."

Fredric closed his eyes, tilting his head back until it touched stone, wishing he had lived through just about any time in history but this. "I cannot, in good conscience, arm men and women to serve me only to reward them with starvation. *I cannot.*"

"How can we be sure that our years of famine were not themselves the work of the Uthuk and their warlocks?" asked Salter, raising one prickly white eyebrow.

"Then send to Greyhaven for runemasters to find the bedevilment and cast it out," Fredric cried, suddenly angry, for they had argued this before and would again. "Send to Vynelvale and the Cathedral of Kellos that the Disciples of the Living Flame might cleanse our fields, and from there to the Weeping Basin for the priests of Aris to bless the ashes with fecundity."

He bit his tongue, fighting down the bitterness of knowing that he and others had attempted all these courses and more. The land refused to yield. If it was sorcery that blighted them, as Beren feared, then it was something greater than the ability of the Uthuk to work, and of a similar order beyond the powers of mortal magi to undo.

It was as though the world itself rejected them.

Fredric slumped.

"Then what?" asked Urban, softly.

"I cannot pull my people from their lands. But perhaps *I* could take a detachment of soldiers and ride out in person."

Salter looked mortified. "I would ardently recommend against that, my lord."

"And I," Trevin added. "Albeit in plainer words."

"It would not be the first time I have led an army," Fredric countered, a little too hotly.

"But if anything were to happen to you. With your daughter still so young…"

Fredric's mouth twitched in frustration, but as Trevin had no doubt been expecting, knowing him as well as his own wife if not better, the appeal to his family found its mark.

"It is a bold suggestion," said Trevin, in a mollifying tone. "But I fear it would do little good in any case. Take too few men and you would be a target for every would-be usurper that's crawled out of the hills and dubbed themselves lord. Too many and they would melt away as though they were never there. And worse, you would be leaving Kellar looking very tempting indeed."

"It would take an army," said Urban. "A big one and probably more than one." He produced another growl-sound that was as close as the lord-commander could come to acknowledging impotence, recognizing the fact that they were arguing one another round in circles. "Which we haven't the manpower or the provision for. I know, I know."

"I might advise sending Litiana Renata away with young Grace," Salter murmured, whispering as though such defeatist talk might be heard above the tramping and bugling from the bailey beneath them. "I fear that things will only worsen before they improve. Whether through a peasant rebellion or, gods help us, an invasion from the Ru, I see no quick solution that does not end with Kellar besieged. Baroness Magrit would gladly take them in, I am sure, and her castle at Dhernas is but a short ride over still reasonable country. Or better yet convince the baroness to return to her family's estates in Alben for a spell. Grace is an inquisitive girl: I am sure she would not resent the opportunity to board a galleon and visit her mother's homelands, particularly if you frame it to her as an adventure. And would the Queen not herself be overjoyed at the chance to meet her granddaughter? Pleased enough to worry for the lands and title she is due to inherit through her father's side?"

Fredric managed a smile. "Sly."

"I live to be useful, my lord."

"And you are. I understand you have already sent your own family to your half-brother in Highmont." The chamberlain stammered for a moment before Fredric interrupted her. "I don't hold it against you. I would do it myself in a heartbeat, but…" He hung his head and sighed. "If I were to pack away my household and send them west what message would that send? I would be saying that Kellar is unsafe even for my own family."

He stared across the battlement. For a long while no one spoke.

There was precious little left to be said.

"Where then does that leave us?" said Brant, ill-tempered at any decision that counselled inaction.

"What do we do…?" Fredric whispered to himself. Then he

lifted his gaze and spoke louder. "We send to our neighbors, and to the Citadel; we send to the dwarves at Thelgrim. We ask them again, no, we *beg them* for their aid."

"They will say no," said Salter. "They will say that a little banditry is Kell's own affair. So long as it doesn't cross their borders."

"Then I will remind them what happened two hundred years ago in Otrim in the winter of 1662, the last time the barons made that argument."

Salter smiled, clearly pleased that her tutelage in the histories had not gone entirely to waste.

Trevin shook his head. "They will still say no. They always say no."

"Send the messages anyway," said Fredric. "Maybe things will have got worse by the time they get there."

CHAPTER FIVE
Trenloe the Strong
Hernfar Isle, the Borderlands

"Smell that?" said Dremmin as the Companions of Trenloe and their civilian train rumbled from the barbican tunnel and into Nordgard Castle. The dwarf took a deep breath and beat on her broad chest. "Smells like money."

The courtyard about them was mud, scattered with straw, rutted by the wheels of heavy wagons and busy with sunken hoof prints. Thoroughfares had arisen that allowed them to wind their way around stacked crates and heaps of dung that had been in place for so long as to become permanent landmarks. Mangy-looking birds hopped from one leg to the other, eyeing the soldiers passing by on their horses like nobles turned out to watch the long walk of the condemned to the gallows.

"It doesn't smell like that to me," said Trenloe.

The dwarf tapped her forehead with one well-chewed finger. "That's because I'm not sure there's anyone entirely at home up there. Look around here. This is the only good crossing between Terrinoth and the Ru. There should be five times as many soldiers as there are." She leant towards Trenloe and lowered her voice. "We could charge Dame Ragthorn twice what she's promised."

"We won't, though."

"Oh, won't we?"

"No."

Dremmin scowled. "She'd pay it. You'd better believe she'd pay it. We'd turn around and march right on back to Trast, thank you very much."

"Dremmin…"

But the dwarf wasn't listening. Her eyes were glittering and distant, her mind dreaming about gold. "Or maybe we'd just take the castle for ourselves, what do you think?"

"Dremmin!"

Trenloe was never sure if the dwarf was entirely serious when she made these sorts of suggestions, or if she just enjoyed teasing him.

"I'm not saying we'd keep it." The dwarf's attention snapped back, her manner becoming suddenly defensive. "Who'd want to live with their back ends hanging out over the Ru? We could ransom it or something."

Trenloe sighed. "We're not taking Dame Ragthorn's castle."

"Helka's Eyes," Dremmin muttered, fixing her eyes forward. "I should've left you in the army."

"Smells like dung anyway," said Bethan, the corporal trotting up from behind to join them.

Dremmin turned in her saddle. "Who asked you?"

Bethan shrugged. "It does smell like dung."

"It's a dungy country," Dremmin agreed. "What do you expect?"

Looking back over their journey thus far, and as much as Trenloe might have wanted to argue the place's unappreciated virtues, it was difficult to disagree. The downs had been desperately bleak with their endlessly rolling hills and scab-like heath, but the isles of Hernfar were somehow worse. The sun was a vague suggestion of something better beyond the clammy mists, and the ground was so squalid it was possible to lose a horse up to its fetlocks if you were incautious. Hernfar was a boggy eyot, caught in the middle of the Lothan, its fords the fairest crossing between the baronies of Terrinoth to the west and the Ru Steppes to the east. It felt sometimes as though they had crossed some invisible boundary to pass out of Kell and arrive in a strange realm not entirely of the mortal plane at all. It was like one of the weirder songs that Bethan claimed to have learned from a drunken Latari about how the first elves had been tricked across the bridge of the Aenlong and into Mennara. Mist and mud had muted the clop of their horses' hooves on the trail, and yet every step deeper had been shadowed by the sawing of insects, the belching of toads, and the crowing of wading birds.

Despite old Maeve's assertions it had taken them three days.

With better kept roads, and without the refugees' wagons to escort to safety, it was possible they might have made it in the one that had been promised, but Trenloe was uncertain even of that. He'd spent too much of the time looking over his shoulder. Dremmin had spent most of it complaining, and she had not been the only one. Even the Gwellan townsfolk seemed to have found the sight of Nordgard's mist-wreathed battlements and crumbling walls a disheartening end to a long journey.

"Aren't you from somewhere around here?" asked Bethan, wearing a bright smile and quite alone in her rugged good humor. "I know you're not originally from Trast."

"Thelgrim is far to the north of here and high in the Dunwarr," Dremmin grunted, as though divulging some great secret of her people which all in earshot ought consider themselves greatly esteemed by the dwarves for having heard. "Compared to this dung pile it might as well be in Ghom."

Trenloe raised a hand and clicked his tongue for a halt as

soldiers in the purple and gold of Kell emerged like wraiths from the mist to greet them. They walked with the peculiar gait of people who had had nothing to do yesterday and did not expect to have anything more important to do tomorrow. At their unhurried direction the wagons ground past the idling mercenaries and away into the mist.

"I'm glad this lot are on our side," Dremmin muttered.

"They just need a song." said Bethan.

Trenloe turned away from them, not exactly keen to hear more, as Maeve rolled by in her wagon. The old woman leant from her raised seat in the front. "Thank you, Trenloe, for everything you have done for us. I only wish I could have persuaded more to join us. I fear for what will become of them if the Greyfox is not stopped."

"I'll see that she is," said Trenloe.

Maeve's face creased into a warm smile. "You are a true hero, Trenloe. If ever you have the need, or the time, come seek us out in the castle. We of Gwellan will be at your service."

"Promise her nothing," Dremmin muttered once she had driven out of earshot. "We're lucky to be finally rid of those beggars."

"It would be nice to be paid once in a while," Bethan mused.

"We helped her folk because it was on our way regardless, and kindness costs us nothing," said Trenloe. "And because it was the right thing to do."

"And who's to judge what's right and what isn't?" said Dremmin.

Trenloe frowned.

The dwarf's question sounded like one of those clever riddles that were meant to seem complicated when you first heard them but were actually fiendishly simple once you thought about them for a little bit.

"Everyone," he said.

Dremmin looked nonplussed by that answer. Then she started to laugh. Trenloe was not sure why.

"Are… are you Trenloe the Strong?"

A group of soldiers approached. All wore purple surcoats over gilt-edged breastplates, steel vambraces gleaming wetly from their arms. The livery was dirty and blotched with mold. The steel could do with an armorer's polish. But Trenloe was impressed all the same. There was a prominent school of military thought in Trast that a soldier really ought to carry a weapon, and so Baron Rault tended to provide his enlistees with at least a spear, but they were lucky to have armor unless they happened to have been wearing it when they joined. The leader of the group, as declared by the golden epaulette on his puffed gambeson sleeve and by the fact that he was the one who had spoken, carried his helmet in his hand, smoothing his hair back with the other hand as though nervous in front of a lady.

"You're talking to a six and a half-foot-tall man riding on a farmhorse," said Dremmin. "Of course he's Trenloe the Strong."

The soldier stammered for a moment, then pulled his helmet back on over his head. That seemed to steady him.

"Follow me then, sir. If you please."

Civilization had withdrawn from Nordgard. That much was obvious wherever Trenloe and his Companions looked as they were escorted further into the castle. Something had *driven it back*. The bustle of the gatehouse, however muted and coarse it might have been, dwindled quickly and soon became entirely absent. The odd apparition shuffled through the cloying fog like a ghoul in search of bones to gnaw. Soldiers? Civilian laborers? They never drew close enough to the column of riders for Trenloe to be sure. Mist concealed everything beyond the occasional clang of a smithy's hammer or the squeal of a grindstone wheel. He had never been blessed with a tremendous sense of direction and very soon after losing sight of the gatehouse Trenloe was thoroughly and irredeemably lost.

Fortunately Marns, as the sergeant assigned to be their escort had introduced himself, turned out to be an affable guide. As their horses clopped mutedly from one dilapidated pile of dark granite to the next he would point out a flicker of firelight where breakfast could be found, where the latrines were, how to find them and (almost as importantly) how to avoid them when the fog came in thick. From him, they soon learned where and how the castle laundress could be hired, from whom luxuries like beer, bedding, and new socks could be bartered in exchange for silver and, lastly in the minds of all, where the armorers and smithies were.

Trenloe did not expect to be able to retrace his steps to find any of these locations again, but Dremmin had an innate directional sense that he had trusted his life to more than once.

"And here we are," said Marns with a flourish having led them on a tour of the outer wards for about forty minutes. "Your new home."

Trenloe squinted into the steadily thickening fog. Large, blockish shapes squatted in the murk like river trolls.

"Stables," Dremmin gruffed, barely even bothering to look up.

Marns dismounted from his horse. Trenloe and the Companions followed suit, passing over their reins to hostlers who came trotting in from the still half-recognizable stable yards to take them. Trenloe looked around, slowly closing and reopening his eyes in the vain hope of making the buildings out, as Rusticar was led away with the promise of food and bedding.

Bethan reached into a pocket for a silver coin embossed with Fortuna's sign and clutched it tightly in her hand. "Is this what the world is like in the Charg'r Wastes, once you go far enough into the great east and the world disappears into the nothing of Syraskil's scales?"

Dremmin gave a bark of laughter. "No."

Irritation displaced the young corporal's superstitious fears. "How would you know?"

"Terrinoth is a young country. It's no secret that my own culture hails from far out to the east. As did yours. Or so I've read."

"What have you read?" Bethan pressed, as avid a reader as she was a hoarder of stories and a singer of songs, but at that the dwarf became tight-lipped and would say no more.

"How long have you been here?" Trenloe asked Marns.

"A year and a half. I think." He pointed to the sky. Trenloe looked up. The fog was so thick it could have been a gray day or a brightly mooned night. The farmer's son in Trenloe shivered at being so divorced from the cycles of the day. "You lose track."

"How do you bear it without going insane?" said Bethan.

The soldier grinned at her. "Are you sure we do?"

"You shouldn't joke about such things," Bethan shivered.

The man laughed. "But how then would we keep from going insane?"

"Where is everyone?" Trenloe asked, turning back from his fruitless survey of their surrounds.

"Sent home." Marns shrugged. "We don't complain. The garrison at Nordgard Castle has fared better than most. Or so I hear."

"Why is that?"

"Strategic importance." The solider leant conspiratorially in. "Most of those that serve in Hernfar didn't exactly *choose* to be here. If you catch my meaning."

Trenloe straightened.

He disapproved of penal service on principle. A garrison of murderers, sheep rustlers and thieves might have had the wits to choose the baron's colors over the noose but they weren't folk that Trenloe would willingly entrust with a sword.

Oblivious to his thinking, Marns stepped away to beckon for another soldier.

At the sight of Trenloe the newcomer stumbled, looking up and managing a cursory salute.

"This is Bannit," said Marns. "He'll show you where you're to be barracked."

"Go with him," Dremmin grunted at Bethan. "And don't take the first leaky old hovel they shove you in. There's hardly a shortage of space around here."

The Kellar soldier and the corporal hurried off together, hunching as though the mist bore some great weight or portent of menace that would press down on them the further they went. Marns turned back to Trenloe.

"For you, sir, if I may. Dame Ragthorn extends an invitation for you to dine with her at the keep. As soon as your company is settled and your affairs here are in order."

Trenloe turned to Dremmin who produced her nastiest smile and winked.

"Head on, lad. I can bed us and feed us well enough and there'll be no real work discussed up there." With a jerk of her head, she gestured with inhuman certainty to where Hernfar's keep presumably loomed in the mist. "She probably just wants to shake your hand and tell all her friends back in Archaut how she met a real-life hero."

CHAPTER SIX
Kurt
Gwellan, South East Kell

"They came right out from the forest. Bold as daylight."

Holger Thorenburgher spoke with the air and manner of one who'd pronounced on this dark omen – or dark omens much like it – more than once before, but wouldn't be so vulgar as to make meat of it now. With the livestock markets empty, the magistrates closed up, and foot traffic through the town's wooden gate going all the wrong way, the aged timbers of the Black Lamb were one of the few places in Gwellan where folk could still congregate for news. This, despite the emptying of the town, they continued to do in some number, since Holger was to gossip as a high priestess of Aris was to alms for the poor. The stout chestnut bar was his altar, the greasy apron his chasuble, and the spit-rag and tankard in his meaty hands his scepter and rod.

Most soldiers were natural gossips. Anything to escape the dullness of their own day-to-day routines. But Holger's morbid fascination with recent events put Kurt's nose out of joint.

"Ain't natural," he muttered, shaking his head. "Ain't right. The Downs is for folk like us as works the soil, and the forest is for the tree spirits and the fae and the dragon half-breeds that old

Baron Roland, may he rest easy at Basin's bottom, weren't able to kill. Something in the forest has kept their numbers up, they say, made them grow bold and strange. More alike to the old ghosts of the wood than the dragons of the Molten Heath. A man who enters so far as to gather deadwood or hunt for small game will be paying the forest back tenfold in the end."

Nodding heads greeted this statement.

Woe betide him or her who failed to concur with Holger under his own roof.

"The Greyfox is one of those Primalists as still worships the spirits in the Howling Giant Hills, I'm telling you. Leastways that's my reckoning on it, you can take it or not. She's bargained with the wood for a share of its powers, the old sorcery of the elder world, and all our lives is the price she's promised in return. Either that or our allegiance to the wood."

A fearful, angry muttering swept about the crowded taproom as Holger stuffed the rag into his apron's breast pocket, set down the metal tankard, and crossed his big, heavily tattooed arms across the bar top.

"What do you say on it, Stavener? You're closer to the forest than anyone, except for when Yorin is in his hut up in Latwood."

The muscles across Kurt's jaw twitched as he battled the urge to brain the man against his own bar. "I don't know how you do it, Holger. Really, I don't. All I asked from you is if you knew anyone with sheep to sell. That's all."

"What good'll sheep do you now?" called a drinker from his long trestle.

"Aye," said another. "S'like feeding a bear and hoping it don't take your hand."

"You'll not find anyone selling," muttered a third.

"Not unless you're looking to buy from the Greyfox," said Yorin, bleakly.

The old woodland ranger was fetched up against the far end of the bar with his boots up on a stool, dressed in a tough outfit of dark browns and pale grays with a feathered hat on the counter beside him. Kurt had known of him from the army, a Darkland Ranger for Dame Ragthorn of Hernfar, and apparently a good one, but he was more often to be found in the Black Lamb these days, or laid out somewhere nearby to it.

"Everyone with land north of Gwellan got hard hit," said Holger. "Most of them were through here before joining the west road, and not a one of them had aught but the clothes on their backs. We've not seen days like these since Margath the Unkind led his dragons here during the Third Darkness. Something big is coming. Something bad. You tell me now if you think I'm wrong."

"You ain't wrong," someone dutifully answered.

Sarb leant along the bar to nudge Kurt's arm. "Perhaps we shouldn't have left Elben in the house on his own."

"He'll be all right," Kurt whispered back. It was half a day's gentle riding to the farmstead from Gwellan and it wasn't often that he would leave Elben there alone. Ordinarily he would have brought his younger son with him and left Sarb to mind the dogs. Elben loved the bustle of the town. Like his mother had. Almost as much as Sarb hated it. But there'd been nothing else for it. Kurt needed to replace his lost animals if they were going to see the winter through and he didn't think much of the idea of letting Sarb out of his sight. The boy was still hot from the previous night. The odds of him getting it into his head to do something rash like setting out to track the Greyfox into the Whispering Forest were uncomfortably high. "Provided we can find someone who'll sell to us we can be home again by dawn. And in any case, I doubt the Greyfox will be back any time soon."

"Why do you say that?"

"Because there's nothing left for her to have."

Sarb slumped over his elbows, staring sullenly at the counter.

"We should fight back," he muttered after a while.

"With what?" said Holger, overhearing. "The baron's no help. Dame Ragthorn can't, or won't, with the Uthuk stirring again in the east. And Sheriff Jolsyn is, well…" He picked his tankard back up off the counter and resumed polishing. "She's as handy as a cup with no bottom isn't she?"

"We'd do it ourselves," said Sarb. "That's what the Greyfox did, isn't it? Take hungry and desperate folk and bitter old soldiers and turn them into an army?"

"Speaking of bitter old soldiers," said Holger, raising an eyebrow, "what *did* you do in the army, Stavener?"

"Sing a lot of songs," said Kurt, to a smattering of laughs.

"She took herself half of Kell," said Sarb, angrily, banging on the counter with his fist. "All I'm saying is we defend Gwellan properly and patrol the downs."

"And why not run the Greyfox to her den in the forest and dig her out while you're at it?" said Kurt.

Heads around the taproom nodded.

"And why not?" Sarb countered. "If the forest spirits have already sold the bandit queen their powers then there's nothing left to fear from the woods."

Elben had withdrawn a lot since his mother's death. He barely spoke of her. Sarb was just angry. Kurt frowned.

Why oh why couldn't he have grieved more like Elben?

"It's two thousand years since the Locust Swarm brought Darkness to Kell," said Kurt. "As far as I can figure it nothing worse has hit Terrinoth since that Terrinoth didn't somehow do to itself. Waiqar was the great hero of the day before becoming Waiqar the Undying. And the Third Darkness was the Dragonlords' punishment for the hubris of the Elder Kings, or so the stories tell it, so don't be so keen on being the savior of Kell."

Sarb swore under his breath, imaginatively enough for his father to wonder who he'd been speaking to, but made no argument.

Kurt turned his attention back to Holger

"I've a ton of work waiting for me back home. A roof to mend and Fortuna only knows how many bodies lying in my yard to be buried. I know you know everyone and everything around here."

Holger massaged his chins. "It might be I know of someone looking to move some pigs. They'd help you with that other job of yours as well."

"Sheep," said Kurt.

"Beggars can't be choosers."

Kurt looked down and muttered. "Katrin always liked sheep."

Holger fell quiet a moment.

Sarb got up without saying anything and walked away.

"I don't know the first thing about pigs," Kurt mumbled.

"I don't know the first thing about people and yet here we both are. Anyways pigs is all he's got. Take 'em or leave 'em."

The sound of raised voices reached through the stout oak of the Black Lamb's door. A few heads turned towards it as Kurt slid a brown coin across the bar.

Holger picked it up and held it to one of the yellowish beams light that fell through the holes in the thatch. "Not been through the Greyfox's paws yet. Traders from the north don't much like her coins. Best they start getting used to 'em, I reckon."

"Where can I find these pigs?"

"The old livestock market up top. Hoping some fool like you'll show up. A friend of mine, Pranten, is looking to take the road west and with coin enough in his pocket to buy passage on to Fort Rodric, so he'll sell if you offer him twice what they're worth."

Kurt sighed, then nodded.

"Fine."

"And what'll you do when the Greyfox comes for more?"

"That's not your problem."

"So that's it, is it?" said Yorin, still slumped back with his feet up. "Your own first and everyone else never?"

"Isn't that why Baron Fredric sent us both home?" Kurt shot back.

The ranger stared at something invisible in the hanging dust. "Maybe we'd all be better off with the Greyfox."

Holger frowned, and the inn fell into an uncomfortable quiet.

It was the familiar sound of a large group of people neither openly condoning, nor entirely condemning, something that even a day or two ago would have been unspeakable.

"To the bandit queen," someone said, raising their cup.

A few folk drank.

Yorin himself just stared sullenly into his.

"Well, I'll leave you all to it," said Kurt, getting up and looking around for Sarb. The boy was nowhere to be seen. The door was open and a couple of men were huddled either side of the frame, out of the cold and the drizzle, and peering onto some kind of a kerfuffle outside. It didn't take him long to figure out where Sarb had got too. "My son the hero," he muttered as he pulled on his old coat, picked up his old bow, and stepped out into the rain.

CHAPTER SEVEN
Andira Runehand
Gwellan, South East Kell

Andira staked her long poleaxe into the earth and lowered herself to the road. Her knee plate squelched into the thick mud, filth and grime sliding from the blued dwarf-forged steel like water from an oiled sheet. She held out her hand, wincing in familiar pain as the rune inscribed into her palm crackled to life. A ghostly yellow light glowed through the blood and skin of her hand, showing through the back as a cross, or perhaps a sword, bound within an incomplete circle.

The Gwellan townsfolk who had been watching her and her entourage of pilgrim-soldiers with fear started fleeing up the hill road and screaming of sorcery the moment the first rays spilled from her hand.

Andira did her best to ignore them. She always expected a little unease when she exercised her rune-powers, but her first impression of the Kellar was that they were a more-than-usually suspicious and mage-fearing lot. She approved, although their fear was regrettable. There was a good chance that she would need local guides if she was to pursue her quarry across this unfamiliar northern territory.

With a grunt of effort and another flare of pain, she returned her focus to the rune, tracing the lower half of the circle with her mind. Harnessing the bound magic of a rune required no special talent. That was what made them so sought after, and so valuable, but only an expert runemaster had the expertise to manipulate the components of the rune shape to enact the full spectrum of effects. That Andira was capable of such feats told her that she had once been rune-trained. Perhaps. But how, where, or when such a time in her life had come about, she had no recollection at all.

Through eyes limned with runic sunlight, she blinked and saw the town anew.

"What do you see?" asked Sir Brodun, her protector, a billion leagues away by her side.

"The Ynfernael..."

The clouds above the town were thick and torn, the yellow of bad blood and wreathed in multicolored fires that would burn without end. The spikes of the town's stockade grew lengthy. Teeth sprouting from a demonic mouth, splintered and bleached, as if by hard acid, even as the world about it became dark. The fleeing townsfolk were shades caught in tar, wriggling worm-things about which ragged crow-things flocked like starving birds for an after-storm glut. The Ynfernael was the plane that existed parallel to and below the mortal realm of Mennara, a world where hatred and prejudice were physical things and where demons dwelt in a constant state of war. Words of some sort rumbled through its tormented sky like the echo of another world's thunder. Andira could not understand them. The language of the Ynfernael was spoken not with the consonants and vowels of human speech, but in torment and horror.

She shuddered, her fingers stiff as mummified claws as she

folded them in, dousing the rune again. She blinked, her mortal sight retuning slowly.

Hamma Brodun was holding her shoulder steady.

The former knight was a large man, and a hard one, his features coarsened by a grizzle of white hair. His breastplate was dinted and absent any knightly heraldry. His long-sleeved coat of mail, while at least as old as he was, was immaculately kept and oiled. In one hand he carried Andira's holy standard. In the other he led a dirty gray horse with the off-hand ease of second nature. He was the only one amongst Andira's procession of pilgrim-soldiers to possess one. Out of humility, however, he seldom rode. Sir Brodun had forsaken his rank and its privileges, sold off his holdings to outfit her in arms and armor, and given his ancestral seat in Carthridge to the Church of Kellos, much to the chagrin of a few disinherited heirs and an embittered wife, of whom he spoke little.

Andira did not recall much about their first meeting as it was the earliest memory that she had. They had fought, she knew, for apparently she had strayed into a tomb complex that lay under his family's protection and he had mistaken her for a Mistlands grave-witch. She had won.

His hand was on the hilt of his sword as he stared at her hard in the eye.

"Andira?"

She gave a weak smile and nodded. "It is still me, Hamma."

The knight's grip on his sword loosened. He did not, however, remove his hand. "You have been looking too far and too often into the Ynfernael. The demon will start to take notice."

After recruiting her first pilgrim-soldier in Sir Brodun, Andira had wandered aimlessly for a time: silencing a restless wight here, driving a wyrm from a ruin there. But she had always been certain that she had a destiny. How else to explain the power she had acquired given that she had no memory of obtaining it? All she needed to do was keep going, keep fighting, and eventually it would reveal itself. It had done so quite by chance, while exploring the demon-tainted ruins of Sudanya in northern Frest, where she had vanquished the demon lord Prutorn, and learned the name of *Baelziffar*, its master.

Now, she felt her purpose.

"We gain on him," she said, rubbing at the back of her hand as pain settled down and became one more ache. "My sense of him grows. There are times when I feel as though I can almost glimpse him. The Ynfernael is a distinct plane but one that parallels our own from beyond the veil. He strikes north from his domains over Sudanya, marching his legions towards another site of power twinned with somewhere in Kellar, I am certain of it."

"That could explain the rumors of Uthuk rising in the east?" said Hamma, still the soldier, even after two decades of restless questing.

Andira nodded. The Uthuk Y'llan had consorted with demons for so long that every aspect of their culture had become corrupted by it. When nightmares racked the Ynfernael, it was the tribes of the Charg'r Wastes who woke screaming. "And the banditry and famine we have heard of as well. Be vigilant."

Hamma grunted and nodded ahead. "I'm always vigilant."

Townsfolk with the look of provincial marshals, outfitted in stiff wools and boiled leather, armed with a rough assortment of axes and staffs and the infamous Kellar short spear, were filling up the road ahead of them. Some gestured towards Andira. The word "sorcery" appeared on several mouths, and a stranger one, "Greyfox", on others. They seemed in no hurry for violence, however. The majority of Andira's pilgrims were clad in nothing more threatening than old robes and sandals. A few carried bows, and a talented handful that Hamma had begrudgingly trained bore swords, although they would storm the Black Citadel of Llovar itself if Andira were to lead them, and feared neither hardship nor pain. But at two hundred strong, with dragon runes inked onto their faces in imitation of the one that Andira had unwittinly branded onto Hamma Brodun in their first encounter, they were an intimidating force for any peasant militia.

"Long have I yearned to see the legendary Shield of Daqan," said Hamma, with a sour flourish. "The embodiment of martial excellence. The great defenders of the east."

"Strength comes in many guises. Do not be so quick to judge."

Hamma gave an idle shrug, his hand still light on his sword hilt as the crowd ahead of them continued to grow. "Who's this Greyfox they're in such terror of?"

"I do not know."

The knight turned to her. "*Is* it you?"

Andira turned her gaze inward, but her memory of her life before the rune was empty, a blank wall without pictures. "I... do not know that either."

Hamma sighed. "All the ground we've covered, something like this was bound to happen sooner or later."

Leaving her poleaxe stuck in the ground Andira held up her hands. The townsfolk took a collective step back, warding themselves with the protective sigils of Kellos, Aris, and lesser deities that either Andira did not know or whose symbols the townsfolk drew incorrectly.

"My name is Andira Runehand. I mean this town no harm, and I will be gone soon enough if anyone here can point me towards the shortest road to Castle Kellar."

The peasant mob fell to muttering, apparently caught unprepared by that explanation and uncertain what to do about it. While Andira waited for them, Hamma gave her a nudge and directed her attention to a large timber-frame building that fronted onto the street. A faded wooden sign displaying a sheep or a donkey hung from a sagging portico and a second, smaller, angry crowd was spilling out of it.

"They say the Ynfernael is the root source of all the world's evil," said Hamma. "And taverns are the wellspring of all its angry young men."

A tall, wiry youth with a thin fuzz of dark hair over his head raised a long knife. "We're not afraid of the Greyfox here!" The drunken mob cheered him on and, buoyed by their response, he charged.

"My lady?" Hamma asked.

Andira nodded. "But be gentle."

Passing his lady her standard and leaving his sword in its sheath, Sir Brodun walked casually towards the running boy. The youth slashed his knife towards the knight's face. Hamma bent aside, caught the boy's arm as it flew past, and had him disarmed with his face in the mud before he could have realized he had missed. The knight knelt on top of him and twisted the boy's arm behind his back, locking it at the brink of snapping between his gardbrace and his knee.

"Hands off my son."

The voice was unraised, strikingly calm. Andira glanced to the tavern door where a man, similar in appearance to the boy but twenty years older, stood with a flatbow nocked and fully drawn.

"We've had our fill of outside trouble here."

The bowman loosed, and then several things happened at once.

Andira drew her finger around the circle border of her rune, the arrow bursting into flame as it a shield of sunfire and exploded in midair. Townsfolk ducked as burning motes rained down.

The bowman gawped.

"Sir Brodun," said Andira, lowering her steaming hand and grimacing in pain. "Release the boy."

The knight did as he was bidden, and the youngster flopped to the ground. Crunching over bits of fire-blackened arrow that now littered the road, Andira walked towards him. She knelt.

"What is your name?"

He looked over his shoulder at her. Fear of her made his eyes weak. "Sibhard. My... my father calls me Sarb."

"Do not be afraid, Sibhard. Fear is one of the many spheres of the Ynfernael. It is to be overcome and eventually ignored. Remember instead the bravery that drove you to attack me to defend your village." She smiled at him. "Although you should probably know that Sir Brodun was once the most famed knight in Roth's Vale and I bested him in his prime." Hamma grunted that this was so, but she knew it was a story he did not enjoy sharing. "I said I wished you no harm and I meant it. Let me prove it." She laid her hand on the boy's head. Pain crept into her wrist and up her forearm, but she held her hand where it was as warming light rinsed across the boy's face, closing the cuts and bruises from his altercation with Sir Brodun, as well as a few other, less recent wounds, that he had earned elsewhere.

Andira flexed her fingers and withdrew her hand. The boy gasped.

Returning her standard to Sir Brodun's keeping, she stood, walked to her poleaxe where it had remained, stuck in the soft mud of the road, and pulled it free.

Slowly, Sibhard got up. He touched his face, his jaw, the fear in his face replaced with worship as he gazed up at Andira now. Townsfolk who had just moments before been warding themselves against evil sorcery dropped to their knees

"Now," said Andira. "Who is this Greyfox? And who can point me in the direction of Kellar?"

CHAPTER EIGHT
Kurt
Gwellan, South East Kell

The sun was sinking over the moors, tearing at the clouds with pink streaks. The cleaner light and fresher winds of the west, of the Kingless Coast and the unspoiled lands of Terrinoth, threw off the drizzle and the long gray cloak of the day. In spite of the hour Gwellan was abuzz. Andira Runehand was already being hailed in most quarters as a hero. It might have been all quarters, if not for those hailing her as a prophet, an avatar of Kellos, or (amongst the most predictably excitable) a new goddess for a new and evil time.

Kurt could only laugh. Even if he had no one but himself to laugh with.

Any hedge wizard with the right set of runes in their pocket could mend a split lip. The runemaster at Bastion Tarn, Kurt couldn't remember his name now, could do miraculous things with frostbite and wound rot. What he'd mostly treated of course were hangovers, if he could be moved to sympathy by a hard enough push of coin.

If he looked very carefully, and borrowed from his small store of imagination, then from his vantage at the top of the Gwellan hill Kurt could almost see a blueish flash of metal from the north road. It was a drovers' trail really, a minor tributary of the Great Forest Road that ran out east, the long way around the forest's borders, towards Kellar. The old soak, Yorin, had volunteered to lead Andira and her little army of fanatics north.

Good riddance, was what he thought.

To the lot of them.

"I hear I missed a bit of excitement in town," said Pranten, the pigherd, shooing the last of his animals into a snuffling, ill-tempered group churning up the mud of the road around Kurt and his already cantankerous black horse. The man had the washed-out look of too much worry and too little sun. His skin was pasty, and with a clammy sheen. His hair was long, but thinning. A huge wax coat swaddled him.

"Better off out of it," said Kurt.

"That's excitement for you. It's always better after the event or when you're not there."

Kurt nodded in agreement. "You might be one of those fools out there with her now if you had been."

"My marching days are long done, though I fancied myself quite the adventurer in my day."

Kurt looked the man up and down and decided to take his word for it.

"I heard that hero was quite beautiful too."

"I think those days are long done too."

The pig-farmer sighed. "You're probably right."

"Besides." Kurt crossed his arms. He'd barely looked at another woman since Katrin, which made no sense at all, because while she'd been alive he'd looked at them plenty. Sometimes he thought that strength of feeling just wasn't in him any more. Like Katrin had taken something with her when she'd gone. "I can't say I noticed."

The other man gave him a look. "I heard she put you in your place, Kurt Stavener."

"Give her to me with her back turned and I'll put an arrow in her same as anyone."

"You're a proper hero, you are."

"No such thing as proper heroes," Kurt grunted. "And if I *had* shot her then I'd have spared a lot of gullible folk around here a lot of wasted breath."

"Maybe. Maybe. Or maybe they'd have been calling you a hero now."

Kurt snorted. If that didn't sum it up just perfectly then he didn't know what would.

Pranten gave his herd a last look over as if putting off the moment of parting now it was here.

Kurt wished he knew what he was supposed to do with them.

"Where's your boy?" Pranten asked.

"A quick errand in town, he told me. He'll be back soon."

"You're set on leaving tonight then?"

"The Greyfox won't trouble Gwellan again so soon, and it's not so far. I can be there by dawn and Elben will be sure to fret if I'm not."

"Not like your eldest. I don't suppose being roughed up a little by someone old enough to be his granddad will teach *him* any lessons."

Kurt frowned in thought.

Sometimes he wondered if a good lesson was what Sarb needed. But if the last night on the farm hadn't provided it then he wasn't sure his brief and humiliating run-in with Andira Runehand's henchman was going to do so.

"No. I suppose it won't."

Approaching his horse, he gave his baggage a final look over. He had picked up several packages of salt, honey, vegetables and grain, in addition to Pranten's pigs, and spent several minutes pulling on straps and tightening buckles to ensure that all was secure.

It was then he noticed that his bow was missing.

"Damn," he muttered, going cold in his chest, and spent another anxious minute rummaging to reveal the absence of a blanket, a cook pot, a tinderbox, a pouch filled with a half dozen recently purchased onions, and a spare set of Sarb's clothing. "Damn, damn, damn."

"What is it?" said Pranten.

Kurt bared his teeth, unable to make the words to answer, and looked back to the north road, desperately seeking out the blueish glimmer he had almost convinced himself he'd seen amidst the heathers. He could no longer see it, gone the way of the sinking sun. His thoughts raced. The old knight had been the only one in Andira's company with a horse. Her warband would be going by foot, and even with a half day's head start on him Kurt knew he could ride them down without pushing his horse to raise a lather. What he'd do when he got there was another matter. He'd slap some sense into his son, for starters, drag him home if he had to, but whatever he thought of Andira's supposed godhood, he wasn't exactly chomping at the bit for another run-in with her. Or with her knight.

He thought of the pigs he'd just spent the last of his coin to buy.

He thought of Elben, waiting for him at home, alone.

He closed his eyes and cursed silently.

Then he looked up, tears threatening in his eyes.

Why did you have to die, Katrin? he thought. Neither of them ever listened to me.

"Kurt?" said Pranten.

"It's nothing." Kurt angrily stuffed what was left of his belongings back into their bags and climbed up onto his horse. "Just realized I've one less mouth to worry about this winter. That's all."

CHAPTER NINE
Trenloe the Strong
Hernfar, the Borderlands

Sergeant Marns brought Trenloe to a wooden door. The oak was rich and dark, but very plain. The handle was simple brass and the stone frame undecorated. The rest of the hall looked pleasantly furnished, insofar as Trenloe had the sophistication to judge it, albeit with a sort of bare-knuckle hardness you rarely saw in the homes of southern lords. Aside from Marns and himself it was also eerily quiet. There was no legion of aides or flunkeys going about their private business. There were hardly any soldiers. Just the occasional curl of mist that had somehow snuck in over a door jamb or through a window. The emptiness had been unnerving at first but Trenloe found he rather liked it. This was frontier décor. Lordship without its airs.

It was refreshing.

With a curt salute and a smile that might have been sympathetic, Marns withdrew to attend his other duties.

Trenloe knocked on the door, waited a moment and then ducked inside.

A highly polished oak table sat in the middle of a modest chamber. Places had been laid for two, but Trenloe thought that it could comfortably seat four or five with standing room leftover for a servant or two apiece. He could almost picture it as the setting for a short breakfast before a battle, or a hurried conference between the castellan and her highest knights over simple fare. Two large platters were presently heaped with crusty loaves. The bread was of an eastern type he did not recognize, black-crusted and studded with nuts. Nevertheless, he had been dreading the sort of dainty he was likely to find at a lord's table – softshell merriod eggs, razorwing tongues, Ghur Highland mushrooms – and the range of silverware necessary to eating it, so the straightforward food was reassuring. Even his father would have felt at home, though he might have grouched at the idea of putting seeds on good bread. Set beside the platters were two wooden goblets, both chipped, a jug of water, and a large breadknife with a serrated blade and a plain wooden handle. A fat tallow candle produced a smoky light and a strong scent of cooked mutton. There was a single window, and since the room was quite high above the castle it was pleasantly large, but the evening was gloomy, even above the fog, and the candle was the only source of light.

Lured by the scents, Trenloe drifted towards the table.

He'd not had a proper meal since the crossing from Dhernas. Dremmin would probably have finished off both platters by now. Even Bethan, though she would have been more convincingly guilty about it afterwards. But Trenloe's father had taught him better manners.

He pursed his lips in thought.

As he had never been introduced to either of his lieutenants' parents he decided that that was probably unfair.

But he *remembered* his manners better.

Mentally tightening his belt, he moved to examine the shelves that lined the walls.

In amongst the decorative tea sets, small portraits of hard men in serious armor, and the strange fetishes of ivory and feathers that had to be trophies claimed from battles fought beyond the Lothan in the Ru, were several books with cracked, faded spines. Trenloe ran his finger along them, but did not pick any one to look at more closely. He had never learnt his letters. Though not for want of effort. The skill just didn't seem to want to go in. But he'd always felt… the best word he could think of was *enlightened* in the presence of words. There was something civilizing about them. Something better. Even in this small room they seemed to stand above and apart from the rough décor and bestial totems.

A second door behind him creaked, and Trenloe turned.

A large woman in the last years of her middle age walked in. She was wearing a richly padded doublet and an embroidered cloak with a fur trim. A heavy signet ring was squeezed over the little finger of her left hand and a scepter that looked sturdy enough to double as a mace swung at her hip. Her eyes had a sharp look that might have appeared knowing, even wise, if not for the sudden widening of startlement as she caught sight of Trenloe.

"My word," she whispered, after the moment of shock had passed. "Trenloe the Strong. You are even bigger than your reputation. That is saying something." With an embarrassed cough, the woman swept out her cloak and seated herself at the table. There, she poured herself a goblet from the water jug and, disregarding the knife entirely, tore off a hunk of bread. With the bread in one hand and the goblet halfway towards her lips, she caught sight of Trenloe, still hovering by the bookshelves, and paused. "I take it I am somewhat more or less than what you were anticipating as well." She lifted one eyebrow. "Would it be indecorous to ask which?"

Trenloe cleared his throat, feeling oddly like a boy with his hand caught in the honey jar, and stood to attention.

"Dame Ragthorn?"

The woman sat back in her chair and smiled. "You were expecting some waifish dilettante, I wouldn't wonder. Or some over-promoted imbecile. All chins and braid." Trenloe shook his head, but the castellan raised her hand to forestall him. "No! Don't try to deny it. I shan't hear it. It comes with the territory of being distantly related to aristocracy, and so I am hardly offended. Baron Fredric is my cousin, you know."

"I didn't, my lady."

"Oh." The woman appeared briefly deflated. "Well, second cousin actually. We share a great-grandmother. But blue blood is thicker than red, as they say." Trenloe didn't think he had ever heard anyone say that, but then he was a simple man and so said nothing. As if marking his reticence, the castellan sighed. "Sometimes I think that no matter how far I climb people will assume that it is because of Fredric. Or how quickly I fall, I suppose. So there is that." She set down the bread roll and extended her hand across the table. "Forgive my manners, sir, but this is a plain house. Dame Marya Ragthorn, Lady of Hernfar."

Trenloe took the offered hand, swallowing it in his.

"Trenloe," he said.

Marya snorted. "I know who *you* are. I envy you a little. Common boy. Self-made. Master of your own destiny." She gave him a look and Trenloe again caught a glimpse of the sharpness he had thought he'd seen. She was a strange woman, but then most nobles tended to be. Being consigned to the eastern shoulder of Terrinoth had undoubtedly left her more than a little starved for conversation. But there was a shrewdness underlying it that Trenloe felt it best not to ignore. "But now I look at you I see that you were probably always destined to be a hero. As much I was destined to be lady of some out of the way castle far away from Kellar." She picked up her bread. "So. Which was it?"

"I'm sorry?"

"That you thought I'd be. Dilettante? Moron? Senile old mouth-breather stashed away in a border castle where she won't bump into any of the Daqan lords?"

Trenloe smiled. He thought he rather liked the lady of Hernfar. "I hadn't thought much on it, my lady. My partner, Dremmin, generally handles that sort of thing." He shrugged, thinking back to his home in Trast. Unlike the majority of sellswords and career soldiers, and even the handful of self-declared "heroes" he had met in his time, his childhood had been a happy one. "I mostly just fight."

"We all have our talents." She gestured towards the chair opposite. "Would you please sit? Ordinary men loom. You…" Her eyebrow climbed slowly as if to encompass his stature. "Just sit, will you."

"Yes, my lady."

"And that's enough of the 'my lady.'"

"Yes… er… my lady."

He eased himself carefully into the proffered chair and wedged his knees under the table, wobbling the crockery. Dame Ragthorn caught the water jug before it spilled and grinned. Mumbling his apologies, he picked up a whole loaf and broke it in half.

He tore off a bite and closed his eyes, giving a quiet moan of pleasure.

It was good, just slightly warm, and softer inside than its dark crust made it appear. Foreign spices infused its texture, leaving the inside of the mouth warm long after he had finished chewing and swallowed.

Dame Ragthorn nodded approvingly as she watched him eat.

"I'm sure it doesn't compare to southern tables. But we do our humble best. There has been famine here as I am sure you have heard, hard frosts as if this were Isheim or the northern Dunwarr rather than a barony of fair Terrinoth.

"This Dremmin character handles the books, I believe," she said, sharply changing the subject. "I recall her signature on the contract my agent conveyed to me ahead of your arrival. And as daring a piece of brigandry as any I've seen committed to parchment. May I ask how you ended up as a mercenary?"

Trenloe shrugged. Dremmin was forever scolding him for being too free with his life story. By the time Trenloe was eleven years old there was no highwayman or bully left within twenty miles of his father's farm that had not felt Trenloe's fists. Their neighbors had hailed him a hero and, as any boy would have, he had reveled in it. But his father had always disapproved of easy violence. *The bigger man wins his way with words,* he would say. In the end though even he had come to accept that fighting was the one thing in which Trenloe excelled and had given his blessing to Trenloe joining Baron Rault's army. It had not taken him many months to realize that patrolling the safest border in the richest barony in Terrinoth was not the sort of good he had envisaged himself doing.

He and Dremmin were technically still deserters, but they had both battled enough evil in the barony since that the legal technicality was almost never brought up.

"Was it the gold?" asked Marya.

He shook his head firmly. "No. Never. Not that."

The woman frowned. Lines formed across her forehead, dimpling the corners of her eyes. "No. I suppose I didn't really think that. For all Dremmin's profiteering I am sure you could have earned twice as much elsewhere. You'll forgive my prying but I wanted to know the man I had hired. Mercenaries come in all stripes, bad and good. Heroes likewise I suppose, though I swear you're the first I've had the fortune to run across. If it's not too obvious can I at least ask why you are called the Companions of Trenloe?"

"It was Dremmin's idea."

She gave a faint smile. "Of course it was. Silly me. But imagine my delight at securing the sword arm of the renowned Trenloe the Strong! So you see I had to meet you properly. Informally. To see if you were mad, or an imposter or…" her hand flapped about her like a wounded bird "…or I don't really know what. But no one comes to Nordgard Castle by choice. Not unless the other choice is a noose around the neck, if you follow me."

"I do," said Trenloe, thinking back to his earlier conversation with Marns and Dremmin and feeling the soft glow of appearing informed.

"Do not misunderstand me," Marya added, quickly. "They can fight. You had best believe they can fight. Woe betide the demon that scales these walls and runs into one of *them* on a dark night. But I have as many soldiers busy keeping them in line as I do watching over the fords." She took another mouthful of bread and spent a while chewing. "You don't talk much, do you?"

"I suppose not, my lady."

"Dremmin takes care of that, I suppose."

Trenloe thought about it, and realized that it was largely true. "Yes."

The castellan near choked on her bread. "That was meant as a joke!" She took a sip of water, and then another, until she felt comfortable breathing. "Tell me Trenloe. Was it Dremmin's choice to give up the pleasant climes of Trast, parading Baron Rault's flag up and down the Lorimon border, in exchange for Hernfar?"

"No."

"Why am I unsurprised?"

"She handles the details, but I decide which commissions we take."

"Why this one?"

Trenloe shrugged. "A feeling. I wanted to be where I could make the most difference."

"Is this something that comes upon you often? These feelings?"

"My father told me I've a good sense for what's right."

"Well," Marya pointed at him sternly. "I've got you contracted for twenty-four months. In case any more *feelings* come over you while you're here."

For a while they chewed their bread and supped at their water in silence. The square of visible sky in the window darkened from deep gray to truer black. A scarlet tinge undertook the easternmost clouds. The candle smoked and sputtered.

"How much do you know about this fortress and its history?" she asked, at length. "What do you know about the battles of the First Darkness?"

Trenloe considered. Most of his history came from his father's bedtime stories, or Bethan's songs. "I know we won."

Dame Ragthorn laughed, thumping hard on the tabletop. "Answered like a hero. My word, it's as though the last great wizard Timmoran Lokander has stepped out of one of those old books and come to dine at my table. If you will allow me then, I will give you a somewhat *fuller* idea of why we are all here."

She paused, considering how and where to begin her tale.

"There was no fort here then, of course. There was no Terrinoth. It was Talindon still, as it was called in the Penacor reign. The Uthuk could cross the Lothan here as they pleased. That was what they called themselves by the way. The great enemy from the east. *Uthuk Y'llan.* In their own tongue it means Locust Swarm and as I understand it the name was apt. They swept across Talindon and only the greatest fortresses of the age, our own Kellar amongst them, were able to hold out though they spent many years besieged. Even the great citadels of the Latari and the mountain strongholds of the dwarves were beset. Indeed, were it not for their fixation on conquering Thelgrim, the capital of the dwarven realms, then all lands east of the Kerdoshan Divide would have been his long before Timmoran and an army of Sundermen arrived from across the sea on behalf of the caliph of Al-Kalim to turn them back."

She coughed and took a long drink.

"Anyway. The alliance of elves and dwarves and the two great nations of humanity were enough, *barely enough*, to break the Locust Swarm at Thelgrim. This castle, and the watch forts built north and south of it along the length of the Lothan, were raised to watch for their return. Those in Frestan lands, I am told, are still garrisoned, though not to the strength necessary in King Daqan's time. There have been raids across our border, skirmishes fought on both sides of the water, but little to threaten Nordgard Castle itself. Even when Terrinoth found itself beset by other evils during the Second and Third Darkness the threat from the Darklands has stayed quiet. Some say that threat is gone forever and that the tribes will never again gather in such number as they did in that time."

Trenloe lent forward, the spread and his own hunger forgotten. He had heard these tales before, albeit in simpler forms, but hearing them spoken aloud here, within watching distance of the endless steppes of the Ru, felt like an illicit thrill.

"And what do you think, my lady?" Trenloe breathed.

"I think the Greyfox is not the greatest or only danger to Kell. I see things here that I have not seen before and, if I am being honest, things that I had never thought to see. People flee westward from Last Haven in their hundreds. Most of those you will have seen at work about this castle are those refugees we have taken in from across our border in the last few months. They speak of demons again bestriding the Charg'r Wastes at will, as has not been possible for them in a thousand years, of flesh ripper packs attacking walled settlements in broad daylight and devouring all within. My own scouts fail to return more often than not, and so I no longer send them. On a clear day I can see well enough with my own eyes that something is not quite right upon the Ru. Sometimes I see great numbers of horsemen, vast like a migrating herd, but it is the stillness of it that terrifies me the most. The animals and the birds fall quiet, as if before a terrible storm. Mennara holds her breath, I can feel it."

Trenloe found that he was holding his breath too.

Marya looked at him and smiled suddenly, as though shaking off whatever darkness her mind had wandered to and the sight of him came as great relief. She waggled her finger at him.

"Twenty-four months, remember?"

"There is nowhere else I'd rather be, my lady."

"Perhaps it will all come to nothing. That is what my cousin would like to think." Marya turned towards the window. "But he and those around him do not look upon the Ru with their supper."

"I don't think I've seen any Uthuk in Kell," said Trenloe. "But on the road east from Dhernas we did run across more than one bandit force. They showed little fear of us. Or this castle."

Dame Ragthorn frowned down at her table. "I regret the condition of the roads. I haven't the strength here to discourage the bandits from using them, much less force the legendary Greyfox into open battle. Even if I had twice as many soldiers as I have now, I might hesitate. I have a nagging suspicion that it's a battle I'd lose." She looked up at Trenloe and smiled ruefully. "Heroes come in all stripes, as I said. Bad and good – is that not right?"

Trenloe nodded. It was sad but it was true. "Isn't that why I'm here?"

The woman grinned. "What would you say to a ride tomorrow, Trenloe? You and, say, half your warriors. Hernfar Isle is not large, that part of it that can bear the weight of a horse anyway, and it would be good for you to know the isle a little better when… if… the need comes for you to defend it. If you were to take over the garrison at the eastern ford for a few weeks then I might be able to spare enough real officers to show our presence on the Downs."

Trenloe nodded. "I am yours to command, my lady."

"Good," said Marya, with a smiling breath, as though already filling her lungs with fresh morning air. "Is this how it is, I wonder? To be in the company of heroes? I do declare, Trenloe the Strong, that I feel better about my future now than I have done in years."

PART
TWO

CHAPTER TEN
Trenloe the Strong
Hernfar, the Ru border

It was still dark when they gathered the next morning for the ride east.

Thirty Companions of Trenloe, a few bodies shy of half the company's full strength, walked out their horses, looking more like dangerous vagrants than soldiers in their mismatched leather wargear and full beards. Meanwhile, up and bored, a third that number again of Nordgard soldiery sat slouched in the saddle, wrapped up tight in their purple cloaks with their faces covered.

Even the presence of the Lady of Hernfar, Dame Ragthorn herself, did not seem to enthuse them much.

Her dappled warhorse trotted about the courtyard with a nervous energy it shared with its rider. The powerfully muscled animal wore a heavy caparison, baronial purples made black by the pre-dawn, silvers and golds brought to life by the contrast, and by the damp fingers of the mist. Despite the unholiness of the hour the castellan must have arisen several hours earlier still to be fitted into an elaborate harness of golden fretwork and enameled plate. Her mood, at least, was undimmed by the weather.

A large ironclad wain rounded out the company. It rode low on its bed, laden with all the goods and baggage necessary to keep the Companions in their garrison for a month. Four strong horses waited in their traces. That the two Borderland Knights remained alongside the wain at all times while Dame Ragthorn clattered about the courtyard at whim told Trenloe all he needed to know about the blight, famine, and brigandry that had afflicted Kell. Of the order of the Borderland Knights, Trenloe knew almost nothing, and nor had they spoken to any of his company except to issue Dremmin a rebuke after wandering too close to their ward. Their heavy armor was quartered yellow and green with a sapphire trim. Demonic heraldry adorned their rondel pieces and visors, and their shields, pennants streaming from their upraised lances.

Spying Sergeant Marns amongst the impatient riders, Trenloe raised a big hand in greeting as he went to claim his own horse.

The young girl holding the reins surrendered them with some reluctance. Rusticar was an amiable beast and appeared to have spent the night working his charm.

Giving the horse a pat, he then took a quick rummage through his saddlebags. Ragthorn's people had prepared them, but he didn't want to be the one caught out without a blanket or a cloak in a pinch. Everything seemed in order. Reaching to the bottom of the bag, from inside an oiled wrapping, the spiced scent of Dame Ragthorn's bread wafted up in reward of his diligence.

He leant in closer and, in spite of the cold stinging his nostrils, breathed in deeply.

"Fine day for a picnic, all things considered," Dremmin grumbled.

Trenloe looked over his shoulder as he repacked his bags. The dwarf was already mounted, bringing her almost level to Trenloe's height. The stiff plates of her armor were covered in a thick cloak, her braided hair glittered like a bed of nettles with pricks of morning dew.

"If we were in Lorimor you'd be complaining it was too windy."

"Sea air dries out the skin."

Trenloe laughed. "I don't think I've ever seen you happy."

The dwarf scowled. "I hate that you're a morning person."

Across the square, Marya Ragthorn loudly cleared her throat.

"For many of you this is as far east as you have ever been. No doubt you are looking forward to an unpleasant ride ahead!" Dremmin opened her mouth as if to comment, but at a look from Trenloe left it unsaid. "Hernfar Isle is no more than three miles across, as the birds of the Lothan might fly, but the going can be treacherous, and there is no real road as such. That said, Runemaster Garlon predicts that the day before us will be dry and fine. If you ask me the fog already seems a little thinner than it was yesterday evening and the wind from the east has a late touch of summer to it." She took a deep breath, her harness creaking as she filled her lungs, and then shook out her reins. "All right then. Chop chop. Get a move on now and all things being well we should make the eastern ford by midday."

Dremmin muttered under her breath.

It looked as though as she was chewing on fog.

"You were saying only yesterday how you wanted your own castle," said Trenloe.

The dwarf's glare was ice. "Be lucky that the lives of the dwarves are measured in centuries rather than decades. Were it otherwise then I might be extraordinarily bitter about now."

With the company ready and as willing as they were likely to get without a hefty rise in their pay, Dame Ragthorn led them out.

The east gate was far smaller than its counterpart to the west, dedicated fully to defense with little thought to its usefulness as a thoroughfare. It was wide enough for the supply wain, but only just, and its metal hubs shrieked along the tunnel's sides more than once. Traversing it became quite the operation, and getting everyone through took most of what was left of the night. The sun was just beginning its steady climb over the distant Ru when the last Companions across emerged to a chorus of sardonic cheers.

But the coming of day put things into a different light. The sun remained a pallid blur, as bright as a coin at the bottom of a wishing pool, but the warmth of it was already beginning to burn off some of the fog. A chain of hummocky atolls extended out towards a river Trenloe couldn't see yet but could definitely hear; bulrush fronds and stagnant pools, trees sticking out from lumps of ground like broken fingers. Somewhere deep in the fog, birds chattered and cawed.

Trenloe had a feeling that Dame Ragthorn's runemaster had called this one right.

"Trenloe!" Ragthorn called, waving furiously from further along the boggy trail. "Ride up front with me. I have lived in this castle forever. If anyone can guide you better then let them be castellan for a day, I say, and I shall put my feet up in Kellar."

"Get on then," said Dremmin. "I'll be sick of you in a few days and by then there'll be nowhere to be rid of you."

With a nod and a smile, Trenloe spurred Rusticar into a canter until he had caught up with the column's van. Dame Ragthorn smiled brightly as Trenloe reined in alongside to match her walking gait. The expression took a decade off her face. The armor already appeared to have removed another. "Your dwarf friend is exactly as I pictured her."

"She is not as bad as she likes to look."

"And I think that you are one of those people who determined to find only the best in people. Is it that, I wonder, rather than your strength and size, that makes you the hero you are?" When Trenloe simply looked at her, at a loss for words, she laughed. "Relax, Trenloe! I'm second cousin to a baron. Not a dragon."

"I think I might be more at ease with the dragon."

Grinning, Dame Ragthorn looked ahead, enthusiastically pointing out every sluggish rill or still pond that caught her notice. "A desolate looking isle is she not? But believe it or not, she works as hard towards the defense of the realm as you or I. The only credible ground is that which King Daqan built his castle on. Everything else winds through marshland from ford to ford, and can be remade by a single day's rain. Only I and a handful of scouts know it well. Still, better to be watchful. Small groups of Uthuk Y'llan are forever looking to sneak across in boats. They tend to hide out in the hollows hereabouts to cause mischief and poach livestock and make the crossing west where the opportunity presents. I'm resigned to the fact that one or two will always slip the net. Fredric knows my needs and as he's not sent the soldiers I need to meet them, I can only assume that he's resigned to it as well. He's a good sort, my cousin. He cares. Kell could do worse, but ..." her gaze drifted across the marsh, and she went on, "we used to patrol the island regularly, but, as you know, I have not had the manpower to spend on that kind of exercise in some years. I console myself instead with the knowledge that the western ford is watched far more heavily. The Uthuk may cross in dribs and drabs, but not in any significant number and ... Remind me, Trenloe, what was I saying?"

Trenloe smiled. "Be watchful."

"Ah, yes. Ironically, the Greyfox and her brigands have probably done more to keep the east clear of Uthuk than General Brant and my cousin."

"I heard rumors in the Downs that the Uthuk could be behind the Bandit Queen somehow."

"Pish. Every spy and whisper I have says that the Greyfox is nothing more than a common girl from the Downs. Or was. Before she decided to make herself a queen. I could believe a lot of a young woman like that. Damn, I would like to meet her. But this is Kell, Trenloe. That might not mean a lot to you, free man of the south that you are, but we live every day with the Ru on our doorstep. You only have to face east and feel the danger on the wind. Even the light tastes differently at dawn. Believe me. No man or woman of my land would ever ally with the Uthuk. It's unthinkable."

Trenloe nodded.

"You're a clever man, Trenloe. If you did not delegate *all* your dealings to Dremmin then you might surprise yourself."

"I prefer to keep to myself, my lady."

Dame Ragthorn regarded him slyly. Trenloe felt himself squirm. He was well accustomed to being the center of attention, but it was generally a case of folk wanting to stand back to back and measure themselves against him, feel his muscles in extreme cases, or ask him to lift or bend something. Dame Ragthorn's determination to find something of deeper worth was unsettling.

"We'll see," she said at length.

Trenloe changed the subject. "How long has it been since you last heard from the garrison at the ford?"

"About six weeks." Trenloe looked sharply at that, but Marya waved away his concern. "No news is not ill news, I assure you. We may not have soldiers to spare riding needless messages back and forth, but some of my fastest horses are stabled at the garrison, and the warning beacon burns brightly enough that you could see it at noon through the thickest fog."

After a time, even Dame Ragthorn ran out of geography to talk about or past battlegrounds to draw attention to and the ride lapsed into silence.

As the day matured, the sun continued to peel away at the fog, leaving the copses looking spindly and denuded, but far less otherworldly than they had appeared at the ride's outset. For a moment, Trenloe even fancied himself warm, and a discernable picnic mood came over the company. Warriors began to talk quietly amongst themselves, and after a while Corporal Bethan struck up her zither and sang "The Host of Thorns" twice through. Trenloe did not know if there was any genuine bardic magic in her, the very nature of it made it difficult to be certain, but, if nothing else, Bethan was at least exceptionally good. By the end of her second rendition even Dremmin was humming tunelessly from further down the column.

Trenloe turned in the saddle to see this miracle for himself, just as the dwarf paused, squinting into the fog where it still lay thick over the east. She rode ahead to join Trenloe. "There's something up there."

Dame Ragthorn leant aside from Trenloe to confer with Marns and one of her scouts. "You have a keen eye in fog. If ever you wish for a permanent commission as a Hernfar ranger, I will make you a generous offer." The dwarf growled something without translation, and the woman went on. "That is the eastern watch fort that you have seen. We call it Spurn."

"An endearing name," said Dremmin.

"It has high walls, a thick gate, and a good hearth. There are worse places east of here to spend a season."

Dremmin grunted something to the effect that she could imagine it well and would not wish to overnight in any of those either, but otherwise showed sterling restraint.

Trenloe was proud of her.

"Herald!" Dame Ragthorn called, and a liveried soldier who had been paying Bethan special attention sat straighter in the saddle. "Announce us."

The soldier put his curling brass horn to his lips and blew. The long note lingered in the heavy fog. Trenloe waited for the answering hail.

He waited.

Nothing.

The horses walked stolidly on.

Trenloe shared a worried look with Dremmin.

"What did I tell you?" said Dame Ragthorn, seeming less concerned than embarrassed. "Excellent fighters and appalling soldiers. They'll be drunk and passed out in front of the hearth, I shouldn't wonder. Everything will look brighter once we are closer."

CHAPTER ELEVEN
Andira Runehand
The Whispering Forest, South Kell

The boy came hurrying from the wood as though trailing something terrible he could not see, his strung flatbow over one shoulder, his leggings strangled in stickyweed and holly. He panted something that aspired towards speech, waving a hand that appeared to contain a few threads of white fleece.

"Spit it out," said Hamma. The man stood tall in the tangled gloom, his battered mail further scored by the shadows of the wood. "Unless snorting on the ground like a wounded stag was your sole intention."

Sibhard shot the older man a glare and then, opened up his trembling hand. Hamma leant in to look.

"Sheep's wool, my lady," said Sibhard, looking past Sir Brodun in favor of Andira. "I found it stuck to a piece of tree bark. About a quarter mile that way." He turned to point back the way he had just come. "There's no sheep in the Whispering Forest. Not alive anyway. It's got to be from one that the Greyfox took in her raid."

"What does Yorin think of it?" said Hamma, straightening his back and wincing, immediately suppressing it. The infirmities of age were for lesser men.

"I came straight here." The boy bowed his head. "I thought Andira would–"

"The next time you find something you take it to Yorin first, boy," said Hamma. "Andira made him her chief scout for a reason. He'll decide if it's worth Andira's attention or mine."

"But..." said Andira, and held out her hand. "Seeing as you have come all this way."

Sibhard gazed at the rune that had been inscribed in her open palm, equally fascinated and repelled. He pressed the scrap of fleece into her palm, brushing her skin with as little contact from his own as he could manage and as much as he dared.

Paying him no more heed, Andira closed her hand over the wool and shut her eyes.

She could feel the tickle of the wool against her skin. The way it scratched the uncanny lines of the rune. The cloying odors and rustling whispers of the old wood receded, like the sounds of a distant sea heard from a quiet bedchamber after the shutters had been closed. The forest's gnarled and tangled spirit grew like a long shadow in her mind, primal and cold, but rooted fully in the rocks and soil of the mortal plane and with no trace of the Ynfernael that her rune's powers could detect. There was a power in old places like this to resist such encroachment. A pity then that they tended to harbor so little love for humanity. The collective weight of the trees' souls shuttered her from any sense of her demon quarry, much as their physical mass prevented her scouts from locating the Greyfox, but the wool in her hand was a physical focus, similar to the wands and rods that sorcerers employed to simplify their castings.

She drilled her focus towards that itch in her hand.

A memory flashed through her mind.

It was simpler than her own. Painted in different colors. Interpreted through different senses.

She is confused. Afraid.

She is in a strange place. Different to the place before.

Tall things loom over.

Close.

Whispering.

Others like her talk and jostle. They are comforting. She follows them. Gray shapes run alongside. Showing them where they must go.

Another gray shape waits for them. It is bright in the dark place. Its face is ageless. Neither young nor old. One ear tapers into a mist of silver-gray hair. There is no other. It makes it look crueler. But no less beautiful. Its garb is one of many colors.

A bit of her coat tears off on a tall thing.

She hurries on.

The gray shape is already forgotten...

Andira blinked open her eyes.

Sibhard was back on his feet, staring at her in wonder.

"The fleece was... I don't know, it was glowing."

"I was borrowing the thoughts of your lost sheep."

"Did you see where the bandits took them?"

Andira smiled "Better. I think I saw the bandit queen herself."

The boy's confidence slipped. Andira could not help but be intrigued. She was not an easy woman to follow, she knew, but people tended to do so regardless because she had power and because she had a purpose. She could be as terrifying as all but the most unholy of creatures she had made it her life's mission to battle, but nevertheless this phantom of the wood that no one in Kell appeared ever to have seen still had the power to frighten the boy.

"It is good that you are afraid," she said, softly. "Fear is the first enemy that a warrior determined to confront the world's evils must face. Better to face it just you and it together, rather than when real enemies of flesh and blood surround you."

"You are kind, Lady Andira."

"I can be. Sometimes."

She returned him the tuft of fleece.

He looked at it in wonder as though it had been blessed by the goddess Aris.

"Now get lost," Hamma growled.

The knight raised his fist as if to administer a slap and Sibhard bolted into the woods.

"Were you never young?" Andira asked him, a smile testing at the deeper muscles around her face.

"No," said Hamma.

"He is brave. I hope you don't feel threatened by him."

The knight gave a laugh, too amused to be offended. "I think the boy is infatuated with you. Nothing more."

Andira studied her champion's hard face. Her eyes, for all their perspicacity into the arcane realms above and below, were no more adept at reading the man beside her than they were the trees or the great horse he led. She was envious of the ability that others wielded so casually, the ability to understand *people*, and she wondered sometimes how much of her power she would surrender to have that gift. "People come to heroism by many paths. Who can say how you came to find me near death in a barrow in Roth's Vale with this rune in my hand? Or why it was you who found me there? If the loss of my life before this quest has taught me anything it is that our past selves have no sway over us. Those people are the ghosts of ourselves. Not dead. But *gone*. Because they lacked our purpose. It is what we do today and in the future that is all-important."

The knight bowed his head. Suddenly, she was half again his height and too fierce for him to look upon.

"Sibhard will serve to the fullest of his gifts, whatever they may be. Come," she said. The golden halo that she had unconsciously begun to project faded, and she coughed, embarrassed, her commanding aspect diminishing. "Before we lose him in the wood."

At her movement the pilgrim-soldiers who had been gathered silently in prayer around the nearby trees rose with her and followed.

"You told the boy you saw their Greyfox," Hamma muttered, a little nervous of her still and keeping his distance as he beat a path through the undergrowth. The trees of the Whispering Forest were the descendants of an ancient world. Andira understood that from somewhere even if she did not quite know from where. They recalled an age when their wood was but another unnamed outpost in a primordial expanse stretching from the Blind Muir Forest in the north to the enchanted Aymhelin wood in the south where the Latari elves made their homes and as far west as the sea. They were prisoners in their own lands, and they were resentful. Branches tussled overhead, crowding the floor of air and light. Roots had an uncanny way of tripping even the wary. The knight kicked at a root and stepped over it, his horse following less assuredly on its lead. "Will you say no more about her? Why we waste our time on her, for instance?"

"Partly because it is the right thing to do. Partly because if I wanted to cross the Whispering Forest then I needed Sibhard and Yorin's help. And partly again because I *feel* Baelziffar's hand behind this bandit queen somehow."

"What did you see?"

Andira closed her eyes and recalled. "It is… difficult to say. The eyes I saw her through were not my own. She is an elf, I think."

"You think?"

"Something in the way she seemed. An aura. It reminded me of the old legends. Of how the first elves purportedly journeyed to this existence from their true home in the Empyrean."

"The dark places of the world have always treated elfkind with a softer glove," Hamma agreed, and shook his head. "But no elf would ever involve themselves in the designs of a demon."

"Not usually. At least not knowingly."

"Leave these eastern peasant folk to their woes, I say. Strike east for the Forest Road while we still can."

"You are a hard man, Hamma Brodun."

"And you're a hard woman when you need to be."

"When I need to be," Andira agreed. "But in the Darklands beyond the river the Uthuk raid again. An Ynfernael lord makes his play for Kellar. And at the same time, an elf commands an uprising that leaves half the barony lawless and unwatched. Do you call that coincidence, Sir Brodun?"

The knight grunted.

"You disagree?" said Andira.

"With you? Never."

Sibhard came into view once more, propped up against an immense tree that five men together could not have spread their arms around. He was whispering animatedly with Yorin. The one-time Darkland Ranger who had volunteered his services as guide following the altercation outside the Black Lamb tavern in Gwellan was clad in forester's attire, tough hides for turning thorns and natural shades that blended well into the gloom.

Uninterested in what the locals might have had to argue about, Andira crouched, bringing her perspective closer towards that of an animal's eyes.

She touched the tree beside her.

They were close now.

She felt it.

"Keep your voices down," Hamma growled, now someway off behind her.

"Yorin's afraid to go further," said Sibhard.

"That's not what I was saying," said Yorin, with an exasperated breath. "But I'm cautious. This is far deeper into the forest than I've ever gone, and we're still in its outermost fringes yet. If the Greyfox is laired further this way then she's more courage and guile than we've credited her with."

"Not so much more, I think," said Andira. "She is not far. The trees have not yet forgiven humanity for the loss of their domains of old. I do not think the most persuasive of elves could charm them into accepting a host of human outlaws into their heartlands."

"And what about us?" asked the ranger.

"Whatever law holds for village braves and common adventurers does not hold for Andira Runehand," said Sir Brodun.

"Then we'll trap her between our bows and the wood," said Sarb, with a gleam in his eye. "Like the fox she is."

"The Greyfox has shown she has some cunning in her," Yorin warned. "Greater generals than you have failed to bring her to heel.

Sibhard drummed his fingers on the limb of his flatbow, apparently not listening. "I only hope I get to see the look on her face before she falls."

Both men looked to Andira for a comment, but she was already heading off.

Silently she moved through the forest, in spite of her heavy armor. She did not walk with any particular stealth or deliberate care. Branches that might have snapped under the weight of an armored woman, or beds of leaves that would have rustled had she crossed them, were simply not there where her boots fell. The trees themselves recognized her as a power and gave way. On some level they intuited her purpose and saw in her a kindred. At a ridge built up from tangled roots and layers of quilted mosses, she dropped again.

The small rise overlooked a narrow dell that seemed to have been made when the tree at its center had died. Through its snaggle of gray and leafless limbs the sun fell on a carpet of wildflowers. The sky was overcast, interrupted by fits of drizzle, but after the gloom of the forest it looked and felt like a glimpse into the Empyrean. Several hundred sheep and goats and a number of horses grazed around the dead tree, watched over by a handful of men and woman in motley attire. The tree itself was huge, one of the largest Andira had seen, though larger undoubtedly existed in the deeper regions of the wood, and was within a natural hollow in which the bandits had erected their camp. Rope bridges and wooden platforms spread out through the remaining branches; potted tomatoes, strawberries, and a few Daqan banners captured in battle provided the dead wood with a new life of a sort. More bandit fighters stood sentry there. Others patrolled the bridges and gangwalks. Their lair may have been well hidden, but they were wary just the same. Either they had been forewarned somehow or they were very well led.

"It's a castle," Hamma muttered.

"We do not fight because it is easy, or because it is hard," said Andira. "We fight because we must."

In the branches above them, a bird began to sing.

Yorin was the first to look up.

"It's just a bird," said Hamma.

"No," said Andira, rising. "It is an omen."

CHAPTER TWELVE
Greyfox
The Whispering Forest, South Kell

The bright little bird twittered at the end of its branch, shuffling about agitatedly as it sang. Sitting cross-legged at the thicker end of the same branch, clad in a jester's motley of patched-together squares of colored cloth and armor, Greyfox listened. Although she was, in truth, far older than the teenage girl she appeared to be, she was light enough that not a single leaf was disturbed by her presence.

"Two hundred fighters?" she murmured, speaking in the language of the birds that she had mastered long before she had learned to understand the grunting sounds of her human father's language. Her mother had been a wealdcaller and had taught many of the animals and trees the Latari tongue. She had also taught her daughter some of the magic, but her own skill was less than she would have liked. Too few opportunities to practice. "This I know already. I have followed them from the borders of Latwood and have informed my men as such. But *why* is what I want to know? Who is this blue knight that leads them? To be armored like that. To be walking around in my wood carrying power like *that*. She is somebody important, surely. A knight of a great order. Or a countess." Greyfox drew her knee up and lounged back against the tree trunk. She had always wanted to kill a countess. Ever since she had been a little girl and a countess had hanged her father as a horse thief. "Should I kill this one, do you think?"

The bird swiveled its head as though surprised to see her there sharing its branch.

With a fluttering of wings, it took off.

Greyfox looked at the empty branch, nonplussed.

"Well. That was just rude."

That was the problem with dealing with birds.

They were so… flighty.

She watched the blue knight and her entourage of peasant soldiers move into the clearing, humming a tune to herself as she idly attached a string to her longbow. The string was elf hair and it was the only one she owned. It had been her mother's. Her own hair lacked the delicacy and the strength. When the work was done she removed her fingers from the knot and ran them down the intricately carved upper limb from nock to grip. The pale wood shimmered like pieces of the moon. As if by magic an arrow appeared on the string. The moonstone head twinkled like Latariana's last gift to the world. Elves, even half-elves with thick Kellar accents, were rarities this far north of Aymhelin and south of the Salishwyrd. Even to sensible folk, her abilities were practically indistinguishable from magic. It had come in useful, once she had decided to start taking back just a little bit of what life had taken from her.

She stuck her tongue out the side of her mouth as she aimed.

The blue knight was, rather amusingly, walking brazenly towards her hideout.

She almost felt guilty for having warned her men of their coming.

The woman was not even trying to catch them off guard.

"I think I will shoot her first after all," Greyfox murmured speaking now not in the language of the birds, because that would have been silly, but in her own common tongue. "Better to be safe than sorry."

CHAPTER THIRTEEN
Trenloe the Strong
Spurn Castle, Hernfar, the Borderlands

The door to the Spurn fort was unlocked. It creaked slowly inwards against Trenloe's shoulder. He ducked beneath the stone lintel.

The flooring was scuffed. A thousand years of heavy boots and shifting furniture had left their mark. There was a hearth in the middle, built up with a wall of blackened stone, a cook pot hanging over an iron grate. Several big chairs were set about it, draped with furs. A smaller number were set off to one side, near a private table cluttered with coins and dice and a few leather cups. Personal oddments lay here and there. A piece of bark with a picture of a woman drawn on it. A pair of worn boots next to the hearth. A captain's dress coat hanging from the back of a chair.

The quiet made Trenloe's breathing quicken.

He stepped inside as lightly as he could, but the floorboards still groaned under his bulk.

Dremmin crept in after him. The dwarf was taking no chances. Her winged helmet was pulled firmly down over her head. Her Dunwarr war hammer was gripped in both hands and ready.

"Hello-*ooooo*."

No answer. Not even an echo.

Trenloe peered inside the hearth while Dremmin stood watch. "It's cold."

"For how long?" said Dremmin.

Trenloe shrugged. "How do you tell?"

The dwarf scowled, then gestured towards the pot. "What's in there?"

Trenloe pulled off the lid. "Nothing. It's burnt down."

"I don't like it," Dremmin muttered. "There're two things a soldier won't abide: going cold, and going hungry."

The rest came in behind them.

Corporal Bethan muttered a few verses of a prayer, her hand in her pocket, playing with her lucky coin, as she looked over the deserted guard room. While the Companions explored, Dremmin crossed to the table and its abandoned game. She prodded a small stack of coins, baring crooked teeth in a grin that Trenloe knew well enough from an ancient dungeon or two. The dwarf picked up a cup. Its contents sloshed about. So, not empty. She lifted it to her broad nose and sniffed.

"Is that the first thing you can think of?" Trenloe hissed. Despite the emptiness, his abiding instinct was to remain quiet.

"I've always said you should drink more," the dwarf countered.

"I don't drink at all."

A man as big as Trenloe couldn't surrender his inhibitions like that. Someone could get hurt. It was a small sacrifice to make.

"My point exactly." Dremmin swallowed what was left in the cup. She pulled a sour face, sticking her tongue out and setting the cup back down. "If you're asking me these cups haven't been touched in days."

"I'd listen to her," Bethan murmured from across the room. "If it's a song you want then go to a bard. If it's a question about ale then ask Dremmin."

The dwarf patted her leathered belly and leered. "What did I say, Trenloe? Drink more."

DameRagthorn stamped inside, and Trenloe whirled towards the sudden noise.

The Lady of Hernfar was red-cheeked stamping the mud from her boots as she turned to Marns and her herald, Barden, coming up behind her. "Wait outside with the horses. It's getting crowded in here."

Trenloe let out a slow breath, his heart reluctantly slowing its beat. "You should wait too, my lady. Until we can find the garrison. Or what's become of them."

The woman snorted. "I'll not be seen fretting in the courtyard of my own castle. I told you what this lot were like. Miscreants to a man." She looked around the grubby guardroom. The coins, Trenloe noticed, were no longer on the table. He glanced at Dremmin who looked innocently elsewhere. "Had the door been broken in or the horses missing I might have worried. But no, we will trip over them somewhere around here, you have my word. If they have not been celebrating the changing of the guards by putting away the next three weeks of beer ration in one night then I'm a Loriman."

"*Our* three weeks of beer ration," Dremmin grumbled. "The storeroom's downstairs, is that right?"

"That's right," said Ragthorn.

"Go take a look," the dwarf said to Bethan. "If there's been a party and we weren't invited, then odds are it'll have been there."

The corporal brightened appreciably at being handed responsibility for securing the beer cellar.

Dremmin turned to Trenloe. "You and I had better have a peek up top."

Across the guard room stood another door. It wasn't locked either, and opened onto the narrowest of stairwells. Trenloe looked up. The stair wound upwards into ominous gloom on a right-handed spiral. He would not have wanted to fight his way up those steps. Not even if he had been Dremmin height and Bethan's width. A decently armed soldier could hold it forever.

He swallowed nervously.

But again, there was no sign at all that anybody had.

"You should go first," he hissed back to Dremmin.

The dwarf scoffed. "That's not the way we do things."

"Your eyes are better in the dark than mine."

"What's to see? Face forward, put one foot in front of the other. If you walk into me then you're going the wrong way."

Trenloe swore under his breath. He led the company because, as Dremmin put it, his name was golden. It had been Dremmin's idea, and Trenloe had long accepted that Dremmin made most of their decisions.

He took a deep breath and squeezed his right hand around the outside handrail, drawing reassurance from its existence.

"All right," he said.

And then he climbed.

The fortress may have been a small one, a few cramped rooms and a tower, but its walls were still high. High enough to peer across the full width of the Lothan on a clear day. High enough to see nothing at all of its ramparts from the ground when the day was not quite so fine.

He pushed open the door at the top of the stairwell.

Light that seemed to have come to him through a dishcloth laid its wet hands on his face. The wind rushed and snuffled about, pulling at his tabard and nipping at bare skin as he stepped into it. The Lothan, as wide here and as powerful as at any point on its thousand-mile run, hastened by under a coverlet of fog. The sound of it gurgling over the shallow bed of the ford was the only reassurance that the river was in fact still there.

Llovar's star was a twinkling spot of red, a smear just beyond the deepest fog.

A soldier was standing on the east-facing ramparts with his back towards them. His cloak fluttered in the wind, steel helm aglitter with wet. Trenloe felt a sense of relief go through muscles he had never imagined could be so tense. He would have to tell Dame Ragthorn that her opinion of her soldiers was unfairly low. The man was merely intent on his duty, so fixed on his watch of the east that he had not even heard the castellan's herald.

"Greetings, friend," he called out.

The soldier did not hear that either.

It was only when Trenloe was close enough to smell his rotting flesh that he realized why. His hand went to his mouth.

"Blessed rock and vengeful earth," Dremmin muttered, emerging onto the battlement behind him with her hammer gripped tightly in both hands. "I hope the poor sod was already dead by the time this was done to him."

The soldier had been driven onto his own spear by something tremendously strong. His face, unhelmed, had been pecked by the birds, and the sight made every muscle in Trenloe's body cringe anew. He felt physically ill. He had killed before, of course he had, but only in battle, as a last resort. This… Someone had delighted in this.

"Who…?" he managed, shaping the words around the gag reflex in his throat.

Dremmin came to join him. She looked along the rampart. "What did Dame Ragthorn say the strength of the Spurn garrison was? Twenty?"

"Twenty," Trenloe confirmed, placing both hands on the crenulations, looking steadfastly at the battlement-walk and breathing. "Do you count twenty?"

Dremmin peered into the fog as though afraid of what might come out of her mouth were she to open it. "Aye."

There was a clatter from the stairs.

Man and dwarf both whirled.

"My..." said Ragthorn, looking about her. Her expression twitched like that of a person talking to someone in their sleep. "My word."

"Tell me again how long it's been since your last word from Spurn?" said Trenloe.

"How long *exactly*," Dremmin added.

"I... I..." Ragthorn blinked and turned to them. "I don't know exactly. I would have to ask Marns, or..." Her gaze drifted back to the impaled soldier. "Six weeks, I would say. Yes, six."

"The ford has been unwatched for *six weeks*?" said Trenloe.

Dremmin shook her head. "No. No. It's not as bad as all that just yet. This one's not been gone more than one." She tapped the side of her nose. "The beer downstairs tells the same story."

"All right," said Trenloe. "One week then. How many Uthuk could have crossed in that time?"

"I... I don't know," said Ragthorn.

"Hundreds of Uthuk could have made it into Kell."

Dame Ragthorn did not try to argue. For the first time since Trenloe had met her, she seemed at a loss, confronted by a situation she had not predicted and could not overturn with charisma alone.

She nodded like a broken woman.

"They could."

Trenloe made to say something more, but Dremmin's hand shot up to demand silence and Trenloe closed his mouth. The dwarf shuffled back to the battlements, giving its grim sentry a wide berth, and peered down. "Something's crossing the ford as we speak."

"What?'

Trenloe joined his friend at the ramparts and looked down

A chill ran through his bones. A ghost story of the First Darkness, when all that was good in the world had been one heroic deed away from annihilation, wrapped itself in the shroud of Hernfar's mists and breathed down his neck.

He stared into the gray until his eyes began to water.

Then he saw it, and somehow on this occasion the reality was far worse than the fear of it.

"Golden Kellos almighty," he breathed.

"What?" said Ragthorn, still stood by the door. "What is it?"

Trenloe was too stunned to answer her.

"Uthuk Y'llan," said Dremmin darkly. "It's happening *now*. They're crossing." She turned to Trenloe. "Just my luck to be stuck here for this."

"How many?" said Ragthorn.

"It's called the Locust Swarm!" Dremmin snapped at her. "Work it out!"

Trenloe tried to get his mind to think. A battle was coming. He was a soldier. But he could not overcome the first mental hurdle he came to which was that this simply could not be happening. The end of the world. "I… I only see a few hundred."

"There'll be more behind them."

"We can hold them," said Ragthorn, to their disbelieving stares. "We can! The ford is narrow, and the river is vigorous. The Uthuk won't be able to charge across it. Nor will they be able to come at us in good order. Set my soldiers up here, on the walls. For all the poor choices they have made in life to bring them here, they are warriors of Kell. There are none better this side of the sea with spear and bow. If the Uthuk dare cross then it will be into a hell of arrows, and to find Trenloe the Strong and the Lady of Hernfar waiting with a proper Terrinothi welcome."

Trenloe took a deep breath and nodded. His mind was still struggling to conform to the enormity of what was happening below, but a fight he could understand. His body felt ready for it even if his mind was not quite there. He had come north to make a difference.

He was ready to save the world.

"I will hold the ford," said Trenloe. "Your place is in Nordgard Castle."

"What are you saying?" Dremmin wailed. "We should all ride back to Nordgard."

"It took us half a day to get here, but a faster rider could be there in under an hour and have reinforcements back here in four."

"I'm not the lightest of riders, Trenloe, though bless you for not noticing," said Ragthorn with the stiff grin of martyrs and the very finest of generals. "Even if I was as swift as a verdelam scoutrider I would have sent someone else in my place. I'm not about to miss the chance to stand alongside Trenloe the Strong!"

"*I'll* go," Dremmin interrupted.

Trenloe and Ragthorn turned towards her.

"I'll go," she said again, more forcefully. "We're mercenaries, Trenloe," she said, her gruff voice becoming wheedling, and she shifted as though to make a bolt for the stair if either of them disagreed. "I'm not fighting the entire Uthuk Y'llan for these people. We don't do last stands. Nobody gets *paid* after a last stand."

"Go," said Trenloe, though it broke his heart to think of this as a farewell.

"Ride fast!" Ragthorn called after her.

But the dwarf did not answer.

She was already gone.

CHAPTER FOURTEEN
Andira Runehand
The Whispering Forest, South Kell

"Runehand!"

Warrior-pilgrims streamed from the wood. Arrows zipped at them from the roof of the great tree. A pilgrim fell with an arrow in her chest. Then another. And another. The handful of pilgrims carrying bows, mostly those led by Yorin of Gwellan, dropped to one knee as their comrades ran past them, then drew, aimed, loosed. The rattle of bow-fire looped up towards the platforms, thudding into wooden mantlets and clattering off clay pots. The horses and livestock who had been grazing in the clearing bleated in sudden fright, as some captain amongst the brigands waiting in the hollow trunk shouted a charge.

The two groups ran at one another, like fighting dogs set loose in a pit, smacking together with a thump of meat and mail and a snarl of blades. Screams rang out, men and women bowled over, as the mess of fighters broke into a hundred individual contests of strength.

Sir Brodun ducked under a swinging axe, hamstrung its wielder with a neat low blow, then swept out his legs. Yorin sent an arrow whistling into a woman's chest as she ran at the knight.

From there, Hamma rose to block a sword-thrust to his eyes, kneed his assailant in the groin, then sliced open his throat as he knelt before him. He moved to engage a third, the other fighters still bleeding to death behind him.

A tall woman screamed something incoherent as she ran at Andira.

Her face was half-hidden behind a bandana, long hair drawn back into a ponytail. She was carrying a short spear that she wielded overarm like a javelin. Andira let the shaft of her own weapon run out through her fingers as she swung. Power pulsed from her rune and coursed the length of her poleaxe. The bandit's spear disintegrated before Andira's axe-blade even touched it and the bandit went flying, her leather cuirass coming apart as though savaged by a four-armed makhim berserker. Dead the moment the blow landed.

No.

Sooner.

She had been dead the moment she had decided to attack Andira Runehand.

Three more came at her.

Reining in her poleaxe, Andira took it two-handed and gripped it tight. Rune power infused her body and enveloped her. It spilled outwards into a bubble just as the bigger of the three, a bearded man with an axe in each hand, struck. Both axes swept down together, meeting the arcane barrier an inch before they could test her armor. One axe went spinning as though the wielder's hand had been cuffed by a giant. The other exploded. Its owner reeled back as though shot in the shoulder, landed on his face and refused to rise.

The other two leapt over him, confident in their weapon skill and their numbers.

Andira gave ground.

Hamma was often criticizing her for failing to practice as she should. She relied too much on the power of her rune, he would say. Trusted too much to destiny.

The first of the two raised her shield. Andira's poleaxe tore it roughly in half and ripped it from the woman's arm. The blade's serrations caught on the tattered hide and dragged the fighter to the ground with a yell. The last man took advantage, striking high while her weapon was trapped low. Andira ducked her head back and brought up her open hand to meet it.

The sword hit the rune drawn into her as though striking marble.

Andira screamed in vicious pain as the blade scored her palm. Blood ran down her wrist and into her vambrace. The force of the impact drove her to her knees. The rune itself was not indestructible, not by a long way, but it was far beyond the power of some yokel brigand to unmake. Through gritted teeth she channeled its magic and pushed back, sending the swordsman flying. His limbs paddled madly until his flight ended abruptly against the side of the great tree.

Andira felt faint for a moment as the strength drained from her limbs. Her hand throbbed like dying flesh. She hissed, smothering it into a fist until the ache passed. The rune in her hand was powerful, and not it her only source of strength, but her magic was not inexhaustible. She had used so much of it tracking the demon king Baelziffar, and now the Greyfox. Drawing on it was starting to feel like pushing against an already tired muscle.

Pilgrim-soldiers belted out songs and shouted prayers. While she had fought, the battle had moved on from her, the bandits pushing her warband slowly back from the foot of the tree. Numbers and blistering hot belief in Andira kept them steady, but the bandits were bigger and heavier than they were, better armed, better fed, and they died hard. Bowmen dueled from thirty yards apart, her lightly armored followers dropping over the open grass like cut flowers.

"Fight on!" Sir Brodun bellowed, whirling his bloody sword through a figure-of-eight above his head, his hoarse voice cracking like old leather. "For the Runehand!"

Andira looked up to the south-facing platforms. They bristled with archers, roughly cut wooden handrails and vegetable pots sheltering them like a parapet. Ragged volleys of fire scythed her warriors down.

It had to go.

Taking a deep breath, Andira rooted herself, drawing her focus inwards. She felt the power in her hand swell as she she traced the crossed interior of the rune to activate its offensive powers and reached out as if to grasp the tree from afar.

They had been ready for a fight.

She was confident they were not ready for this.

She made a fist.

Dead wood crunched around the base of the trunk. The brigands sheltering inside screamed as their supposed castle turned to splinters. And then the tree began to list. It had been dead since the Third Darkness, but even now it was stubborn. It came down with a tremendous lack of urgency, men and women grabbing after railings or flinging themselves from the walkways as it went. Its gnarled body thudded into the canopy of its nearest neighbor with sufficient force to knock the pilgrims closest to it from their feet, shredding leaves and branches and sending a cascade of both down over the dazed fighters' heads.

"*Runehand!*" the pilgrims shouted in religious joy. "*Runehand!*"

Fighting back tears of agony, Andira let the hand drop at her side. It felt like she was holding onto a hot coal. She had to let go of her poleaxe and manually uncurl the fingers one by one

"Fight on!" Sir Brodun roared. "They're on the run! Keep on fighting! Keep on f–" There was a hiss, a thud, and the knight's eyes grew wide. He stuttered as though the word was stuck in his mouth. "F-f-f…"

He looked down at the arrow sprouting from his breastplate. His lip twitched with disdain even as his knees wobbled groundward.

"F-f-f…"

CHAPTER FIFTEEN
Greyfox
The Whispering Forest, South Kell

"Damn," Greyfox swore, watching the arrow smack home in the gray-haired old knight's chest, fully six yards from its intended mark. "Missed." The tremors from the felling of her tree were still running through her vantage. It had not quite sunk in just yet. She had had other homes, but this one had been good to her. She peered down through the tangle of branches. Her warriors were crawling out from under heaps of dead wood, stuck up neighboring trees into which they had thrown themselves, or else standing about dumbstruck. The blue knight had done that. She had done it with a gesture. Greyfox's lips parted. She *definitely* needed to shoot her first. And then cut off her hand. "Don't fret now, it's all right," she murmured, running her fingers along her bow stave's intricate carvings and laying a light kiss on the string. "It wasn't your fault."

As the old knight she had accidentally hit puffed and snarled and stumbled to his knees, the blue knight turned towards her. The woman looked up, an expression of utter fury on her face.

Feeling no safety from that fury whatsoever in her treetop vantage, Greyfox stepped off the branch and fell. At the end of the twenty-foot drop she landed on all fours like a cat, and then rolled. She slid to her knees. Her bow came up. She nocked an arrow, pulled it taut. She did not pause to aim. At this distance she could shoot a fly between the eyes, and her mother's bow would not allow her to miss twice.

She loosed.

The blue knight made a swatting gesture and the arrow careened off target like a sycamore seed in a hurricane. Greyfox skipped another few steps forward, readied another arrow and loosed it. The woman snarled and dismissed it as she had the first. Greyfox grinned, advancing as she launched arrow after arrow. The blue knight deflected them all, pain furrowing deeper and deeper into her features until at last she staggered, sinking to her knees with her brilliantly glowing hand clutched to her breast. Her face was stricken, her short blonde hair stuck to it with sweat. Her chest heaved under a great mass of shining plate.

Greyfox prepared another arrow.

"So, you're not all-powerful," she said. "That's a relief."

A wild yell from her right made her look around.

A large, scrawny boy, weasel-thin and whipcord strong, ran at her from the scrum of fighters in the clearing and tackled her to the ground. They rolled together, the boy grappling for her arms, but she was lighter than he had been expecting and stronger than she looked. She punched, scratched and wriggled free, rolling apart and springing to her feet.

The boy whipped out a long knife. Greyfox bent back. The blade whisked across her. He stepped in, wise to her now and eager to make hay of his greater size. His knife traced a series of elf-shaped silhouettes in the air, Greyfox giggling as she wove through them like a circus tumbler through burning hoops.

"And who do you think you are, boy, to challenge the Bandit Queen of Kell?"

The boy snarled at her and lunged.

"I'm sorry, I didn't catch that."

She dropped under his swing and rolled, gathered up her bow where it had fallen. He stabbed for her, his arm reaching. She rolled across it, drawing an arrow from her quiver and stabbing it up into his armpit. The boy shrieked and crumpled on the spot. Greyfox pulled the arrow out and set it to her bowstring, swinging her aim back towards the blue knight.

"I am the Greyfox. Perhaps you have heard of–"

The blue knight's poleaxe smashed her bow to smithereens. Greyfox screamed as she was thrown back, showered in her mother's splinters.

"My name is Andira Runehand. Perhaps you have heard of *me*." The blue knight came on, haloed in golden lines, blonde hair bristling from her crown, the rune in her hand glowing with a ferocity that scorched its pattern into the backs of the elf's eyes. "I am the Savior of Terrinoth." Greyfox threw herself clear as the poleaxe pulverized the ground she had been standing on. "I am Fortuna's Champion." Dragging the heavy weapon from the ground, the blue knight looped it overhead, building power, before chopping diagonally across Greyfox's knees. The elf leapt over it, shouldering what was left of her bow while still in midair and drawing a narrow sword as her toes touched back to the ground.

"You look tired," she hissed.

The woman's face was grim. "I am the Ruin of Evil."

Greyfox laughed, although in truth she had already come to the decision that this woman was rapidly proving more trouble than she was worth.

"No wonder you are tired."

Putting two fingers in her mouth, she whistled.

Andira gripped her poleaxe. "Is that some kind of spell?"

"I'd look behind me if I were you."

A look of mocking pity shifted the tiredness on the knight's face.

It lasted about a second.

In the next, her face was flat to the ground and Starchaser was trampling over her armored back.

The dappled gray courser whinnied, the stolen Daqan banners hand-stitched into its caparison fluttering like long skirts. The horse had been a twelfth birthday present from Baroness Harriet of Frest to Lady Grace of Kellar. That had been Starchaser's own story anyway. And horses, as everyone knew, were pompous scoundrels and liars.

Greyfox made a tutting sound as she sprang lightly into the horse's saddle. "I'm sorry. Looking back, that probably wasn't enough warning. I'm beside myself." Fishing in one of the pockets sewn into her trousers she pulled out a large bronze coin. Baron Fredric's face had been struck out and the letters *GREYFOX* scratched crazily around the edge. She tossed it to the flattened knight who didn't move. "For your troubles," she said, looking over her shoulder at the peasant mob rushing towards them and urged the horse into a gallop.

CHAPTER SIXTEEN
Andira Runehand
The Whispering Forest, South Kell

Andira groaned.

She had no idea how long she had been unconscious. Every muscle in her body ached and her head was ringing. It felt as though she had been wrapped up and rocked to sleep by an ogre. Pain exploded from her runehand as she positioned it underneath her body and pushed herself up. Magic was still crawling from the rune and into her arm without her bidding it. She could feel it knitting together broken ribs, smoothing out great horseshoe bruises as though with a rolling pin made of broken glass. With a final heave she got herself upright. The memory of being bested by a glorified thief returned to her like the taste of something foul.

Scowling to herself, she looked around.

The dell seemed to have been largely cleared, although pockets of fighting persisted around the stump of the stricken tree. She squinted. The figures involved were stick-men, woozy and unclear, and it was hard for her to tell who was fighting, or indeed winning. She shook her head, to no great avail.

She needed proper rest. She could not remember when she

had last allowed herself to stop. The rune could substitute for sleep to an extent. It allowed her to forget, sometimes, that the her body still had human needs.

A coin lay face-side down on the ground beside her.

She picked it up and turned it over. Saw the name scratched over the baron's likeness.

"You look dreadful, my lady." Sir Brodun stumbled towards her. The silver-feathered fletching of the Greyfox's arrow stood six inches proud of his breastplate. He lowered himself as though kneeling was entirely by his own free choice, sticking his sword into the ground and leaning against the crossguard. His breath came in wheezes. "If you'll permit me to say so."

"Hamma," she said, pocketing the Greyfox's coin and starting towards him.

He shook his head as she raised her hand to his wound. "No. You're already too weak. Weaker than you were after you broke Baelziffar's rule over Sudanya." He grinned, his teeth smeared red. "Weaker even than after your fight with me. Don't waste your strength."

"I can heal you. It is my strength to waste."

The knight snorted. It seemed to shiver through him. "You think I'd let this finish me. A little girl's arrow? After the things we've been through? I'll still be here when you drag her back to me."

Hamma had been with her from the beginning. A father. A mentor. A paladin. Her earliest memory was him screaming as she branded him.

Reluctantly, she withdrew her hand from his chest.

She made to say something, but no words seemed right.

"Go," he hissed. "I don't take an arrow for just anybody."

"She will not escape. I promise you."

Hamma reached out and took her arm. His grip had the

strength of sudden desperation and the look in his eyes was fierce. "When the quest is finished. When it's finally finished. See that my weapons go back to my children. They are all that I have… that I…" His eyes became cloudy. "I…"

Andira stood as her champion slid down the upright of his sword and slumped, unconscious, at her feet.

Her quest was to save Terrinoth from evil.

It would never be finished.

"I will," she lied.

CHAPTER SEVENTEEN
Ne'krul
The Borderlands

The warrior-grotesque, Mikran Izt'har, dragged the sacrifice to the river's edge by his ankle. He was a creature of bone spurs and poisonous purple-gray flesh, a sculpture of iron hard musculature and jagged bone crafted from the blood-tattered remnants of a human host. He was one man, but the harsh gaze of the Ynfernael had rendered him inhumanly strong and tall. The sacrifice, a Ru tribesman of no name, fought impotently as Mikran Izt'har bent down and, with one arm only, lifted him off the ground.

"*Jan'na a uethy'yre kisthe'hye ke,*" said Ne'Krul, the syllables flowing over her tongue like a hot liquid. The shadows that slunk and coiled always about her emaciated frame trembled, responding to the power and command inherent in the language of demons. "*Is'v'aan perys ke jedra.*"

The sacrifice kicked furiously at Mikran Izt'har's hard carapace.

He knew what was coming. He was the last.

The grotesque bore him towards a wooden post. Mist wreathed its base. The top had been roughly hewn to make a spike.

Ne'Krul extended a bird-like talon.

"*Veth'a ak T'mara T'rusheen ak'vala.*"

Mikran Izt'har halted before the post. Taking the sacrifice by the shoulders, he raised the squirming man up high. The tribesman screamed and kicked to no avail, and then gave a final blasting shriek loud enough to pierce the iron walls of the Ynfernael below as the grotesque rammed him onto the stake. It was a moment of absolute, transcendent pain. One that was all too brief before the man's head lolled and he became still. Blood leaked down the wooden post towards the desecrated ground.

"*Eneshr'aa Baelziffar. Baelziffar. Enethr'aa.*"

Ne'Krul closed her eyes, seeing instead through the red veil of her eyelids as the spilled magicks of pain and violent death worked another fraction of an inch into the walls between barriers. With her outstretched talons she traced a mark in the air. It was not one of the dragons' runes, but of the older, more visceral magic of demonkind. The dragon, Mennara, had created the world and arrogantly named it for herself, but before the coming of the world there had been the Ynfernael.

The air sizzled with her mark before it darkened into shadow and faded. She breathed in the plundered strength of her sacrifice, bit her lip with fish-like teeth, and shivered. She already felt swollen. Sick with strength. As though she could break the world with an accidental word and drown it all in blood.

The power of the Ynfernael was indeed great.

Her great challenge lay in *not* wielding it.

Soon, the shadow whispered.

At its unspoken urging, she looked up.

Before her ran the Lothan.

Always it had been the western frontier of the fractious Uthuk empire, the horizon to which the dreams and ambitions of the tribespeople turned and across which their vengeance would, in time, ultimately spill. It had always been her dream. For generations the Blood Coven of Kaylor Morbis had sought a successor to Llovar, one with the will to travel the Ynfernael, the guile to uncover the hidden fastness of the Black Citadel, and the strength to unite the warring tribes. Powerful witches like Kethra A'laak, Malahyndri of Yrg, and even Q'aro Fenn herself, the bone witch, lieutenant of Llovar in ancient times, had Ynfernael patrons and designs of their own, but of them all only Ne'Krul was here now.

At some unspoken signal a great roar went up.

Ne'Krul turned.

A forest of sacrificial dead studded the river's bank, a hundred bodies deep and vanishing into mist well before the ranks of stakes came to their end. Exulting in their shadow, a heaving sea of bodies and mutated limbs turned the grassy steppes of the Ru the pallid purple-gray of Uthuk flesh. Warriors with the might and blessing of Mikran Izt'har were one in a thousand, but it was a host hundreds and hundreds of thousands strong that had gathered on the far western plains. And this, she knew, was but a drop in the great sea of grass compared to that which would flood from the Charg'r once her sisters had been bent to her will.

The road to get here had been long and bloody, paved for her by the sacrifice of friend and foe alike and the promises of demons. But her sisterhood would soon recognize her as the greatest of their number. She would anoint herself the heir to Llovar and they would praise her as the goddess she fully intended to become.

She glanced over her shoulder. The coterie of bond witches averted their gazes, lest the petty hatreds they harbored failed to amuse her and earn censure.

"The Ynfernael is ready to spill upon the mortal world," she said, addressing a stick-thin woman bound like a mummy in a crimson shroud. Her face and hands were the only flesh exposed, and these crawled with tattoos of demonic eyes and runes of prophecy. Re'Kaan was a psychosis siren, a master of far-speaking and far-scrying, and in the infliction of madness from afar. "Visit our brothers and sisters beyond the Lothan in their thoughts and in their dreams. Tell them that the time is now."

Re'Kaan risked an upward glance, a flicker of wiry lashes. "And our other... *friend.*"

Ne'Krul smiled at her sister's awkwardness. Neither the Uthuk nor the Ynfernael had a native word for *friend* and so she uttered it in the deep growl of the masters of the Molten Heath.

"He will join us when it suits him, but by all means, sister. Reach into the monster's dreams if you dare to. Tell him that the Fourth Darkness begins."

CHAPTER EIGHTEEN
Trenloe the Strong
Spurn Castle, Hernfar, the Borderlands

Trenloe had never seen a flesh ripper before. He had certainly never seen a hundred of them, powering across the shallow waters of a river ford, more like huge, flayed men loping along on all fours than the hounds he might have imagined from the old songs. Their bloody physiques repulsed him, red-scaled monsters as fast as horses and as massive as lions, the powerful flow of the Lothan causing them no difficulty at all. Dame Ragthorn splashed into the shallows, the water running up to the gilded discs that protected her knees.

"Shields and spears!" she yelled, and soldiers, anchored by the two Borderland knights, formed up around her to present a wall of round, iron shields. A second rank stepped in behind them, thrusting their short, heavy spears through the gaps. Their discipline was inspiring. Companions made up the third, fourth, and fifth ranks. Trenloe himself stood front and center, taking up the space of one and a half men and stabbing the pointed base of his huge kite shield into the riverbed. Bethan struck up a song, low and fierce, striking out the martial tempo with hammer and shield.

"Shield of Daqan!" Ragthorn roared.

The soldiers responded with a hoarse cry.

"We stand!" Trenloe bellowed above them all, raising his axe high. "We stand and give not one inch."

And then they came, through the mist and the river spray, like nightmares of blood and bone given form and voice. A rattling volley of arrows hissed down from the castle and clattered off bone armor. The demons charged through it. Trenloe lifted his shield and took half a step forward. There was no time left to think. He swung his axe. It crunched into a flesh ripper's chest. The creature whined like a kicked dog and fell with a great splash of water onto its side. He stepped back into line as another dropped onto its muscular hind legs and lunged, rising out of the water and crashing into Trenloe's shield. The monster's weight bore him down. The cold Lothan rushed over his head and flooded his armor. His world became fast and loud. Scrabbling claws. Churning limbs. He hauled his head above water with a gasp. The flesh ripper gnashed for his face. He ducked just out of its reach. Its fangs were the color of bone and the length of knives. Its eyes were lidless, the yellow-red of Llovar's star.

Dame Ragthorn's mace crunched into the side of its head and the creature splashed sideways. Sergeant Marns and another soldier helped to pull him up.

"Thank you," he breathed, but the soldiers were already pulling back into line.

A flesh ripper with a studded iron collar stove in the shield wall, using its head like a battering ram, and sank its jaws into a spearman's leg. The soldier screamed. The river spray turned bloody. "Hold the line!" Dame Ragthorn bellowed, Bethan leading a wedge of Companions to pull the mauled soldier back. "Hold the line! Help is coming! Heroes of Daqan!" Demon hounds shrieked like raptors as they galloped from the fog.

Soldiers screamed and wept as they held them at bay. The heavy blades of the Borderland Knights glittered and flashed. Arrows hissed about them like rain.

Trenloe roared and swung his shield. The blow smote the inch-thick bone plating of the flesh ripper's ridge head, cracking it and leaving it dazed. It opened its jaw dumbly as Trenloe planted his boot on its shoulder and struck its head from its neck with a single blow from his axe.

He stood over its corpse, bloodied and dripping, and roared until he was hoarse.

"My beating heart!" Dame Ragthorn cried, allowing her knights to draw her back. "We will all have reputations to earn today!"

"I think Dremmin might have been in the right mind all along," Trenloe yelled back. "We should have all fled to Nordgard Castle."

"We could not have outrun the Locust Swarm. They would have swarmed us in the marshes. It is too late now at any rate."

Trenloe turned at the sound of an arrow thudding into human flesh.

The Uthuk berserker grunted, his upper body swaying with the impact of the arrow to his chest, and ran on regardless. More swarmed after him. Many more. Lilac-skinned. Yellow-eyed. Their faces were long and contorted by savagery. The occasional hulking champion sported a cracked helmet made from the skull of some personally bested monster or a plate of dented steel strapped across one shoulder, but the majority were semi-naked and feral, clad only in strips of red-dyed cloth and the slave brands of their demonic masters. Spurn's arrows fell on them like rain. A few fell. Most simply ran on with arrows sticking out of their bodies. They were less men than demons themselves. They felt no pain.

Trenloe's muscles bulged, his grip tightening over the haft of his axe.

He would show them pain.

Aggression rolled ahead of the Locust Swarm. The way a man's hair might stand on end in the seconds before a lightning strike.

"They are flesh and blood!" Dame Ragthorn yelled, breaking the spell. "Hold the line and let the Lothan have them!"

The first wave of berserkers slammed into the wall of Daqan shields. Uthuk screamed and howled and kicked up water, raking, chewing, clawing even as they were run through with spears and lay dying. A warrior flung herself at Dame Ragthorn. The Uthuk's knives were made of knapped flint and shimmered as though stained with old blood. Trenloe intercepted her with a blow from his shield. She did not get up. More Uthuk swarmed over her. Trenloe felt his fury rising. A high, looping axe-swing split an Uthuk berserker roughly in two. He roundhoused another with his shield. The warrior went six feet, sending another three sprawling to be trampled under the rest of the swarm before splashing clear of the shallows. As an afterthought he broke a warrior's face with his elbow. He fought like a bear baited by dogs, felling two with every swipe of his mighty paws.

"We are the Companions of Trenloe!" He beat a scythe-wielding Uthuk to the ground. "We hold this ford until Dremmin's return." He hammered his axe deep into a warrior's skull. "I will hold it alone if I have to. Let no man or woman stand with me who does not wish to do the same." He kicked the body off his axe. "If Lluvar himself came to force this crossing then he would find me still here." He beat his axe's flat against his shield. Both were slick with blood and the sound they made was that of a wet drum. "So come test your strength against mine, Darklanders! Come shift Trenloe the Strong if you can!"

A hulking warrior pounded on its chest and bellowed. Trenloe looked up at thing that had once been human.

It stood a foot taller than Trenloe and its shoulders were huge.

Its arms were stupendously muscled and ridged with spikes of bone, and were far, far too long for a man its size. "I am Mikran Izt'har," it said, knuckling towards him. "I will test my strength against yours."

Trenloe turned a punch off his shield, but its strength was outrageous. A normal man would have felt the bones shattering in his arm. Gritting his teeth, he struck back. His axe gashed the brute's forearm. The other fist dropped like a hundredweight from a cargo crane. Trenloe raised his shield. The punch crumpled it. Metal wings lifted up around the grotesque's fist, and Trenloe sank to his haunches. Summoning all his stubbornness and strength, Trenloe pushed back. Bits of bent metal flew off his broken shield as he beat it across Mikran Izt'har's near-human face.

The grotesque roared and staggered, unable to lift its gargantuan arms quickly enough as Trenloe buried his axe in its neck. It crashed backwards in a geyser of bloody water, the enormous muscles of its arms standing clear of the water like rocks.

Trenloe lofted his weary axe above his head and gave another roar.

"Trenloe!" Dame Ragthorn shouted.

"Trenloe the Strong!" his Companions replied.

For several long minutes that lasted a heroic age, Trenloe was everywhere at once between the shield wall and the Uthuk, an invincible champion of an elder time. Something from a song. Where berserkers threatened to break through the wall of Daqan shields, Trenloe was there with his axe to beat them back. Where flesh rippers were driven by Uthuk whips to flank the slender Daqan shield wall then Trenloe had the brawn yet to wrestle them to the ground and throw them into deeper waters. Fighting was all that Trenloe had ever been good at, though he had lacked the stomach for baronial warfare and his heart balked at casual violence. But for all that, he had been born for this fight, a hero alone at the edge of the world, and he fought as such, as though the fate of all that was good rested on his broad shoulders.

But the men and women who battled against the swarm beside him were not cut out to be heroes.

They were just soldiers.

A Companion fell to an Uthuk scythe. Then another to a punch from a spiked glove. A Borderland knight stood before a second lumbering grotesque and was crushed, armor and all, with a single blow from its fist.

"To me!" Dame Ragthorn bellowed, soldiers rallying to her side before a bone-tipped spear found its way between helmet and gorge and slid into her throat. The Lady of Hernfar gagged and blubbered, blood welling up over the golden gauntlets she brought up to stopper the flow, and folded unsteadily to the riverbed.

Trenloe watched her fall with a wrenching tightness in his chest.

Dremmin gone.

Now Ragthorn.

It all depended on him now.

He laid into the swarm in a frenzy and for a moment at least he drove the Uthuk singlehandedly from his friends.

But he was only one man.

That was true even of the mightiest heroes.

Marns cried out, his shield torn from his grip. Bethan screamed as a flesh ripper fell on her. He remembered the day outside Dawnsmoor when the bard had first strolled into his camp and for some reason had simply never left. Her song ended in savagery.

"Fall back!" he roared, tears and river water mingling in his eyes. "Fall back to Spurn!"

He made a wall of himself between the Uthuk Y'llan and his fleeing Companions.

He would hold this ford until the Lothan ran dry. He would hold it until the god Nordros burned hot and Kellos cold, until Aris fell hungry and Fortuna's luck expired. He would hold it until the warring of the Stormlords drove the Torue Albes under the waves and the hunger of the Chaos Snake devoured the Charg'r Wastes.

A serpent hissed.

Pain flared suddenly in his arm and Trenloe stumbled.

He looked down.

An arrow stuck out of his right bicep. It did not hurt at all.

He looked up.

Sinuous shapes, all flowing robes and recurved bows, slithered through the fog at the back of the swarm. His vision turned watery. He became acutely aware of the sound of blood pulsing though his ears. Another arrow thudded into his thigh. He grunted. The leg collapsed under him and he dropped onto bent knee with a splash.

Poison, he realized. The arrows of the Uthuk are poisoned.

He tried to lift his axe, but he could no longer feel the fingers of his hand.

The weapon slipped from his grip.

A third arrow banged off his breastplate. A fourth again found the meat of his arm. He sank a little deeper onto his haunches.

Something in the sky above him issued a triumphal blast.

Trenloe looked up as a great darkness swept overheard. It was a shadow and an ancient dread, armored and terrible, head horned and long tail barbed, the colossal span of its wings broader than the keep at Artrast.

Trenloe felt himself sink into the mud under his bent knee.

A dragon of the Molten Heath.

The winged terror circled high above the castle's tower. Arrows rattled off its black scaled underbelly. A ballista twanged and undershot. Fire ignited in the dragon's deep throat as it flapped its wings to brake and climb. A torrent blasted the entre run of battlements from the tower's top. Trenloe saw bowmen silhouetted in flame before dissolving in ash. The dragon delivered a trumpet so loud that the baked stones of the tower shivered and cracked. Then it rose higher, wreathed in the fires of the yrthwrights, before delivering a contemptuous breath of fire that brought the entirety of the castle down. Trenloe heard the wild screams of horses before the stables were mercifully buried under a mountain of fire-blackened rubble.

Trenloe screamed for Rusticar, but his tongue had become chalk in his mouth.

With a feat of strength surpassing all others, he defied the Uthuk poison in his veins and made himself stand.

He would stand before the dragon. He would measure his strength against the terror from the northern skies and he would break it across his knee. He would stand.

He would–

An arrow thudded into his uninjured shoulder.

He blinked and staggered.

His eyes opened long enough to register the Uthuk berserker hurtling towards him.

It swung its club.

And then the Lothan took him.

CHAPTER NINETEEN
Kurt
North of Gwellan, South East Kell

"I wonder what Sarb is doing now." Elben lowered his cards to stare mournfully out the window. The little steading faced north. Under a bright moon and a clear sky the southern outriders of the Whispering Forest might have been just visible from there. If it had been possible to make out even the new pigsty on the other side of the stream through the cheap slab of leaded glass.

This had always been Kurt's least favorite part of the day: too late for more chores, but too early for bed, nothing left to do now but to eat the little he had, dwell on thoughts he didn't want, and sit with sons he didn't understand.

A son, he corrected himself.

"It's your bet," he grunted.

Elben returned his attention to his cards.

Something on the downs howled.

Kurt gave it no mind. Some fools had broken the forest's peace and it'd be taking its due tonight.

The howl came again. A little closer.

Elben added to his neat stack of coins, deliberately setting each one with the defiled "face" side up. The Greyfox pillaged right across southern Kell these days, but she seemed to just scratch out and then throw away everything she took. A child could find her coins anywhere. They had become so commonplace as to be almost worthless.

"I'll call you out," he said, and with the seriousness of a general deploying his model soldiers to battle he moved the coin stack forward. Then he laid out his hand. "Frontal assault."

Kurt spread his own cards across the table.

His djinni countered Elben's naga priestess, his two Weik warriors bettered his son's goblin pair, and an Undying King thoroughly outscored a Queen of the Elves.

"You're awful at this game," he said.

"I don't understand the scoring," Elben admitted, leaning forward to admire the cards on the table. "I just love the pictures."

The game was called Cradle. Kurt had no idea why. He'd picked it up at Bastion Tarn. How Sibhard and Elben had come across his pack and learnt to play he couldn't remember. Katrin, probably. His heart gave a twinge.

He pulled the spread cards together and shuffled them back into the deck.

"Why don't you teach me a game?" he suggested.

"*Me* teach *you*?"

"Sure, why not?"

"What kind of a game?"

"Any kind." He shrugged. "What did your Aunt Larion play with you while I was in the east?"

Elben deflated, his initial enthusiasm in the idea faltering as he thought. "I can't think of any."

Another long howl rattled the window frame.

It sounded close enough to freeze the milk in his belly. Just over the far side of Old Gray. And familiar too. Disturbingly familiar. He'd never faced the Uthuk himself, there was no crossing at

Bastion Tarn, but he'd been trained for it, and he'd heard them. Kellos, he'd heard them. Like something crossed between the growl of a bear and the cry of a hawk, yet more alike to neither.

Kurt turned towards the window. He eased his chair back from the table.

"What is it?" said Elben.

"Probably nothing. Stay there."

He stood and crossed to the corner where he kept his bow stave. Remembering why it wasn't there any more, he said a word that Elben was too young to hear, and then lifted the old sword and battered shield from the mantle

"Stay here. Get under the table."

"What's going on?"

"It'll be all right, just ... just do as you're told and stay there."

He went to the front door.

He slid his shield over his forearm so that it was secured by the straps leaving his hand free, and with it he lifted the latch.

For a moment he was sure he had fallen asleep at the table and was dreaming.

He was at watch, on the high tower of Bastion Tarn, overlooking the southern Dunwarr and the Borderlands. Same sword. Same shield. An oft-recurring nightmare of a monster he had briefly glimpsed on the Plains of Ru came scrabbling down the loose-bound soil of Old Gray and into the yard. At the foot of the hill it sniffed and snorted. Its eyes burned like coals in the night. Its body was huge and blood red, emitting a deep growl the way a man would breathe. The pigs in their sty squealed in terror. From the back of the house, Boxer was barking. It was all Kurt could do not to slam the door.

It was not a dream.

This was not the Ru.

He was not in a castle.

With shaking arms he inched the door carefully shut, not daring to breathe even as the sounds of savaged wood and pig screams rang out from the other side of the yard. He closed his eyes and leant back against the door.

His breath came in a shudder.

Not a dream.

"Father?"

Elben ran to him, the hobby bow in his hand with a clutch of arrows.

Kurt caught him by the hand, terror making his grip so strong that he pulled the boy down. He pressed a trembling finger to his lips. "Stay down. Not a sound."

"What *is* that thing?"

"A flesh ripper," Kurt answered in a low voice.

Demon hybrids of the most distant east, so the campfire tales went, monsters born not from the union of beasts but from blood magic and Ynfernael sacrifices.

Elben's face went white. "Uthuk magic. Like in Yorin's stories…"

"Go," Kurt gestured him back to the front room. Yorin drank too much and he talked too much. "Put out the light. Then meet me at the back door."

"What about the pigs?"

"Pox on the damned pigs."

"They cost us everything."

"Only what I'm willing to pay. Now *go*."

They scrambled together into the front room, close to all fours, keeping under the line of the little window. Elben licked his fingers and pinched out the candle flame and the room fell dark. Kurt nudged open the door to the pantry. A dozen wheels of white sheep's cheese sat on the side. Too big to take with them. Elben joined him, snatched a knife off a chopping board and nodded.

The pigs had stopped screaming.

Kurt turned the handle and pushed open the back door.

Boxer and Whisper ran up with their tails between their legs. Boxer gave a loud bark that made Kurt's heart leap for the moon.

"Quiet," he hissed.

Elben threw a frightened glance over his shoulder.

The big dog sat on the ground and whined.

Kurt half-ran to the stall at the back where his horse was waiting anxiously, pawing at the straw and throwing his mane. He unbolted the stall door and led him out. There was no time to saddle him.

"We'll have to ride elf style," he said, turning quickly to Elben.

"We're… we're leaving the house?"

"A flesh ripper isn't an animal, Elben. It's a demon in animal shape. And worse. They're the heralds of the Uthuk Y'llan. Where the flesh rippers hunt, the Locust Swarm isn't far behind."

"But… our house."

Kurt physically lifted his son and sat him on the horse's back. "It's just a house," he said, burying his own pain for Elben's sake. "Nordgard Castle must have fallen. If the castle has been taken then our house isn't going to last to morning." He climbed up hurriedly and set himself behind his son. "If the Greyfox wants to call herself baroness of what's left when the Uthuk are done, then she's welcome to it." He kicked his heels in. The horse snorted in fright.

Boxer gave a frenzied bark.

Kurt turned his head back, towards the house, *Katrin's* house, and an arrow whistled across his ear, thudding into the back wall. The horse reared. Kurt threw his arm instinctively around Elben, covering the boy with his shield. Two Uthuk careened into the back yard. Their chests were bare, their purple-gray skin like stone under the white light of the moon. They shouted something in the broken language of the Charg'r and more arrows flicked towards the house. One slashed Elben's arm. He hissed as blood welled up.

"You'll live," Kurt yelled, and kicked the horse harder. "Yah!"

This time, the charger leapt into a gallop, flying over the picket fence. Its turn of speed confounded the Uthuk who had been slowing down as they approached the house. Holding tight to Elben, who was in turn holding tight about the horse's neck, Kurt looked back over his shoulder. The Uthuk were not even bothering to give chase.

Boxer's wild barks ended with a piteous whine. Whisper, as always, was quiet. Kurt hoped he had been bright and run away.

The first flicker of fire appeared against the dark hills.

The scent of smoke came to him on the wind.

"Where are we going?" asked Elben.

"I don't know."

CHAPTER TWENTY
Fredric
Castle Kellar, North Kell

Princess Litiana Renata, or "Anna" to most in court, stared icily over a bowl of mallard broth and several platters of crusty bread. Her skin was a pale brown, her hair a long black that tended naturally towards curls. Her expression was one of deep and ongoing disappointment, as though whatever she presently beheld was something she had seen better of in her home country. Detesting Kell's courtly garb, she was wearing baggy pantaloons tucked into a pair of sturdy wayfarer's boots, and a leather corselet rendered in bright colors that the tailors of Terrinoth simply could not reproduce outside the cosmopolitan quarters of Tamalir, Dawnsmoor and Jendra's Harbor.

Fredric tried to smile at her.

Her frown deepened.

He coughed, slurping at his broth, well accustomed by now to handling spoon and bowl in steel gauntlets, and looked away.

Seated further down the table, the gaggle of master craftsmen, reeves, and merchant guilders he had invited to discuss the barony's troubles picked silently at their breakfasts. The clink of spoon on bowl echoed through the empty spaces of Fredric's great hall. The long table could feast two hundred knights. The hall could host a thousand dancers. Its walls were cut from glittering gray stone, a type of granite hewn only from the Howling Giant Hills, and paneled with dark oak imported at vast expense from less haunted forests in Forthyn. Thick mullions barred the windows and sturdy crossbeams bowed low under the ceiling. It was a grand space, but a cold one when empty, and intimidating to those who were ill-accustomed to it.

Fredric wondered if a minstrel might have set his guests more at ease. He shook his head. An entire circus troupe would have struggled to cheer this hall.

From behind his chair there came the harsh note of steel being delicately ground across steel as Grandmarshal Trevin Highgarde, fully armored and tall, shifted position.

"Say something to them, husband," said Anna, in a bored tone. "If they do not stop looking at me like that then I am going to kill one of them."

Fredric smiled through his teeth. "We don't do that over here, beloved."

"We do not do it in Alben either. We have not the need."

"Dig in, friends," Fredric called down the table, his voice sounding out like a drum over the empty quiet. "You should see this hall when my knights come in from the provinces to tourney. Or when Magrit, Harriet, or Adelynn bring their courts to feast. If you had, then you would know that there is little ceremony at this table. And none at all at breakfast!" His laughter fell flat. He coughed again, affecting seriousness. "It is plain fare, I know, but plentiful enough for it. No one in Kellar will go hungry while I sit as baron." A handful of burghers rapped their knuckles on the table in support of that. "Banditry and blight plagues much of this great realm, it is true," he continued, warming to his speech. "But not here. Here, by the strength of our arms, the roads remain open to trade. We have sympathetic friends and good neighbors. And we have strong allies abroad." His wife scoffed. Subtly, if loudly. "But I did not invite you here solely to feed you, or to give you a lengthy speech and impress you with my chivalry. No."

He set down his spoon and his bowl as though with intent.

Fredric looked down one side of the table, and then back along the other, firmly wishing to look every man and woman present, however lowly, in the eye. Few, however, were prepared to meet his.

"The lords of Kellar live here in this castle, but you, my friends, are the lords and ladies of the guildhalls and the marketplaces, of the courthouses and the workshops and the coaching inns. I would hear from you as I would from any of my own advisors. So speak! Tell me! What troubles afflict your regions of my land and my city, and what might your baron do to allay them?"

For a long while there was quiet.

Men and women glanced nervously at one another, as if affirming some compact of silence. One man, an artisan from one of the Free Cities dressed in golden doublet, cherry red hose and a folded cap, was even drinking determinedly from his soup as though intent on pretending that he was not being spoken to at all.

The urge to bang his fist on the table and have Trevin haul the artisan from his chair and throw him at Fredric's feet to explain himself became almost too great to manage.

He set his palms flat on the table and took a deep breath.

"Speak, I said. You have been invited to share your baron's table. In what other land of Terrinoth, at what other time in our history, would that have been possible for folk of your birth?" He rose to his feet in a snarl of heavy plate. The burghers shrank into their chairs. The artisan of Pollux dropped his bowl suddenly and looked fearfully up. In the seat beside Fredric, Anna smiled.

"I ask you for your counsel and instead you sit there like lambs. I hear from my counsellors about shortages of fuel and salt, of iron ore and of cloth. I hear about the rising cost of imported bread and the hardship that has brought to many. If I can hear all of this from the safety of my keep then why can I not hear it from you?"

Anna gave a loud sigh. "They do not want to sit here in the great hall of their lord and trouble him with the price of grain," she said, her Alben accent decorating her simple words with barbs. "They do not want breakfast and a pat on the hand."

"I would hear their concerns and have them know they will be acted upon."

"The ancestor of yours, the Dragonslayer whose portrait hangs in every great hall from Jendra's Harbor to here, he who slew Margath the Unkind in single combat and saved Terrinoth. Do you think bread was cheap that year?"

"Please! Gods! Give me a dragon to fight!"

"Do you think my mother, the queen of the Torue Albes, would suffer this Greyfox or her like? She would not. She would have hounded her down, burnt her out, slain every third woman and man if that was what it took to make an example of any who harbored them."

"You speak of slaughter as though it is a casual act."

"Of course it is not. If it were, then all would do it. Everyone would be a baron or a queen, and no one would be content to be ruled. So maybe people will go hungry." She shrugged. "If they cannot feed themselves maybe they deserve to go hungry. Or maybe hungry people will fight harder if their baron can point them at those to blame for their empty bellies."

Fredric pinched the bridge of his nose, but he had no words of argument left. He slumped back down onto his seat as though exhausted by his family harness's weight.

"Since I arrived here I have heard nothing but how strong the armies of Kell are, how hard its folk are, and so stubborn against the evils of north and east," Anna continued. "The cruelest man can be good when times are easy and there is no evil." She reached across, and with unexpected tenderness laid her fingertips on his pauldron piece. "You are a good man, husband. Everyone knows it. It does not need to be proven. But it is less easy, I think, for a good man to be cruel when the times need it."

Fredric glanced down the table.

The guests looked uncomfortably at their nibbled breakfasts. If they had been ill-disposed towards an audience then they fancied being party to his marital disputes even less.

"Would you care for me to step in, my lord?" asked Trevin, deadpan, no steel visor of Terrinothi make adequate to concealing that wry grin.

"Do not tempt me."

There came a knock on the oaken doors at the far end of the hall.

Fredric did not care enough to conceal his relief.

"Enter!" he shouted.

The guards opened the doors, and Chamberlain Salter swept in, trailing a brocaded overgown and close to three dozen pages and scribes. Without a word to anyone, the old woman strode the length of the hall to where Fredric sat at the long table's head.

"Well?" said Fredric.

"News, lord. May we speak of it privately outside?"

Fredric considered. "No. We can speak of it here." He threw a dismissive wave down the table. "Get rid of this lot. Trevin."

"Yes, my lord?"

The warden of Kellar lurched forwards. The burghers hastened at once from their seats, like rabbits startled by sudden movement, and streamed out through the open doors followed by the guards until it was only Fredric, Litiana, Beren Salter and her servants, and the grandmarshal himself left in the hall.

The princess put her boots on the table.

Fredric gave her a despairing look.

"I am sorry, husband. But I do not like these small people." She waggled her finger at him. "They will respect you more for having the stones to throw them out than they will for your kindness. You will see. Maybe next time you call them here for counsel they will speak up."

Fredric shook his head.

He loved his wife.

Almost all of the time.

"What is so urgent, chamberlain?" he said. "Before my wife and I come to blows and my champion at arms is forced to intercede on my behalf." Anna snorted. Fredric smiled weakly. "I would hate to deprive the Sacred Order of the Yeron of their grandmarshal in these dark times."

"The times are darker than you think, my lord," said Salter, without humor. Even the servants that tended on her with parchment and quills looked grave

The smile drained from Fredric's face. "Well spit it out then, Beren. For pity's sake."

"It is Hernfar, my lord. Nordgard Castle has fallen."

Anna pulled her boots off the table.

Fredric sat forward. "How? There has been no word of a siege from my cousin."

"Which tells me that it must have fallen swiftly indeed, and to a great host. But riders fly this way on every northbound road with word of Uthuk Y'llan. Brant was right, my lord, and I beg forgiveness for what might have been done to prepare ourselves had I not doubted. The Greyfox, if she still lives, is no longer a concern to us. If the Uthuk Y'llan have indeed come in force enough to sweep the defenses at Nordgard Castle aside, then they have come as a force to threaten all of Terrinoth. And beyond. I would strongly recommend you find local people who can carry word to the bandit lords still at large in the north of the country. I would entreat upon their humanity to stand with us against this evil."

Fredric's mouth worked dumbly. His entire body tingled as though to fight or run, and his thoughts could find no way through to his mouth. His right hand patted for his sword, and did so for several seconds before it occurred to him that he was not yet in the habit of sitting armed to breakfast.

"*Yes*," said Anna.

"Agreed," Trevin added. "The time for grievances is past us."

"I have already spoken with General Brant," said Salter. "And after he had reminded me several times that he had been right and I wrong he concurred as well. He forwards his apologies by the way for his absence. He thought it wisest to look at once to the defenses of castle and town."

"Quite right," Fredric murmured.

"The forest will slow them," said Trevin.

"Undoubtedly," said Salter. "It will buy us some days to prepare, though it may simply turn one great horde into many. Elements of the swarm may split west and pass into Dhernas, Pelgate, and Frest. But history tells us that the full might of the Uthuk Y'llan will head here, and precedent tells us that our futures are grim."

For a long time Fredric remained too stunned to speak further. He had thought himself bowed by the weight of his family pressure. It was as nothing to this news.

He found himself picking up his spoon and his bowl and staring down the length of the empty table.

"Fredric!" Anna snapped. He turned to her. "Now is the time for good men to be cruel."

"You are right," he said slowly. "Take Grace. Go west. Magrit will give you shelter."

"No."

"This is me being cruel! If we were in Alben and this your court then I would obey without question. But this is Kellar. I told you to take our daughter and flee."

"Respectfully, my lord," said Salter. "I fear it is already too late. If the Locust Swarm does fragment and send a portion of its strength south of the forest then Dhernas Keep may itself come under siege before we do. The westbound roads will almost certainly become impassable."

"I would not have gone anyway," Anna smiled.

Fredric could not help but return it. He offered his hand.

The princess took and squeezed it.

"Then send out riders on every road while they are still open," he ordered. "Our neighbors might not have troubled themselves with our banditry, but the Uthuk Y'llan is another matter entirely. Have others ride to every town, village, and large farm in the north. Everyone of an age to fight is summoned to Kellar to be armed."

Anna gave him an approving nod.

"And everyone not of an age to fight, lord?" said Salter.

Fredric drew a deep breath, felt the cool air in his lungs harden his heart.

"Point them in the direction of Forthyn and Highmont, chamberlain. Tell them to run while they still can."

CHAPTER TWENTY-ONE
Greyfox
The Whispering Forest, South Kell

Starchaser was blowing hard, eyes wide and nostrils flared, tossing his head this way and that. It was the forest. It terrified him, and rightly so. Greyfox had lived in or near it all her life and it still terrified her. Exhausting all her gifts to calm the poor horse, Greyfox vaulted lightly from the saddle. Wading a short distance into the thick carpet of moon-dappled ferns, she lowered her good ear to the hard earth and listened.

Roots creaked as they delved deeper into darkness. Oaks, birches and yews that had weathered the coming and going of three Darknesses, and the cataclysms of the elves before them, armored themselves in lichens and mistletoe, and drew their spirits into harder woods. Somewhere nearby, a stream gabbled with unseemly haste, while in the canopy, high above, dark-feathered and ill-omened birds twittered of evil tidings. She breathed in. Moss and bark filled her nose with their scents. A slow fear filled her heart, but could not quite do away with the grief.

Her mother's bow. It was all she had had left except for memories.

At least she had been able to save the string.

She eased herself up off the ground, making less noise of it than a furtive rabbit in the undergrowth.

Trees stalked away from her in all directions, in ranks a thousand years deep. The stream was to her left. It was not one she knew and she had thought she knew them all. The forest was changing, reordering the paths through it as it hardened its boundaries like a nut before a long winter. The Whispering Forest was one of the last refuges where the "Lays of the First", the song that had made the universe, embittered and fragmented though its notes had become, could still be heard. Its grumbling and creaking was a lament for the end of a world already lost to time.

She had come too deep.

It was dangerous for her to be here, even had she been fully elven, but there was no helping it.

All the talk of the wild was of the Uthuk Y'llan.

If she meant to reach her friends and allies in the north ahead of the swarm, then she had no choice now but to be bold and brave the forest's knotted heart.

Even the assault of the blue knight on her hideout was starting to seem providential. Without it, she might never have got out in time, and been caught between the Uthuk Y'llan and the forest for better or worse.

The evil would pass. Of course it would. As evil had in the past and would do again in the future. Whatever fears the forest and its creatures held on the matter. There would be blood. Naturally. There would be anguish, and upheaval, and anarchy – and Greyfox intended to profit mightily from it all because, as far as she was concerned Terrinoth's Twelve Baronies were past due a little anarchy. When Harriet the Willful had led her peasant uprising to power in Frest, Greyfox had looked south across their shared border with expectation and envy. How many times had she dreamed of some similar revolution sweeping Kell? But she had been disappointed. However much muck Harriet's commoner ancestors had or hadn't shoveled over Frestan fields the "usurper baroness", as she was quaintly known by the rest of the Twelve still lived in a castle and garbed herself in silk and jewels.

Power had changed her, Greyfox thought. She was no different than what had come before.

But when there were no more jewels? When there were no more fine clothes, no more castles, when the Uthuk Y'llan had swept those things into the western sea and all that was left was Greyfox and her band of believers, kept safe by the Whispering Forest, then the few folk who were left would be ready for a new way.

Greyfox's way.

A creak shivered from the darkness of the wood. It lingered a moment, distinct from the low song of the forest, then died away and was taken up again elsewhere. She turned. There was a low chittering, as of an insect or a reptile, the snap of a twig underfoot.

Greyfox felt for the grip of her knife. It was bound in leather, by a human tanner in Carregolt, with a black iron spearpoint blade stuffed into her breeches.

She missed her mother's bow.

The night was dark. Heavy branches crowded the moon from the sky. But elven senses were as keen as anything that walked or flew or sniffed along Mennara's ground. Something in the darkest depths of the old forest was stirring. Something with wrathful blood and scaled bodies. Something with no love of the forest but neither, some elven intuition told her, any friend of the Uthuk Y'llan. It awoke as a reaction, not to a summons.

For the good or ill of Greyfox, she did not know.

For the good or ill of Kell, she did not much care.

The thick layer of ferns behind her rustled.

She grinned, stretching the scar that ran through her face and the ruin of her ear. The dull pain as it pulled reminded her of the first and last time she had ever been caught.

She swung around, drawing her dagger.

Her pursuer stood beneath a moonbeam, golden haired and pale skinned, her eyes the same sharpened blue as the edges of her plate. The forest did not appear to have touched her in her passing. Even Greyfox harbored a scratch or two and a leaf in her hair. The woman put her hand over the knife blade and spoke a short word in the draconic tongue. Smoke plumed from her closed fist and the iron blade melted in her hand.

"You followed me," said Greyfox. "How on Mennara?"

The blue knight tossed a coin to the ground beside her. "With this," she said, and struck the knife edge of her hand across the elf's temple.

And then Greyfox knew only the ground.

CHAPTER TWENTY-TWO
Andira Runehand
The Whispering Forest, South Kell

Two heavyset men in tattered robes and worn sandals hauled the unconscious elf up against a tree. Once there, the men sat her up and bound her. Half a day in Gwellan had been enough for them to imbibe every possible fairy tale about the bandit queen and the supernatural powers she held over moors and forest, and the pilgrim-soldiers that followed Andira Runehand were nothing if not superstitious folk.

They were taking no chances.

Andira leant wearily against a nearby tree while they worked.

Whether it was the elf's doing or not, the forest did feel uncomfortably close. As if to warn them that they were unwelcome here. She could hear a stream running somewhere nearby, and that brought with it mixed solace. It should be easy enough to find, come the dawn, and to follow it from there to its outlet in the Lothan or the River of Sleep to the west. But either course would be wrong. Insurmountably wrong. Her destination was north. The same titanic pull that she had felt since encountering Baelziffar's plans for the mortal plane still drew her by the hand. And when she looked around her, in that arboreal and earthly place, she heard not the sibilant whisperings of an old forest but those of Baelziffar the demon king, mocking her failure to oppose him in the proper place. Looking upwards, where the silver tracts of stars and moon pierced the canopy, she saw only the rents made in the firma dracem by his claws.

Another might have seen such omens and been fearful, but Andira could not recall ever having felt such a thing. She was not certain she was capable of it, as if there was something inside of that was fundamentally missing or she had been made better by being who she had become. Perhaps that had even been part of the bargain she had struck to acquire this power. She did not know, and sometimes when she was still like this it bothered her that she did not even know what the price of her powers had been. It was a strange thing, she supposed, to wonder what fear felt like. Most of her followers would no doubt gladly have given theirs away too if they could.

With the rest of her followers seemingly content to mill about in the forest without guidance, she sat down against the tree bark and allowed herself to close her eyes, telling herself it would only be briefly. She put her head back and was soon asleep.

How long she remained that way she was not sure, for none of her followers would dare disturb her without Sir Brodun there to put them to it, and it was still night when she awoke, still sitting against the same tree. She gave her head a shake as if to cure it of sleep. The Greyfox's horse, who had been set, unwatched, beside her, lowered his nose to her forehead and snorted through her hair.

For some reason, the unwarranted affection made her smile. She stroked his head absently. "Do not think I have forgotten who broke my ribs," she told him.

"Andira."

Sibhard stumbled through the undergrowth toward her. She

was not sure what had become of the ranger, Yorin, only that he was no longer with them. She had sacrificed a great deal, more than she could remember, to the battle against Baelziffar, and it was only just that she allow others to make what sacrifices they would to the cause.

She supposed that put the boy in charge.

"The elf's coming round," he said. Even then, speaking of the captive Greyfox put a quaver in his voice.

"Good," said Andira. "We will see now what part she plays in all of this."

The bandit, as promised, was wide awake, struggling viciously at her bonds and snarling at the two men stood watch over her.

"Do not be so dismissive of your captors," said Andira, lowering herself onto bent knee as one might before a sick animal. "They are simple folk but they brought you low."

"You're being too modest," said the Greyfox. "It doesn't suit a woman whose armor shines like yours."

Andira touched her mortal hand to her breastplate. The most sought after blacksmith in Castle Talon had labored for six months to create it. Hamma had bankrupted his family to commission it for her, and then sold a castle to pay for the addition of the runic engravings that had made the metal not only practically unbreakable but surpassingly beautiful. "My armor was a gift. From a man you killed."

The bandit queen turned her head to display her ruined ear. "So was this. From a man *I* killed."

"You are a flippant creature."

"I try to be."

Andira pursed her lips. She found conversations even this long tiresome. "You are an elf."

The smirk appeared again, fast and furtive like her namesake. "Are we to play a state the obvious game? My turn…"

While the elf made great show of pondering, Andira studied her face, some buried well of lore noting the gentler taper of her remaining ear, her fuller shape, the roundness of her jaw.

"You are a *half* elf," she said.

The Greyfox's expression froze briefly. The corners of her lips twitched, but it seemed she had nothing to say.

"Such unions are not uncommon in the free cities of the south," Andira went on.

"They *are* uncommon here in the east," the Greyfox muttered.

"I believe you. You could not lie to me."

The elf snorted. "We'll see."

"When you attempt to deceive, even with the best of intentions, you are calling in some small way on the Ynfernael. That is why I never lie. Now, what is your real name?"

The Greyfox buttoned her lips.

"Are you one of the Daewyl elves?"

The elf's eyes kindled with a sudden anger. She leant into her bonds, suddenly enough to startle the two guards, and spat on Andira's hand. One of the men stepped forward, brandishing his club, until Andira stayed him with a glance.

"Don't insult me," the Greyfox hissed, venomous and low.

"If you are not one of that Ynfernael-worshipping tribe, then what are you?"

"What do you know about the fallen Eleventh tribe?"

"More than most humans. Less, probably, than you."

"How?"

Andira struggled for a moment "I… do not know."

"Or won't say."

"No. I do not know."

"How can you *not know*?"

"I do not know that either. I wish I did."

The elf looked around as if waiting for the laughter. Her

eyebrow lifted, a smile skulking about the borders of her expression, but something in her gray eyes conceded. Andira had the unpleasant sense of a kindred heart, though she could not explain where it came from, another wayfarer content to go where the gusts of fate carried them

"Elves who dwell in human lands don't always hold onto the old tribes," said the Greyfox. "They tend to have good reasons for letting go. But then, learned as you are in the culture of the elves, I'm sure you knew that." The Greyfox's smile faltered. She looked down and gave a small sigh. "But they have long memories. My mother was a wealdcaller of the Latari but she only ever spoke of it in the songs of the Aymhelin. Such beautiful songs. Like a sunset playing on the strings of a harp. But you know how the songs of the elves can be."

"Riddles with poetry, metaphor and lies," Sibhard snarled, standing over Andira's shoulder.

Andira turned slowly to glare at him and he turned quickly away.

"Then your father was human," she said, turning back to her captive.

"Did you work that out just now?"

"Was he Uthuk?"

The Greyfox spat on the ground. "Are you *trying* to insult me? Or just my mother?"

"Where is he now?"

"He died."

"How?"

"He got old."

Sibhard scoffed at that. "You look younger than I do."

The Greyfox tilted her head towards him. "Where did you find this one?"

The boy drew his knife. With the wound that the Greyfox had

done him in the battle for the glade, he wielded it now in his left hand.

Andira threw up a hand, and he lowered the weapon.

"Bad dog," the Greyfox sneered at him.

Andira cocked her head. "You are lying. How did your father really die?"

The Greyfox glowered for a moment, then relented. "He was hanged as a thief."

"What we come from matters less than where we go," said Andira, gently. "I know a little of elfkind, but more than you appear to think. I have had some dealings with the Latari of the Aymhelin forest, spent some months fighting alongside them in the Athealwel before returning north, to Frest. Even the little I know is rare lore for one of my race. More than the Latari themselves would willingly share, even amongst their own. But if you are not one of the fallen Daewyl then tell me this: what business have you with the Ynfernael?"

The elf laughed. "None at all!"

"Why do you laugh?" said Andira. "No one here is joking."

"Yes." The Greyfox looked around the watching faces. "I see that."

"I hunt Baelziffar. A demon king of the Ynfernael. What his ambitions in Terrinoth are I don't yet know, but his rise and yours are too closely aligned to be coincidental."

"Korina's Tears and the Lothan are in close alignment too," said the Greyfox. "For all that they are hundreds of leagues apart, spilling from different sources and running to very different places."

Andira paused. She was not ordinarily given to doubt but there was a poetry to the elf's argument that touched her. "Who benefits from the weakening of Kell but the daemon king, and his mortal instruments in the Darklands?"

"I didn't weaken Kell," the Greyfox answered. "I happened because Kell was weak. I *am* the benefit to Kell."

"And your insurrection takes no support or instruction from the Uthuk?"

"None!"

Andira shifted back, shaking her head. Aside from the fact that the elf told no lies she was not certain what to believe. She wished that Hamma had been here to advise her, to challenge that certainty. He had always understood human nature better than her.

"You believe her?" Sibhard asked in disbelief. "She's a thief and a murderer."

"I swear it on the silver spires of the elfhome of fair Lithelin," said the Greyfox with exaggerated somberness. "I swear it by the Lord Protector of the Light and the crown of the First King." She looked up and managed to make a pair of complicated signs with her bound hands. "By the Lady who looks down on us now."

Andira smiled. "Truly, your mother did not neglect your history."

"I don't believe this," Sibhard scowled. "Are we going to kill her here then? Or take her back for Sir Brodun as we promised?"

Andira glanced over her shoulder at him.

She wondered if she had ever been that innocent.

"Hamma did not honestly expect me to return," she said, as softly as she understood how. "No more than I would have expected to find him alive and waiting for me if I had honored that promise."

The Greyfox tutted approvingly. "Cold."

"When I need to be," said Andira, and then raised her voice enough for all to hear. "I am satisfied that she is not tainted. Nor do I believe her to be in league with the mortal enemy from the east. Whatever her earthly crimes might be, they are not mine to punish."

"You've killed plenty of her followers already," Sibhard argued.

"Battle and cold murder are quite different things. I will take no part in the latter."

"We can't just cut her loose."

"Then you kill her."

"What?" said Sibhard.

"*What?*" said the Greyfox.

"I will not," said Andira. "But I absolve myself of her. Her power is broken, for the doing of good or of evil. Her fate no longer has any bearing on mine."

Sibhard raised his knife again and brought it to the Greyfox's throat. The elf turned her head aside and closed her eyes, but the knife stayed still. With the last fractional inch left to cut, the boy hesitated. As most people who were not wholly lost to evil always did. The knife point wavered for a long moment, as if looking for a way around whatever invisible block was stopping it, until with a curse he pulled it back.

He spun around and kicked the tree with a yell.

"You… you knew he wouldn't be able do it," the Greyfox breathed in relief. "Didn't you?"

"No," said Andira. "I honestly harbor no further interest in you."

The elf's smirk faded. "I am not entirely without power of my own you know."

"You have abilities that, to those unfamiliar with elfkind, might appear magical. But you have no real power. I," Andira said flatly, "am a power." She spoke without exaggeration or pride, the way one might express the greater height of the Broken Crags relative to the Shadow Peaks, or that Tamalir was objectively the larger city than Frostgate. She turned to Sibhard who had fetched up against the neighboring bole with the hard, determined breathing of one who expects at any moment to be violently sick. "Think nothing more of her. Her power, such as it was, is broken, and this part of our quest is over. Yorin promised to lead me north to Kellar in exchange for that, but he is gone. I need you now, Sibhard. Can you guide me to the capital?"

"No," Sibhard answered, at length. "I don't think Yorin could've either. At least … not from here."

Andira frowned in thought. She was not entirely surprised, which was why she had asked the question. She had felt the power of the wood grow as she intruded deeper, sensed its attempts to mislead them.

"What if we turned back? Could you retrace our steps and find another route that would take us north?"

"You have no idea at all what is happening, do you?" said the Greyfox. "You could have left a trail of corpses arranged behind you head to toe and still not found your way back to my camp. The forest talks. It *whispers*. You can overhear it, a little, if you had a wealdcaller train your ears to it, and you know something of the language of the trees. The Uthuk Y'llan have crossed the river, you fools. There is no *back* any more. They will be everywhere soon enough. Perhaps even here, in the old places. But I was making the crossing in the hope that they might not."

The pilgrim-soldiers began muttering.

Sibhard stared at her dumbly.

"The Uthuk have crossed the river?" said Andira.

The Greyfox nodded. "It is all the trees can talk about."

"Baelziffar makes his move," Andira whispered to herself.

"What was that?" said the Greyfox.

"Can *you* guide me north?" Andira replied.

"Not from this tree," the Greyfox answered, leaning forwards until the ropes binding her to the tree creaked.

Andira considered a moment, and then nodded.

At once her pilgrims began to cut her free.

"But–" Sibhard began, before another sharp gesture silenced him. The boy turned instead to the pilgrims currently lifting the Greyfox from the ground. "Keep her hands bound," he said. Andira said nothing to contradict him, and so the pilgrims obeyed. As they had obeyed Hamma Brodun before him. He turned and pointed a finger at Andira. "If she sees us faithfully to Castle Kellar then we'll hand her over to Baron Fredric and his justice. Agreed?"

"Agreed," said Andira.

"Now wait a m–" began the Greyfox.

"But if she leads us false then I *will* kill her."

"I would expect nothing less, Sibhard."

The boy grunted and sheathed his dagger. "I think you should start calling me Sarb."

CHAPTER TWENTY-THREE
Kurt
North of Gwellan, South East Kell

"Where are we going?" Elben had asked.

Two hours later, Kurt still didn't know.

Gwellan was too obvious. It'd be the first place to be smothered under the Locust Swarm after the fording at Hernfar. If he rode there now he'd probably get there in time to find the Uthuk Y'llan still sharpening the last sacrificial stakes.

North then? To Kellar?

South to Aerendor?

Or west, to Dhernas?

Castles and borders weren't going to slow the Uthuk Y'llan.

In the night behind him something demonic howled. Kurt rode on. *West is best*, as the old rhyme went, with good reason.

The land to the west was an unruly estate of jumbled stone overgrown with cornel and broom, hemmed in by forest and hills as though they had something to hide. Hundreds of tiny rivulets and streams trickled between the rocks, draining off rainwater that might otherwise have made a tract boggy or swept off good soil to the River of Sleep and to Frestan farmers downriver who could live well enough without Kell's charity. Kurt could even remember there being cattle there. In more prosperous times. When he'd been as young, or thereabouts, as Sarb was now, and Katrin had lived with her parents and sister in the house on the rocks. It was just his sister-in-law there now.

He drew in as the ground beneath them became a proper path, and the homestead came into view on the hillside.

He tried not to let himself feel anything as premature as relief.

The place had been built up over as many generations as there'd been men living in Kell, a drystone pile sprawling across a dozen rooms and ringed by waist-high wall except for where the ground became too craggy to allow or need it. Kurt could still remember where there'd been a smokehouse and a cheesery, a barn and a covered latrine. But the Greyfox had been this way, to Kurt's shame, and little of them was left now but bones. Kurt hoped that that'd be enough. That the Uthuk would think it derelict and pass it by.

Kurt could see no light spilling from its windows. No smoke curling from its chimneys. There were no animals left to disturb.

No sound at all emerged from the property.

Or from the land.

Where at first the silence had been a reassurance, now it left him troubled. He wiped his sweating palm on the horse's rear and rested it on the grip of his sword.

There ought to have been *some* sign of life.

"We shouldn't be bothering Aunt Larion so late," Elben murmured, swaying with the motions of the horse. "There'll be milking to be done first thing."

Kurt held his son close. With the other hand he held on to the horse's rump. Elben was becoming increasingly delirious and wasn't doing anything to hold on for himself any more. The cut to his shoulder had stopped bleeding. Almost straightaway. But it had gone black, and gooey to the touch, rather than crusty like a scab, and with a foul smell. Kurt had seen wounds go like that, but only after several days untreated

This had been bare hours.

In spite of the heat coming off him, Elben shivered. "It hurts, Da."

"It's all right, son," Kurt said, hugging him closer. "It's just a little nick."

"Sarb hit me with his sword again."

Kurt gave a pained smile and shushed him. Elben gave a clammy sigh and lapsed again into a shivering half-sleep. "It'll work out all right," Kurt said again. He could feel his body beginning to panic. His heart was racing, his thoughts whirling. He couldn't think further than the next hill, just as he needed it most. "Look, we're here now. A bed for the night and a fire, and you'll be all right. Larion will look after you. Just like she did after your mother... after she and I went away."

He peered ahead, and tentatively raised his hand.

A figure stood out by the front door, under a silvery wedge of shadow cast by the gable of the house. A long dress fluttered in the night wind. Gray hair frayed about it, loose.

And still, there was no sound.

No sign of life.

Kurt could almost physically feel his heart in his chest.

It hurt.

"Damn it."

His sister-in-law stared out over the path with glassy eyes. Her toes dangled an inch above the ground, and that ground was stained dark in a circle about her with blood. As his eyes improved to the darkness he noticed that her long dress had been cut with evil runes, her body mounted there on a spike.

His lips trembled. He could say nothing more.

"What is it?" Elben murmured. "Is she angry?"

"No," Kurt managed to say. "No, she's sleeping still."

Elben yawned. "I'm sleepy too."

"Not yet," said Kurt, shaking him gently awake. "Not here."

He looked around quickly. He could see a certain sense to waiting out the night someplace the Uthuk had already attacked and left, but even he didn't think he could be so cold as to sleep a night in this house. Nor did he think it would trick any flesh ripper, or worse, that crossed their scent on the downs.

He needed somewhere the Uthuk wouldn't follow.

Somewhere Elben could get help.

"Where's Sarb going to sleep?" said Elben. "This bunk's too small for two. And he fights in his sleep."

"Sarb…" said Kurt.

He lifted his gaze north.

A permanent veil lay across that horizon, a dark and whispering band that was as evil-looking by night as it was by day. But while the rough and essentially imagined lines that carved the Barony of Kell from those of Dhernas and Frest meant as much to the Uthuk Y'llan as they would to the farmers who followed their herds back and forth over it everyday, they might just be wary enough of crossing *that* border.

And that was where she had gone.

The hero who had mended Sarb's broken face with a touch of her hand.

"Where are we going, Da? It's late. I want to sleep."

"Soon," he said, hugging his son close and praying fervently to gods that had not heard from Kurt Stavener in many a long year. "Very soon. I promise."

CHAPTER TWENTY-FOUR
Trenloe the Strong

"Donit'hrava, ek a aj'aava."

Trenloe was alive. Every breath he took felt like a mockery of that small blessing, and no one was more surprised than him. He groaned, the movement of his face hammering pain into his head like a doctor with a trepanning drill. His body felt fat and heavy. His arms wouldn't move. Or his legs. The attempt sent pain stabbing through them. His eyes wouldn't open. But he could smell smoke and blood, hear the mad cackling of dancing flames.

"Esken'kenr ar vatnr ek rekaar."

And that chant.

He wasn't hearing it the way he heard the flames. It was inside his head. Ignoring the pain that the movement caused he shook his head to get it out.

"M'lala 'n kek nat'yra."

The language was incomprehensible. It was not even made up of words as Trenloe thought he understood them. Rather, it was a string of clicks and grunts. More alike to the sound of someone's windpipe being crushed than any spoken tongue.

For some reason that thought excited him He felt his heart beat faster.

"*Mekek'kree sala ak Prutorn.*"

At that final word, that name, Trenloe groaned. The words and their meaning reached out from their source like the clammy hands of the condemned. Claws made of uncanny syllables reached into his ears and rooted around inside his mind. He scrunched his face and whimpered at the feeling of their digging through his head, pulling violently on his arms, but they still couldn't be moved.

They were bound behind his back. Around some kind of wooden rod.

Or a stake.

"*Prutorn! Akek an'aat Prutorn!*"

As though bidden by something irresistible and immense, Trenloe opened his eyes. Heavy lids peeled back from stone-dry orbs.

He recoiled from what he saw, banging the back of his head against the pole to which he had been bound.

"Trenloe the Strong," said Dame Ragthorn. "You really are alive."

"What?" Trenloe stammered. "How? I don't understand."

He looked sharply away.

Everything apart from the woman in front of him was grainy and raw. He saw rubble. Fires burning. He could not place it. It looked like a ruin, and Terrinoth had hundreds of them, even this far east where fewer structures of stone had ever stood but where the foundations of civilization went deep. Bethan's last song played round and round the rubble like someone torturing an out of tune violin and from somewhere in the shadows of his head he heard laughter.

Dame Ragthorn sighed. She was sitting on a rock with her arms around one knee. The golden pieces of her armor glittered under the light of many fires. "I'm really not surprised. You never were that bright. I knew that as soon as I met you. It is always the stupid ones, isn't it? That survive. You would think that it would be the other way around, but no, look at any event in your…" She caught herself and smiled, a hard thing full of dangerous teeth. "… *our* history and you will see the same: heroes perishing while lesser peoples return to their farms and rebuild. The torch of civilization gutters a little dimmer against the outstretched hand of the dark that would snuff it out." Without moving she appeared to have become closer as she spoke, or else in some similar manner grown larger.

Trenloe jerked back but there was nowhere to go. "You died," he rasped. "An Uthuk spear to the throat. I saw you fall."

She leant forward until her breath was on Trenloe's face. It was like nothing from a human mouth, rancid and hot, like meat roasted over brimstone. "Why would the Uthuk Y'llan wish harm on their ally?"

Trenloe shook his head. "No."

"Yes! I have been in the pocket of the Darklands from the very start."

"No," Trenloe said, more firmly.

"Yes," Ragthorn laughed. "My only regret is that I could not somehow sell my cousin out to Waiqar as well as Llovar. That would have served the swine right for consigning me to that godsforsaken swamp."

Trenloe shut his eyes. "You're a good person. Brave. And true. *Listen to your heart, Trenloe,* my father used to say. *It always knows what's true.*"

He reopened his eyes and started doubly.

Dame Ragthorn was gone.

In her place, Dremmin scowled. "If I hear another of that old man's sayings, I swear it'll be my end." She grinned evilly. "Or someone's end." The dwarf looked much as Trenloe had last seen her, helmed and armored, with her war hammer resting head down on the ground beside him. Her dreadlocks appeared a little singed and her armor carried a few scorches, but nothing more.

Trenloe opened his mouth, but there were no words. His head was spinning, fire bright in his eyes wherever he tried to turn them.

Suddenly, Dremmin was in his face.

"So, maybe she *was* true. Aye, and maybe she was brave as well. But she's still just as dead, isn't she, and you couldn't save her. Throat cut by an Uthuk spear, you say?" She spat on the ground. "Nasty. But still, at least it was quick. Not like poor Bethan. Did you see that? Eaten alive by a flesh ripper."

Trenloe shook his head. "You don't know that. You weren't there."

"You should have heard her screaming. But of course, you did. I heard them all the way away in Hernfar." She grinned and her entire face appeared to distort to accommodate it, fire reflecting off her brown teeth. Her hair was starting to smoke, the smell of it filling Trenloe's nostrils and making him gag. "Did you hear her scream, Trenloe?" she said, her voice cracking and breaking. "I did." Trenloe heaved on the thick ropes binding his wrists behind his back. He felt them give, just a little, and roared like a penned animal as the Dremmin-thing laughed. Her hair was now fully aflame, her skin turning black and peeling. "You were never anything more than a figurehead, a useful prop for shaking coin out of tight pockets, a neat front to the old business of killing people for money. Be my figurehead again, Trenloe," she said, her voice like an open door on a furnace. "We will kill so many, and never demand a single coin as our due."

"Never!"

The Dremmin-thing opened its mouth, but it was no longer

human, words were tumbling out of it. *"Urun'kairn ja leke'mair eken lak uryn'mkex."* It was the speech of the ancient and the vile, of fire and shadow, a thing of such infinitely pure hate that it had kindled its enmity of the mortal world before there had been a mortal world made for it to covet.

"Prutorn," it said.

Trenloe closed his eyes and roared.

The ropes keeping his hands tied snapped.

He stumbled from what appeared to be some kind of stone plinth. Two lengths of frayed rope swung from his upraised fists. Tendons stood proud of his naked muscles like steel bands riveted across armor. He hurt everywhere, but it would take more than a few tainted arrows and a blow to the head for Trenloe the Strong to surrender his will to a demon lord.

He looked around as though newly sighted.

The appearance of a great and smoldering ruin remained, but the space immediately around him was clear. Braziers stood atop bronze pedestals, burning a sweet-smelling fat, while censers carved from human skulls, their eye sockets glowing from the herbs smoldering within, hung from chains bolted onto broken walls.

Dremmin was gone.

As was Ragthorn.

In their place was a crooked figure with papery gray skin, long red hair worn in a topknot, and a staff threaded with the mummified remains of a menagerie of beasts, birds and fish.

The unholy chanting had stopped.

The rubber-faced Uthuk warlock produced a snarl and jabbed an accusing finger. *"Y'kann etak Prutorn etak k'taan."* He did not seem at all alarmed by Trenloe's freedom.

Trenloe put his fist through the Uthuk warlock's chest as though it was a bird's nest.

He had been beaten, poisoned, spiritually mistreated, but the scrawny creature flew back from him all the same, landing in a broken sprawl in the midst of the ritual clearing.

A maddened hiss told him that the warlock had not been alone Uthuk Y'llan poured into the circle of firelight, ritual knives and sacrificial blades twinkling. Their skin was a pale purple-gray, studded with bony lesions ranging from bumps and spikes to horned skulls. Male and female, they were equally emaciated, sparsely clad in scarlet rags and ringlets of bone.

Trenloe took a deep breath.

This, he thought, *is better.*

An Uthuk witch shrieked as she leapt on him from behind and stuck her knife in his shoulder. He grunted in pain. There must still have been some poison in his muscles. He did not remember being this slow. He stumbled back a step, turning it neatly to his advantage by headbutting the woman and shattering her jaw. Gritting his teeth, he yanked the knife out of his shoulder. Another warlock swung for his throat. Trenloe jerked back by instinct, snatched the arm by the wrist and pulled, dragging the scarecrow figure to him along his toes, then buried the stolen knife in the warlock's chest. The Uthuk screamed as Trenloe threw him to one side.

The last blood witch drew back to the light's edge and began to mutter. "*Ynkarn anat'aan ek an.*" The flames within the braziers sputtered and grew tall and Trenloe felt her invocation as a tingling in his veins. The socket eyes of the hanging censers turned red. The Uthuk brandished her knife and, teeth bared, ran it across her own wrist. "*Sank ekek nah…*" Blood welled up under the cruel knife, but rather than run down her arm it solidified into a clutch of whipping tendrils.

The witch's voice climbed to a shrill laugh.

"Look out!" someone who was not the Uthuk witch yelled.

Trenloe leapt to one side as a blood tentacle groped towards him. Another darted out. He beat it aside on the back of his fist. A third stabbed at him in the same moment. He slashed the Uthuk knife across it. The thing burst like a jellyfish under a heavy stone, splattering him with vast quantities of blood. Far more than the witch's act of self-harm had spilled and far more than the Uthuk woman could even have conceivably contained.

Trenloe threw the knife at her.

The blade broke her nose and sank into the middle of her face.

Her eyes crossed to look at it and the ruin of her face gave a bubbling laugh. The tenor of her voice shifted downwards. Fire limned her mouth and the whites of her eyes turned black. An ecstatic look of horror remodeled her face, even the bone of her skull snapping and mutating into something goat-headed and obscene.

Trenloe looked on in revulsion as the witch changed and grew.

This, he realized, with a sick feeling in his stomach and a crawling horror in every square inch of his skin, was what the Uthuk had had in mind for him.

Trenloe looked around for a bigger weapon.

He had never faced a demon before, never encountered one outside of songs. He had no idea how to kill one. Spying the thick wooden stake he had been bound to he returned to it. It was buried deep into the ground, but he gripped it between both hands and pulled with all his might until the length of wood snapped off. He stumbled, then used both hands to swing what was now a heavy wooden club with a crude point at either end back towards the demon, impacting its transforming host so hard that her head snapped back into her shoulders. She scuttled about on the spot, her face buried upside down between her expanding shoulders, and with the ink black eyes of a demon, she grinned up at him.

"It is a rare host that the blood sister Ne'Krul and my lord Baelziffar offer to me," it said, in the breathless rasp of the bent corpse it was. "Perhaps too rare. This is respite, Trenloe the Strong, not victory. The days when the great Prutorn must clothe himself in mortal flesh are numbered now as the breaths of the dying. Savor them."

Rotating the spar in his grip he used it like a conventional spear and drove it through the witch's back, bursting her black demon-possessed heart. The witch twitched and slithered, still changing, cackling occasionally and hawking up black bile, until at last she became still.

Trenloe held onto the spear for a while longer, until he was certain the demon was dead. Then he let go and tottered backward, finally allowing his abused body to feel its weariness. He looked around, searching the heaped rubble and the more distant, low-burning fires for signs of Uthuk. But nothing came. The ruin, wherever it was, appeared to be empty.

"They are all gone," said the same voice from before.

Trenloe turned.

Beyond the firelight he could now see, arranged in a half-ring behind the stone pedestal, another line of wooden stakes. To each of these another man or woman had been stripped and bound. Their bodies had been daubed with baleful sumbols drawn in blood. Some of them appeared to be people of Kell, but many more had the dark hair and pallid skin of Uthuk tribespeople. What they were doing there Trenloe could not imagine. As well as being bound they had been gagged too, but one of them appeared to have worked hers loose in the fighting. Her heritage was difficult to make out. Her skin was preternaturally pale, but with only the faint lilac pigment to tell of some distant Uthuk in her bloodline.

"Where?" he asked.

"North and west," she replied, in a heavily accented form of the western tongue.

"And where... where are we?"

With her head, the only part of her that was free, she gestured around her. "This was Nordgard."

Trenloe felt as though he had been struck. "The castle?"

"Yes."

"That's impossible."

She shrugged.

He looked around him again. Rubble and fire. The smell of baked stone. His memories of the battle at Spurn were jumbled but vivid enough. He recalled the dragon. Suddenly everything made a terrible kind of sense.

The old woman from Gwellan.

His Companions.

Dremmin.

All of them gone.

He sank to his knees and for a moment he remained there, head bowed.

What would it take to fight a monster like that? Or an army of them? What kind of a hero? It had been pride, or so the bards sang, that had brought the Dragonlords from their homes in the far north to end the reign of the Elder Kings. Was it pride too, he wondered, that had brought the dragon to Spurn to inflict the same on Trenloe the Strong?

"How long has it been since the battle?" he asked.

"I do not know," the woman said, "but not long. The Uthuk don't keep prisoners for long." Her voice lowered. "The demands for sacrifice are too many. And too frequent."

Trenloe took that in. "You were to be sacrificed as well?"

A number of the other captives, though still gagged, began to weep.

"We were offerings to Prutorn." At the name, Trenloe shuddered, the taste of its breath still clinging to his face. "He is a demon of the Ynfernael, but a mere servant of the great Baelziffar. I am told that he was banished by some mortal hero in a great battle to the south of here. An unholy place called Sudanya. Offering you as his new host was a gift to appease him, and tighten Baelziffar's ties to Ne'Krul."

Trenloe pinched his forehead.

There were too many new names for him. Too much strangeness.

"You know a lot. You are Uthuk?"

"Yes and no," she said, in a harder tone. "I fled here from Last Haven with everyone else. But I speak the language."

"I don't suppose you overheard anything about my weapons?"

"Sorry."

He bent to pick a knife off the ground. It would serve.

"Are you going to cut us free?" the woman asked.

Trenloe thought about it a moment.

For most men, the purple color of her skin alone would be reason enough to leave her, and everyone with her, exactly where she was. Dremmin would certainly have argued that. Dame Ragthorn might have too. But Trenloe had been raised better. And he had to make his own decisions now.

He cut her down.

Then he proceeded to free the others.

Wincing, the woman rubbed at her abraded wrists. "Where will you go now?"

"North and west," Trenloe replied.

"Why?"

"That's where the Uthuk have gone."

"Would you mind if we came with you?"

Trenloe looked over his fellow captives. There was not a small knife or a stitch between them, and most looked in far worse a way than he did. "Why?"

"Because that's where you are going."

Trenloe thought about it for a while and then nodded.

"My name is S'yarr," said the woman.

"Trenloe."

The Uthuk woman smiled, as though he had said something adorable. "I know who you are."

CHAPTER TWENTY-FIVE
Ne'krul
Gwellan, South East Kell

The dragon, Archerax, descended on spread wings the color of black marble, conjuring devils of ash and chipped bone from the flattened town. With the slow grace of something inevitable and cruel he settled onto a pillar of shattered stone, black talons the length of greatswords crunching deep into the burnt rock. The outline of the structure was just about visible beneath the dancing ash. Tells of stone and melted nail heads describing rooms that no longer existed, bone-white lumps lightly buried under black sand, mourning people that no one alive now remembered. A wooden post, incongruously unburnt and upright, stood outside where a front door had previously been, a fire-blasted sign hanging from a crossbar and swaying madly in the dragon's downdraught.

Tucking in his wings, the dragon lifted his horned head, its immensity briefly eclipsing the moon. A low grumble rose up from his deep throat and smoke seeped through his teeth, like a threat issued from the deep earth.

"I thought you would never catch up," he said, speaking the Uthuk tongue with a liar's eloquence, but in a voice of thunder that rolled and rolled and would not end. It ground bones in sockets, pressed skin to faces and squeezed organs in their soft bags of meat. "You Uthuk Y'llan speak highly of yourselves, but you are slow." A number of tribal chieftains and blood mages quailed as Archerax lowered his long neck towards them. He sniffed and growled. Flames licked his nostrils. "Where is the little witch who dared go inside my mind to summon me? It is dangerous, little witch, to treat a dragon as one would some lesser being. Our thoughts are older than the stars and as perilous to hold too near."

"I was the one who commanded her," said Ne'Krul, refusing to be cowed.

The dragon's head was the size of a chariot, armored and horned like the bier of a demon lord. His eyes were a hard and blistering white. His nostrils flared as he took in her scent, then exhaled heat that set her long hair blustering. She could have reached an arm into each nostril and never touched the back or the sides. She could have lost herself in his mouth. Truly, Archerax was amongst the oldest and mightiest of his kind. But she did not fear him or his kin and she would suffer no insolence in view of her sisters. She stood proudly as he sniffed at her, the hunch of her back lending her a posture that might have been judged subordinate were it not for the crook of her lips and the scarlet gleam in her eyes.

She licked her white lips, empowering her next words with the cajoling, coercing, insanity-inducing gifts of the blood-siren. "If you desire recompense for the value of your sullied thoughts then you will have to exact it from me."

Archerax rumbled, apparently amused. "You speak to me in the voices of ancient kin long dead. Have a care, Ne'Krul. Your blood magicks hold little sway here. I have burnt two castles this night and eaten many men and horses and it is not yet morning.

Test me and I may yet come to think that my need of you and this alliance is less than at first I conceived."

"Test *you*?" Ne'Krul hissed. "I have the power to break you one bone at a time and make you beg for me to be merciful and end you swiftly."

The dragon laughed.

A number of less stable ruins in the vicinity collapsed into ash and dust.

"Yes, but you will not use it, however much such a feat would delight you. The power is not yours to spend. You merely hold it for another. So speak thusly to me again, little witch, after you have spent this power for its rightful purpose, and we will see if you are so bold."

Ne'Krul bit back her reply.

The dragon had proven useful. While she knew the secret names of powerful demons who could have wrought on Nordgard Castle what Archerax had, and the incantations to summon them, such rites would not have come without great personal expense and peril. She could not have pushed so far, nor so quickly, nor elevated herself so high above her sisters in the esteem of the Ynfernael without his aid. There were times when she wondered if the dragon understood the role he played in the power politics of the Darklands, and of the demon realm, but she suspected that he did, and saw some advantage for his own gain. Dragons were wiser than their arrogance suggested, and cunning beyond the understanding of mortal wiles.

"We Uthuk play our part," said Ne'Krul, allowing the dragon a barely perceptible bow of the head. "While you level the great cities and towns, my warriors lay waste to the countryside and make sacrifice. If there is any word of our attack that flies ahead of us then it will be words of panic and fear that will sound as sweet as music to the ears of Baelziffar and his kin."

Archerax growled, dark lips peeling back over his fangs as though discomforted by a corroded tooth. "Speak not that name again."

Ne'Krul smiled and permitted herself a deeper bow. It was gratifying, and reassuring, to know that he was as wary of her patron in the Ynfernael as he ought to be. "We are together now, dragon, and together we can push north on our final goal."

The dragon issued a gout of fire that had the wary gathering of blood witches and champions ducking to the burnt ground.

Even Ne'Krul flinched.

"No, little witch. This is where we separate. We share a common purpose but differing goals. We are not friends, you and I, and your ambitions hold no interest for me."

"We hold promises over one another," said Ne'Krul. "Such promises of pain as are not easily broken."

Archerax laughed. "Nor do I fear you. Not your magic. Not your master. And not all the might of the Darklands arrayed with steel before me. Knowing as I do how much that galls you gives me warmth in this cold land." He lowered his head again to her. The fire about his lips flickered back, and he issued a conciliatory rumble. "Tonight, I fly westward, to the castle home of the Dragonslayer who felled Margath the Unkind and cast my forebear's ruin into the icy waters of the Weeping Basin. Eight hundred years has it been since Shaarina Rex called the dragons back from the Land of Steel, but never in that brief span have our eyes long strayed. They say that the Age of Heroes is passed, ended once and forever with the demise of the Elder Kings and the end of the Dragon Wars. But they are wrong. Heroes arise at need. They may hail from any place, and at any time, but there are places in this world that call out to heroes like a siren to the sea. Kellar is one. I will destroy it now, lest it be allowed to stand and defy us both in future, and by my tooth and flame will I end the Dragonslayer bloodline once and for all and bring its proud dynasty low.

"Your species' ember gutters. Pale imitations and pretenders are you who remain. Even in your Darklands where demons walk and in lands unknown to all but the mind of the First who speaks of them not, this is so. So lend me your swiftest warriors, blood sister, those whose Ynfernael mounts and demonic gifts might allow them to keep pace with a dragon in flight. I will add them to the host I muster for myself there. I will destroy Kellar in a night of fire unseen since my kindred descended on the city of Tamalir and brought down the Soulstone line. This I have sworn. When it is done your warriors will be free to rejoin you, and you will find your own black purpose in the north unopposed by troublesome heroes."

"What do you know of my purpose?" said Ne'Krul.

Archerax gave no answer.

With a deep laugh he threw his wings out wide and extended his neck to its full, awesome length. He beat his wings for lift and Ne'Krul struggled to remain proud under the downwash, bone fetishes and robes flapping about her, shielding her dark red eyes with a bony hand.

"Decide quickly, little witch," he said, climbing slowly towards the distant moon. "Aid me or not, but I go now, and ere the cold sun rises a fifth time over this land Kellar will be no more."

PART THREE

CHAPTER TWENTY-SIX
Andira Runehand
The Whispering Forest, South Kell

The trees grew taller, broader, prouder in the dark green crowns that they wore. Light became a rarer sighting, something smuggled on a gust whenever a breeze distracted their kingly gatekeepers and then taken away just as swiftly. Even the game trails left in the forest floor became narrower the deeper into the forest they went, crowded out by gnarled roots and deep drifts of ancient leaves. The rabbits and small deer that had made the trails showed themselves occasionally, utterly unwary of the spears and arrows of armed men, eyes twinkling in the gloom, before vanishing back into the dense undergrowth. Such trails however, though Andira's pilgrim-soldiers were neither as light as rabbits nor as nimble as roe, were all that there was to follow. As such they walked in single file, slowly, miserably, every whipping branch drawing blood and every stinging plant finding bare skin.

The Greyfox went first, Sibhard after, then a long snaking file of pilgrim-soldiers, with Andira trailing a few paces behind.

The battle with the Greyfox and her warband had tested her. The night-long pursuit that had ended with the former bandit queen their supposed captive had exhausted them all. But Andira had looked to the sky then and judged it nearly dawn, and insisted they march on until dusk came again. If the Uthuk Y'llan had chosen to move on Kell, now of all times and after so many hundreds of years, then she could only imagine that Baelziffar would soon be readying his own final move.

There had been two nights since then. All of her people were as weary as she was now. Unlike the Greyfox herself.

The elf skipped along the narrow trail, in spite of the rope tying her hands behind her back and the occasional angry tug from Sibhard, leaping over roots, dancing over spider webs, maintaining a constant flow of chatter in at least three languages, as though this was a lark that she had come up with for her own amusement. Her vigor seemed boundless, and certainly not a thing that trifling inconveniences like mistreatment, exertion, or denial of sleep could dampen. Sibhard followed behind her with the attitude of an old man holding onto the lead of an exuberant hound. Too tired to pay as much attention to his own feet as he paid to the elf's he suffered every cut and sting that the forest meted out to the other pilgrims twice over. With every furtive glimpse of the forest's wildlife the Greyfox would straighten and pull, startling Sibhard out of whatever brief waking doze he had slipped into, to point and bemoan for the thousandth occasion the cruel destruction of her weapon.

It had been, she would colorfully declaim, a gift from her mother, a rare heirloom of the mysterious Latari no less, and each reprise of the same old back and forth between them brought with it an ever more grandiose and outlandish set of promises for some kind of replacement being offered to her in return.

Her horse was a baroness' gift and could be Sibhard's in exchange for one of the pilgrims' shortbows and a single arrow. Or there was the hidden glade in which she swore to have found buried the crown jewels of Prince Farrenghast, the lost portrait of the infamous Penacor beauty Gissele of Greenbridge, and a cache of enchanted bodkins handcrafted by a huntress of the fae.

All she wanted for it was one minute with a bow.

"I have had enough oatcakes and pickled onions to last me to next winter," she said.

"Then stop eating," Sibhard snapped.

"Tell me you wouldn't rather have a nice piece of venison to look forward to when we stop tonight. *If* we stop. On my word you can have first pick of the cut."

"You could promise to take me to where King Daqan rests and I'd not untie your hands. Much less put a bow in them."

The Greyfox pondered for a long while before finally shrugging, as though deciding to keep that particular treasure to herself, for now, and skipped lightly on. Sibhard gritted his teeth and followed. At the outset of this northward leg of their quest, the boy had drawn some satisfaction from kicking the elf in the calves and watching her stumble when she refused to take a hint and be silent. But the hours became days, the party encroached ever further onto paths made by and for the forest alone, and he grew too weary of it even for that small amusement and feigned to ignore her.

And so the elf smiled, and chattered on, unchallenged, on every inconsequential thing that caught her magpie eye. The monsters that dwelled in the deeper fastnesses of the wood and their natures; how to evade them and how to hunt them. A pink flower that smelled of honey in autumn. The languages of yew and elm. And always the tidings of flight and war, brought to her by the birds and animals of the north beyond the wood; none of which grew any more believable with repetition.

"Enough," Andira sighed, unable to find peace even further

down the line. "If you cannot spend a moment in quiet and you cannot truly offer the boy a runebound shard or the keys to Icegate Prison then tell us something we have not yet heard from you. Tell us your real name and where you come from. You say that you were born in Kell, is this true?"

In all her days of blather, the one thing the Greyfox had not yet spoken of was herself. Even Andira had noted that and had wondered. Despite remembering little of her own past and nothing at all of her early years, even she spoke of them occasionally.

She had expected the question to quieten the elf, but instead the Greyfox sighed and said: "Yes, it is true. I grew up with Kell's legends and its stories, all the folk myths my father would share, and all those that a sharp-eared elf girl could overhear. He was a drover, you know, and a seller of horses before he became a thief of them, and an occasional soldier of the old baron for a time, if you would believe that." She smiled in memory and Andira felt a twinge of envy. "He travelled all over Kell, from Hernfar Isle to Kellar, and knew all the old tales, most of them designed specifically, I think, to terrify young children. My mother's people had their own stories of the forest, of course. She called it the Yarhelin." Here, she peered into the forest, as if to the truth of things, her thin, pale face striped alternately with the light and shade of the wood. "Have you ever wondered at how two people who are otherwise so similar can look on the same thing and see it so differently? One person's hero is another's monster. My mother's sylvan grove, a place of wisdom and old power, was my father's cursed wood."

"I have never thought about it that way," Andira shrugged. "The thing *is*."

"You have never doubted yourself at all, have you?"

"Have you?"

The Greyfox thought for a moment. A smile spread slowly across her face. "If I only had the powers you had. I would never doubt myself again."

Andira held her hand to her face. The rune set into her palm glowed in the forest gloom like a dim torch burning its last embers. It ached, as though the bone were being slowly, slowly squeezed. "It is not about power."

"It is always about power," the Greyfox argued. "Unless you're the one that has it."

"You made much of your abilities in the Downs before my arrival, enough to impress the locals and make yourself a queen. But the world is vast and very old. There will always be someone mightier lying in some near land, or waiting in the wings of history. As it was for Llovar and Timmoran so it was for you."

"And will be for you?"

Andira clenched her hand into a fist, fingers curling over the rune. Light trickled through the gaps and turned the fingers gold. "Inevitably. I have spent every day that I can remember seeking out the one with the power to destroy me."

"Why?"

Andira regarded the elf quizzically. "I do not understand."

"Why go deliberately looking for the one creature in Mennara who could beat you? Aren't there enough kobolds and outlaws for you in Terrinoth?"

"What would be the point of this power otherwise?"

The elf laughed. "Ahh, now I see."

"See what?"

The Greyfox shrugged the question off. "So, are you Timmoran in this story? Or Llovar?"

Andira frowned, perturbed by the questions, and after that gave herself to thought and did not attempt to silence the Greyfox again.

Night in the Whispering Forest came on slowly but arrived suddenly.

The westering sun made little play over the scampering of light and shade over the forest floor, not until it sank completely under the horizon and that which before had been merely gloomy became, almost in the blinking of an eye, oppressively dark. The wan silvery glow of Andira's rune made the trees look even mightier than they had by day, the forest thicker and older by far. The light, almost like moonlight but not quite, glinted across the shiny carapaces of previously unseen insects and the floating specks of seeds and tree pollen that the day had not shown. As though the rune scratched away at the familiar and revealed the layer that existed beneath. The Empyrean, perhaps. It had an eerie beauty that reminded her of the Ailatar and the spires of the elven city of Lithelin. Several of the pilgrim-soldiers signed themselves and muttered prayers when the hour came, believing, or wishing to, that Andira here displayed some new power that waxed greater by night. And perhaps she did. She knew little of her powers, of their origins or their limits, of if they had limits at all beyond those set by her, her own mortal weaknesses and frailties.

Whatever the light's origins or nature, it proved as good as daylight for the Greyfox to lead them on their trail, and so they continued, stopping only briefly to nap and eat, although Andira herself partook of neither before waking them again before dawn. She was weary. Desperately so. But the elusiveness of her demonic rival within this wood worried at her, far more than her growing sense of him ever had.

There would be no rest for her in sleep.

And so she would not sleep. The rune would provide.

"You can't keep this up all the way to Kellar," the Greyfox snapped, just as the dawn of the third day was beginning to trickle through to the forest floor. Her enthusiasm was almost boundless, but Sibhard was not nearly so rested, and his constant tugging on her rope was beginning to rile even her. "What is the point of getting there at all if we are all going to need to sleep for three days afterwards?"

"What's… the matter… elf?" Sibhard panted. "Can't take a little… real… work?"

"Castle Kellar is two days ahead of us yet. See how keen you feel then."

Sibhard scowled but said nothing.

"I am serious, Lady Runehand," she went on, never able to say *Lady* without a condescending smile and a mock courtly flourish. "What does it matter if we kill ourselves to cross the forest in a day and a half or if we take a proper rest now and do it in two?"

"It may matter little or it may matter greatly," said Andira. "Unless you have some foreknowledge of what passes beyond the forest's borders that you have not yet shared?"

The Greyfox considered for a time, perhaps considering another lie in exchange for an hour or two's genuine rest, and then shrugged. Which was wise of her. Andira could not be lied to.

"Why don't you… ask… one of your… trees?" said Sibhard.

"Why don't you go bang your head against one?"

"You're a charlatan," said Sibhard. "Either that or just mad and I… I don't know which is more pathetic. It makes me sick… to think that we feared you so much."

"Then untie me," she said sweetly. "And give me my knife and a bow. Show me how much braver you've become."

For the first time, Sibhard almost looked as though he might.

The Greyfox grinned.

"There is wisdom after a fashion in these trees," said Andira, looking up into the brooding canopy, breaking the dangerous moment. "And power still in the old places. It speaks to me as well although not in so many words. It is great enough to crowd out my own sight, and my sense of the world beyond. Our ancestors came to places like these for protection and guidance. Long before there were universities and runemasters, or even gods as we know them now."

"You think… she… actually… speaks to trees?"

"I think our forebears weathered many trials. They cannot have been wrong about everything."

"I wish… Yorin… were here. I'd feel better for having more than this… trickster's word for the fact that we're headed… north at all."

"If you don't like the path then you are more than welcome to take another," the Greyfox said. "I for one would not mind giving Tomlin over there a go on the leash." With her head she gestured to an aged pilgrim with papery skin and a cassock robe, all thin muscle and sinew, faded rune tattoos and a grimace made of broken teeth. Andira was not sure how the elf had come to know all of their names. She had not yet learned all of their names herself, although she had always made a point of remembering those who fell in the cause.

"But *should* you decide to stay on please tell me this: you have already promised to kill me, what do I possibly get out of leading you astray now?"

"I don't… know. Treachery doesn't come as… naturally to me as it does… to you."

The elf tilted her head back and groaned. "Your going on is giving me a headache."

"*My* going on is giving *you* a headache?"

"I left them all better off, you know. The people I robbed. Their land, their things, none of it was really theirs. It was what made them slaves, cattle that the baron could milk for tax whenever the neighbors across the river got uppity or his foreign wife needed another castle."

"I hope… that I'm wrong," Sibhard said, his voice dropping dangerously low. "I hope you take us to Kellar. I'd hate to… rob the baron of the chance to… hang you."

The Greyfox rolled her eyes. "Blah, blah, burned my favorite auntie's farm, blah."

Sibhard gawped, too dumbstruck to answer.

Gods help her, Andira felt herself smile.

"Enough," was all she said.

After that, Andira thought it wisest to permit them one night's proper rest.

That night, their third under the Whispering Forest's roof, Andira kept a restless watch, neither asleep nor fully awake, while the Greyfox sat back against a tree trunk and slept with open eyes in the fashion of the elves. Sibhard, though as weary as anyone with the exception of Andira herself, seemed to have been stung by her taking the Greyfox's side over his and organized the night's watches. Andira listened to him from across an imagined distance as her thoughts grew separate and slow, her other senses diminishing in order to dwell upon them and their import.

She came to with a start, as a scream rang through the dell. It was still dark, the night lit only by the wraith-glow of her hand. The trees were close and high, mocking her, it seemed, in the hour of their greatest strength.

Andira looked around her.

She had no memory of having fallen asleep and the unaccounted-for passage of time now confused her.

Pilgrim-soldiers rushed around her, crashing through the near forest with weapons drawn and waving torches that bobbed like will-o'-the-wisps between the crowding trees. Two lay still nearby. One had clearly been on watch. His club was still tied at his hip and his throat had been slit from behind. The other had fallen with a javelin in her back. Andira picked up her poleaxe. It seemed to weigh as much as a horse, but at the same time trifling in comparison to the weight of the rune in the opposite hand. She ignored the burden as she had accustomed herself to ignoring the other, and struck out in the direction of the commotion.

She saw no sign of any enemy, beyond the occasional javelin left lying in a fern or sticking from the trunk of a tree. Every so often she would hear a rustle from further off amidst the trees or the chirrup of what sounded like laughter. If she stopped long enough then she might catch the glitter of eyes in the light of her rune, the faint scent of dried skin and saltpeter, but the only signs of battle otherwise were coming from her own bewildered warband.

"Do not be drawn into the forest," she said, speaking calmly, carrying her light with her like a beacon. "Stand together and defy them, as your ancestors once defied the Yarhelin of old and confined it to this final remnant of its old strength." As she passed amongst her people, they rallied to her, the clicking and rustling receding into the forest, and the strange burnt odor that had come with it.

She found the Greyfox fetched up against a hummock of leaves. Sibhard was scowling over her, almost as though the intervening hours had not taken place at all.

"Get up," he said.

"I think you've sprained it," the elf replied.

"It's not so bad as all that."

"What is it?" said Andira.

Sibhard started at her approach.

The Greyfox looked up from the ground. "I turned my ankle in the fight."

"Trying to escape, she means," said Sibhard.

"I was *saving your life*, thank you very much." The bandit gestured towards the javelin piercing the bark at about head height on the tree behind them.

Sibhard muttered under his breath. "Taking the chance to get the slip on me, most likely. I thought elves were meant to be lighter on their feet."

"Half-elf," she grumbled.

Andira closed her eyes and appealed to herself for inner strength. As if the ambush itself were not enough.

"Can you walk?" she asked.

The elf propped herself onto her elbows, stuck her foot out and eased a portion of her almost nonexistent weight onto it. She hissed in pain and sat back down. "I could ride."

Sibhard snorted. "Nice try."

Ignoring him, Andira crouched down beside the Greyfox. She placed her hand over the elf's ankle. The elf winced in pain and pulled back, but Andira squeezed tight. Whatever else she had lied about since their paths had crossed, she was not faking this. "Do not wriggle," Andira said. "It will hurt less if you are still."

The Greyfox set her jaw and turned her face away as healing light rinsed across her, bathing and cleansing her in a watery yellow light that pushed the darkness a little further into the wood. The elf gasped, and Andira withdrew her hand, drawing the light back in and the shadows a little closer than they had been before. Her hand throbbed, as though she had taken on a portion of the elf's pain and added it to her own. Which she had. Andira's existence was one of numerous aches and constant pains, and there came a point when a little more was an inconsequential thing.

She offered her hand. The elf regarded the glowing palm as one might a dragon's mouth or a swollen sea, then hesitantly took it, albeit with her gaze well averted until she was satisfied that Andira was not about to brand the rune into her hand as she had once done to Hamma Brodun's face.

Andira pulled her to her feet.

The elf put weight onto the twisted ankle with an expression of wonder.

"Milenhéir," she whispered.

"What is that?" said Andira.

The elf lowered her voice even further. "My name."

Andira smiled.

"You healed her," Sibhard spluttered. The boy went without thinking to the bandage that one of the pilgrims had applied around his wounded armpit, the days-old dressing dark with sweat and blood.

"I need to save my strength where I can," said Andira. "Hamma understood that and it cost him his life. You can serve me with one arm, but I cannot have a scout who can't walk."

The Greyfox gave an uncertain grin. "Can I have a bow too?"

Sibhard shoved her.

"What was it that attacked us?" Andira asked.

"I don't know," the Greyfox admitted. "There are many creatures who call the forest home. Not all of them are consciously evil, and not all of them wholly a part of the mortal plane. It would be a task beyond the lifetime of a pure-blood Eolam elf to know them all." She turned west, what the elf assured them was west, studying it for a long time. "My guess would be that they are fleeing before the Uthuk, just as the human folk of Kell will be by now. We just had the bad luck of being in their way."

"Because I allowed us to rest," said Andira.

"My lady, no–" Sibhard began.

Andira closed her runehand into a fist and covered it with the other, shrouding the majority of its light, and looked upwards. "You are right," she said. "What is done is done."

Meanwhile, one of the pilgrims approached Sibhard and whispered something in his ear. "My lady," the boy began again. "We lost three in the attack. Another is injured, but not seriously.

Two are still unaccounted for. There's a chance they've been taken by…" He glanced at the Greyfox. "By whatever it was." He waited a while for an answer. "My lady? Shouldn't we go after them?"

"It is nearly dawn," Andira decided at length. She hefted her poleaxe and oriented herself north again. "It is time we continued on."

CHAPTER TWENTY-SEVEN
Kurt
The Whispering Forest, South Kell

Andira and her company had passed this way. Kurt was no scout. He was less of a woodsman. But lucky for him it didn't look as though Andira Runehand was either. Her small army had left a clear enough sign of its passage that they might as well have stopped and paved it. He could well imagine Yorin cussing the lot of them for blundering fools. Kurt crouched to examine the flattened ground cover and bent flowers, wondering where in all this mess Sarb had been. Somewhere to the front of it, he didn't doubt.

While he was low to the ground, the flutter of something wispy and white caught his eye. He reached out a finger and touched a bit of wool that had been snagged on the rough bark of a tree. It pulled in the occasional breeze like an injured bird, or a moth stuck in a spider's web.

"I'll be damned," he muttered, and smiled despite himself. "He actually found the sheep."

He let it go, pulling at the stiff collar of his jacket. It was hot, given how dark it was. The trees were uncomfortably close too, and strange sounds – not so chilling as a flesh ripper in the night, but bad enough – echoed through the rustling wood. Whatever it was making them might not have troubled a hero like Andira Runehand, or a host as big as the one she had been travelling with, but they sure as hell troubled him.

He swallowed the urge to call out for Sarb.

Elben muttered something from the back of the horse.

Kurt had needed to tie him to it to keep him from sliding off. That tiny little nick that the Uthuk arrow had put across his shoulder was sweating like a slice of old bacon on a sunny window and the boy's whole upper arm had gone black. Kurt had done his best to mask the smell, using the crushed petals of the flowers he'd been able to pick from along the trail, but the corruption was still there, still getting worse. While Kurt was struggling to loosen his collar, Elben was shivering, and clearly in pain despite approaching consciousness only in spells. Kurt didn't know what else to do. The Charg'r poison was quite beyond his own meagre herb lore. The thought occurred that he should have somehow found a way back to his steading to recover the arrow that had cut Elben's arm. That was surely what an experienced Darklands fighter or battlefield healer would have done. Wasn't it? How he was supposed to have gone about that or what he would have done with the thing had he done so he did not know, but the thought, once there, nagged him with guilt and refused to be sent away.

Again, he had to bite his tongue to keep from yelling Sarb's name into the wood.

Only Andira Runehand, or a fortunate encounter with a very lost runemaster, could save Elben now.

"Father?"

Kurt wiped the sting from his eyes and looked up. "Elben. Go back to sleep."

"Are we almost there?" the youth whispered. "Listred is tired."

Kurt smiled unbidden. "You named my horse?"

"He wanted one, I think. Why did you never name him?"

"I suppose it never felt important. He always answered to *horse*."

"Well, I think he's a Listred."

"He looks a bit like one too. There was a cook in my garrison called Listred, a highland lad, and we used to…"

He trailed off.

Elben was already unconscious again.

The boy didn't want to hear *that* story anyway. Kurt sniffed. For months he'd not spoken a word to his sons about his time in the army. However much they had pestered. Now, he'd gladly tell his youngest any tale in exchange for a few more hours.

He ground his teeth lest he start to cry.

Damn it.

"Sibhard!"

The shout echoed through the wood.

From somewhere ahead, something gave an inquisitive growl.

Kurt drew his battered old sword and rustled towards it. The forest billed him step for step with scratches. He only felt the deepest of them. Panic seemed to have inured him to the rest. Better than a stiff drink.

After a little way he came to a fallen tree and dropped down beside it. The tree itself had been dead for an age and then some, but it seemed to have fallen only lately and lay in its neighbors' arms like a large drunk being dragged home after several too many. The fall of leaves was enough to obscure Andira's trail, but he could see from the scuffed pile how the tracks became scattered there, as though at this point they had ceased to march in the same semi-orderly fashion that had brought them this far.

He looked up.

The trails led on to a clearing.

He could see sunlight, and vicariously felt wind on his skin.

"Wait here," he murmured to the horse that had followed behind him and was now nosing at his shoulder. "I'm going to take a look."

He stood up.

Leaf fall and undergrowth rustled as they clawed at his leather. He squinted, covering his eyes, staggering into the brilliance of an uncovered sun. The chill of it grew on him slowly as his vision cleared, exposing the sun's cruel lie. The day was as gray as an undyed fleece. Bodies littered the clearing. Dead men. Slaughtered animals. Hummocks in the grass made by bits of both. The crows were busy about them, too much so to raise so much as a croak until Kurt stumbled out to disturb them. Even then, they showed no inclination to leave their feast, certainly not for this old man's sake. They pecked and cawed and ruffled their feathers. Those nearest stuffed their beaks with stringy bits of red meat before taking off in an angry fluttering of black, calling harshly from the bowers of the watching trees. Larger scavengers moved about further away. A pair of gray-coated timber wolves prowled around the lightning-smote stump of the downed tree, while a large black bear snuffled alone around the far edge of the clearing. They regarded each other warily, like lords across some arbitrary border, and occasionally at Kurt too: the less-than-nobody whose land they had decided to carve in half.

Kurt switched from covering his eyes to covering his nose and mouth against the smell.

"Sibhard!"

The bear issued a low growl. The two wolves turned and slunk into the woods.

"Sibhard!"

The bear rose up onto its hind legs and gave another threatening growl.

Kurt had the unmistakable sense, too, of other things close by. Watching. Lacking the bear's wariness of humanity and human steel. But content to watch even so. For now at least. The forest had the feeling of a garrison town whose army has been mobilized to some foreign war and left its walls standing empty. It was a skeleton that stood behind as castellan, an embittered token that would have gladly rent him limb from limb for this trespass had its might been just a little greater.

Satisfied with its display, the bear dropped back onto all fours, gave another growl, and turned from the clearing.

Kurt let out a relieved breath.

Listred, the horse, crunched through the undergrowth behind him.

Kurt didn't turn.

His years in the baron's purple had been spent mostly playing cards. He'd drunk quite a bit of bad ale too, and sung a lot of songs of the sort that Katrin would have disapproved of had she been alive to hear them. He'd stood on a high wall and complained about the cold and the wet to folk that his late wife would have approved of no more, looking out east when by all rights they might have spent the time much better had they been looking back west.

He shook his head at the memory of his wife.

Again, his eyes began to sting.

He grunted it off.

What kind of a man was he, crying over a wound as old as that one?

Kell's army was meant to be the biggest and best in all Terrinoth. That's what everybody always said, so there had to be some kind of truth in it. Couldn't they have guarded against the Uthuk Y'llan *and* the Greyfox? Instead they'd ended up doing neither. No one up on that wall at Bastion Tarn wanted to fight. Except the odd bully that every company had one of and the would-be heroes like Sarb. But it was what they'd all been there for. They'd have fought in a second if it could have stopped half the things Kurt had seen and those he'd had the hard luck to have only imagined. But Fredric had sent them home.

The short-sighted, soft-hearted fool.

"Worst plan in the whole damned world," Kurt muttered to himself. "I couldn't fight the Greyfox on my own."

"Da…"

Kurt wiped his eyes on the back of his hand and looked up.

Elben was looking glassily across the clearing. "What's that over there?"

Kurt turned and walked, picking his way slowly between the bodies, in that direction.

Then he saw it.

He dropped to his haunches and picked it up between both hands.

He held it numbly. It was his flatbow. Or it had been before Sarb had taken it on his way to running off with Andira's warband in Gwellan. The wood was split. There was blood on one limb. The string had been cut. Had the latter not been the case then the tension on the limb would have surely wrecked it as a bow by now. As it was it would probably manage a few more shots before the damage to the wood made it snap. He gripped the limb in one hand, looked again around the clearing, and took a breath so deep it hurt.

"Sibhard!"

He got stiffly to his feet and turned over a body with the same short dark hair as his son. A woman's pecked sockets stared up at him.

He felt no relief.

"Sibhard!"

He ran to a stockier man that looked nothing at all like Sarb. Desperation made him blind.

He went to another.

Another.

The body he ran towards kicked out before he got near, took out his legs and put him on his back. The wind flew out of him, surprise as much as the blow, and the body got to its feet.

It was an old man, gray-haired and grizzle-bearded, haggard and pale as an old bird and clad in battered mail with half an arrow sticking out of his chest. He hissed at Kurt, something unintelligible, spittle flying from his clenched teeth as he stumbled drunkenly sideways, corrected, and then hacked down with his sword.

Kurt rolled out of the way.

The blade chopped into the clod where he had been sent sprawling.

He cursed himself *again* for leaving his shield on the horse.

Some soldier he was.

"You'll not pick at *this* corpse, brigand," the old man snarled as Kurt backed hurriedly away and got his sword up between them. The man swayed. Kurt felt himself smile as the initial shock turned to something like relief. An old man with an arrow in him was about his level.

"I'm looking for my son. I don't want a fight."

"When Fortuna throws arrows then sometimes a man gets hit." The old warrior gave a guttural cry and hacked out with his sword.

Kurt raised his own sword: a passable drill yard counter to a downswing from on high.

The old knight shifted his footing at the last moment, dragging his blow an inch left and forcing Kurt into a hasty adjustment of his own. He overcompensated, all his weight on his left, and the gray-haired warrior pivoted, turned, sword blinking as it changed direction again. Kurt couldn't keep up. He gave ground, the other man's sword chopping methodically away at his earlier confidence and his guard. He'd faced off against better swords than his own on the training yard, plenty of times, but the feeling of being so utterly and ridiculously outclassed was a new one.

"You've had a little training." The old knight pushed Kurt's sword this way and that until his hands were numb. "But not nearly enough practice." There came a brief flurry which Kurt blocked about half of and retreated from the rest, the routine finishing up with Kurt's sword quivering point-down in the earth and the knight's pressed against his neck. Kurt gave way, stumbled over a body, and fell. The old man kicked the rusty sword over before Kurt could get any ideas about it. "Pathetic," he grunted. "If Highmont and Forthyn hadn't stood between you and my old castle then I might have conquered Kell myself and done Lady Runehand and Terrinoth a mighty favor." He swung his sword up high, ready to chop down.

The point glinted red where the stained metal caught the sun.

"No!" Kurt wailed. "Please no."

"Stop begging. You made your choices, brigand, now die with some dignity."

"I'm not with the Greyfox! I'm not! I'm looking for Andira Runehand."

The old man bared crooked teeth. "You said you were looking for your son."

Kurt shut his eyes.

The warrior grunted in pain and Kurt opened them again. He gasped in relief, the painful rush of *life* pushing through his veins to every part of his body. The old knight's sword arm buckled and the man himself soon folded after it, descending to one knee. His breath shuddered out through clenched teeth, one hand to his side near to where the arrow had entered his chest. Kurt didn't need a second invitation. He scrambled to where his sword lay and snatched it up. He took it up two-handed and swayed to his feet like a drunk holding a chair. The old knight glared up at him, hurt and self-loathing written in gray across his hard face, and made no effort to defend himself.

"Kill me then, if you've the stomach for it."

Kurt glanced over his shoulder to where Elben lay slumped against Listred's neck. His eyes were vacant. Kurt couldn't even be sure he was awake. He lowered his sword with a grunt.

Damn the boy and his belief in heroes. Damn them both.

"No wonder one little elf girl took half your country," the old knight panted.

"Shut up," said Kurt, and peered more closely at the warrior's face. Now that he had time to think about it, he realized it was one he recognized. The dragon rune drawn into the skin in burnt flesh was as singular as a true knight's heraldry.

"Brodun?" he said.

The old man's eyes narrowed, almost perfectly mirroring Kurt's. "The yeoman. The archer who shot at Andira in Gwellan." He laughed roughly, then grimaced at the pain it brought him. "No wonder you're so bad with that sword. I've never seen a bowman that knew what to do with a real weapon. Sibhard is your son, isn't he?" He glanced towards Listred and Elben. "Your other son?"

"Yes."

Hamma grunted, a little empathy in his dark eyes. "I see why you're looking for Andira."

"Do you know where she went?"

The old knight winced, then nodded.

"Is Sarb alive?"

"When I last saw him. But that was heading north with Andira

Runehand, and I can't think of more dangerous company for a boy that dreams of being a hero. Believe me..." Levering his weight against the upright of his sword, he pushed himself back to his feet, pain digging ever deeper lines into his thin face. "I know. Let me share your horse with your son for a while, yeoman, and I will lead you to her. Maybe she can mend us both."

"What happened to dying with dignity?"

The old knight gave a bloody grin. "I'm a knight of Roth's Vale. That is what we tell the peasants."

He took his sword by the blade and offered it up to Kurt.

Kurt thought for a long moment.

Then he sighed and took it.

CHAPTER TWENTY-EIGHT
Greyfox
The Whispering Forest, South Kell

Greyfox studied the prints in the ground. She lowered herself to her knees, her hands still tied behind her back, to sniff around them and mutter. They were booted and she could see the deeper indents left by hobnails or rivets. The earth underneath them was cracked as if by heat, the undergrowth similarly wilted. If it was a forest creature that had made them then it was certainly not one *of* the forest, nor one with any great love of the wood. But she was close to where she wanted to be. She stuck out her tongue and licked the soil.

Sibhard made a disgusted look. "What are you doing?"

"More of the creatures that attacked us passed this way, I think," said Greyfox.

"Are they still headed west?" asked Andira.

West-ish.

"Yes," she lied.

"Then leave them. We are bound north."

Sibhard and more than a few of the pilgrim-soldiers looked troubled. Clearly it did not sit well with them to leave their own behind.

Greyfox stood up and shrugged. "Yes, Lady Runehand."

They continued that day as they had the previous three.

Greyfox led, walking more and more with her face turned up towards the sun that blinked at her through the heavy screen of leaves. The wittering birds, miles away yet but already clear to her elven ears, carried the songs of northern hills and upland dales. The refrains were similar enough to those of the forest to fool the untutored ear, but not to one as familiar with the forest's voices as its beloved bandit queen. In the same gradual, barely discernable way, the swathe of the forest's carpet shifted from the yellows and oranges of the forest's stifling heart to the dull purples and whites of a lingering winter. Even the air began to taste different. It was fresher, sharper, redolent of the rocks of the Howling Giant Hills and the ice of the Dunwarr. The humans did not appear to be conscious of the change, even as they began to huddle nearer together in spite of the widening of the path, stamping their feet and rubbing their hands in the chillier air.

"The world starts to taste clean at last," Andira murmured. Greyfox was grudgingly impressed by the keenness of the other woman's senses. She had only become aware of the changes about an hour ago herself. "The shadow of the forest lifts from my mind. I can almost feel the power of the demon king, and he mine, but…" She paused, her coldly perfect features locked in a frustrated grimace. "Only not quite. The stain of the Uthuk Y'llan grows in the forest's place. I fear there is little hope of us reaching Castle Kellar ahead of the Locust Swarm now."

Greyfox nodded her head, lending her face an appropriately regretful expression. "We are well into the forest's northern boundaries now. As to the Uthuk, I really couldn't say. A Daqan army could not have marched the Forest Road in the time it has taken us to cross its heart, but perhaps the Swarm could. They are said to be swift."

Andira's expression became impossible to read, and Greyfox winced as her gaze nudged briefly towards *actual* north, like the arrow of a magnetic compass, before drifting back to the course that Greyfox had, in fact, been setting for her these last three days.

She breathed a sigh of relief.

"Assuming Kellar is even their object at all..." Andira murmured.

"What do you mean?" said Sibhard.

"I..." Andira began, then waved the question away unanswered.

There was something about the woman's manner that sent a shiver down even Greyfox's neck. She wasn't quite *right*. She certainly wasn't entirely normal. There was a nobility to her, but the real kind, the kind a person earned rather than the sort that a handful might be lucky enough to be born with. And she had a... reach, as if she extended somewhere beyond herself to touch those around her and share a small bit of whatever destiny she had taken on herself. Greyfox shivered as if to shake it off. From what little she had been told she wanted none of that stuff on her.

"How long until we are in sight of Kellar?" Andira continued.

Greyfox picked her words with care. "We will be leaving the forest behind us soon. In fact we have already started to, though I doubt you have noticed it yet. We should be able to make better time from here, perhaps enough even to see the sun set over the Howling Giant Hills."

Andira nodded but said nothing.

Greyfox took that as permission and led them on.

The sky began to darken. The air turned cold, the forest too thin now, on its northern hinterlands, to hold onto the heat of the day past evening. It was then that one of the pilgrim scouts, a tall Frestan woman named Penn who had once called the Applewoods her home and, by her own reckoning at least, had some wood craft, returned. There was a clearing in the forest ahead, she said, a rocky knoll with a wooden tower, and some kind of camp ringed by a palisade. Greyfox smiled when she heard her report. Despite the best efforts of the forest to lead her astray and of Sibhard to look over her shoulder she had brought them to the right place. Penn and her scouts had ventured only as far as the forest's verge, to the foot of the knoll, but even that had been vantage enough to glimpse the open country beyond the forest and the glitter of the Lothan from afar.

"Doesn't the Lothan run much further east of Kellar?" asked Sibhard.

"You have never travelled north of the forest, have you?" Greyfox put in quickly. "Several wide streams feed down from the Howling Giant Hills. Most of them would be great rivers in their own right if they weren't tributaries of the Lothan. Chances are it is one of those that your scouts have spotted, rather than the Lothan itself."

Andira nodded. It sounded plausible.

And it wasn't really *lying* as such. Greyfox felt rather pleased with herself.

"The old baron had a string of forts built along the forest's northern border," she said, falling into her habitual way of talking as though she was not nervous. A woman who could use her rune-magic to sense the evil of the Ynfernael when a person lied was not, she was learning, a person she was comfortable being around. Particularly given that she had been lying on and off for the better part of three days. "For his huntsman and his loggers. There are kobolds and goblins, and worse, that lair in the forest's outskirts. And legends of feral dragons and hybrids, leftovers of the old war, in the deeper woods. Though I've never seen one, and even in the Whispering Forest a dragon would be a thing to hide. With its walls and its armies, Kellar has almost forgotten its fear of the forest. Almost. But not quite."

"You gave them a reminder, I'm betting," said Sibhard.

"It was others who claimed this country north of the forest, but yes. The baron and his father feared his own people more than they feared the Uthuk, or even the forest, and kept these keeps manned while the border forts sat empty or crumbled. How wise he must feel, sitting in his great castle now."

"Hindsight will make fools of us all," said Andira. "I have heard that Baron Fredric is able and just."

"To someone looking in from Carthridge or wherever it is you're from, *milady*, perhaps he is."

But Andira was not listening. Her eyes were on something that no one there could see but her. "If this is one of the baron's outposts then we will make for it now while the light holds out. We may yet be in Kellar before the sun sets tomorrow."

"It might be wise to scout the castle first. We still don't know how far west the Uthuk Y'llan have come." Greyfox raised her bound hands. "I would volunteer to..."

Sibhard gave a snort, almost amused now by her persistence. "I'll go."

Greyfox shrugged as if to say *Don't say I didn't try.*

"If you insist."

CHAPTER TWENTY-NINE
Andira Runehand
The Whispering Forest, South Kell

Sibhard called back that the way was clear.

The Greyfox stiffened and murmured something under her breath.

Andira turned to her, probing. "You seem surprised."

"Surprised? No. Should I be?"

Andira smiled. "You know you cannot lie to me, Milenhéir."

She pronounced the Latari name perfectly, and yet the Greyfox winced at her use of it. The elf shifted, apparently uncomfortable, but not prepared to say anything more, as Sibhard returned to their side. He was red-faced and breathless, his underarm wound torn again from the exertion and leaking into the bandages, flanked by a pair of pilgrim scouts carrying short Frestan bows.

"We've gone right up to the wall," he said. "No sign of Uthuk Y'llan. Or anything else. The gate's wide open. We walked right up to it."

"Is it abandoned?" said Andira.

"I don't know, Lady Runehand. I … I didn't dare go further."

Andira felt a shiver of anticipation at the report. "Why? Tell me everything."

"There was just a … a bad feeling about the gate, my lady," said Sibhard.

"Some evil that pitted its will against ours," said the archer to his left, a tall woman in the mottled reddish garb of an Applewood forester.

The second scout signed himself. "It was the same evil I felt at Sudanya."

At that, all three fell quiet.

Andira turned to the Greyfox and smiled again. If anything it conveyed even less warmth than the first. A pair of pilgrims took the elf roughly by each shoulder and together they walked towards the abandoned fort.

"What did happen at Sudanya?" the Greyfox hissed.

Andira thought back.

Perhaps it was because she did not have years of needless childhood memories cluttering her thoughts, but there was little of the subsequent years of adventure she could not instantly recall.

"I had been fighting in the Bloodwood," she said. "Beyond the southern border of Frest but before the Aymhelin truly begins. After two years the Latari and I finally had a victory to celebrate, having driven the Tangle and its servants from the verdelam outposts and many miles back towards the old city of Athealwel. Only when it returned again in full force the following spring did I understood what Sir Brodun had been telling from the beginning – that the Tangle is a thing of the Ynfernael, and that it can never be fully beaten in this realm. Endless battle could not have been my destiny, so we left the Latari to their struggle and went north, to where Hamma had heard of a place where the walls of the Ynfernael were broached once and remain weak. There is a village there now in its shadow, best known as the site where the lords of orcs and elves and humans and dwarves convened to plot the defeat of the Dragonlords. But the ruins of the original were home only to darkness, an evil that had been there long before the coming of the dragons, before the Age of Steel. The villagers were wise enough to keep away, but I wasn't the first hero to try and conquer it. A demon called Prutorn, I learned, had made it his castle. What had happened to steep the city so deeply in the Ynfernael I can scarcely imagine, and I doubt even Prutorn himself was powerful enough to have had a hand in it. He was a vassal of greater powers, potent though he was. I banished him, though he almost got the better of me, while Hamma slew his mortal followers. Ever since then I have had Baelziffar the demon king, his master, in my thoughts. I have felt the Turning as it brings about the waxing of the Ynfernael and I have felt it draw us nearer."

She paused and glanced at the Greyfox. "You are quiet."

"I'm wondering what happened to the Latari you left in the Bloodwood."

Andira frowned.

That was the price of having a heroic destiny, she told herself, the knowledge that you could save anyone but that you could not save *every*one.

"I think about that too. More than I would like."

"Do you really hope to defeat him?" said Sibhard, as if in awe of her all over again. "If his lieutenant was almost too great for you."

"I've heard stories," said the Greyfox, "very, very old stories, of entire armies being raised to take down one of the kings of the Ynfernael. They don't always succeed."

"Time will tell," said Andira.

She had prepared herself for death from the moment she had set out from Roth's Vale with Hamma by her side. It was the only conceivable end to her quest that she could see. There was a small part of her that was almost looking forward to it. It would be nice to rest. She wondered too, if she would be reunited with her lost memories when she died, the way many people seemed to think they would meet lost loved ones. She had always meant to talk to a disciple about it. But there had never been time. Always too much to be done. She turned and called for her poleaxe and banner.

The pilgrims who had assumed the honor of bearing them on her behalf hastened forward to present them. Andira took the weapon. The standard she passed onto Sibhard. He clutched it as though it might otherwise take flight and rejoin the firmament alongside Latariana's stars.

"I'll not dishonor it, my lady."

"There's no need to be afraid," she said. "Victory or defeat, whatever must be will be."

There was another two hundred yards to cover before the forest thinned out sufficiently to make out the encampment that Sibhard and the other scouts had described. Pale, jagged stumps took the place of mature trees while those still upright were younger, with fewer branches, warier roots and less pride in their leafy crowns. The rocky knoll at the center of the forced clearing was natural enough and might even have been a site of significance and sanctuary in bygone days, back when the forest had dominated the continent and the threat from the Ynfernael was still unrealized except by the most dark-hearted of elves. Heavy logging had extended it to create a long oval killing ground of pale wooden stakes, and to source the raw material for the raising of the small keep and palisade that now fortified the hill. It was rough work. Even for bored Daqan soldiers.

A shadow lingered over the vastness now. It had nothing to do with physical light or its lack. Indeed, with the forest diminished and the open vistas of the northern dales before them, light felt uncommonly abundant. Rather it was a darkness of the spirit. As though it was the thing that the First had sung into existence at the moment of Light's creation to be its opposite that dwelt there on that hill. Andira felt it as a throbbing in her hand, almost as a pull, drawing her towards the gate as if a hand had reached out from it to take hers, and despite her earlier words of encouragement she felt uneasy at the sensation.

"My lady?" said Sibhard, concerned.

Andira drew her aching hand forcibly to the stylized steel device of her pectoral plate, leant her poleaxe against her shoulder, and then massaged the back of her hand with her fingers. She had never confided, even to Hamma, who had been the nearest thing she had to family, if not a friend, just how much pain the rune brought her. It was a constant ache at rest, like a burning spear pushed through her hand when called.

He had always known though, of course. He had been no fool. But he had respected her enough, and loved her in his own cold way, never to ask.

"What do you see in front of you?" she asked, letting go her hand and retaking her weapon as though it was just a little stiffness there, nodding instead towards the eerie quiet of the hilltop fort.

Sibhard squinted towards the distant walls. Some measure of the shadow that Andira felt crossed into his face as though the sun had passed behind a cloud. It had not, though. It shone brightly, if coolly, and the boy shuddered, with no sense at all of why. "I... don't know what you want me to say, my lady. Is he here?"

"It seems... insignificant for a king of his power. I had expected to face him at Kellar itself. That seemed more in keeping with his sense of majesty. And yet..." She paused, turning her head slightly as if to catch a scent on the wind. "I do feel his presence here. If not the demon king himself then another of his Ynfernael servants."

"Another Prutorn?"

She raised her voice so that the entire pilgrimage, spread out around the rough-hewn stumps and arming themselves with bows and staves, could hear. "Be wary. We are close now, whether he is here to face us in person or not."

"I'll be the talk of every outlaw in Kell," the Greyfox murmured. "None of them have ever battled a demon before. Fredric might even have to pardon me, eh, Sibhard, rather than force himself to hang an elf of such renown."

"Stranger things have happened," the boy replied, but he did not appear to be listening.

The open gate admitted them.

The ground beyond was rugged. Steps hewn roughly from the bare rock wound towards the keep on its promontory. Several wooden huts clustered around the edges of a narrow courtyard, presumably guardhouses and stables, with flat roofs and smoke holes. No smoke climbed from them now. All were empty and silent, but for the wind that whispered through far-off trees, making a sound like a sea heard from faraway, and the calls of northern birds.

Andira turned to the Greyfox. The keen-eared elf shook her head. Her expression was drawn. Unasked, the pilgrim-soldiers spread out to secure the courtyard. Hamma may have trained them reluctantly, but he had done it well. Sibhard and the same two archers he had been sent out with earlier hung back between the gates with the Greyfox and the two horses. The Runehand banner fluttered in the wind that came in off the dales and fled through the open gate.

On her guard, Andira walked alone to the foot of the stair.

"Where are the banners?" one of the pilgrims called from behind her. Korace, she thought his name was, a soldier of Pelgate once upon a far-off time. He was one of the men that Hamma had trained to wield a sword and had a little skill. The scrap of mail he still wore was decorated in the faded golds and greens of Riverwatch. "If this is a fort of the baron then where's his emblem and colors? Where's the purple and gold, and the Owl of Kell that always looks east?"

At the foot of the steps, Andira halted.

She raised her hand for quiet.

She turned slowly, drawn by intuition, towards the narrow berm of rock that encircled the revetment about the keep's walls and found her answer.

All her answers.

A forest of blanched and pointed stakes ringed the wall. At first glance Andira had taken it for an abatis, another defensive structure to add to the revetment and the wall. In a sense it was – an abatis of men and women staked out in forester's garb. But the real barrier was not a physical one. Its purpose was not defense. Andira grunted, the death energies and last moments of pain of so many that she been unable to cross the forest quickly enough to save crashing over her like a torrent of ice. The rune in her hand burned, the pain suddenly as sharp as Nordros' spear. She gave an involuntary cry and staggered back from the stair. The laughter of something ancient and profane rang through her spirit, delighting in the crack that that small moment of dismay had opened to the Ynfernael plane. She clenched her hand over the rune and looked hard into the source of the pain.

"Where are you, Baelziffar?" she hissed.

She looked up again to the staked-out remains of the garrison and this time did not look away.

This sacrifice had been performed recently. Within the day, she thought. But the power of the Ynfernael was not a thing to linger. It was an impatient force, always moving, always acting, and the magicks drawn into the world by this offering were already beginning to leach away. She could sense it, the way someone who knew the geography of a place could look on it in drought and see where the rivers would have flowed and known the path to the sea.

North.

Where would it end, she wondered? Was she being led to anywhere in Kell at all? Or would destiny guide her ever northward, on and on, across the mountains to the Weik, and onwards to whatever mysterious lands or sea lay beyond that realm?

But these were questions for tomorrow, and beyond even her powers to know.

It was frustrating, after so many years spent searching, but she consoled herself that she was closer than she had ever been.

Behind her, her pilgrims moaned as they noticed the castle's unholy fortification.

"Impossible," said the Greyfox, shaking her head. "Impossible."

Sibhard glanced at her, as though surprised that the murder of Kellar troops could affect her at all. He swallowed as he turned back to Andira. "Was this the Uthuk?"

"No one else would do this," said Andira.

"Is this what they would have done to Gwellan?" he asked, plaintive suddenly, and no longer the hero he strove to be. "And Nordgard Castle?"

Andira turned to him and smiled sadly. "I am afraid so. I know it is hard, but try not to grieve too much for them. Even the pain of your heart is a feast for the Ynfernael. You could not have helped them had you been there, but you are alive, and that is a victory of a kind. You can avenge them, if that interests you, and you can ensure this happens to no one else."

"How… How am I supposed to not grieve?" Sibhard wailed.

Andira thought, and then sighed. "Practice."

"Kellar is going to be surrounded already," said Sibhard,

turning away, from Andira and from the appalling view. "We'll never reach it now."

"It might just be possible…" the Greyfox began, "that we're a teensy bit further out from Kellar than you think."

Sibhard turned to her. "How *much* further?"

"I…" The elf looked around the defiled stronghold. Her shoulders slumped. "This isn't one of Fredric's watchposts. At least it hasn't been for a long time. It was the hideout of a bandit chief I knew called Captain Beltran." She gave a small laugh. "He had been a soldier once. But he was never any captain."

"You mean to say you have not been leading me north at all?" said Andira, her eyes blazing suddenly like ice fire.

"Mostly north. And just a little bit east."

"East?" said Sibhard. "East? Never mind that you've taken us miles from Kellar. You've put us right onto the Forest Road and in front of the Uthuk Y'llan!"

The Greyfox, already a waifish thing in her gaudy trappings and too-large demeanor, visibly shrank. Sibhard looked almost ashamed for having yelled at her.

Andira wondered if this, too, was a part of the elf's subtle power.

"This wasn't supposed to happen," the Greyfox hissed. "The Uthuk weren't supposed to come this far into the forest. Why would they attack a fort flying a bandit's colors when the road would give them Kellar in a day or two?"

"You mistook the Uthuk Y'llan for an army of the more familiar kind," said Andira, "led by sane captains with rational goals. Undoubtedly Baron Fredric and whoever was once lord at Hernfar made the same mistake."

"You were hoping this Beltran would kill us and free you," said Sibhard.

"A girl can dream, can't she?"

Andira sighed. "Give the elf the bow she has been begging for."

"What?" said Sibhard.

"What?" the Greyfox echoed.

"She's only just confessed to betraying us," said Sibhard.

"And I think she sees now how much good that has done her." She turned and waved her still-glowing hand towards the defiled keep. "This is her future." While Sibhard did nothing, the two pilgrim archers that flanked him quietly cut the Greyfox free. "The Locust Swarm will make friends of us all yet," said Andira, almost softly. "Perhaps that is *their* purpose in all this."

"That's a very optimistic outlook, my lady," said the Greyfox, rubbing her wrists where for the past few days the rope had been chafing.

Andira smiled. "What lies north of here?"

"North of here?" The Greyfox shrugged. "Nothing. We're almost straight west of Kellar now."

"There is always something."

"Nothing but cold hills and heathland until you get to Forthyn and I've never ridden that far. Apart from…" She looked thoughtful. "Apart from Orrush Khatak. It's a pass leading though the Barrow Dales, a particularly empty part of northern Kell. I've never been there. Nobody ever goes there. Not even adventurers."

"Then that must be the true purpose of the horde…" Andira murmured.

"I told you there's nothing there," said the Greyfox. "Not even a ruin. Just an old road."

"Whatever the Uthuk are planning we have to go to Castle Kellar first," said Sibhard. "The baron needs us."

"He's not *my* baron," said the Greyfox.

"Nor mine," Andira murmured, though she felt as though she was coming to some agreement with herself rather than mediating between Sibhard and the bandit queen. "Baelziffar is north. That is where I have to go."

She turned attention north. Always north. The stench of evil beckoned. The pull on her hand grew.

"But if we can help Fredric, can't he help us?" Sibhard argued. "Didn't the elf say it'd take an army to slay the demon king? Well the nearest army is in Kellar, isn't it, fighting the Uthuk Y'llan?"

Andira thought. She did not like choices. The First had created fate as a straight path. Choice was an illusion created by ignorance.

"I am an army."

"Please," said Sibhard. "We can't save Kell by sacrificing Castle Kellar."

Andira kept her gaze north. She could not look at him.

"I am not here to save Kell. I am here to save the world."

CHAPTER THIRTY
Fredric
Castle Kellar, North Kell

Fredric struggled up the winding staircase in the dark, one hand running along the stone wall, the other on his sword hilt to keep the scabbard from interfering with his legs. Grandmarshal Trevin Highgarde and six Knights of the Yeron followed close behind, filling the narrow ascent with their clatter. The deep voice of the Roglun Horn, named for the first Kellar lord to bend the knee to Arcus Penacor, sounded again as Fredric pushed against the tower's highest door and almost spilled onto a wide rampart. The night was chilly, and he shivered as he emerged. The warmth of Litiana and their bed clung to him only weakly, and his bleary-eyed squires had draped his out-garments over him with noticeably less care than they had applied to the fitting of his armor. A ballista turntable stood, uncovered, at both ends of the battlement. Two full crews and a unit of archers braced themselves against the cold winds with wool-lined helmets, thick cloaks, and a canteen of some kind of spiced cider between them.

He leant back against the door frame for a moment and gulped down the cold air.

Kezian Tor was the highest point in Castle Kellar, six hundred steps above the inner bailey, taller than the keep itself, and almost at parity with the lower heights of the Howling Giant Hills to the north-west.

Collecting himself, he pushed his way through to the parapet. The archers and weapon crews parted for him. Sir Highgarde and his knights followed.

Kellar, castle and town, spread out for him like a drawing on a map.

Pennons and torches fluttered from every rampart. Purple and gold. It might have been mistaken for an Elyana's Day carnival, the grand celebration to mark the last day of the week-long fast, or an outpouring of pageantry for a visiting lord or a hero of high esteem. Were it not for the threat in the air. The lingering murmurs of the Roglun Horn.

The mood was tense. A man only had to stand out in the street to feel it. Even from its highest tower, Fredric could not ignore it. The city was wound as tight as a crossbow. Twenty thousand pairs of eyes looked eastward, along with every thought, every fear, every unspoken prayer. Every child in Kellar would have heard of Nordgard Castle's fall by now. It was impossible to keep a secret that big in a castle. And in any case, these were hard folk. They would not have thanked him for trying. Even then, at that late hour, Fredric could see last-minute preparations being made. Ballistae were being oiled and tested. Rune golems were being awoken. Fresh units were armed and armored and sent to the walls. Those walls already shimmered silver and gold by torchlight, the helmets of so many men-at-arms making the ramparts appear as though they ran with metal.

To his surprise Fredric felt no particular sense of apprehension about what was to come or how he would be measured against it.

What he felt in greatest abundance, looking down on his city in its darkest time, was pride.

Here was the might of Kell, mustered in its fullest strength as had not been called upon since the first incursions of the Dragon Wars.

He found himself wondering if his generals might have been right all along.

What chance would Kell's robber barons have had against a host as great as this?

He shook his head. It was one thing to hold a castle against the ancestral foe of every man and woman of Terrinoth. To subjugate a fractious land by force of arms was quite another. And raising these kinds of numbers from an impoverished country in such short order would bring problems for later. But later was *later*.

Fredric would call it a victory to have a later.

For the sake of his family, if not himself.

He turned to the captain of the watch.

"Show me."

The officer passed him a long brass tube.

Fredric took it and put it to his eye. He trained it on the eastbound road.

The seeing glass was an innovation from the Torue Albes, a tool of piracy some called it, and one of the many toys and trinkets that Litiana had brought with her from the court at Alben.

Within the lenses of the seeing glass the haze on the eastern horizon became the dust kicked up by a marching column.

Somewhere in the distance, quite visible by day but hidden even from the Alben glass in the dark, the road forked into two. The Forest Road went south and east around the Whispering Forest, towards the Crimson Downs and the barony's southern counties. Straight east went the ancient highway to the rocks at

Orrush Khatak and the Barroway. No one knew who had built the road, or by what ancient sorcery it had been maintained when all trace of its builders had disintegrated with the passing ages. There was nothing there, and it was a road seldom taken unless the hour was late and the need desperate.

"Is it Constan with the army from the south?" he asked.

"It is too soon for him," said Trevin. "And it was only ever a slim chance that he would return at all."

"And yet he went anyway," Fredric muttered, his resolve weakening, but only for a moment. "Then it is the Uthuk Y'llan. They run like a wind from the Ynfernael. More swiftly even than General Brant feared." He turned to the captain of the watch. "Is there some way to see them more closely?"

Mumbling his apologies, the soldier took the glass from Fredric's hands and showed him how to adjust the lenses.

He returned it.

Fredric put it back to his eye.

And gasped as for the first time he saw the oldest of civilization's enemies.

A strange thrill went through him. It was like seeing something from an old text take physical shape, or a phantom from another person's nightmare. He had always privately suspected the outlandish descriptions and eye-witness illustrations from the old histories to have been exaggerations. But they had all been true. The histories had overblown nothing. Fredric might have been better prepared for the reality of the Uthuk Y'llan if they had done so. No treatise read in an airy study, accompanied by an amphora of Al Aluaham wine, could recreate the curdling of the gut evinced by the real thing.

They were naked but for thick greaves that guarded their shins. Their skin was a grayish purple, like parchment under an arcane light. Their faces were long and cruel, their mouths unnaturally wide and filled with sharpened teeth, their hair long and whipping black.

The hand that held the glass wobbled and he took it two-handed and then lowered it. He found himself thinking again about the old histories, the genealogies of Timmoran's *Legendum Magicaria*.

Could the people of Kell and the Charg'r truly share common blood?

Were the Uthuk Y'llan even human at all?

"There are so few of them," said Fredric. The Uthuk were several miles away yet, but nevertheless he found himself whispering lest they might somehow overhear. He thrust the glass back to the captain of the watch. "Not nearly enough to storm Castle Kellar."

A trumpeting bellow blasted from the south.

Louder even than the Roglun Horn.

Fredric gripped the battlement and turned in the direction from which it had come.

There was no thrill this time.

The blood ran cold.

A dragon, as large as a hill and as dark as the Aenlong bridge, climbed above the forest's roof. One of its lesser kindred rose behind it, flapping hard to match speed and flank it as a knight would ride alongside his king. This smaller dragon was the green of aged copper, thin and scarred, as if from forgotten battles, and covered with mosses. It was no more than half the colossal span of the black dragon, but still seemed like a small castle taking flight.

Two dragons would be enough to break almost any castle, if not Kellar. The Uthuk Y'llan still approached from the east.

And the dragons had brought an army of their own.

A host of reptilian foot soldiers marched or, for those with vestigial wings and armor that was light enough to be borne, flew beneath their masters' shadows.

For the longest age Fredric could not form words in his mind, until the two came that filled him with dread.

Dragon hybrids.

He had fought them before. They could be found all over the wild places of north-eastern Terrinoth, but they had always been a rabble. Little better than kobolds or brigands, and supposedly of lesser intelligence than either. He had never heard of them marching as an army, or clad in dragon mail. He had never heard of them aligning with the Uthuk Y'llan. The lords of the Heath and the Locust Swarm had both menaced Terrinoth's frontiers many times, but always separately. Not since the dark days of Hellspanth and Llovar had they found common cause, and even that, supposedly, had been in defiance of the great Dragon Rex.

The black dragon bellowed as arrows from the city's outer walls and towers began to rattle off its armored belly.

Fire turned the southern skyline white, and when Fredric could see again there was a hole in the city's wall. He gripped the rampart, helpless to do anything about what he was seeing as, with a single flap of its wings, the dragon arrested its flight and swept aside. The downwash turned an already weakened corner tower to rubble and the dragon banked, flying off before any surviving bowmen could return fire. Its smaller lieutenant attended it closely, dropping low to broil the battlements it overflew in a torrent of greasy green fumes.

A few moments later the hybrids were over the walls.

Screams spread ahead of them. Faster even than the flames could go.

Fredric greeted the sight at a strange remove, as though his heart had taken the moments of inaction to clad itself in armor. The uncertainty left him. He would listen to no more screams.

With a rasp, his sword came free of its sheath.

In a singular hiss of Joulnar steel, the Knights of the Yeron each simultaneously drew theirs.

"Rally every soldier. Man every wall."

He turned to Grandmarshal Highgarde.

"And have somebody ready my horse."

CHAPTER THIRTY-ONE
Archerax
Castle Kellar, North Kell

The rising heat of a sea of fire filled Archerax's wings. The city's southern quarter was a steaming caldera of heat-fused rock and running metal. Such strongly built stone buildings as still stood were blackened and brittle. The screams of those within had brought a flicker of warmth to Archerax's vast heart, but one that had faded with every ponderously slow beat until it was cool and hard once more.

He swooped low.

These were the children's children of those who had stood against Hellspanth and Avox and Gehennor and who had seen Margath the Unkind so cruelly slain.

No man or woman would be left unburnt.

This he had vowed, and this would be done.

A company of archers scurried like rodents in the charred bones of what appeared to be a temple to one of the human gods. Black lips pulled back over hard gray teeth and steam emerged. *Human gods.* The idea amused him. A lazy sweep of his wings showered the ruin in sparks and embers. The humans sheltering there screamed, dropping their weapons in favor of beating on their burning clothing and rolling about in the soil like the ferreting little creatures they were. He chuckled, smoke pouring from his nostrils as he peeled right and climbed.

He could not be harmed by bow and arrow. The mightiest lance thrust could not pierce his scales, nor the broadest shield withstand his breath. The larger spear-throwers that the humans, towards the end of the Wars of Steel, had learned to construct could do him injury if he were to allow it, but they were unwieldy and slow. Humanity was not the only race in Mennara capable of adaptation. Archerax had learned well the lessons of the last war. To keep his distance. To spread his terror wide. To overrun the spear-throwers with hybrid soldiers and disposable allies, and only then to commit his own wrath to the fray.

He engulfed a towering three-floored stronghouse in flame as he soared over it. Its roof rose on a white pillar of fire, a hard rain of rubble and brick crushing the soldiers that sought belatedly to flee the neighboring buildings or clogged the roads beneath.

Kellar was a place of deep gray and grinding cold. It burned reluctantly, but burn it assuredly would.

This, too, he had vowed, and this too would be done.

He bellowed his triumph to the city below him, shattering windows and bending steel, the human legions directly underneath him clapping their hands to their ears and dropping to their knees in terror.

"I am Archerax the Great. Archerax the Terrible. Kneel, for I am your death. I am your god now."

The green dragon that flapped on moss-covered wings alongside him gave an eager trumpet of her own. Golden eyes glittered madly from beneath a deep ridge of emerald scales, flecked by silver rheum and as good as blind. Her nostrils trembled as she took in the excitements of the burning city. The feral creature was barely intelligent, another wastrel of Margath's legacy, like the hybrids that had worshipped and feared her as a god-queen of the wood for the past eight hundred years, abandoned as a hatchling when Shaarina Rex had recalled the Dragonlords to the Heath. Archerax had dubbed her Grievax, for that had been the name of her mother, whom the children of Kell had brought down over the forest and been too fearful to pursue, not even for the runebound shards she had borne with her to ground. It was a name that the dragon appeared to revel in, though what she had called herself in the centuries before, if the need or notion of doing so had ever even arisen, Archerax did not know. Or care.

"Spread devastation," he commanded. "Draw out the Dragonslayer's Heir or burn him out."

Grievax hissed her assent, and with a turbulent wingbeat turned herself away, descending gracelessly on the inner city.

CHAPTER THIRTY-TWO
Fredric
Castle Kellar, North Kell

The knightly orders of Kell thundered down the cobbled highway, bannerol fluttering from their lance heads, caparisons flying about their clattering hooves. The bright steel of their armor shone, the emerald, turquoise and gold of a dozen heraldries burnished red by flame.

Fredric did not lead from the tip of the lance as he might have wished. Sir Highgarde would not allow it. He rode two back from the grandmarshal and to the right of the wedge, his sword upraised and shining golden, rallying the men and women that fled in the opposite direction. Soldiers threw themselves to the sides of the road as the knights galloped past. Some came running from the ruins of the lower city, but many more walked as though exhausted, dragging themselves and injured comrades, trudging doggedly towards the keep at the very summit of the hill. To the last however they turned, raised their weapons in salute and cheered as Fredric and the hardy winter flower of Kellar chivalry charged past.

This ward of the city was not yet burning, but the ragged skyline of ramparts and steeply sloped slate roofs was lit a cherry red, an enormous mouth gaping wide to swallow the heart of his city.

It almost broke his heart. Kellar could have withstood the Uthuk Y'llan. At least until the full strength of the Locust Swarm had passed the forest. It could have driven back the dragons.

But was there a fortress in Terrinoth that could have defied both at once?

Perhaps it was his ancestor's armor, some reckless courage in the runebound shards that were activated only by battle, but he found himself excited to show that Kellar was one.

Trevin Highgarde barked an order.

The grandmarshal's armor was elaborately gilded, fretted with lattice wings that screamed with the rush of air. A white fur cloak stitched with golden fleurs-de-lis snapped over the cantle of his saddle. His visor was up. His huge moustache pulled in the wind of their charge. His massive sword, *Unkindness*, was held in two gauntleted hands, while he commanded his muscular destrier with the understanding of close comrades and the occasional instruction of his knees.

Sixty knights couched their lances.

The multitude of wooden shafts rattled like a lowering drawbridge. Steel heads spat like points fresh drawn from the fire. There was an almost imperceptible sense of acceleration. The beat of the warhorse's hooves became rhythmic.

Fredric roared.

"Charge!" Trevin bellowed.

"For Kellar!" Fredric cried out from the third rank, beating his sword on his Owl-emblazoned heater. "For Terrinoth! And for Daqan!"

The horses leapt.

Or so it felt.

And the knights' charge hit home.

Armor split. Bone cracked. Flesh tore.

Dragon hybrids croaked and wailed as the knights of Kellar trampled over their lines and on, urging their horses forward as if through a thicket.

No infantry formation in the world could have stood against a charge of Daqan knights. Had it been the deathless legions of Waiqar the Betrayer or the demon-possessed berserkers of the far east that stood before Fredric now, they would have been swept aside just as easily. A well-drilled company of Kellar militia or Dunwarr warriors, perhaps, soldiers of exceptional discipline and courage – they might have managed an orderly disengagement, but the dragon hybrids were a rabble. They were beasts that rune magic and cold-blooded genius had bidden to walk upright and take up arms to wage war like men.

They buckled.

Then they broke.

And then they ran.

A red-scaled hybrid with a proud frill of yellow bone and a coat of dark iron spun away. Its wings were just pulling its heels from the ground as Fredric's sword came down on its shoulder. A coat of dragon-forged metal could turn a blow that would crush dwarf plate and not show the mark afterwards. It was the dragons' ancestors, the yrthwrights, who had created the world and their craft was second to none. But Fredric's family sword boasted dragon magic of its own, a Rune of Fate plundered from the lair of the lesser Dragonlord, Vrarnir, and it clove through the weaker points in the dragon's armor as though through unwoven mail. The hybrid screamed like a shot goose as Fredric's sword cut into its shoulder. Blood, darker than that of humans, sprayed from the torn scales and his horse's hooves trampled it to the cobbles. Another nearby attempted to take off. Fredric swung eagerly for it, but the knight immediately behind skewered it with a solid thrust of his couched lance.

This was the reason why, for eight hundred years, every knighthood of Kell had favored the lance.

The blocks of hybrid warriors slowed the knights slightly, but it was not until they neared the colonnaded Soulstone playhouse at the foot of the road that their charge was halted. Its heavy stone outwalls stood bestride the fork in the highway like a fortress, grand oriel windows looking out over hooting Uthuk raiders rampaging up from the east and the bonfires of the south. Under its decorative cornices the charge turned into butcher's work. Knights cast aside lances and took up swords. Trevin laid about him like a frenzied bull, the rune magic of *Unkindness* and its special hatred of dragonkind seeing shields beaten in two and heads stricken from bodies. The greatsword's long-forgotten maker had quenched their still-hot blade in the blood of dragons before applying its runic charms. Twenty generations of grandmarshals since had sharpened its edge each day with a scale cut from the back of Margath the Unkind.

Fredric turned his horse, using the animal's armored bulk to knock over a hybrid caught between him and another knight. Another thrust its spear at him. He took the blow on his shield. The runebound shard set into the metal shimmered the painted owl device as though he were viewing the emblem from the bottom of a shallow pool. The dragonkin recoiled and Fredric rammed his sword through the hybrid's eye socket. He looked up then, looking for more enemies to slay, only to find that the work was done. Most of the hybrids had been slain already or fled, forcing a way into the playhouse where the knights could not follow or been caught by the infantry returning to the fight on the south road.

Fredric wheeled his horse about, soothing its temper as it snorted and stamped.

The soldiers filling both sides of the road cheered.

Fredric saluted them with his blade, the first flush of victory in his chest.

"Fredric!" Trevin roared, his voice hoarse from the exertions of ten men. He took one hand from his sword and pumped the air with his fist. "Dragonslayer! Baron of Kell!"

"*Baron of Kell!*" the soldiers shouted in return. "*Dragonslayer!*"

The latter became a battle cry.

A chant as their formations rallied and their spears hewed into dragon flesh.

"Dragonslayer! Dragonslayer! Dragonslayer!"

A rider clattered up the southern road. He was young and unarmored with a tonsured head, clad in baronial heraldry and the livery of Fredric's own select company of message riders. Soldiers made way as the rider pulled up in a clattering of hooves. The horse panted, wild-eyed and manic. The man was red-faced, his flesh burned and his skin peeling.

"What news?" said Fredric.

"The dragons have levelled the entire quarter," he said, breathless, but concise. "Nothing stands, be it man or building."

Fredric bowed his head but held back his grief. "Very good. Ride back to the keep."

"My lord?"

"You have been burned half to death and your horse is little better. Go back. Eat something. Have your wounds seen to. There will be fighting left for you afterwards."

"Yes, lord." The message rider wheeled his horse about, then turned back in the saddle. "There is one other thing, my lord."

"Speak."

"The Uthuk Y'llan are no longer keeping pace with the dragons' advance. I don't know why. But I have heard rumors from other riders in the city that some other force assails them from the Forest Road."

Fredric's masked grief gave way to a treacherous flicker of hope. "Thank you. Now go."

The rider spurred his horse and galloped off up the hill road.

Fredric turned to Trevin. "Captain Constan and the Southern Army?"

"Too soon, sire. I would caution against hope."

"A man needs hope, Trevin. A baron needs enough of it to share." Standing in his stirrups he called out to the soldiers that his charge had rallied to the fight. "Fall back by units. Withdraw to the castle while they are in rout. We have been caught between two mighty foes today, and that would test the mettle of any hero of Terrinoth. But this is Kellar!" He beat his sword's flat on his shield and the soldiers roared their love for him and their country. His heart swelled big enough for all of them. "We will break them against the walls of our castle. As we have broken everyone fool enough to make themselves our enemy before them. This is Kellar!"

"*Kellar!*" they roared.

"Dragonslayer!"

"We should go back as well," Trevin muttered. "We can sally again if we must, but this is infantry work from here on."

Fredric nodded reluctantly. "I leave it in your hands, grandmarshal."

Trevin barked instructions

The knights drew back into formation and came about.

Fredric was amongst the last.

He turned in his saddle and looked back at the playhouse. It wrenched him to abandon it. He recalled taking Litiana for the first, and last, time two years before, to see the Orisson Players perform their famous tragedy, *Mirror Lake*. He smiled, bittersweet, recalling how Anna had entirely failed to understand the point.

He was still watching as it was destroyed.

The roof collapsed as though a castle had been dropped on it. Dust and rubble from its shattered walls blew across the turning knights, bowling over horses and unseating their riders. Trevin Highgarde went down under his flailing horse. The green dragon bulled its head through what was left of the front wall and bellowed.

A fatty spark struck up in the back of its throat.

Fredric spurred his horse without thinking.

He raised his shield, its embedded runestone throwing out an invisible barrier just as the dragon exhaled. The monster's breath attack struck the runic shield and blasted outwards. Soldiers ducked and cried out as black smoke struck across their heads and savaged the stone fronts of the buildings on both sides of the road. The dragon bellowed its frustration as it clambered out of the ruined playhouse.

A dismounted knight tried to run away.

The dragon crushed him underfoot.

It built towards a charge.

Fredric gasped, astonished to be alive, lowered his aching shield-arm and turned his horse to face the dragon, the charger awing him then with its courage, and struck with his sword. Its fated edge, sharper than any metalcraft of elves or dwarves could fashion a blade, chipped emerald scales and drew brackish blood. The dragon howled at the unwelcome novelty of pain. Sheer bludgeoning mass threw Fredric from his horse. He hit the ground with a crash and a clatter and skidded out from under it. The horse cried out as the dragon trampled it. The monster turned its long, snaking tongue towards Fredric, nostrils flaring as it rediscovered his scent, and roared.

Fredric struggled against the weight of his armor to stand.

He raised his shield over him.

"Bows!" came Trevin's frantic bark. "Bring me bows!"

In the years before the Dragon Wars bristling squares of spearmen and massed archery had been the best way to deal with the rogue drakes that occasionally menaced Daqan lands. Against the ordered legions that had emerged from the Molten Heath in later centuries, the tactic had proved dangerously flawed, but to fend off a single rampaging beast it was what the military instructors of Kellar and Archaut still taught.

The dragon swung its savage lump of a head as deep blocks of silver-armored and purple-liveried spearmen formed up around it, archers ranking up behind to pepper the beast with arrows. Most snapped against toughened scales, a few sticking like splinters in the gaps between plates, or in the mossy regions around its joints and wings. It roared like a pestered lion and threw out its wings. The stench of grave mold and leaf mulch sent knights reeling. Craning its long neck towards the spearmen, it exhaled.

Black fumes washed over the Kellar soldiers and smashed though the frontage of the building across the way. Men and women screamed as their armor cooked them, turning them into heat-fused skeletons that the dragon then casually dismantled with a beat of its wings. Archers continued to break their arrows against its hide as it lifted off and climbed away, even after Fredric had commanded them to stop.

"Back to the castle," he said, choking on the poisonous heat, knowing with a sickness in his chest that it was dead men he was breathing in. He waved in the direction of the castle. "Go. Go. I will be following."

"Never do anything like that again," said Trevin. His eyes were red and his skin was black. The visor had twisted right off his helmet and one side of his moustache was smoldering

"I hope I never have to," said Fredric, and meant it.

"I'm serious. Did you think what it would mean for morale if you fell? Do you know what it would do to my honor?"

Fredric smiled as heavy-armed knights struggled to remount without the aid of their squires and turn themselves around. Twenty had fallen. Just forty were left.

"It pains me to leave their bodies to the dragons," he said. "Or worse, to the Uthuk Y'llan."

"That is the burden of leadership, lord. And the costs of war."

Fredric could bear that burden, but he thought the cost far too high.

Trevin made his way to his own horse. His right leg dragged.

"You are hurt!" said Fredric.

Trevin looked down and grunted. "It's the armor's joint. My leg is well enough." He swung the seized limb up into the saddle, and then turned back, noticing that Fredric was without a mount. He looked around and shouted into the confusion of the retreat. "Is there a horse spare for the baron?"

"Take mine, sire."

A knight in the purple heraldry and polished steel trim of the Knights Griffon drew his arming sword and dismounted. Fredric saluted him, touching his blade to his brow, and climbed onto the warrior's horse.

"Back to the keep, lord," said Trevin.

Fredric nodded. "Back to the keep!"

He spurred the borrowed horse, the lance of knights clattering into a trot and then into a steady canter as they raced back up the hill they had just charged down in glory.

Fredric resisted the desire to go faster.

He would not have the Orders of Kellar be seen as fleeing in rout from his own city.

The gatehouse loomed into view.

It was the most fortified corner of the most fortified site in Terrinoth. It was a mountain of dressed stone wrapped in steel.

The gates were of strong, dark oak banded with metal, and set deeply into the walls to expose any would-be assailant to arrow loops and flues for boiling oil. Two colossal towers flanked it, strung with pennons and mounting the great flags of the Barony of Kell and of the Daqan lords, facing defiantly eastward as they had done for two thousand years.

Retreating soldiers streamed through the open gate. Arrows whistled out in all directions, slackening off and then flurrying again like winter showers. Dragon hybrids with javelins and bat-winged creatures of the Ynfernael, demons with the muscular bodies of men and the faces of dogs, harried the walls like gulls.

Fredric was satisfied to see his soldiers' discipline. Spearmen surrounded the long lines of archers with steel points and round shields. Units of bowmen in turn screened the crews of the castle's ballistae, the siege masters holding their weapons taut and ready, holding their nerve through every probing attack, patiently waiting their chance at one of the greater dragons.

There was no evidence yet of panic.

The city burned, but by Roland, with warriors like these to call upon he would hold his castle. "They have been well trained," said Fredric.

"I take no credit," said Trevin.

"They are a credit to General Brant. And to every man and woman who has stood on this wall before them and held it."

"As are you, sire."

Fredric smiled, and for the first time his immediate thought was not to argue the virtues of some more valorous ancestor. "We will win this yet. If even one message rider made it past the hounds of the Uthuk Y'llan and out of Kell then I would not bet against Kellar stamina to hold until reinforcements come."

"Relief from Dhernas or Forthyn is about all we can hope for now," said Trevin, his voice dropping to a cracked whisper as they passed under the castle's threshold.

Even confidences could carry far through the barbican's stone tunnel.

The column rode for a long minute. The horses' hooves rang alternately off stone flags and metal grates, echoing loudly, the tiny chink of sunlight at the tunnel's far end growing steadily into a second gate that admitted Fredric and his knights into Kellar's outer bailey and a scene of urgent anarchy.

Soldiers hurried back and forth, running errands alone or as whole units rushing to reinforce some embattled section of wall. Horses huddled together, untended, confused and panicked by the mayhem around them. Aged runemasters in the scholarly robes of Greyhaven clutched tightly to cracked tomes of battle spells while harried apprentices fussed with towering golems, etching runes, adjusting charms. Only the golems themselves were unflustered, as fearless as rocks with immense blades, idle for now, in their untiring hands. Somehow, they appeared all the more fearful for their lack of reaction. None but the runemasters whose lore commanded them dared stand near. Even the horses, dogs, and hawks that the Kellar employed in war gave the rune constructs a wide berth.

The bustle parted around the knights to reveal Princess Litiana haranguing some luckless page as he fled back towards the inner gate with an armful of flags. She was wearing a brigandine in her usual clash of bright colors, with a large arbalest of Loriman make in both hands and hanging against her chest by a shoulder strap. Her dark hair had been tied back with a colorful string of ribbon.

Fredric had never seen her looking closer to her natural element.

"You should be in the keep," he said.

"*You* should be in the keep," said Litiana. "You're the lord of the castle. I'm just your wife, and a lord can always get another one of those."

Trevin cleared his throat and leant in. "There can be only one woman for this man, my lady. He is quite taken by you, I fear."

Litiana sniffed. "That is disappointing."

In spite of the battle, Fredric flushed.

"Indeed, my lady," said Trevin, "I'm afraid you will have to refrain from dying today after all."

"Did you at least kill some dragonkin with that thing?"

Trevin brandished *Unkindness* like a proud father. "Some. Though I fear your husband outdid me when he blooded one of the greater beasts."

Litiana turned to look Fredric up and down. "I will be impressed when its head is on our bedchamber wall. I want it to be the first thing I see when I wake tomorrow morning."

Before Fredric could think of an answer a gibbering shout, part manic laughter, part tormented shriek, drew their attention skyward. A demon careened over the walls, pursued by a blizzard of arrows.

Litiana raised her arbalest, sighted down the track and loosed.

"Curses," she swore, as the bolt sailed wide and the demon continued its erratic flight towards the next gate.

"Go back to the keep," Fredric told her.

"If I had hit that thing we would be having a different conversation."

"Brant can keep order here."

"Pffft."

"And so can I."

"Respectfully, sire," said Trevin. "I should escort you *both* back."

"These are my walls! I won't ask another to hold them in my stead."

"Where is young Grace?" said Trevin.

"In the keep, with Chamberlain Salter and the other old people," said Litiana.

"Without guards?" said Fredric.

Litiana looked offended. "I made sure she was armed."

Fredric's mouth dropped open.

Their daughter was a noble, an heir to a barony: it was expected that she would take on responsibilities young, but not *quite* as young as the families of the Torue Albes seemed to demand of theirs.

Trevin chuckled.

Litiana winched her arbalest. "It may not come to that. There is a rumor going around that we are going to win."

"Aye, my lady," said Trevin with a wry smile. "I heard that one too."

CHAPTER THIRTY-THREE
Archerax
Castle Kellar, North Kell

A new moat encircled the keep, an ever-tightening ring of glowing metals and burning stone. Ash filled the sky and covered the moon. Screams rose from the tortured city like smoke. Only the castle itself, perched high on the rocky shoulder of the Howling Giant Hills like a moribund falcon of gray stone, was unburnt. Its walls bristled with spears and bows. The hated spear-throwers sat ensconced in towers a hundred feet high. The gate itself, supposedly a castle's weakest point, resisted the flames that the hybrids hurled at it. The metals gleamed after every assault as though poured afresh from the cast each time. Even the wood was unmarred. Some rune magic rendered them proof against dragon fire. But it was dragon magic that allowed them to defy him, and Archerax would see it unmade.

His nostrils smoked as he pondered.

"I promised the Uthuk witch that Kellar would fall ere the dawning of the fifth day, and lo, it shall. Even if it is by the murder of my own claws that it must be done."

He raised his head on its long neck and split the night with his call.

A moment later the green dragon, Grievax, settled onto the ruin alongside him. She beat her wings slowly, as though unwilling to set great weight on her leg.

"You are injured," said Archerax.

Grievax hissed. "Dragonslayer's Heir," she managed, in the halting dragon speech she had learned from the elder hybrids. "He has claws of his own."

"Such is the reason that I have flown so far from the molten hearthlands of Mennara's Heart. To return you, of course, kindred of mine, lost childe of Shaarina Rex, and to lay low this savage outpost of the dragons' rightful dominion, but to end him also, and his hated line, before the storm from the Heath rises in full."

The green dragon panted and fumed, as eager as a hatchling and as stupid.

Not unlike the Uthuk Y'llan.

"But you have failed me," he said. "The Dragonslayer's Heir has barred his gates and now we must unmake his fastness stone by stone."

"It will be done, lord!"

"You assured me that this one was soft and would not hide behind walls while his city burned."

Grievax hissed, but did not respond.

"Prove your worth to Levirax now. Make me an entrance. I will deal with the Dragonslayer's Heir myself."

CHAPTER THIRTY-FOUR
Fredric
Castle Kellar, North Kell

The gatehouse's left-hand tower exploded into rubble and flame. Fredric raised his shield and flinched back. Lumps of burning masonry rained over the bailey like meteors. Smaller debris rattled off shields and helms and rooftops. Larger chunks smashed men and flagstones indiscriminately. A quarter of the tower's height was gone, gouting flame like a volcano, the immense forest-green drake that Fredric had wounded fanning the flames with each beat of its gargantuan wings. Arrows by the hundred bristled its tough hide already, and no sooner had it alighted than a seven foot-long bolt from a ballista pierced its chest. The monster issued an eardrum-rupturing scream, sending a plume of hot breath rolling across the rampart towards the right-hand tower. Archers screamed as they burned. Another bolt pierced the dragon. The creature arched its long neck back and bellowed.

And then fell.

Its landing crushed another ten yards of the curtain wall. It thrashed violently, once, like a dog with something stuck in its back, flattening a hundred spearmen and the entire span of wall, and then fell still.

Fredric looked at the destruction in horror. Not even during the reign of Margath the Unkind had the inner walls fallen. "The wall is breached!" Fredric yelled.

Spearmen rallied to him, forming up in deep ranks and locking shields. Rune-golems lumbered forward, visible through the thickening pall only by the magic blazing through the joints in their armor. Whatever decided to test that breach was in for the fight of its life.

Fredric raised his sword high. His borrowed horse paced under him. "Kellar has stood for two thousand years. It stands today. Kellar!"

"*Kellar!*" his army roared, as the dragons came.

They came from above.

Ignoring entirely the breach that had drawn the human army's attentions the hybrids descended like autumn leaves gathered by a storm; greens and yellows and silvers and reds swirled as they flew. Soldiers screamed as they shifted to address the new threat, bending the formation's discipline as warriors stationed to the flanks and rear lifted their shields.

Somewhere close by, a second dragon bellowed.

Fredric snapped to life, a lifetime of training to lead his people taking over. "Archers!" he yelled, turning in the saddle to project his voice wherever it might be heard. "Archers. Thin them. Infantry to me. Rear units form schiltrons. Forward units disengage and reform at the second gate." From the vantage of horseback, Fredric watched as the battle slowly began to conform to his command. Units drew back into tight rings of spears, stabbing up at swooping hybrids while others hurried back, clattering past Fredric where he still stood with Trevin and Litiana in front of the main gate before streaming out into new ranks like steel poured into a mold.

Fredric himself was untested and unproven, or so he had

always felt until this point, but the blood of legends was in him, and it stirred at the sight before him now.

The initial shock had been overcome, and the dragons would break themselves on Kellar discipline and Kellar stone as they had always done.

"Now – drive! Drive! Them! Back!"

A flying hybrid in armor the color of molten rock swooped for him. He was a raised target on horseback, harder to protect with spears and evidently important. Fredric ducked its spear thrust and cut it down with a counter from his sword. Another shrieked, circling, waiting, and then dove. There was a twang as Litiana shot it. The bolt from her arbalest punched through metal and scales alike.

Fredric turned to her.

She nodded.

"Go back to the castle," he said. There was an authority in his voice and a stature to his bearing that had not been there before, and she took a backward step even if she did not immediately obey. He would protect her, not that she needed it, but so that there would be someone left to protect Grace should he fall.

Turning back to the battle, he swept his blooded sword up overhead.

"Show them Kellar steel!"

A formation of spearmen had pinned a mob of dragon hybrids in place. More of the hybrids were landing to reinforce them, hoping to overwhelm and overrun the human formation. A rune golem waded into them before they had the chance, setting to work with a gigantic axe in each of its four hands and a sound like a thousand lumberjacks working a single tree. The construct emerged from the melee a few seconds later, splattered in blood and surrounded by broken blades. Elsewhere a lance of knights, their heraldries impossible to make out in the gloom and dust, colors all turned

to gray and all armor to brass by dragonfire, thundered around
the southern edge of the battleground, sweeping away hybrids
and scattering them back to the skies. Archers shot the creatures
down the moment they were airborne, spearmen hurrying up in
the knights' wake to reclaim lost ground and push the hybrids
backs to the wall. Even if the dragons themselves had made no
use of it, the breached wall was impossible to ignore. There were
more hybrids still out there on foot, not to mention the Uthuk
Y'llan.

The rune golem looked around for more creatures to kill,
thinking inscrutable thoughts born of rock crystals and rune-
magic, the cracks in its rugged brow glowing with a faint blueish
light such that they almost resembled eyes.

It turned ponderously towards the breach.

What it sensed there or how it weighed its decisions, now that
it had briefly been given autonomy to make them, Fredric refused
to try to imagine. The magic, frankly, terrified him in a way no
monster could.

A dragon roared.

The archers still left on the wall whirled, but too late, as a second
dragon blasted its breath across the gatehouse's right-hand tower
and swept overhead. Fredric craned his neck to follow it as bits of
ballista rained down over the bailey. For one brief moment peace
fell as every man, woman, and beast in Castle Kellar paused in
their efforts and did the same.

Here was a true monarch of dragonkind.

The dragon descended on the bailey unopposed.

It stretched out its wings and straightened its back. It was
almost as great in stature as the tower that burned against its
back, its wings broader than the entire span of the gatehouse
and the breached wall combined. Brave knights cried out, all
pride and valor vanquished by the expression of such noble

terror. Veterans of a dozen battles broke and ran before the great monster had fully settled.

Fredric felt himself quaver.

The strength left his arms. His weapons lowered. He had been wrong to think himself the equal of this.

He had been so wrong…

"Dragonslayer's Heir," the dragon announced, its voice thick with the awful majesty of power. "I am Archerax the Great. It is my honor to be your doom."

Claws gouged deep into the flagstones as it took a grip on the ground, and then attacked.

It was a massacre.

There was not the strength in all of Terrinoth to deny such a beast.

Blocks of spearmen were swept imperiously aside. Archers were contemptuously ignored, their arrows snapping off its scaled back. A rune golem with a siege-ballista mounted on its back moved to confront it. The dragon swatted the construct like a beetle.

"Die, spawn of Margath!" Trevin Highgarde yelled, spurring his terrified horse into a charge and hewing *Unkindness* deep into the dragon's hip.

Archerax reared and bellowed.

Stone cracked. The metal points of spears bent.

Fredric's hands flew to his ears and he screamed.

"Insolent flea," said Archerax, as Trevin fought to restrain his mount. "Blood kindred to Margath am I, but no lesser than he. Cower, tin man. You stand before a sovereign such has not trodden the Land of Steel since your elder age. Gather all the tools of your ingenuity and your theft, they will not avail you now."

The grandmarshal raised his sword for another swing.

Archerax struck it from his hand. The blow would have

stricken stone. While the knight screamed over his broken limb, Archeron wreathed him in fire.

Fredric watched in horrified disbelief as the ashes crumbled.

All his life he had thought Trevin Highgarde indestructible, the last thing that would be left standing when the world failed, and the one he had always imagined he could entrust his daughter's crown to if he fell.

Unkindness clattered to the charred stones. Its magic alone was proof against whatever destruction Archerax could inflict, but it was glowing red with the heat, the smoke of Trevin's final grip curling from its hilt.

With a cry Litiana raised her arbalest and loosed.

The heavy bolt thudded into Archerax's neck and pierced the scales.

The dragon turned to her.

Before Fredric could react she bent to scoop up a spear that a fleeing soldier had dropped and charged.

As though slapped across the face with a steel glove, the fear of watching this play out snapped him out of his terror of the beast. He raised his shield, his face turning deathly stern, and he spurred his horse into a charge. The warhorse overtook Litiana a second later and Fredric hacked his sword into the dragon's flank. The Rune of Fate blazed as it sought out the weakest point in a monster without weakness, but there was no harm it could do that *Unkindness* had not done. Litiana yelled as she rammed her spear up into the pit of Archerax's foreleg. The dragon growled, pulling the spear from her grip as he raised his foot and then brought it down with crushing weight across her legs.

Fredric felt as though he had been run through the chest with *Unkindness'* still-hot blade. "No!" he yelled, striking the dragon's side again and again in a frenzy.

Turning from Litiana's still body, Archerax struck his snout across Fredric's shield. Power burst from the runic device and was broken. The runestone embedded in the metal exploded. The discharge hurled Fredric from his saddle.

Archerax grunted and shook his head, armored lids blinking slowly, then idly snapped forward his neck to rip Fredric's horse from the ground and hurl it bodily into a nearby wall.

Fredric dragged himself back.

"All that is yours or that you hold precious I will take until there is naught left to you but your life – and then that too will be mine," said Archerax. "Heir to Dragonslayers you may be, but Roland you are not. No winged horse of the elves have you to match me in flight. No Soulstone Shard have you to leach the might from me as we battle. Both were lost in Margath's fall, and no craft do I see about me by which they might be replaced. The lesser descendants of unexceptional men you are. I will dismantle this citadel piece by piece and when I am done there will be left not a single stone to mark you." A huge, smoking black tongue emerged from behind the dragon's fangs. He licked his lips. "And then I will find the hole where your offspring cowers and I will eat her."

Fredric howled his defiance, throwing off the scraps of his ruined shield and taking up his sword two-handed as he fought his armored body back to its feet.

Like a lion being attacked by a cub, Archerax cuffed the baron onto his back.

"Nevertheless, a part of me had hoped to face something greater. But I see now…"

From his stupefyingly great height the dragon looked down.

The malice and disappointment of ages filled his eyes with hate.

Fire flickered about his jaw.

"Humanity is weaker even than I had thought."

CHAPTER THIRTY-FIVE
Greyfox
Castle Kellar, North Kell

Greyfox never would have thought it possible. She was tired of shooting Uthuk Y'llan.

The Uthuk had been thick over the Forest Road, and all over the hill country north of it. It was as if every land east of the Lothan had emptied itself into Kell. They had been too many even for a hero to fight through, effectively forcing them to head west instead of north and to the relief of Kellar town. Sibhard and a pair of Andira's pilgrim-soldiers wrestled with a seven foot-tall creature made up of pink-pale rolls of skin and wobbling blubber. The rest of the company fended off the rest of the ragtag horde, battering them from the burnt road with flails and cudgels and clearing a path for Greyfox and Andira on their horses to get by.

The elf shifted on Starchaser's bare back, drew her bowstring with a bored expression, and, for variety's sake, lined up a shot on a yellow-scaled dragonkin that was fleeing the castle's walls. The arrow fell woefully short and she cursed the peasant shortbows and the rushed craftsmanship that had gone into her borrowed quiver. Andira had destroyed her mother's Latari bow and she had grieved the loss, but there had been no opportunity to properly miss it until now. She lined up a second arrow, but the dragonkin was gone behind a belfry before she could loose it. She sighed.

She had heard the old tale of the Dragon of the Whispering Forest, but no one, barring a few of the more superstitious locals from her former band, had ever given it much credence. She wondered if perhaps Sibhard had been right and that she was mad and did not really hear the voices of the forest at all.

She shrugged.

Something to think about.

"I see a way through to the castle," Andira shouted to her. "With me, Milenhéir."

Greyfox was starting to regret sharing her real name with Andira. The hero was surprisingly adept in Latari pronunciation, and when she said it, it reminded Greyfox too much of the only elf beside herself who had ever known it.

Starchaser tossed his mane and turned, hooves clattering on the baked flagstones, breaking through the disorganized packs of Uthuk and leaping over a culvert that had been cut through the main road by dragonfire.

"*Lady Runehand!*" Sibhard called out, wrapped up in the folds of the obscene thing as he struggled to stab at it with his knife. The demon-possessed Uthuk monster chuckled jovially, like an old man playfighting with a favorite grandchild, as the other pilgrims beat uselessly at it with clubs.

Andira ignored them. "Get me to the castle, to where Baron Fredric fights," she said to Greyfox. "If this is where I am forced to be then let it be for good reason."

Greyfox marveled at how the woman could adopt a position entirely contrary to her original intention, but then adopt it so wholeheartedly it was impossible to recall how it differed. It was a genuine gift.

"Yes, Lady Runehand," she said, with a bow and a flourish and galloped on, clattering over flagstones strewn with charred rubble and bones.

The paths through Castle Kellar were no longer things that one could blindly follow, courses that one took to thread between the great stone frontages and monuments of a proud old city, but those patches of it where the ground had cooled enough to be ridden across. There was no ordering hand at work in its layout. It was woodland after a wildfire had raged through, or a village after a spring snap in the Dunwarr had caused the Lothan to burst and swept the majority of it downriver. If not for the castle ahead of her, high on its hill as though it had clambered there to escape the rising flames, she might have looked on it all and struggled to match it to the picture of privilege and power she had carried since she had been small.

It was almost funny: she had always wanted to see Kellar.

A flesh ripper with a spined frill and two rows of bone spikes running down its muscular back bounded out of the rubble. Its demonic hide was black with ash. Its eyes were bright with reflected hate. It closed on Starchaser with an easy, slobbering lope.

"Bored now…" Greyfox sighed and shot it through the neck.

It carried on running, until Greyfox gave a reedy whistle and Andira's yellow-white Carthridge courser, galloping behind her, veered abruptly sideways to slam the demon hound into what remained of a corner wall.

"Never do that to a horse I am trying to ride again!" Andira yelled, struggling to regain control.

Greyfox yipped and the bigger horse thundered after her and Starchaser, fighting off Andira's pull on the reins and leaving the hero to shout her curses into the wind. She grinned.

She had found something that Andira Runehand was not good at.

But the hero had been right about one thing.

She had been wrong to lead Andira astray, and it was an error she did not intend to repeat. They would ride into Castle Kellar and save the baron.

Because there was no way Greyfox was following her into a fight with a demon king without an army in front of her.

CHAPTER THIRTY-SIX
Andira Runehand
Castle Kellar, North Kell

Andira clung grimly to the saddle pommel, Hamma's horse pounding enthusiastically after the dart-swift shape of the Greyfox. The road steepened markedly as the elf led her on. The ground became hotter, its destruction all the more recent, their hooves kicking up flurries of sparks as the horses flew across it. The broken walls of Castle Kellar reared from the smoke. A huge dragon, gnarled and green as an ancient tree, lay slumped in the wreckage of the outer rampart, like a Stormlord beached on the rocks of Tigh Higard, cloaked in the ash and debris of its ruin.

For one reason or another, her adventures had always taken her to the most desolate corners of Terrinoth. Abandoned castles. Forsaken woods. She wondered now if it had been deliberate, to spare her from seeing sights like these: the human cost of her devotion to her quest. The Greyfox's mount scrabbled up the heaped spoil around the fallen drake, as agile and as eager as a Joulnar goat up a rockslide. Andira did not have to urge her own steed to follow. She simply held on tighter as it climbed. The smell became acrid.

The smoke was burnt meat and charred rock, burning the back of the throat as soon as it entered the mouth and stinging the eyes. The rune in her hand shone with a clear blue-white light. It burned a hole in the pall. Dust shimmered in the air around her. The ground beneath her glittered. Pale debris. Dark ash. Discarded metal reflecting her light. A field of fallen soldiers stretched out beyond the reach of her light, flowers poking out from volcanic soil. They had been crushed, burned, brutalized by teeth and claws. The ground steamed like a sulfur lake. The shattered earth groaned.

Ahead of her, and high, high above, the dragon rumbled.

Fire wreathed its titanic maw, drawing the huge wedge shape of a head like a god revealing itself from the clouds. The greater bulk of the behemoth was a fear of black, obsidian and glittering, shrouded in a meeker, subservient dark.

The ache in her hand became a pain.

This was not the foe she had set out from the Bloodwood to challenge: it was of an entirely different breed although, she sensed, of similar standing within the great hierarchy of Mennara's powers.

She quailed before it and then smiled.

So, she could feel fear after all.

The Greyfox let go a cry and veered, loosed an arrow that vanished into the smoky pall to no discernible effect, and then peeled off to one side. Divorced from the elf's guiding hand, Andira's mount shied, but even in his most abject terror some instinct told him that it would go ill for him if he were to throw Andira Runehand. She raised her poleaxe like a battle standard and the rune in her hand blazed with a sudden brilliance, throwing its light out over the entirety of the courtyard. Daqan soldiers and dragon hybrids, freshly exhumed from the pall, tussled in the gritty light at the illumination's edge, but there at the dark heart of the storm all was terrible and calm.

The dragon reared up before her in all its awful majesty.

Its scales were glossy and black and steamed with heat. Long spines curled from the sides of its body and the backs of its limbs, less like the malignant outgrowths of the Uthuk Y'llan than the jeweled ornaments of a monarch. Horns and barbs crowned its vast head, limned in turn by an effervescent flicker of fire and a halo shimmer of heat. It exhaled slowly, menacingly. The inner heat brightened, turning from a ruddy orange to a fierce yellow, as if in counter to the growing strength of Andira's runelight.

She amused it. But in the fact that it had not yet slain her out of hand she deduced that it was wary of her too. For all its unknowable might the idea of encountering an equal was not entirely beyond its imagination.

And it knew one when it saw it.

"A frightened little girl on a frightened little horse," its voice rumbled. "Which shall I devour first?" It sniffed, nostrils flaring, and the horse clattered backwards in panic. In the Greyfox's absence it was all Andira could do to keep him from bolting. The dragon chuckled.

"I smell you, little girl. I smell the power in you, and I know whence it was taken. Mine is greater. It was bestowed upon me in ancient days by beings you can scarce imagine and by right is mine alone. Go, child. Flee from me. The Ynfernael rises and it is the duty of all to challenge its power or concede. Do this and I will be gracious and tell you where your nemesis' earthly throne might be found. My sole promise to you in exchange is that I will end this one swiftly."

One colossal toe of one gargantuan foot raised, briefly revealing a body draped in a rich purple surcoat, and then lowered again. Andira gripped the reins tightly. It was Baron Fredric. He looked dazed and half-conscious. His armor was scorched. His shield arm looked unnaturally bent. His face was reddened and hairless, beard and brows replaced with burns.

"And after I have devoured his wife and his daughter and any others I deem precious to him, after I have plundered his treasuries and gathered to myself all therein that I judge desirable, then I will depart this city and bring ruin to no other. On this you have my word."

Andira paused briefly, surprised only by how little she was tempted.

She was no storybook hero, she knew. Although she had had no recollection of ever reading or hearing those old tales herself, somehow she knew. To lack a past was to be without the inner voice and moral guidance that directed most folk, whether they chose to accept that direction or not. Instead, she had her quest. Whether it was wresting perilous relics from the hands of vile necromancers in Roth's Vale, scouring the Bloodwood of the Tangle, or bringing retribution upon the legions of Baelziffar, whatever she decided it must be it was all that she had. *That* was her moral code. She had forsaken innocents before. Gwellan had not been the first. Surrounded now by devastation on an inhuman scale she was most disturbed to find that she was not in fact so heartless as she had always supposed.

She dismounted.

The horse bolted the moment she was clear of it. But Andira no longer cared. She had not been trained to fight properly from horseback in any case.

She gripped her poleaxe.

The dragon rumbled with mirth.

"So be it."

With a deafening roar, the fire buried under its black scales growing fierce, it threw its bulk towards her.

Andira drew her hand from her poleaxe.

The runelight withdrew from the air and returned to her hand, hardening in her grip as steam would turn into water and then into ice. She clenched her fist and then swiped it across the dragon's jaw. The blow connected with a crack like thunder. The dragon's head snapped to one side, the endless length of its body turning across her as its smoking jaws ploughed into the stone girth of the castle gatehouse. The structure had been standing firm despite the destruction of its supporting towers and the onslaught of dragonfire, but it fell then. Thousands of tons of stonework tumbled over the dragon.

It did not stay buried for long.

The mountain of rubble shifted, avalanches sliding off the dragon's back as it lifted itself up and turned its long, dust-grayed neck around.

Fury lit the night-dark rings of its eyes.

"You were not made to contest with one such as I. Not with the borrowed might that you possess. The power to make and break worlds is my birthright. The will to bend them is in my blood."

It opened its jaws wide, fire igniting in its throat and issuing forth on a gale as it threw its jaws towards her.

Andira raised her hand up to the onslaught, her mind tracing the outer circle of the rune to throw out a rippling shield against which the dragon's fire blasted and burst. Andira gritted her teeth and leant into it. The heat, even from behind the rune-barrier, was ferocious. She felt the ground beneath her shift as the fury of the assault ground her ankles back.

The dragon was an order mightier than the Greyfox. He was greater even than Prutorn had been, and the demon of Sudanya had come closer than anyone to besting her and ending her quest.

The pain tore a scream from her throat. Whatever came for her after this battle, whether the glow of triumph or the oblivion of defeat at the last, after this she would finally rest. Just as she sensed the approach of her long-theorized limits, the moment at which she could bear to resist no longer, the onslaught of flame guttered away, the storm of fire petering to nothing across her wobbling shield.

Her hand dropped to her side and she gasped.

The dragon grumbled.

It drew another breath.

Gathering her own body's last strength on a shuddering breath, Andira swung her poleaxe high and leapt.

The dragon was too vast a target to miss. It relied on size, the crippling terror it inflicted upon all mortal creatures, and unassailable power to destroy its foes utterly. Against those foes, vanishingly few, against whom that was insufficient it could count on armor scales thicker than a man's hand and harder than dwarf-made metal. Andira's blade smashed into its shoulder like a pickaxe into stone. Scales chipped and flew from the wound.

The dragon bellowed in pain.

Andira screamed in more.

Power spat from her hand and arced the weapon's length blasting a crater of meat from the dragon's thigh. Half mad with pain, it swiped at her. As it had been too big to avoid her blow, so was its foot too large to miss her. She threw out her hand to block it. The dragon's foot impacted her barrier, encompassing her in rippling lines of energy and doing nothing at all to prevent her being hurled like a pebble a hundred yards across the bailey yard and through the thin walls of a stable block. Her shield fizzled and disintegrated as the roof came apart around her.

The pain was indescribable.

With a staggering statement of power, the dragon dragged itself back into the air. Every sweep of its wings brought more of the ruined stable down on Andira's head.

"You will *pay* for this injury." Its voice boomed like the anger of the black sky. "With the blood of your kin you will repay me a thousand-fold."

Andira struggled back up, pressuring the agony back into her by clenching it tight around her poleaxe. "I have no kin. None that I know. Direct your wrath wherever you see fit."

"And this is what the Land of Steel would call a hero."

"Many have. It is nothing I have ever claimed to be."

"You were born into the wrong skin, Runehand. You should have been dragon, with cold blood in your veins and dark scales over your unfeeling bones."

There was a twang, as though the tension in the air had caused it to snap, and an arrow sprouted from the underside of the dragon's wing.

Andira turned, expecting, or perhaps hoping, to see the Greyfox returned. But the elf was long gone. Instead she saw Baron Fredric, swaying on his knees over the armored body of a woman, leaning over her in order to aim up at the dragon with a crossbow that was still strapped around her neck.

The dark sky pealed with mirth as the dragon laughed.

"Stay down, Dragonslayer's Heir. Play dead. There is a real hero now in Kellar. She may yet salvage something of your kingdom if you allow her. But I think not." It gathered its fire to it, as Andira stood amidst the wreckage of the stables. She stared defiantly up at it. Her entire body felt as though it burned. "I think *not*!"

Flame spiraled from the dragon's throat, blasting like a calamity from above.

The joints in Andira's hand cracked and protested as she forced her fingers wide and re-conjured her shield.

It manifested this time high up in the air, and the dragon roared in surprise as his fire erupted into white heat against the barrier mere feet from his gaping jaws. Andira clenched her jaw and moaned, the pain multiplied many times over by the effort of projecting the barrier so far from the source of her power. The shield fizzed and crackled under the onslaught. Streamers of irreplaceable strength squirmed off from it as the dragon bent his inconceivable might and the prodigious well of his fire towards its destruction. She felt it buckle and, through it, herself. She had tasked herself too harshly. The bar of this final challenge had been set too high. Another might have surrendered and seen an end to it. Andira raged on regardless. It was all that she knew to do. Her thoughts had become heat and flame. The walls burned and sparks rained down. Old memories emerged from buried chambers and fled the collapsing halls.

For a moment she remembered.

She knew who she was.

Her mouth shaped a wordless roar as she pushed back.

The dragon's fire broke against a barrier that had become suddenly unassailable. It broke off, bellowing in surprise and fear, and strove to climb beyond her reach.

But too late.

Andira's rune-barrier struck the dragon like a spiked boss of scalding light, driving the dragon's beaten fire before it and through its gaping jaws. The dragon's throat swelled. Smoke spewed in thick plumes from through its clenched teeth and from its nostrils. With a deep roar of pain, its head snapped back and its impossibly gargantuan body listed over in midair. It fell to the ground like a stone that had been bestowed the power of flight and had it taken away, levelling utterly a swathe of the outer bailey and cracking its jaw against the second gatehouse.

Andira turned and sprinted to where it lay.

The dragon lifted its dazed head from the rubble of the inner wall.

Her poleaxe came down.

The dragon jerked, bringing down another dozen yards of wall.

Andira had cut halfway through its neck.

She clambered onto the dragon's shoulder, even as it bucked and writhed beneath her, and swung her poleaxe high above her head. It flashed with the lingering traces of energy and Andira screamed for the searing emptiness it had left inside of her, and brought it down once.

The rune-sharpened blade completed the task at the second attempt.

The dragon's head thumped to the ground and rolled away.

Andira's body was a moment behind it, her memories gone forever.

CHAPTER THIRTY-SEVEN
Fredric
Castle Kellar, North Kell

The castle was ruined. The dust refused to settle. Soldiers stumbled about as though through a fog blown across the Howling Giant Hills on a rising wind from the Ynfernael. They gazed about themselves with numbed expressions and raw eyes as though unable to accept the magnitude of the destruction, or that so titanic a force could be meted out onto Castle Kellar and that they themselves had somehow managed to endure it.

They had won.

The dragon hybrids had broken with the death of their godlike masters, flying back to the forest to carry the bitter memory of Kellar steel to another generation. The Uthuk Y'llan, Fredric had not even seen since the withdrawal from the city, and appeared to have been slain to the last. He was not entirely sure how, but he was assuming the woman with the rune on her hand had something to do with it.

Castle Kellar had stood as it had for two thousand years.

But their triumph had a distinctly hollow feeling.

Fredric felt as though he had been thrown off the edge of a cliff and had, by some miracle, survived. There was a persistent ringing in his ears and the taste of blood in his mouth. He had not yet tried to move. The one time he had considered it he had almost passed out from the pain. Turning from the gargantuan corpse of Archerax the Great, half buried in the ruin of his castle and rinsed in the faint blue glow of the hero's rune, Fredric looked down.

Litiana's nose was broken, her lips torn. Her face was purple with bruising and smeared with blood and ash. Her hair had pulled out of its tight braid and, in many places, from her head altogether. She breathed, but shallowly. The slight rise and fall of her chest brought with it rippling shifts in hue as the metal plates sewn into her brigandine caught and then lost the glinting light. He dared not look at what remained of her legs. He doubted very much that she would ever walk again.

Holding back tears, for the sake of his soldiers, he leant down and brushed her cheek with his own cracked lips.

"The city is safe," he murmured.

He did not know what else to say, but he had been told that a dying person could hear that which was said to them and even in their last moments be comforted by it.

Or perhaps the comfort was for himself.

"The day was won. Archerax the Great is slain. When you are well enough…" Here his voice threatened to break, but he went on. "When you are well enough, we will all take a ship to Alben and spend a season or two in your mother's court. The year, perhaps. The queen would love to meet her granddaughter, I'm told. And I hear that sea air is restorative. By the time we return Kellar will have been rebuilt. I will commission the most expensive landscapist in Lorim and have them dig the sailing lake that you always claimed the city needs. I will call it Lake Anna and it will be the wonder of the east. To hell with Urban and his demands for an army.

"Anna?" He bent towards her again. The faintly mild touch of her breath spread goose bumps across his cheek. He gave her a gentle shake, as if through doing so she might wake. The tears he held back pushed their way through. "Anna?"

He sensed something moving towards him through the murk.

He looked up and sniffed back his tears.

Soldiers in grimed and war-battered armor were gathering around him, emerging from the pall of dust like the wraiths of men slain in battle recalled to their master's side. Their postures were those of weary souls, but there was a certain glow to their faces. They lived when they knew full well they had no right to it. They had survived a battle that children unborn would sing of and they had seen a monarch of the Molten Heath brought low by a hero's hands.

A swordsman in a bent kettle helm, the simple owl device burnt from his breastplate, raised his fist to Fredric in salute.

"Dragonslayer!"

On a sudden rush of pent-up elation and sound, every man and woman still alive within Castle Kellar picked up the chant.

"Dragonslayer! Dragonslayer! Dragonslayer!"

Fredric did not know what to say.

So he said nothing at all.

It did not seem important enough just then to correct them.

PART
FOUR

CHAPTER THIRTY-EIGHT
Trenloe the Strong
The Forest Road, East Kell

The survivors of Hernfar toiled north. They spoke little. There was little to say.

Purple and brown hills, clad in scruffy winter coats of ling and broom, rolled northward, growing progressively older and meaner as they did so, the wind tugging at them with ever greater menace until they appeared to shiver like dogs cast out into the cold.

The road they followed was winding and narrow, for all that it was the main arterial way from Kell's south to its more prosperous north, occasionally paved with stone, but most commonly comprised of packed dirt that sleeting showers had made squelchy and treacherous. On his way into the barony from the west Trenloe had regularly spied sheep grazing on the heathers, smoke curling from some isolated steading, or even, on occasion, the silhouette of a watching rider on a nearby hill. He had seen these things and thought the place desolate. Now even they were gone. Nothing living stirred the landscape besides grass, and that only at the behest of the cold wind from across the Lothan, and he did not know what to think. The ravages of the Uthuk Y'llan had been indiscriminate and total.

Walled hamlets lay like the ruins of some other age. Crofts dotted the hillsides and the near bank of the river, studies in absolute stillness, blemishes on an otherwise pristine land.

After several days of joyless travel trailing the Uthuk army northwards, keeping the steel-gray tendril of the Lothan always to their right, they happened upon a crossroads.

There was only one real road here, Trenloe knew, and it was the Forest Road, skirting forest and river and hill to join one edge of Terrinoth's bleakest frontier to its other. The other trails most likely joined up some of the smaller outposts they had passed. One wriggled up into the hills and swiftly disappeared while the other, it seemed was destined for the forested eyot that sat in a froth of freezing white water about a mile over the Lothan. It looked nearer to the Borderlands' side than it was to Terrinoth's. Its isolation had not spared it. The familiar scarecrow figurines of the Uthuk's sacrificial offerings stood on its banks under the hanging canopies of junipers and rowans. The crossroads itself was strewn with entrails, joined together in tangled knots to please the Uthuk's unholy patrons.

Trenloe's skin squirmed at the trace of Uthuk magic and he scuffed them out with his bare foot.

"I feel I should say something."

S'yarr shrugged. Unlike Trenloe, far broader and taller than the narrow-bodied Uthuk norm, she had managed to find herself some suitable clothing and was garbed now in a stiff leather jerkin with a bloodstain on the breast and a pair of wiry woolen trousers. "Then say something."

Trenloe thought. "I can't think of anything."

The woman shrugged again. "After what you've been through I'm surprised you can still speak at all."

Trenloe shook his head. Yesterday's trauma. Already forgotten. He bore it because he could.

After that they went on. Foot by foot. Yard by yard.

The hills became higher and less rounded, their character aligning ever more with the snowy granite peaks of the Dunwarr that faced them from across the river's channel. The Lothan itself grew louder and more boisterous. It foamed white for long stretches, dissolving into tricky cascades where the rock became too tough even for the river to break down. The road became steeper and more sinuous in order to circumvent the harder country, their path now most commonly flanked by crumbling cliff walls of slate. Trees stalked them over the western slopes. These were not the blackthorns and spindles that had infested the marshes of Hernfar but lindens and whitebeams and oaks, true forest giants, broad-leafed and dark-trunked. No roads at all veered off that way. There was no evidence of habitation of any kind, nor of grazing or even of Uthuk Y'llan. And yet, as far as Trenloe could tell, no one had sought to flee that way. There was an older menace to the woods that urged Trenloe to avoid it, even at the cost of ending up like those poor folk at the crossroads.

When night fell, and with the forest to their west it fell suddenly, they rested, ate a little of what they had and drank. Fresh water, at least, was plentiful in eastern Kell. They slept fitfully, too weary from their travels to keep a watch, the moon chowing through speeding tatters of gray cloud.

Trenloe woke with the dawn, but the others were slow to rouse. They were malnourished and footsore, miserable and cold. As intent as they were on following wherever he led, they would have been falling by the wayside long before then if he had allowed them. And so he had not allowed them. *Look after those folk as are weaker than you,* his father had often told him. Which, Trenloe had learned since then, had meant most folk. Each day, he had set them a slightly slower pace than the day before, but he knew he could not keep that up forever. The road was simply too long, the country too unforgiving of frailty.

"You may have to think about cutting them loose soon," S'yarr murmured.

She, alone amongst the survivors of Hernfar, had some vigor left to spare. The Uthuk Y'llan did not feel the cold. Either that or through some act of resilience they chose to ignore it. And preternaturally thin though they were, they seemed able to cross vast tracts of country with great speed.

"No," said Trenloe.

"It would be for their own good."

"They won't fare any better left here."

"Better to die of hunger and cold than whatever the Uthuk can come up with."

"I can protect them," said Trenloe firmly.

"If you really wanted to protect them then you would have gone south instead of north."

Trenloe frowned. There was a little truth in that. But north was where the danger lay, and so that was where Trenloe had to go as well.

A few hours later however he was laughing at an unexpected stroke of luck. The others looked at him as though the desolation had finally driven him mad as he left them in the road and jumped into the ditch that ran alongside it.

A hay wain lay abandoned in a bramble thicket. The mutilated remains of a dray horse were harnessed between its wooden shafts and jagged sigils had been scratched into its low sides, but the cart itself appeared undamaged. At Trenloe's urging his companions cut away the horse's tack and harness and watched, bewilderment at the Trastan hero's taking of the animal's place between the shafts turning quickly to amazement as he gave a great roar of effort and hauled the heavy wain out of the ditch and back up onto the road. A few of them clapped, and Trenloe laughed aloud, reminded of happier times, as though the hard pumping of his heart was not only feeding his muscles but purging them of some more pernicious foulness.

"You really are a miracle, Trenloe," said S'yarr, as the others climbed onto the back of the wain. "Even a demonic possession can't keep you down."

After that, with Trenloe drawing the eight of them in the cart by hand, they made better time than they had since the first night out of Nordgard Castle when the terror of their ordeal and the zeal of the chase had still been on them. He even sang a little, snatches of the travelling songs that he knew, but Trenloe had never been able to hold a complete set of lyrics in his head, much to Bethan's amused despair, and the verse of one ballad merged easily into the chorus of the next and repeated often. His audience listened in contented bewilderment, watching the landscape drag by, and did not seem to notice.

The strange sense of equanimity with desolation lasted until around midday when they saw their first Uthuk Y'llan north of the Downs.

It was a scattered war party, spread out over the flank of a hill and disappearing over it, lithe warriors all armed with recurved and tasseled bows, clad in spiked harnesses and with long hair worn in topknots that flapped like vipers in the wind and wet. Each one of them walked at the head of a small train, three or four hunched slaves strung out behind them and laden with goods. Trenloe tensed. S'yarr had plundered an Uthuk hookspear, and most of the others were similarly armed with weapons taken from the dead at Nordgard Castle. Trenloe himself was unarmed and unarmored, roughly clad in a few scavenged rags and the dirt, mud, and soot of the forest road.

To his surprise, the Uthuk did not immediately attack. Some

of them even raised their long, bird-thin hands and waved, baring sharp teeth in grins and calling out in their equally sharp language. S'yarr barked something back and their laughter rang across the barren hills.

"What did you say to them?" Trenloe asked.

The Darklander would not meet his eye. Her expression was haunted. "You don't want to know."

After that they passed many more, and closer. They were stragglers and scouts, rearguards and raiders, warbands with their own chieftains and only notional allegiance to the Blood Sister and who trailed the horde out of fear rather than loyalty or for their own opportunities to plunder. As they continued on north the trailing elements of the great Locust Swarm became so numerous that the hills moved with them, as though crawling with ants. Huge and unruly columns of barbarian infantry filled the road, and just as they were nearing the point where it began to bear west, hugging the shape of the forest towards Castle Kellar, the numbers became so great that they were driven from the road altogether.

Trenloe watched the Uthuk march by. It dawned on him. He and his companions were so grimy and haggard, dressed in their enemy's clothing, that the Uthuk Y'llan could not tell the difference. They did not expect to see anything but more Uthuk coming up behind them, so more Uthuk was all they saw.

He drew up the wain on a patch of mossy scrub, set the shafts down and rolled out his sore muscles. He turned his neck to push out the stiffness. The wind cut across him, dry and cold and flavored like stone. S'yarr sprang out of the wagon and came to join him. She planted her spear in the ground.

"You should rest before we go any further," she said.

"I'm just a little stiff in the shoulders. I'm not tired."

The woman nodded. She knew him a little now, enough to

know that he did not know how to lie. She gestured towards the road. "The army split here. The cavalry and their flesh rippers went west. The infantry left the road and went north."

Trenloe looked out over the craggy hills and wind-scraped gravel stretches. The wind pinched tears from his eyes. He was not entirely certain where he was, maps had never held the same fascination for him as they had for Dremmin, but he had the feeling that S'yarr's home of Last Haven had to be directly east of them by now. He looked at her. She was not looking that way. But then, of course, it was not there any more. He wondered if prior warning of its fall might have better prepared the castle at Nordgard for the coming invasion. If only anyone in Terrinoth had cared enough about folk so low, about events so far beyond their eastern frontiers, to even look.

"Were you a tracker, back in the Darklands?" Trenloe asked.

"My father was. He came to Last Haven hunting a bounty, met a half-Uthuk local woman and decided to stay."

"Your mother?"

S'yarr grinned. "No. But that's another story."

"So," said Trenloe. "Do we take the road west? Or do we fall in with the rest of the horde and carry on north?"

"You're asking me?"

Trenloe frowned. He had been making his own decisions for over a week now. It had not become any easier with practice. "North," he said. "If that's the larger force, as it seems to be, then that's where Ne'Krul and the rest of the Uthuk witches will have to be." He thought a bit longer. "And that's the bit we can still catch."

It was a strange thing, to harbor such hatred towards a woman he had never met. Hate was a strong word, and it was one that Trenloe did not lightly ascribe to himself, but he *hated* Blood Sister Ne'Krul. She had been the author of the battle that had resulted in the massacre of his Companions, and who had commanded the destruction of Nordgard Castle and with it the death of his best and oldest friend. Every cruelty he had witnessed on his northward trek in pursuit of her had been afflicted with her blessing. He hated her, and yet despite every real injury that she had done him he was not entirely convinced it was vengeance that drove him now. Perhaps it was his unfamiliarity with the feeling. But he wasn't sure. All he knew was that Ne'Krul needed to be stopped.

"I wanted to thank you," said S'yarr, softly.

"For what?"

"For never asking if you could trust me."

"It never occurred to me."

S'yarr smiled suddenly. "How far away from home are you?"

"A long way."

"What's it like?"

Trenloe thought. "Warmer. Greener. Flatter. Trast is all fields and farmland, from Summersong to Brightvale, up to where the Lorim's Gate Mountains strike up out of the flats. And not a bit like the Dunwarr. The Lorim's Gate are gentle-sloped and clad in trees all the way to their crests."

"It sounds beautiful."

"It is."

"Why aren't you there?"

Trenloe shrugged and bent to pick up the cart. S'yarr took up her spear.

Someone had to be here.

And if not Trenloe the Strong, then who?

CHAPTER THIRTY-NINE
Kurt
The Forest Road, East Kell

The woodland frayed like an old coat, giving out to hill country, gray and still and with a thin tatter of mist at the sleeves even at noon. He knew they called the south the breadbasket of Kell. He'd always assumed it to be a tasteless joke.

Now he'd seen the north.

He looked left, which had to be west, and then right. Nothing in either direction. Just road. It was wide and well paved, with hexagonal stones, a raised curb for passing wagons and a ditch for drainage. Here and there, creeping buttercup and dandelion stalks poked through gaps in the paving. For the most part though it was well laid and well kept. That was a good sign. Had to be.

He turned left again, west, and ran a short way down the road. He stopped when he ran out of breath.

Still nothing.

"This is it," he muttered to himself. "Got to be."

They'd lost Andira's trail almost at once after they'd left the Greyfox's glade, and never got it back. Hamma talked a good fight, but it very soon became obvious that the old knight had no idea at all where the hero had gone and was simply using Kurt for the ride. He still wasn't sure why he hadn't dumped the miserable old man and gone without him, except, maybe, to prove to himself, and to Elben, which of them was the better man. Not that it had yet dawned on the boy that they had a new travelling companion. He slept most of the time, wandering in and out of consciousness, stirring only for increasingly brief and desperate spells to scream that it hurt and to beg Kurt for his mother. He was asleep now. Kurt hated himself for being glad.

"This is the road to Castle Kellar," he said, louder, as if that made him surer. "If we follow it from here then we can still catch up to Andira."

"Damned Andira."

Kurt turned to look back as Hamma slid himself off Listred's back. He managed a few tottering paces before collapsing in an embittered heap on the grassy verge. He lay on his back and didn't move.

"Damned Andira…"

Torn between cajoling the knight back onto the horse one more time or finally leaving him to rot at the last step, Kurt swore and started back.

"You need to get up."

"You need to leave me alone."

"You're going to just lie there and die on a bit of road in Nowhere County, Kell?"

Hamma looked as though he wanted to laugh, but hadn't the strength for it. The wound in his chest was still bubbling air every so often and his breath was rattling. He bared his teeth at the scudding clouds as though he knew something they didn't and was enjoying holding it over the aloof fools in their precious sky. He closed his eyes. "I like it here. Better than the forest. Better than a lot of places I've seen men die in."

"Is that it then? I thought you were tough."

"The toughest you'll ever run into." He opened his eyes, and for a brief moment they shone like steel. "Roth's Vale. The Mistlands. Tanglewood. Sudanya. Anyone else would have given up and died years ago. But not me…" He growled and closed his eyes. "I gave up everything for her, you know. Everything. I gave my lands to the temple of Kellos and my own children disowned me. But I believed in her cause. She was so… righteous. I thought we were going to save the world from the demon king." He coughed, face marred with pain. "Damned Andira. This is what comes of following a hero. Even for a man like me."

"Shut up," said Kurt. "Sarb isn't you. Don't you *dare* try and make me feel pity for you now."

"East," Hamma whispered.

"What?"

The knight's eyes were still closed, but with his hand he was patting the surface of the road. "East. Coming."

Kurt looked up and glanced right. He couldn't see anything. An odd twinkle in the mist perhaps, or a faint murmur on the wind.

"I'm sorry…" Hamma sighed. "About your son."

"You don't *know* he's dead."

The knight made a vague gesture that he didn't elaborate on. "I was… not kind to mine."

"You did what you thought was right at the time."

Hamma smiled. "Damned… Andira…"

He breathed out.

The smile stayed fixed. His eyes stared unblinking at the sky.

Kurt gave the knight a nudge.

He hung his head over the one man in all of Terrinoth he would never have pictured himself grieving for. The Turning put everything on its head, it seemed.

With a sniff he stood and walked quickly back to Elben and Listred. His son was still asleep. He lay forward with his face in the horse's mane, his arms hanging either side of his neck. His son's entire shoulder was black and sweet-smelling. A solitary fly buzzed over it, disturbing Listred even if it did not seem to trouble Elben in the least, the big horse periodically twitching its ears to try to shoo it.

"Elben?" Kurt gave him a gentle shake.

The boy swayed limply, side to side. His skin was soft, cool.

Kurt pulled his hand away.

He blinked, ashamed that he had no tears left for his son. But his heart was empty. It had been raided and ransacked for grief too many times and now, when he wanted it most, there was nothing.

With one hand on Listred's back he glanced west. He could probably still make it to Kellar, but he couldn't see what the point of that would be now. Katrin gone. Elben gone. Sibhard gone. The bow left on the battlefield surely proved that even if he'd found no body, and Hamma, who surely knew better than anyone, had clearly thought so. He didn't know what he could take from Andira Runehand now except the satisfaction of punching her in her heroic mouth. The thought did not enthuse him. He couldn't move himself even that much.

As though dragged by a counterweight, he turned back east.

There was definitely something there now as Hamma had seen. A clear twinkle. More than a murmur.

He drew Hamma's heavy sword.

The old knight was right. Nothing good ever came from chasing off after heroes. And this really was as good a place to die as any.

CHAPTER FORTY
Andira Runehand
Castle Kellur, North Kell

Some scholars believed that when a person slept, their thoughts travelled abroad of their bodies to the Empryean and touched the Sphere of Dreams. Andira did not know if that was true, but she was certain it was not where her mind walked then. Her dreams were of terror and of torment, and for once the pain she felt on waking was less than that she had experienced while asleep. She came to with a groan, her eyelids fluttering, and felt for a weapon that was not there amidst the crumpled bedsheets that lay over her. It felt as though a beast of fire and brass was standing on her hand, grinding its heel into her palm.

A hand touched her shoulder. A voice spoke her name.

"Lady Runehand…"

She looked up.

An old woman stood over her, with the frail elderly look of seafront glass. Her long silvery hair was threaded with a handful of fine jewels, a brocade gown with a high collar drawn up to her chin as though to keep out a chill. Only then did Andira realize that on top of everything else she felt cold. She turned her head against a flat pillow. A sliver of light entered through a tall slit window. The walls were stone, and bare of all but dew. Thyme and rosemary had been tied in bunches and scattered across the floor to ward off sickly odors, though they gave off little smell of their own in the cold, while the door had been thrown open to better air the convalescent chamber. More restorative by far, Andira felt, were the sounds of bustle rattling from the corridor beyond, armored soldiers and servants in the baron's purple livery hurrying to and fro past her door.

"The healers told me you were well enough to be woken," the old woman said.

Andira turned from the door. "You know my name?"

"Your followers told us."

"They live?"

"Some. Many fell in the battle with the Uthuk."

Andira nodded absently. "Their victory will outlive us all."

"Your elven jester survived."

Andira smiled. "I never doubted it. Surviving, I think, is her special gift."

"Then you know who she is?"

"Does that upset you?"

The woman looked uncomfortable. "No. Not really. I don't think you could do anything to upset anyone around here for a while. Rest assured that the Greyfox is being looked after. As for the rest of your following, most of them have been conscripted by General Brant for the rebuilding, but that is a conversation for later. You have been asleep for days. You must be famished. Allow me to summon you some breakfast before taking you to see the baron." She reached for the small bell that sat on the bedside table.

"Days?" said Andira, sitting up painfully. She looked down, into the palm of her hand. The lines of the rune throbbed. Cold and blue. It had never looked so listless, so tired. Not even after her battle with Prutorn. The draconic emblem, the sword and shield that she believed the lines to represent, were only slightly more vivid in her flesh than the bluish threads of the veins that surrounded them. Saving this castle had cost her so much, and in time not least of all. "Take me to the baron now."

"Ordinarily the baron would be supervising the reconstruction efforts, but at this time of the morning he would be–"

"Now. Please."

"Even heroes need to eat."

Andira narrowed her eyes on the woman. "Who are you, exactly?"

The old woman gave a nervous cough. "Forgive my manners. I have been at or by your bedside this whole time and spoken with all your companions so I feel almost as though I know you well. I am Lady Salter. Lady-Chamberlain of Castle Kellar. As the hero of the day, it would be appropriate for you to call me Beren, should you wish to be informal."

Andira dipped her head to indicate that she just might.

"Do you feel strong enough for a walk?"

"I can fight."

Beren shook her head and gave a fragile laugh. "Heroes. You're all the same, whatever the age. You have fought and won enough already to earn yourself the freedom of Kellar thrice over. Even for your half-elf friend. Walking will be perfectly adequate for the time being. However..." She cleared her throat, raised her eyebrows, and nodded diffidently towards Andira's bedsheets. Andira peeled them off and looked down at herself. She was dressed only in her underclothes, a padded arming jacket, and a pair of grimy white socks of Aymhelin silk, unchanged since Frest. She had presumably been removed from her armor while she slept. She owned little else by way of attire.

"I need to see him *now*," she said, and folded her legs defiantly out of the bed.

Beren colored slightly and managed to stammer "Very well," before being ushered out of the door and into the passageway. A surcoated servant swerved smartly to avoid her, as though accustomed to such obstacles appearing suddenly in his path. A pair of chatting maids carrying soiled linens parted in turn to admit him through, curtseying neatly to the lady-chamberlain and her guest, before carrying on with their burdens, and their conversation, further down the corridor. "The castle has become a little… crowded since the rest of the city was destroyed."

"I had heard the baron was generous."

"He is."

Beren gestured down the corridor with a courtly flourish.

Andira strode on.

"Look at them," she said in disbelief, as servants of all ranks and duties buffeted them in both directions. Soldiers stood guard over every door. "They act as though the world has suddenly returned to normal."

"A victory *has* been won here."

"The first sortie has been challenged," Andira corrected her. "That is all that has been done so far. These people should be girding themselves for the nightmare that is going to follow it. Not… laundering linens."

The chamberlain looked ahead and ventured nothing more.

They came to the door a few minutes later.

Heavily armed knights stood to either side of the stout wooden frame. The elaborate plates of their armor had been etched with gold and engraved to appear as though feathered, the pauldrons flared into the wings of yeron in flight. Fluted helmets, lengthened in facsimile of the face of a golden horse, turned to look down the corridor as the two women strode towards them. If they were at all perturbed by Andira's uncourtly attire, their discipline did not allow them to show it, unlike the third sentry at the door who stood so sharply she knocked over the stool she had been sitting on and almost drew the sword from its scabbard. Her mail was overlain by a heavy tabard bearing heraldry marking her as one of the baron's personal heralds. A small trumpet lay in a leather pouch on the opposite hip to her sword.

The chamberlain walked towards the herald, whispered a few quick words in her ear, and then turned back to Andira.

"Is *Lady* your official title, or an honorific?"

Andira shrugged. "I do not know."

Beren regarded her quizzically, then turned to the herald and shrugged too.

The younger woman puffed her cheeks, as though worse things happened in wartime, and pushed open the doors. The Knights of the Yeron bowed their heads as Beren and Andira swept between them.

"The Lady Andira Runehand, Dragonslayer of Kell, and the Lady Chamberlain Beren Salter," the herald announced, dropping to one knee and scraping the floor with an elaborate bow.

The chamber might have been a larger version of the one in which Andira had awoken. It was better furnished, but not greatly so, a small cupboard and a dresser against one wall and a set of tapestries that came as a pair, but the majority of the space was taken by the large four-poster bed and the grave-looking crowd gathered around it.

Baron Fredric she recognized immediately. He looked older than she had imagined. From his benevolent reputation, she had expected something other than the worn-out campaigner in his middle forties who sat despondently in his state robes before her now. The burns to his face had mended a little over the intervening days, the skin peeled and beardless where they had been. A girl of similarly dark complexion sat on the chair beside him. She was dressed in a child's armor, padded felt and bright gold heraldry with purple hose, and a face full of cares that she seemed also to have inherited from her father. This, Andira guessed, was the young heir apparent, Grace, the daughter of Baron Fredric and the Alben princess Litiana Renata.

An older, grayer, harder man sat nearby but not too near. His hair was a frizz of steel gray, a pair of bushy sideburns framing a battered face. He was still in his breastplate. The Owl of Kell had been almost entirely scuffed away. A drawn sword, an uncompromising length of edged metal, sat on the chair between himself and his baron as if reserving it for a better man. General Brant, Andira assumed.

The rest of the crowd had the distracted look of healers with news they did not wish to be the bearers of. Instead, they muttered to one another about light, humors, and beneficial lunar phases, busying themselves with herbal titers or arguing over the opened pages of Loriman or Ghomish treatises on natural medicine.

The baron looked up. His eyes ghosted over Andira's state of partial undress, then appeared to blink it out of mind. "Your followers say you are a healer."

"When the circumstances demand it of me," said Andira.

"My doctors say that Litiana is well, but she will not wake. Furthermore her legs were broken under the dragon's fall and, they warn me, are beyond the power of human medicine to restore." Grace squeezed her father's hand. "If she was never to walk again I would not grieve: I would thank all the gods and commission a temple to Aris here in Castle Kellar that she lived, but… can you do more and heal her, Lady Runehand?"

"I am still weary…" Andira began.

One of the healers, their senior judging by his wispy white beard and supercilious manner, muttered something disparaging about faith healers and charlatans to his apprentice.

"Can you?" Fredric said again.

Something in his desperation softened her heart and she nodded. "I will look."

Fredric rose from his stool, making room, scattering the flock of physics as Andira approached the bedside. She ducked under the lace curtains and sat in the baron's vacated seat. There, she leant over the bed and touched her rune-hand to Litiana's brow. It was cool, not feverish, the rune's faint glow bathing her in a shimmering radiance.

"I can heal her," she said. Fredric let out a sob, but quickly smothered it, making a fist of his hand and covering his mouth with it. He closed his eyes and nodded as if to some inner doubt. "I can," Andira said again, withdrawing her hand. "But I have a favor to ask of you in return."

Fredric's expression hardened. "You would bargain with me for my wife's life?"

"The greater part of the Uthuk Y'llan has ignored Kellar to continue north. You know this, I am sure. It is the only reason we are still alive having this conversation. What have you heard from the south? Has any word at all come to you from those settlements lost to the Uthuk Y'llan?"

Brant shook his head. "We've too few riders. Those we have out are all at work recalling the baron's armies to Kellar, or trying to get word to our neighbors. As you'd imagine, their focus has been on the north."

"I passed through one settlement on my way here. It was a small fort on the forest's north-eastern border, a short ride from the western stretch of the Forest Road."

"It sounds like one of the watch forts," said Fredric. "What of it?"

"I thought them abandoned," Brant muttered.

"It had been claimed by a bandit chief named Beltran," said Andira, "but it does not matter much now. The whole camp was slaughtered and ritually slain. Their pain was captured and *bent* from there to some greater working." She paused a moment, eyes fluttering closed as though it only just escaped her sight. "It is so close to us here I can almost feel it, an agony just outside my reach. This is why the Locust Swarm has moved less swiftly than they might have. And why they have chosen not to assault Kellar directly as yet. You assume that if they have a goal then it is our destruction. Our destruction is simply the means by which their true goal will be achieved."

"Which is what?" said Fredric.

Andira hesitated. "I do not know."

"Get to the point then and tell me what you want from me."

"I am going after the Uthuk Y'llan. I will be going alone if I have to, but you have an army and I could use one. There are many reasons a blood witch might seek to weaken the natural barriers between planes. Few of them are good. This is not some petty coven of dabblers at large in your barony. This is a blood sister of Kaylor Morbis in allegiance with a demon king of the Ynfernael realm. Whatever they are seeking to enact it will be of a magnitude as befits his majesty."

Fredric flung up his hands. "But you don't know what. Can you at least say where?"

Andira glanced towards the slit window and felt a darkness that was barely perceptible at all pass across her eyes. For the first time that she could remember, Baelziffar was not north of her, but east. The realization was almost giddying. She had him. "According to the Greyfox…" A number of the faces around the chamber, Fredric's included, darkened at her casual use of the name, "… the only place that lies in that direction is a ruin called Orrush Khatak."

The mutterings that her naming of the Greyfox had brought fell suddenly quiet.

"The Barrowdales," Beren murmured. "There is nothing there. Unless you count the road. And it goes nowhere, unless to some prehistoric ruin in the far east."

"Or its destination was never part of the mortal plane," said Andira.

Fredric shuddered, his hand questing for his unconscious wife's and squeezing it. "I have been there."

Brant looked at him sharply. "You have?"

"I was very young. My father thought it important. His father had done the same, he told me, as I would have taken Grace one day." The young girl looked up at him. The baron looked for a moment as though he might weep, and he held Litiana's hand more tightly. "The Gate is too huge a thing to have been made. And yet too perfect to have been entirely natural. The stone is the red of blood, and though it was dry to the touch, as stone should be, you could *feel* that blood had once been spilled there. It is not thirty miles from this castle. With a fast horse and no baggage you could be there in an hour. But it felt like another world."

"Or a gateway to it," said Andira, growing excited. "One, perhaps, that knew better than to open."

"I believe her," Brant muttered. "I've fought the Uthuk, on our side of the water and on theirs, and the things she says, they..." He frowned after the right words, then gave a frustrated shrug. "I believe her."

"I believe her too, Father," said Grace.

Fredric frowned. "Then wake Litiana from her bed. Do this for me and you will have your army."

Andira returned her hand to Litiana's forehead and sighed. The yellow light emanating from the rune brightened slightly, but except to those, and Beren Salter by her quiet gasp seemed to be one, who had been schooled in the manipulations of the

Verto Magica it was so subtle an effect as to be invisible. If one were paying very close attention then they might have noticed a sparkle that engulfed the princess' sleeping form and then was gone.

The room was still looking at her expectantly when she pulled her hand back and looked up.

"There," she said. "It is done."

CHAPTER FORTY-ONE
Greyfox
Castle Kellar, North Kell

"So…" The lumpen scar of Kellar granite seated against the wall of the adjoining cell leered through the dividing bars. "So, what did you do?"

Greyfox crossed her arms nonchalantly behind her head and leant against the stone wall. The floor was a filthy mat of straw. A tin pot that was stained yellow and reeking sat in the cell's furthest corner. Thereupon the catalogue of her worldly possessions came to a crashing end. She'd been in worse though. Back in Nordgard or Gwellan, the county sheriff would have had her fingernails out by now. And she would have been sharing that mat. She sighed, looking up at the ceiling. It was true what people said. Baron Fredric really wasn't as bad as she had always believed.

Given everything she had done on the basis of that belief, it wasn't a pleasant realization.

"How long have you got?" she said.

The petty crook bared an unpleasant half-moon of toothy pieces. "Tough girl, eh?"

"I'm not here to make new friends."

"Why not?"

"My imminent hanging probably has something to do with it."
The man chuckled.

Greyfox turned away from him as something in the corridor issued a muffled squeak.

"Rats," said her unwanted companion. "You'll get used to them."

Greyfox saw them, sharp elf eyes piercing the desultory flicker of torchlight that masqueraded as gloom. There was a pair of them at the stair up the guardroom, picking at the crumbs where the gaoler, through clumsiness or cruelty, always managed to lose half of their daily bread. Greyfox listened to their chittering for a while, then mimicked it with a click of her own. The larger of the pair drew back onto its hind legs and turned towards her. It twitched its whiskers. A second later, both of them came scampering towards her cell, squeezed under the bars, and ran up to her outstretched hand to sniff at her fingers. She turned her hand over, the rats arching their backs as she stroked them.

"Nordros freeze my bones…" her fellow prisoner murmured.

Startled, the rats turned tail and scurried away.

"You're one of them spirit-talkers from the north hills, aren't you? What did they say?"

The elf glared at him. "That they pine for something fresher to eat. Preferably human."

Before the crook could answer, a key rattled in its lock and the jail door swung open on ungreased hinges.

The marshal of the watch descended the stair with the tramp of a disciplined man. His boots were bright. His metal breastplate glossed by torchlight. The marshal, and Greyfox knew the type well, took the same pride in his appearance as he took from his service to the baron. His features were hawkish and sharp, the temperamental zeal of a man who enjoyed his work while also wishing it were something grander. No one rose through the ranks of the watch to become marshal without having once dreamed of glory in the baron's colors. The day he had assumed custody of the infamous Greyfox had probably been the sweetest of his long career. *The Bandit Queen of Kell*, he had likely thought, with a shiver of delight, *here in my gaol*. A pair of watchmen followed him down. They were considerably rougher in appearance. Men who dreamed of being street-level bullies and thugs tended to find their niche and stay there. An old man came after them. There was nothing showy about him, just a large man in a coat, but there was something deliberate about his lack of airs that made Greyfox ignore the more ostentatious watch marshal and pay attention.

The rattle of the marshal's truncheon along the cell bars roused the sleeping drunks. "It's your lucky day, you unworthy lot." He gestured back with a sharp crook of the head towards the shaggy old man stood behind him. "This here is no less a personage than General Urban Brant himself." Greyfox could almost see the man's words straightening themselves up and standing to attention. "And he has a baronial pardon for anyone here who'll avail themself in their baron's time of need. Frankly, I'm tempted to have these two here arrest me so I can march with him myself. Don't think too hard though. The baron marches tonight and so his leniency lasts until the moment General Urban walks back out that door. "So…" The marshal looked around. "Who can I interest in a clean slate?"

There was a sudden clamor as three-score rough-voiced crooks and felons waved their hands through the bars and shouted their love for Baron Fredric at once.

Greyfox remained where she was.

She'd rather take her chances with the noose than Andira's demon king. The old general peered from under his bristly eyebrows.

"Is this her?" he said.

"The Greyfox," the marshal answered, proudly.

The garrulous crook in the adjoining cell backed slowly away from the bars, suddenly regretting their association. "You're *the Greyfox*?"

Brant approached her cell.

"What do you say to the baron's offer?"

"I'm thinking it over."

"I'm told you know this country well."

"Who told you?"

"How well do you know the hill roads to the west?"

"I… Wait, did you say *west*?"

"I'm told you can ride. None better."

Her eyes narrowed. "Did Andira put you up to this?"

"Strangely enough the hero hasn't mentioned you once. Your plight must have somehow slipped her mind."

Greyfox blew out her cheeks. "Sounds like her." She looked up. Whatever the general wanted from her, if it meant going west then it was starting to sound a lot better than hanging. "What do you want me to do?"

CHAPTER FORTY-TWO
Kurt
Castle Kellar, North Kell

It had taken a while, but at last Kell was moving. Long, weary columns of soldiers and conscripted refugees snaked out along the Forest Road, marching under the banners of the southern counties. When Kurt had first spied them coming on him from the western road he hadn't believed it. A part of him had refused to accept that another human being could exist in the world. It had taken three of them to subdue him. Kurt barely felt it, armored in his own grief.

They had buried Elben and Hamma by the roadside. As a knight, Hamma had warranted the time and effort of a small headstone, but the two bodies lay close enough together in the ground that Kurt liked to imagine it was Elben's. He did not think the old knight would mind. He had already given everything away but his title, after all.

And then they had marched. And Kurt, for no better reason than momentum, had marched with them.

On the fourth day Kellar rose in the east.

Its town was sticks and mud. It looked like a campfire that had been kicked over and stamped out. Perhaps by one of the giants that were supposed to live in the hills above it. A number of soldiers cried out as the dusty castle came in sight of the road. They obviously cared more for it than Kurt did. It was just another place. One more faraway place. The man marching on his right, a youngster from one of the southern border villages, a place called Trenton if he remembered, pointed up at the castle's promontory and said something.

Kurt grunted, didn't listen.

He wasn't interested.

The man gave up.

"You're as cold as Nordros' stare, Kurt Stavener."

Sabe Constan, lord of Downs County and captain of the south, rode up alongside. His exhausted mount settled gratefully into a walking gait. The captain looked to be about half Kurt's age, late twenties to middle thirties, but his face told a shorter and happier story. Wind and sun hadn't turned his skin to wood. Pain and loss hadn't dulled his eyes, nor pinched his smile. His armor was mud splattered, but lordly, painted in the baronial purple and edged with silver and gold. The heraldic owl stared wide-eyed from the pectoral, the rondel discs, the caparison of his horse, and from the tricolor banneret that snapped from the neck of his upraised lance. If his beard had been permitted to grow overlong, then this too was all a part of his extended adventure into the north.

"You were a real soldier, weren't you?" he said. "Before all this." He gestured vaguely as though *all this* were something too ephemeral to be put into words or for proper soldiers like them to talk over.

Kurt nodded. He hadn't spoken much since his last words over Elben's grave. There wasn't a lot left for a father and widower to need saying.

"I can see it in your face. In the way you walk. I've been thinking about giving you a unit to command when we continue on."

Message riders had been galloping back and forth from Kellar, or what there still was of it, since the early morning. By now, even the dimmest of the horses had to know there was going to be no respite for them before they were marched back into battle. If they were lucky they might have the opportunity to find a latrine and change their socks before new orders and new officers came in.

"Stavener?"

Constan was still there, still waiting on his answer.

Kurt thought it was a terrible idea. He wouldn't want to be in a unit commanded by him. He shrugged.

He didn't even care enough to tell the man "no."

The captain smiled, seeming relieved. "I like you, Stavener. The troops like you. They look at you, cool as Forthyn in winter, and think that maybe the thing they feared isn't so terrifying."

"I'm not scared of the Uthuk," Kurt muttered. "They've already done their worst."

For the first time in his life, he was getting exactly what he wanted. How ironic that it should be a battle. But then what else was there? Elben was in the dirt. Sibhard too. Hamma's last words had brought home the madness of following in the footsteps of heroes. All he wanted now was to punish the invaders that had brought him this pain. Vengeance. It was dirty money, but it was a bill he meant to see the Darklanders pay.

The Shield of Daqan was coming together, and it was turning east.

Even through the cold sheath of mail he wore over his heart, there was some small pride that he felt in that.

Constan threw him a salute. "I'll see if I can't rustle you a set of corporal's epaulettes before we leave Kellar."

He spurred his horse and trotted on ahead.

Kurt shrugged.

He doubted there'd be time to sew them on.

CHAPTER FORTY-THREE
Andira Runehand
Barrowdales, North Kell

Andira had quested over half of Terrinoth, from the disputed county of Roth's Vale, wedged between Carthridge and Rynn and the haunted mistlands of the Thirteenth Barony, to the far south and beyond humanity's borders into the ancient woodland of the Aymhelin. In all those years of travel she had never crossed a land so bleak, so ill-disposed to life in all its forms. The hills were naked and ashamed, brooding in their cold stone. No crofts stood amongst them, no bits of wall, no grazing livestock. There was not even a bird. The only feature that the eons had changed was the sky. It was a bowl, vast and variable in its gray shades, ringing to the hoofbeats of two thousand mounted men-at-arms bearing east along a metaled roadway that had no right to exist at all except by Ynfernael decree.

Each senior knight, and there were hundreds, commanded their own lance of a dozen or so lower ranking knights, squires and armed retainers. The thundering mass of the heavy cavalry shook out a dark haze from the old road, obscuring the proud heraldries and banners of the martial orders and turning the evening prematurely to dusk. Horn blasts sounded out like wolf cries from the hills as the lances signaled their movements to one another. Fredric's own lance company, in which Andira rode along with Kellar's noblest sword captains and heroes, was particularly well provisioned with bards and heralds, and the clamor of trumpets and clarions was all the more cacophonous for it.

It was a certainly a mighty showing. Andira doubted it was all strictly necessary, but if it bolstered one warrior's courage for the battle ahead then the din would have been worth it.

Fredric himself was clad in plainer armor, the baronial harness ruined beyond all hope of recognition, if not eventual repair. He was properly helmeted so as to obscure the burns to his face while the visor was down and a long comb of purple and gold feathers traied it. Andira wondered if he realized that it was Starchaser he rode, or who it was that had ridden the proud gray before him.

All circumstance was running towards its confluence and it was there, at the end of its literal road at Orrush Khatak, where all heroes and their adversaries were being drawn.

It was not just the demons of the Ynfernael that worked their hands in Mennara though they were the most overt. Andira did not know how the gods chose to operate, only that it was for mortal heroes to heed the silent call when it came, and to interpret the paths that had been laid for them as best as they could.

"Two thousand knights," said Fredric, looking everywhere but at Andira Runehand though there was little else to be seen. Broken earth and iron shoes seemed to echo and transform his words. *Not enough,* was what it seemed to say to her. *Your hand has vanquished Archerax the Great, but the might of Baelziffar Demon King shalt undo thee.*

Andira grunted, her eyelids flickering, and swayed in the saddle before firming her thighs around the horse's barrel and gripping the reins tightly. She had never heard the voice before, never communicated directly, but she had spent so long with the demon in her thoughts, and with the awareness of being in his, that she knew his words when he spoke.

"Out of my head, Baelziffar. I will speak to you from the other side of an Ynfernael gate as I close it against you."

"We should have waited for the infantry," Fredric went on, oblivious.

"There is no time," she said, addressing the baron.

"So you say."

"Because it is true."

"What in the name of Kellos' Justice do you expect me to do with two thousand knights against the entirety of the Locust Swarm?"

Naught but anguish and bitterness in death.

Andira shook her head.

"Distract them for me. I will destroy the demon king," she said, with a conviction that would have turned a sword. "All you need to concern yourself with is the Uthuk Y'llan."

Fredric laughed. "Is that all?"

Even if by some means thou couldst best me here I would outlast you, mortal, and bring thy ruin some other day.

"Some other day does not concern me," Andira murmured.

"What?" said Fredric.

"Forgive me I was… thinking aloud."

She raised her hand aloft, adding it to the tumult of banners that flew around the Baron of Kell and his champions. The gritty air turned white around her, like falling snow around a half-shuttered lantern. Her blued armor sparkled like water in its light, her own banner, reclaimed from the battlefields of Castle Kellar by Urban Brant's resourceful pages, snapped from the head of her poleaxe as she thundered over the Barrowdales on Sir Brodun's old horse. Baelziffar would know her in any guise, but now that the moment was at hand she wanted all his servants to *know* who it was that had ridden in answer to the call. Let them see the hero who cast the great demon king back into oblivion and exult in her.

It was almost dark.

A good rider with a fast horse could cover the thirty miles from Castle Kellar to Orrush Khatak in an hour. A fully armored echelon of knights took considerably longer. They were close though. Andira willed them closer.

"The evening grows warm," said Fredric. "Strange. With night falling."

"We are close to the Gate," said Andira.

"I remember." Fredric turned to gaze ahead. There was nothing there yet to see, but with one mailed hand he pointed to a spot in the distance where the sky, that great bowl of gray, was starting to break to red.

The Gate of the Furnace lay before them.

CHAPTER FORTY-FOUR
Ne'krul
Orrush Khatak, North Kell

The heart was still beating in her hands, kicking like a newborn foal and soaked in blood and juices as she bore it from the sacrifice's gutted body towards the pyre. It disappeared in a fizz and a crackle and a hiss of black smoke.

The plume rose in the hot air and Ne'Krul craned her cadaverously thin neck to follow it. The smoke twisted and coiled into a horned shape that loomed over the Orrush Khatak, and Ne'krul shivered in ecstasy under eyes as white as hissing solder, until, too vast to hold its shape any longer, the shadow came apart and returned to the wind.

With Ne'Krul's first offering, the best she had been able to conjure had been a wraith of cloud that looked like nothing at all, and had survived for the breath of a single moment. Now, the bridge between worlds had narrowed to the span of a whispered threat or a cruel thought. The skin of reality that sheathed the Gate trembled like an eardrum, *things* squirming at the other side of the membrane as if to push through.

And the shape had undeniably become that of Baelziffar, demon king lord of the Ynfernael.

His coming spilled into the mortal plane in a thousand ways. The air turned red. Blood ran backwards. Eyes perceived the night in color.

There had never been a moment in which Ne'Krul had been unaware of her ally's presence, not in the hundred years since her first sacrifice in his name, but to the warriors of the Uthuk Y'llan he came in a giddying fury of visions, violence, and spontaneous acts of ritual suicide.

Ne'Krul turned from the fire.

The vale of Orrush Khatak forge had been transformed into a carnival of fire and pain. So great were the hosts of the Uthuk Y'llan that the road itself could not contain them, and warriors picketed themselves on the hillsides in dervish mood and filled the neighboring vales with noise. For twenty miles or more, the Uthuk Y'llan had transformed the hills into things of flesh. Spanning the valley at its midpoint stood an arch of bloodstone, an Ynfernael mineral well known to the wise of the Charg'r but long forgotten to the superstitious and unthinking folk of the west. Too perfect to have been crafted by human beings. Too unholy to have been a product of the yrthwrights' flawed making. The Gate of the Furnace, it was called by its old name. And the first people, wiser to the truth of humanity's origins as creatures of Ynfernael taint, had understood its nature and purpose. In the light of the Blood Coven's pyres, arrayed in an unholy vigil around the foot of the Gate, and the hundred unprompted ritual blazes that dotted the valley walls, the rock appeared to glisten as though wet.

The Ynfernael transmuted all. She could *see* pain, *touch* fear.

Ne'Krul lifted her hand as though submerged to her neck in sludge and beckoned with a long talon slick with blood.

"Another."

The corral of waiting victims cried out in vain for mercy, or for the intercession of gods that were powerless to aid them here or had never existed at all. Their terror was the sharp edge of a knife called Hate that quivered in a grip made of Pain. It was the tool with which she would wedge open the Gate to her ally's realm and, with the strength she had drawn from the ravaging of Kell, cast it wide. The distances between herself and her otherworldly ally had shrunk from incalculable to inconsequential. Black mist seeped from the west face of the Gate without appearing to have originated from the east. The clouds themselves transformed as they passed above the ley line it marked, threading out into long parallel streaks that looked like the gouging of claws tearing through a weakening roof.

The next victim was dragged screaming from the corral. She was a Suru'ithar. A Terrinothi westerling. The same word meant *soft*. The people of Kell thought themselves a hardy breed, toughened by harsh living. The Borderlands would have broken any one of them, and even that was as a paradise next to the Ru Steppes or the bloody hardships of the Charg'r Wastes, the true cradle of the Uthuk Y'llan. It had been there, long ago, wandering under the malign star of the Ynfernael atop Llovar's tower, that Ne'Krul had first heard the summons of Baelziffar on a storm of crimson dust. There had been siblings but she did not remember them. Conflict, hunger, and the claws of demons had taken them all. Her parents though, she remembered. When the storm had spoken and promised her life in exchange for her parents', she had paid it without reserve. The cost in blood had grown steeply since those dimly remembered days, but so too had the rewards. And so she paid. The Suru'ithar could not understand such sacrifice. This was why her corral was filled only with captives taken in war rather than the ambitious, powerful and treacherous who generally provided in such grand rites of mass sacrifice. The fear in those souls, unsteeled by the daily hardship and brutal misery of the wastes, cut that much sharper at the Ynfernael's walls.

She prepared the ritual knife she was carrying with tired strokes while the struggling victim was strapped to the board.

"Great Sister," murmured a svelte blood champion with curved blades of bronze for hands and a ridge of bone for hair who appeared from the crowds like a visitation, there to avert her eyes and lower herself to both knees.

Ne'Krul waited.

The prepared sacrifice beneath her panted, short, shallow, like a rabbit in an eagle's talons, staring at the blood harvester with ill-deserved hope.

"Archerax has failed," said the warrior. "The army of the Suru'ithar comes by the western road."

Ne'Krul bared her wicked fangs. Turning back to the woman, she stuck her knife into her belly. The woman's shriek was long and uplifting. Blood welled up around Ne'Krul's long fingers and spilled over the table's sides. "Good," she said. "The final sacrifice is here early."

CHAPTER FORTY-FIVE
Fredric
Orrush Khatak, North Kell

There was no hope of concealing their approach. The road cut a straight tract between the steep mounds of the Barrowdales, wide enough for four hundred men or for two hundred heavy knights riding abreast at a hard gallop. The entirety of Kell's surviving knighthood, all that could be drawn from the four corners of the barony in the time at hand and spread out in ten gleaming lines.

A mile or two on, the body of the Uthuk Y'llan began. Where it ended, Fredric could not say or guess. It spilled over the surrounding hillsides, vanished down the neck of the valley. Their campfires were like moonlight reflecting off waves at sea. Snatches of frenzied music, the Uthuk having an apparent preference for percussive instruments and shrieking horns, rose above the churn of voice and fury but there was no rhyme or meter to it that Fredric could catch. It was an impossible number, defying comprehensions, and Fredric found it surprisingly easy to avoid dwelling on the insanity of attacking such a host head on. Above them reared the Gate.

It was impossible to look at for too long before one's heart began to beat overfast and one's eyes waver. A shadow and a malice leaked out of it, something that made even the steel-tempered Knights of the Yeron that flanked him turn irritable. What Fredric saw when he looked he could not describe: treachery, grief, a land engulfed, and afterwards he took pains to look anywhere but at the colossal monument they cantered towards. Only the supposed hero, sheathed in the golden halo of her rune-magic, seemed unaffected. Looking at her, however, even for a moment, brought him no ease. The knights were more afraid of her than they were of the Uthuk Y'llan.

Fredric did not know what to think of her.

"I hope when this is over you will tell me the story of how you came by that," he said, over the pound of hooves, refusing still to look her in the eye. "I am no scholar, but I have read something of rune lore. I have never seen a design quite like that one in your hand, nor heard of a rune being written into the body of a living person."

"I dream of it sometimes," said Andira, looking down into her bare palm. "I seldom remember it when I wake, and it comes to me less now than it used too. I do not know what that means, if it means anything at all."

"They must see that we are coming by now," yelled the nearest of the Knights of the Yeron. Her name was Sathe Caldergart. The electors of the Order had recognized her seniority for the purposes of the battle but had yet to ordain her properly as grandmarshal, and thus she retained her old rank of lance marshal and had refused the honor of wielding *Unkindness* even in Kell's dire need. She rode with her visor up, revealing graying hair, a face cleft by a diagonal scar and with one eye covered by a felt patch. The wind practically screamed through her spurs, through the golden wings of her helmet and the elaborate flutes in her armor. "Why don't they react?"

"They are a barbarian horde," Fredric shouted back. "To my eye they are overconfident in their strength. Their focus is on their unholy ritual instead of on the west road."

Fredric felt himself flush with excitement. Here was a chance at real battle. A purer battle. There were no walls to fight over, no civilians to fear for, just two thousand of his best and noblest, and a single charge for death and glory. He allowed himself a grim smile inside his visored helm. If the Uthuk thought themselves triumphant over Kellar then he would be at the forefront of a rude awakening. He would break the Swarm under the lance and hooves of his knights, and all without a single sword in aid from Dhernas or Forthyn or the corsair soldiers of his mother-in-law's island fiefs. He would carry this day, and it would be his name they hailed when next the lords met in Archaut.

"Do not be taken in," Andira warned, reading his thoughts even through the steel of his helm. "Be ruthless, but be cold. Pride and ambition are the domain of the Ynfernael. Hatred feeds it, in thought or in deed, and regardless of righteousness. The Uthuk Y'llan will no doubt feel differently, but to the demon king of the Ynfernael it does not matter who bleeds in the greatest number today."

Dame Caldergart scoffed. "This is not a joust, lady. Would you have us blunt our lances too?"

Andira regarded her coldly. The knight shrank visibly from her light. "I would have you strike with true purpose, strike your lance cleanly through the heart of the Swarm and do not allow yourself to be distracted. However sincerely the Uthuk Y'llan invite you to slaughter. Strike for the witches that command this horde and strike hard, slay them before they can conjure the demon king from his ivory palace in the Ynfernael. Fail in that and this battle will become one that is wholly beyond you."

"I will not fail," said Fredric, as though he had suddenly

become the itinerant knight and she the baroness.

"I will hold you to that."

"You are certain that the summoning of the demon king is their intention?" said Fredric.

"I am," said Andira. "Nothing less than the massacre of a nation would be enough to herald the return of Baelziffar to Mennara."

Again Fredric felt himself grow angry, but it was a purer hate, arising this time from within himself rather than from the ire washing out from the Gate.

The Locust Swarm seemed without number. His knights would deliver an almighty cull, but he had read enough yellowed treatises, and experienced enough battle of his own, to know that a host as great as this one would eventually bog down even the mightiest cavalry and overwhelm them. They needed infantry to secure a position. They needed archers to harry the Uthuk, to hem their flanks, to pin their own cavalry and demon flyers and support the knights' attack. They needed what he had implicitly known he had been lacking since he had looked out from the walls of Castle Kellar and wondered at his barony's normalcy on the eve of war and that was *more time* and *more soldiers*. Andira did not care. She said as much, and Fredric could only admire her bluntness.

They would win this battle now or they would lose it forever.

"We will prevail!" he yelled, as much to bolster his own courage as to inspire his knights.

"My powers will be needed to make us a path to the Gate," said Andira. "For your own good and the good of all, it is on you to be sure that no sword or arrow can strike me down until the queen of the swarm lies broken under the bodies of her sisters."

"For Litiana." He nodded to Sathe Caldergart, who in turn drew her horse closer to Andira's. He drew his sword and held it aloft to ride amidst the streaming banners of Kell. The slow leach of the Ynfernael winked crimson along its golden edge, the natural magicks of the dragons spitting violently in competition from the Rune of Fate beaten into the base of the blade.

"We are the Shield of Daqan!" he roared. "We face the fire and the shadow, emblems bared and proud, daring death to strike us as it may and knowing no fear. We do not ask for more than this. We do not question. We do it because for two thousand years we always have. We are the first people. We have fought off all the monsters of this world and we have won. We will fight them again today because it is not in our blood to lose. We are the Shield of Daqan. We are Kellar!"

His warriors responded in like voice, a triumph of fierce shouts and strident horns. "*Kellar*!" they yelled back "*Dragonslayer!*"

"There is no retreat!" Fredric cried. "I for one will not die an old man in Dhernas."

The knights laughed as they couched their lances. Two thousand of them. It sounded like a forest falling, trampled under a stampede of avenging hooves.

CHAPTER FORTY-SIX
Ne'krul
Orrush Khatak, North Kell

The horsemen of the Suru'ithar rolled over the furthest elements of the horde. It was like watching a demon storm, all sand and metal and furious energy, crashing against the palisades of an oasis town. She witnessed, protected by bargains made and blessings given, while others were mauled and slain and left to rue their life's inadequacies as destiny passed them by wearing skins of metal. The Locust Swarm was sufficiently huge that it could absorb a battle without affecting her unduly, but its screams and convulsions reached even her. She felt every death, tasted every flare of wrath as a bone knife turned on a stool plate, and saw every blossoming of pleasure as a warrior was trampled, run through, or gored. She took equal delight in it all. For every superficial distinction in color and culture between the Suru'ithar and the Uthuk Y'llan, they were all still kin. They were all human, and when they failed, they failed in the same human ways.

Their souls fled and found Ne'Krul in their path.

Her knife drew an endless web of sigils though the sultry air of the murder pyres, capturing those lost flies one by one. Their

terror at their damnation brought an edge to her smile, but she
could not laugh. The long ritual had taken all of her strength.
The energies she had taken from the murder of Kell and held in
trust for this moment were gone. She was weak, as she had never
been before, and would be until the moment that Baelziffar was
able to fully manifest and complete the ritual from his side of the
Ynfernael veil.

"They get too close," she hissed to the warriors still around her.

A bulging prominence was forming in the Kellar line, a fist of
purple and gold, sheathed in a gauntlet of yellowish light that
seared Ne'Krul's eyes to look upon.

Someone amongst the Suru'ithar was remarkably intent.

Turning from the gutted woman on the board beneath her, she
addressed her guardians.

Two-score and four they were in number, the numeral of
Baelziffar. Each was a battle-swollen obscenity and grotesque,
her personal champions and protectors, secured in bondage of
blood and demonic favor. Each one was the victor of a hundred
battles and could themselves have been the warleader of a horde
within her horde had their proclivities for carnage allowed them
to share a field with others. Ne'Krul had never needed them
before, but she had bought their allegiances, held their strength
at its proper number, knowing she would need the protection of
such warriors now.

"Go," she said, stabbing a claw towards Kell's flags where they
struggled to stay afloat on the maelstrom. "And do not hesitate to
kill them swiftly."

The demon-made killers snuffled and growled as they left the
Orrush Khatak, pushing through the lesser warriors that stood
between them and battle. With their departure, Ne'Krul put the
knights of Kellar from her mind.

They would not be a threat to her for much longer.

She smiled ghoulishly.

Dozens of additional warriors strode up to the fires, looking, as the ambitious always would, to fill the positions of honor that the departure of the coven guard to battle had left open to claim.

"*Ne'Krul*," said one, in an accent that the Blood Sister could not place.

The warrior was exceptionally well built and muscular, with a bald head and skin painted entirely in conquered earth and blood. He bore no weapon, appearing to favor his two massive hands as his killing instruments. It spoke of conviction, and Ne'Krul admired that.

"What is it?" she said, the moment before the warrior's fist broke her skull open.

CHAPTER FORTY-SEVEN
Trenloe the Strong
Orrush Khatak, North Kell

The blood witch went down like a peg beaten into soft ground. She collapsed at his feet, her blood splattered over his knuckles. He shook them off as though they were tainted with something unwholesome.

"Easier than I expected."

He looked around. The rest of the Hernfar survivors were falling on the witches that had been attending to Ne'Krul around the larger fire, staving in heads with rocks and bits of wood, or simply throttling them with their bare hands and drawing such satisfaction from the act that Trenloe was almost certain he saw the air under the great arch of stone thicken into the form of a mouth and wobble with laughter. An Uthuk blood warrior of inhuman proportions, an upright snake with vestigial limbs and sharp black teeth, fought off three men with sticks, but as yet the rest of the Uthuk Y'llan did not seem to have realized what was happening. Trenloe had not expected getting close to Ne'Krul to be this straightforward, but if the old fireside tales were anything to go by, then casual violence was hardly uncommon in an Uthuk war camp. Getting out again would no doubt be harder, but Trenloe was not planning that far ahead.

"My gods," S'yarr breathed, coming up behind him and looking down.

Trenloe had been a soldier most of his life. He knew that there came a point where killing could be an act of mercy, and had heard men speak of it often when they had drunk enough to voice their fears for a coming battle. He had never given that kind of mercy himself, and had saved warriors who hours or days before had begged him for it. Now he would have done it without hesitation.

The woman on the torture rack begged him for it with her eyes.

Trenloe clenched and unclenched his hands, but he was not sure what he could do to finish her off that Ne'Krul had not already done.

"What is this?"

"Bloodwitchery," S'yarr spat.

"What for?"

"I'm one quarter Uthuk. I'm not a witch."

"Let's untie her at least."

The Darklander squatted down by the body. With clear reluctance, she felt beneath her. It was impossible even for the bravest to look on such agony and not feel weakened by it. Even a man who claimed to have no fear of death feared pain. How any monster that was capable of feeling pain itself could bear to inflict it on another was beyond Trenloe's comprehension.

After a brief search, S'yarr re-emerged, her hand over her mouth.

"She's not bound."

Trenloe bent to lift her. The weight of the table fought to pull her down and even his strength would not move her. "She must be!"

Ne'Krul rose.

She lifted up off the ground without the use of her arms or her legs, yanked up by the scruff like a scarecrow fallen from its perch and set back aright. Her limbs were crooked, her nose smashed, her head bent back. There was a string of hideous snaps as her bones were brought back into socket.

Her head came last. She glared at him with liquid red eyes, licked blood flecks from black lips with a long pointed tongue and flexed talons that were jointed all wrong. A long drawn-out hiss played out through Trenloe's mind, something frightening in a dark place. A sudden and inexplicable terror made his legs shake and his arms feel weak. His grip on the woman's body slipped.

"*You shouldn't have done that,*" she said in Dremmin's voice.

Trenloe gasped.

"She's a psychosis siren," S'yarr yelled. "Her weapon is fear. Kill her and it will be gone."

With a horrified yell, Trenloe threw a punch at the witch.

She became a blur of shadow, a dark shape whisked from his fist's path like the hem of a duelist's cloak. Ne'Krul whipped up a knife and lashed out. Trenloe blocked it with his forearm, delivered an uppercut that would have stunned a troll but only served to stagger the blood witch before she struck at him again. Trenloe was an expert brawler, a skill he had honed by being altogether too trusting when invited unarmed to parley, but the witch was strong, fast, jointed in no human way, and uncommonly skilled with a knife.

"*Who are you?*" she said using Bethan's voice. The voice came from behind him with an itch of terror and it took all Trenloe had to not turn and assure himself that his fallen Companion was not there.

"You're the first person I've met in Kell who doesn't know?"

The witch's lips stretched into a corpse's grin.

Chuckles echoed around him.

"Have you come to defy me then, hero?" came Dame Ragthorn's voice. "Do you think your strength enough? Was it enough at the ford?"

S'yarr yelled and thrust at the witch's side with her hookspear. Ne'Krul bent aside. Her arm slid along the shaft while at the same time seeming to wrap around it and pull the weapon from the Darklander's grip. The woman cursed as she stumbled back, casting about her for another weapon.

"Get out of here," Trenloe told her.

The Darklander grimaced. "Being a hero now?"

"Gather up the others and run. I'll not see more Companions dead in Kell."

With a reluctant nod S'yarr backed away, then turned on her heels and sprinted the way they had come. Trenloe was relieved to see them go. If his time in Kell had taught him one thing it was that monsters like these were bigger than them.

"You fear me," said Sergeant Marns. "And you fear death."

"It's a fool who's never afraid," said Trenloe.

"Mennara is full of fools."

The witch struck so quickly Trenloe did not see her move. In fact, he would swear forever that she was still there in front of him as her knife slashed across his bicep. He clapped his hand to it and bellowed in pain, then beat his chest, leaving it with a bloody print, and roared. The witch *flowed* across him.

Suddenly, she was behind him.

"*You disappoint me, Trenloe,*" she said, her own paper-dry voice changing, taking on a rustic Trastan accent so broad that even the tenant of the next farm over would have struggled to pick out more than one word from the four. "*You disappoint me.*"

Trenloe scrunched his eyes and clawed at the sides of his bald head. "No!" He whirled, beating the air behind him with his bloodied arm. "Get out, witch!"

"You disappoint me. You didn't save any of them. Not a one. Why didn't you just stay at home?"

With a sob, Trenloe sank to his knees.

He had fought all over the southern baronies. He had faced down evil curses, liberated ancient treasures, fought hand-to-hand with wights who had bedeviled their old lands for hundreds of years, broken goblin raiders, human bandits and Loriman pirates and given most of what he had earned from it away. In that time, despite keeping his base in Artrast, he had returned home infrequently. Because there was one dread he had always harbored through it all and it gnawed at him.

That even now, somehow, standing alone against the ending of the world, it would not be enough.

"No!"

Five long claws closed over his forehead. A knife dug into his throat.

"Mennara is full of fools," Ne'Krul breathed into his ear. "And all of them are afraid of something."

CHAPTER FORTY-EIGHT
Fredric
Orrush Khatak, North Kell

The warrior was seven feet tall. His skin was marble. He did not die like other men. Fredric's sword chipped at him five, six times, before the rune weapon found its mark and clove deep into the Uthuk barbarian's skull. His stone skin cracked as Fredric wrenched the sword loose, lifted it partway high, too tired now to raise the weapon above his shoulder, and adjusted his seat on his horse to strike at the opposite side. The blade hacked into the Uthuk's shoulder. Sand trickled from the wound. The warrior had a flail made of nine severed heads and looped it over his own head to strike. A Knight of the Yeron plunged his lance into his chest and trammeled his body under his hooves. Somewhere in the mayhem a horn sounded an order to rally. Fredric yelled for his warriors to attend. His horse whinnied, trampling over the small heap of bodies and winning him another few feet.

The charge was well and truly stalled. Like a punch into the body of an Ironbound. The battle line had broken into a hundred wedges. Each of them forced their own individual paths through the meat walls of Uthuk Y'llan towards the Gate. Several knights had been dragged to ignominious deaths, buried under a weight of bodies, hacked apart by barbarian glaives. None had yet pushed so far as Fredric and his own lance of knights, or checked so violently.

With a hoarse cry, he drove his sword into the face of a mountain of blubber. He pushed it as far in as the hilt. The obscene chuckled meatily, a new mouth splitting its face across the middle, and began to chew on the blade. It sounded like grinding stones. Fredric almost let go of the heirloom in weariness and horror.

These warriors just would not die.

"Push forwards," Andira called. "Suffer no distractions."

She whirled her poleaxe one-handed, bringing it crashing down between the two heads of a barbarian armored in bone, then turned to Fredric, open palm extended, the crossed-sword mark in the run flashing, and blasted the blubber mountain back into the hordes like a slug struck hard with a hammer.

Fredric nodded his thanks. Without Andira Runehand they would all have been dead already. He did not forget that. Even if it was clear to him, for he had seen how mighty she could be when pushed to it in her contest with Archerax, that she was holding something back.

He did not want to think that the demon king might be something even worse. He feared that if he did, then he would not have the courage to continue at her side.

Hearing again the horn blast, he echoed the hero's urgings and turned in his saddle.

The view to the west lifted his heart.

Sudden exultation from the grip of despair put a fierce grin on his face.

Gold blazed under a crimson sky, followed thereafter by a sea of purple.

Lord-Commander Brant. The infantry had arrived at last.

Fredric watched the infantry battalions spread out to occupy the road, falling in good order out of marching files and forming up neatly into shield walls and lines. Archers assembled behind the rows of spears, and loosed a first volley that scythed through Uthuk warriors armored only in skins and ink. They prepared another. Golems with powerful siege bows bolted to their backs lumbered up to support them.

"The army is here!" Fredric yelled, and his warriors lifted his cry with their own.

With the full strength of Kell's army now taking the field they could withdraw and regroup. The infantry would be the anvil against which Kell's knights could hit the Uthuk Y'llan again and again until their strength broke. It was a textbook approach against a barbarian foe who favored overwhelming numbers and personal valor over battlefield tactics. It had served Fredric's forefathers well in their border conflicts with the Ru. It would work again.

Andira spoke as though reading his thoughts.

"We cannot delay. Do not forget that we have engaged only the smallest fraction of the horde. Give the Swarm time to rouse and they will flank us from the hills and crush us." With her poleaxe streaming banners she turned and pointed. "The Gate is before us. It is there. One more push and it is ours and we can end this, even though it may cost us all our lives."

Fredric lifted his visor from his face. He sought out Sathe Caldergart who was busy dueling with an Uthuk warrior thing so willowy tall he was almost equal in height to the lance marshal on her warhorse. She found the space to nod between exchanges. Fredric's face became stern. For some reason he found that he no longer cared about glory.

He was thinking of all the things that he and Grace had not yet seen and done, about how they never would. He wondered what she would be told of him when she grew up.

If she grew up.

He slammed his visor shut.

CHAPTER FORTY-NINE
Trenloe the Strong
Orrush Khatak, North Kell

The most unexpected thoughts sprang through Trenloe's mind. His father at his milking stool, bent from a hard day. Riding across Hernfar with Dremmin and Marns. The first time he had been taken to Artrast for market and seen the city. The taste of Ragthorn's spiced bread. His small hand in his mother's blonde hair. He could not hold onto them. They ran through his fingers like rainwater. He did not expect it to stop until the knife ran across his throat.

It stopped.

The blood witch released him, her knife scoring a deep descending line into the thick muscles of his neck as she arched back and shrieked. She stumbled, a spear point puncturing her narrow chest, sticky fluids leaking from the wound and down her belly.

S'yarr grinned fiercely. "Did you think I would leave you, Trenloe? After you pulled us, literally *pulled us,* through Kell to get here? Do you think any of us would leave if there was the slimmest chance that this witch might beat you?" She twisted the spear and pushed it down, a combined action not unlike that needed to draw a speared fish up onto a bank and pin it down for clubbing.

Trenloe dropped onto hands and knees, straightening to rub at his cut neck, and grinned weakly back at the Darklander. She laughed, and an arrow shot through her mouth.

She gagged, pawing at the red-feathered shaft, and slowly fell.

Trenloe stared at her, his expression frozen in stunned disbelief.

Not again.

He could not let them all die again.

"You are a failure, Trenloe," Ne'Krul hissed, dragging herself along the ground with the Darklander's spear still half in her. Something that was too far away to be glimpsed and yet intimately near laughed at them both. "That is your great fear come true." She flicked her talons this way and that, drawing the shadows thrown by the sacrificial pyres about her. "One by one they will fall and then you, last, knowing you have failed again."

She dragged herself further back. The shadows broke.

The Uthuk Y'llan came pouring through them.

The first threw himself at Trenloe with a savage howl. Half his face was melted, and the other was frilled and spined like some horrific reptile. Trenloe dismissed him with a backhand so fierce it dislocated the warrior's jaw and snapped his neck. As the warrior went limp to the ground, Trenloe took the next in line by the face, his huge hand swallowing it whole, and lifted her clear off the ground. The Uthuk woman kicked briefly, but could not match his reach, before Trenloe threw her back into the onrushing mob like a weighted net. The first two ranks went down under her. The third leapt over the second, and then Trenloe was amongst them.

Trenloe was a living war machine, a rune golem of flesh and blood, driven by fear. He wielded his fists like hammers capable of splitting stone, and every blow from them broke bones and sent bodies thumping to the ground. He was unstoppable, and yet every glimpse of the greater battle showed him his new Companions falling, overwhelmed by the sheer number of their foe or overpowered by warrior-obscenities three times their size. And so he snapped spear shafts, punched through bucklers, pulled clubs from clawed grips, forging his way like a frenzied bull to where Ne'Krul continued to draw herself back towards the red stone of the arch. Every step and blow redounded across the horizon of the archway and rang like thunder. As though the gods rose to their feet in applause. Bethan the Bard would have thrilled to witness it had she not fallen under a flesh ripper's jaws. He roared, bestial, more Uthuk than Uthuk, as the acclaim of *something* from beyond the gate urged him to greater feats of slaughter in defiance of his fears.

In the opening that he bludgeoned for himself he spied Ne'Krul where she lay on the ground. She was shadow-wreathed, but the shadow had grown so massive that it seemed to stand over her. It resembled the knightly statues that he had seen once in an old Soulstone manor, overrun now by the woodland between the Tanglewood and Sern Genslyn.

This statue however was the starkest, most deathly white. The shadow it had previously inhabited had receded to form depthless pools within the hollow spaces of its eyes and mouth and to confer a mist-like definition to its musculature. Its crown was horned. Its back was winged. Its head was bowed, turned towards Ne'Krul as though in reflection. Its turned back was enough to paralyze Trenloe with terror. His arms fell cold and limp by his sides.

Ne'Krul cackled, clutching at the spear in her chest, and so too did the shadow. Neither was the original. Both seemed to be a copy of the other.

"How mighty you could have been had you allowed Prutorn to

inhabit you. You could have ruled all of the west, sat in Archaut as Baelziffar's regent of all the lands from Thelgrim to Lorim, as I will one day rule the Steppe."

"As a demon's pawn," Trenloe spat.

"As his equal," Ne'Krul replied. "They need allies on this plane as much as we need partners on theirs. It is not too late for you. You think you are a hero to the Suru'ithar? Amongst the Uthuk Y'llan you would be worshipped as a legend only one step removed from godhood, and even that might one day be within your grasp. Forget Prutorn. When Baelziffar's ascension and mine is complete he will no longer need your body to walk in this plane. He will do so freely." She laughed. "As Llovar Rutonu Lokander once did in the depths of the Charg'r, when he first broached the boundaries of the world and raised the Spire of Ruin in monument, so too will I do now in Kell. My name will be forever spoken alongside his. I will live forever, and Llovar's conquest will finally be complete. Kell, and all the lands between it and the Spire, will merge with the Charg'r and become one with the Ynfernael."

Trenloe held his head.

It was difficult to think in the presence of that shadow. Difficult to think.

Difficult to breathe.

He fought to hold onto his last breath, his last thought, struggled to remember what that had been. He tried to tighten his hands into fists but failed to command the fingers to move as one.

"Stop... feeding me lackeys and... fight me."

"Not everyone is as mighty as you are Trenloe the Strong. But then," she bared her bloodied fangs, "I am sure you remember. What kind of hero lets everyone fall but himself? What kind but a hero of the Uthuk Y'llan."

"No!" Trenloe roared. Rage burned behind his eyes, and the

force of his fury seemed to ripple the air beyond the blood witch like a pond struck by a feather. "Fight me!"

"Very well."

The shadow lifted its horned crown. Its wings unfolded from its back. Every movement occurred without sound. Indeed, they drew sound and light from the world as if to fashion them, and all around could do naught but stand mute and watch in silent awe as the demon king made his decree.

"As thou hast granted me my desire, allow me to grant thee thine." The demon king drew a sword the color of the last star's dying light. "I will fight you."

CHAPTER FIFTY
Kurt
Orrush Khatak, North Kell

The battle wasn't nearly so terrible, now it was on him. He'd practiced for it, drilled for it. All those half-remembered dawn exercises out on the flood plains at Bastion Tarn, back when the only thing that had come across the Lothan with impunity had been the fog rolling off the lower Dunwarr. The long marches up the endless tracts of nothing anyone wanted that supposedly marked the border with Forthyn. The endless cycles of unit, battalion, and regimental contests, all of it coming to a grand head in Castle Kellar with the garrison champion competing for honor at the Feast of Roland. It had always seemed like a tremendous time-wasting exercise. It was as though the marshals and baronets and so on had decided that since they had all these soldiers they had really better do something with them all, lest the baron take them all away.

And look how well that had turned out.

He saw it all for what it had really been now. It had been for this.

Most of Kell's men and a good number of its women would have been trained. They might not have worn the baron's colors in one of the big garrisons like Kurt had, but they would have served in one of the local militias, the patchwork of county warbands and ranger outfits that held the darkness at bay. They knew how to hold a spear, shoot a bow, stand in a line. Most would have defended Kell in some small way before today. There was a reason that Kell's army was looked on with admiration and envy by baronies with five times the population and fifty times the wealth and it was here, in the oiled war gear and battered faces of the ten thousand infantrymen in grim array spanning the old road.

No one else took the Darkness as seriously. No one else had to. Because the Kellar did it for them.

"Draw!" Kurt yelled.

Three long lines of bowmen, sixty in all under his command with a good arm's length between each, drew arrows from the quivers set up in front of them and nocked them to their strings. They bent backwards, aimed somewhere between the far end of the vale and the sky, and then pulled them to their ears with an audible creak of stressed yew. He didn't call for them to aim. There was no need. He could have ordered them to turn around and shoot backwards and they would all still hit a Darklander.

"Loose!"

Flax strings thwacked against leather wrist guards, rattling down the line of archers as their volley leapt skywards in a staggered sheet. Kurt watched it arc upwards, over the embattled ranks of mail-clad spearmen and golems, before hissing down over the Uthuk Y'llan as though it was raining snakes.

From what he'd heard of the Charg'r and the Ru, they probably felt right at home.

"Draw!"

And they went again.

Beyond the battle lines, the valley rocked and swelled, like a sea goaded to frothing outrage, the bone whites and bloody purples of the Uthuk surging with great and terrible fury around the chinks of silver and gold where Kell's knights were still struggling valiantly on. *Valor*, Kurt thought, and shook his head. They could keep it. This was where the real work was getting done. There was where the world would get saved, if the gods decided it was worth it. For his own part, Kurt wasn't sure he cared. It wasn't as if he was leaving any great part of it behind. Elben, Sibhard, Katrin, his home: all gone. All he wanted now was to do what he could, to be as stubborn and awkward about bowing out as any proper man of Kell ought to be. He felt almost nothing at all, and a curious sense of empowerment and courage came with that fact. As though he was denying something precious to someone he didn't know and who didn't know him, but who despised him utterly nonetheless.

As he watched, a thin streak of gray burst out of the tide swell of Uthuk Y'llan pressing the Kellar shields. The warrior was long-limbed and demon swift, his back hunched under the towering weight of bone spurs festooned with grisly fetishes and pennons. Kurt tracked the thing as it ran, so inhumanly fast it almost flew over the shield wall, to drop in behind and stab its knives repeatedly into the line-sergeant's neck before the warriors around him could reform and bring the berserker down.

Kurt nocked his arrow to the flatbow he now thought of as being Sarb's and drew it back. He could have put an arrow through the Uthuk's heart from there. Easily. But he wasn't one man looking to hold his hill any more. He was one small part of the Shield of Daqan.

"Loose!"

Another volley arced up, arced down. More Uthuk fell, spitted with arrows, and Kurt was entirely unmoved. Someone, somewhere, trumpeted an order. The spearmen clammed up and ground forward a pace before resetting their wall of shields and asserting a new line about a yard ahead of the old one. *Twist and pull*, he thought. Some things a soldier just didn't have to think about any more. It wasn't enough simply to hold and check the Uthuk there. There were too many of them, and the Barrowdale hills were far from impassable. The Kellar army had to force the question. They had to push. Even in defense.

Just then Constan trotted his horse up through one of the corridors that had been left between the formations, his mail jangling and bright. "We're holding them!" he shouted as he rode past, holding his sword aloft, the flames of Kellos etched in acid along the length of the blade visible for anyone to see. "By the gods, we'll win this thing yet!"

Kurt grunted.

It was still a little early in the day for that, but the troops seemed to like it.

Constan rode on, shouting his message to the front where, by the looks of things, they needed it more.

The archer to his left, to the right-hand edge of the third line, turned to him and grinned. She was about Sibhard's age, with long blonde hair worn in braids and from a farm someplace called Zeiholt, further south and west than he had ever imagined he'd need to care about.

"What?" he said.

She shrugged.

"Draw!" he barked.

This time, as he raised his flatbow to turn his arrow skyward, his eye crossed the horizon of the Gate. Since the army's deployment to the valley, it had been there. A strain through the air under the arch that made his heart beat harder and his palms sweat. Something ready to snap. Just at that moment it gave a sickening ripple. The streak patterns that had been prominent in the clouds came suddenly apart and the air, unseasonably warm until then, more Trastan summer than autumnal Kellar eve, became cold. A *thump* reverberated through the old paved road. Then another. Another. A deeply slow heartbeat.

Or perhaps, Kurt thought, footsteps.

Kurt held his shot and strained his eyes, but he could see nothing.

Just a shadow.

His archers lowered their bows and eased tension from the draw, uneasy, as the newly cold wind blustered though long hair, helmet plumes and Constan's banners, bringing with it the murmur of doomed voices and the coming immediacy of dread.

With one voice, the Uthuk Y'llan gave a shout that chilled Kurt to his spirit. It wasn't the sound of triumph. It was a cry of terror. And there was only one realistic way for them to get out.

Through the army of Kell.

CHAPTER FIFTY-ONE
Andira Runehand
Orrush Khatak, North Kell

She was moments from failure, but she refused to accept it. Not while she was so close. The Uthuk Y'llan issued an almighty roar, fear and rapture equally bright in their fervid eyes and came at the Kellar knights with redoubled savagery. Only the aberrant champions, irredeemably a part of the Ynfernael realm long before this moment, seemed unfazed by the sinking of the mortal plane beneath their feet. They threw back their deformed, maned, spine-frilled heads and exulted, yelling out the name of Baelziffar their immortal sovereign and deity, even as Andira stubbornly went on striking them down.

Andira whirled her poleaxe overhead, once, twice, building up speed, and on the third loop struck the head from the iron-scaled neck of a blade-chipped Uthuk champion, using the momentum that granted to turn Hamma's horse towards the sundered Gate.

"Now!" she roared, hoarse with determination. "We must get through now!"

Fredric turned his head towards her. His face was hidden from her but for the little bit she could see though the grid pattern of small holes in his visor. Even that was enough to share in the nightmare that the baron, and soon enough every mortal soul in eastern Terrinoth, was now living. The Ynfernael had been cast open. Reality had been upended. A demon king walked amongst them and all that had once been unheard of was now so. He said it all with his eyes. Nothing came out of him in words.

"Gather your knights!" she shouted. "Rouse them for one last attempt on the Gate. You have brought them this far in glory, do not allow them fade into damnation now!"

For a moment Andira feared that the horrors of Baelziffar's Ynfernael domain had pushed Fredric too close to the edge, but the appeal to vainglory seemed to reach him. His helm gave the slightest of forward tilts as the baron nodded.

"Yes," he said, his voice coming from someplace very deep, and echoing from him like a cry from the bottom of a well. "One last charge. That is how knights and heroes are meant to perish when it comes time for them to falter."

"See me to the Gate and no further. This is no petty demon like those that Archerax threw against the walls of Castle Kellar. This is a fiend that was never meant to set foot in this world. He is beyond all your swords. Get me to the Gate and leave his destruction to me."

"It will be done, my lady!"

The baron gave a shout, rallying his stricken knights to his voice. A few were too far gone to terror to listen and would not be roused. A great bard with power over hearts and souls might have reached them, but Andira did not have that gift and Fredric, for all his honest charisma, lacked that power. There was nothing to be done but leave them to fate, and prevail with the force they still had.

She raised her hand and raised her voice. Light blazed from her as she tapped the power she had been saving, pain filling her as though she were kindling being devoured by a fire. With a crescendo shout she punched the air in front of her, something far greater than her own fist and made of something more than mere rune magic punching a hole into the hordes of Uthuk Y'llan.

Her horse reared in the magical backwash, a glitter shower of light and color as, with the space to gather a charge, Fredric went. Horns blowing, the last two dozen Knights of the Yeron alive and sane were set thundering after their baron. Regaining control of her panicked steed, Andira shouted in frustration and galloped after them.

Her magic had made the breach. Fredric and his knights were the hammer and wedge that split the whole thing up the center. In their own terror of the colossus they had set loose on Kell, the Uthuk almost let them past.

With Fredric still leading, they burst into a narrow clearing that appeared to shadow the position of the Gate as it crossed the valley and the road. Great bonfires writhed, uncannily man-shaped, reaching with their fingertips towards the demented beckoning of the Ynfernael and screaming as though in anguish. Mortal warriors ran about without any obvious direction or plan. Witches sat on their knees, backs turned, hands raised up to the spasming Gate. Fredric had a free run.

"Knights of Kell!" he roared, spurring his horse into a mad gallop.

The vicinity around the bonfire looked like the scene of a parallel battlefield. Fredric's knights trampled over a field of slain in their determination to assail the Gate and expunge the creeping dread of it from their hearts. A twelve-foot high silhouette stood framed before the Gate's swirling fury. It was a shape without substance, an anathema, defined wholly by what it was not and what it denied. It was entirely white, the hard white of emptiness, of light so bright that it blinds and devours, the screaming void against which nothing could stand.

Baelziffar.

Fredric yelled a challenge. None of the knights had retained their lances through the long battle, and all followed suit brandishing swords and maces and battered shields.

Andira was awed by their foolish courage.

These were highborn men and women. They had been given everything, lives that the vast majority could only dream of, and yet they threw them gladly away for the sake of Kell.

Baelziffar was standing over the stricken body of a huge human man. There was no time to wonder who he was or how he had come to be there, lying beaten at the feet of the demon king. Fredric and his knights descended on him like an avalanche of metal.

Baelziffar did not move. Movement was for lesser beings.

The charge broke over him like a wave against a rock. Bodies went flying. Armored men and horses went over as if they had just charged full pelt into a wall. Sathe Caldergart broke her sword against the demon king's perfect form, screaming as a trio of smoking lines appeared across her cuirass and her body slid apart into four smoldering pieces. Those knights who were still alive and horsed galloped on past, raving about the lifetime of horrors they had just witnessed, and did not look back. If Fredric was amongst the dead or the insane, Andira did not know, and did not know which the baron would have preferred.

Still, Baelziffar did not move.

Andira swung herself from the saddle and dismounted at a canter, skipping several paces across the broken road while Hamma's horse wheeled and bolted. She preferred to fight on foot. She gripped her poleaxe in a defensive posture, holding her runehand up before her like a talismanic shield. She was strangely unafraid and unexcited now that the moment she had been fighting towards for so long was here. She was almost surreally calm, focused on what needed to be done. The rune glowed and spat in the demon king's contesting aura. The pain was incredible and the demon king, for his part, seemed to feel something of it too. A snarl smoked across the pristine façade of his expression.

He did not raise his sword, but it arrived there regardless, en garde.

"*Thou art too late, paramour.*" He was gesturing to the transforming corpses of the blood witch's sacrifices ranked up before the gate. Another blink, another flicker of perception, and then he was not. "*Soon my court entire shall make their way to this world. But I would be remembered as the first.*"

"When Kell sinks wholly into the abyss, then, perhaps, I will concede that it is too late."

"I have taken great pleasure from thy hunt, Runehand. I shall keep thee, after thou art slain."

Even anticipating the onslaught to come, Andira was barely prepared for it.

Blows rained down from nowhere and everywhere, all at once. There was no lead to them, no footwork or body language to read and interpret; the demon king simply moved, like a shadow always ahead of a moving light, and the blows fell. She parried by instinct and a vanishing degree of foresight. She punched with an open hand. The rune smacked into the demon's chest like a thunderclap, and for the first time in their altercation she saw the demon king *move*.

He threw out marble white wings and twisted into shadow. Andira whirled as the demon king was behind her, sword striking the horizontal shaft of her poleaxe like a mountain falling across her guard. The grit and pebbles paving the ancient road exploded up from around her feet, and she reeled back as the debris got into her eyes.

The demon king's strength was colossal. Physically, he was smaller than Archerax had been, but there was far more to Baelziffar than his earthly dimensions. Of the two of them, *of the three of them*, he was assuredly the greatest.

"I am godlike." He moved towards her, every flicker carrying him closer. "I am immortal. By what right does a creature of animal kind spar with me?"

Another flicker.

His sword was upraised.

Another.

It turned point down.

Baelziffar's eyes smoked. His smile was the perfection of darkness. One more movement and she would feel hellmetal as the sword split her body in two. Her quest would be over. A part of her would welcome that, but failure she would rage against until the final breath was dragged out of her. She tried to move out of the way, but her mortal body was just too slow.

Suddenly Fredric was there.

The Rune of Fate that emblazoned his sword had done what its draconic creators had intended for it to do: it had found its moment and its place, even at the cost of its wielder's sanity, and his life.

The sword burst through Baelziffar's stomach, the Rune of Fate burning like a sunrise as the magic of dragonkind warred with that of the Ynfernael. The baron's eyes were alive with nightmares that none but he could share, playing out in mirrored reflection against the black film that seemed to cover his eyes. And yet he struck his blow regardless and struck it hard.

Baelziffar roared. Darkness crystalized within his yawning mouth. Reality broke and fragmented as the demon king writhed.

There were two of him. Then there were three. Four. Five. Six. A
hundred. An infinity. All of them a still-life composition in agony.

Then there was only one.

Andira took her poleaxe two-handed, the rune in her hand
glowing brighter than her fated soul, and struck.

CHAPTER FIFTY-TWO
Kurt
Orrush Khatak, North Kell

The battle was lost. All done but for the sticking folk up on spikes. The captain was dead, and his southern companies were running. Kurt didn't know what had happened to General Brant, but he'd seen a giant centipede thing of the Ynfernael, all hooks and teeth and leaking venom, trample his standard and eat his horse. Somewhere in the mad stampede that had overtaken the Kellar lines the general's clarion still sounded. Long blasts repeated the same panicked cry over and over. Kurt couldn't see the musician or figure out which direction the call was coming from. All directions had become the same. People fought everywhere and over nothing, discipline and cohesion lost, sides done away with. It was every man for himself now, whichever way he turned.

The Shield had been broken. Its pieces were being cast aside.

Way, way above Kurt's head, a second battle was being fought on its most terrible scale. Lightning lashed and stabbed across the sky giving short lives to a thousand shadows around every figure struggling to get clear. Around the vicinity of the Gate it became too harsh even to look upon. People were dying in droves and it didn't matter. To the demi-gods dueling over the blasted Gate it didn't matter a damn. Kurt didn't know what he was supposed to do now but run.

Who would have thought it: Kurt Stavener wanted to live after all.

Wielding Hamma's heavy sword two-handed, his old round shield strapped across his back, Kurt sprinted from the front lines with the fires of hell on his back. A handful of his unit were still with him. The blonde woman who had been stood nearest when the line had crumbled and the Uthuk Y'llan had spilled through. The boy from Trenton. A few others similarly kitted out with arming swords and knives, their bows cast aside with their empty quivers. The rest were dead, mad or fending for themselves somewhere else and doing better than he was probably.

An Uthuk swung her scythe at him. He ducked, ran on, didn't bother to counter. He saw no point in it now. The blade struck into one of his soldiers who gurgled as he went down. Trenton rammed his sword into another Uthuk's side, screamed as he ran into him and fell over. The rest left him behind.

The Uthuk Y'llan were fighting like rats to get out of the valley, no different to the Kellar. Kurt hacked, kicked and bludgeoned his way through a dozen minor, brutally significant skirmishes, before falling on a knot of spearmen clustered together behind a wall of Darklander corpses and an upturned supply wain.

At the last moment Kurt held his blow, his remaining soldiers ploughing into his back and menacing the spearmen with their weapons.

The warriors were liveried in the castle's purple, but the Ynfernael made a mockery of a man's colors. Whether it made him see foes as friends, or friends as foes, Kurt didn't know, the end result was blood on his hands. Kurt pulled his sword up, about to simply give the spears a wide berth and keep on running, when the unit sergeant called out in surprise. Gray eyes very like his own widened in his soot-grimed face, and he pulled off his kettle helmet, revealing pale, almost-clean skin and a prominent widow's peak.

Kurt stopped short. His heart fluttered in his chest, unsure if or how it was supposed to beat. The Ynfernael was not supposed to give these kinds of miracle.

"S- Sarb?"

The boy had changed so much in a short time.

He almost didn't recognize his own son.

The bowmen lowered their weapons and ran past him to merge gratefully with the larger group of spears. Their leader's reaction to his opposite number was permission enough for them.

Sibhard put a grubby hand on Kurt's mailed shoulder. Kurt layered it with his. He didn't know what to say. "You're alive," sounded trite. It was all he had.

"Elben?" Sarb asked.

A tear fell from Kurt's eye. He shook his head.

He squeezed his son's hand. They had a moment only, but a moment was more than he'd been expecting when the Ynfernael had opened its gates. He'd take it.

He doubted there were many men fleeing Orrush Khatak just then with more than they'd taken in.

"Run!" Sarb dragged on his arm, pulling him on as the sky above them exploded and a demon raged, and the day rained red stone.

EPILOGUE

CHAPTER FIFTY-THREE
Greyfox
Barrowdales, North Kell

Greyfox crossed her arms and leant forward over the creaking saddle. The horse was one of Kell's sturdy hill breeds with stocky legs, shaggy coat, a mane like wire and stamina in buckets where it lacked in speed. She had developed a certain fondness for the animal after their wild ride west, evading the flesh ripper packs and hybrid scouts that had plagued the border regions to get word of the Uthuk invasion to Fredric's neighbors. The horse had been borrowed. Looking at what was left of the battlefield she had returned too, she was supposing she got to keep it now.

Silver linings.

Sir Hrothgang Liedner trotted his enormous destrier alongside her and peered out from under the beak of his bascinet helm. The wind pulled vainly at his blonde beard. Greyfox did not know how status was measured within the Marshals of the Citadel, the famed knightly order of Archaut, but Sir Hrothgang was something high within their ranks. His plate was silver and gleaming, blustering with blue ribbons, the golden crown of Daqan bold on every shining surface. Even his mount was dressed in mail, not merely caparisoned but armored after the fashion of its rider. No ordinary horse could have borne such a weight of metal so far across Terrinoth so quickly, and it was no ordinary horse. Ten hands taller than Greyfox's steed and barrel-chested, short hair the color of bronze. It came from the finest stock in all of Terrinoth, descended from the horses of kings bred centuries ago from those reared by the orcs of the Ugluk Badlands. Or so it liked to tell her. Whether it was hardship, burden or supernatural peril, the warhorses of the marshals treated it with equal disdain.

The taskforce that Greyfox and the marshal had hurriedly pulled together from the yeomanry of Pelgate and Dhernas, about six hundred horse and foot in disparate, flapping liveries looked anxiously over the silent hills as their commander crunched on ahead.

"This is only my second visit to Kell," said Sir Hrothgang. "But should there not be some kind of arch structure here?"

Greyfox puffed out her cheeks, at a loss. She did not know what to say apart from what General Brant had told her. There was no Gate, no Furnace, no structure of any kind. Just a rubble wall of red stones that spanned the width of the vale. It was broken only towards the center, by a crater large enough to have swallowed the marshal's entire army, which had been partially filled in with jumbled stone.

She licked her lips nervously.

"We should probably head back to Dhernas," she said. "It looks as though we missed it."

Sir Hrothgang was silent a long while. "It looks as though we missed the beginning."

CHAPTER FIFTY-FOUR
Grace
Frostgate, Forthyn

The young baroness of Kell shivered in the cold. She was wearing armor that was too large for her, and carrying a sword that was too heavy. A thick coat feathered with snow was drawn tight, a fur-trimmed collar so high on her that it pricked the tops of her ears. She looked ridiculous, but she did not want to upset her mother who had suffered enough, or offend their host by refusing his gifts. The coat, the armor, and the sword, had all been gifts from the thane of Frostgate. He had thought highly of her father and been genuinely grieved to learn of his fall to the Uthuk Y'llan. Grace had been moved by it, enough to wear the emblems of his city as she set out. The shield strapped across her slender back was all she carried that was her own, the unblinking Owl of Kell bobbing with her gait, looking back down the snowy road towards the city gate already half buried in the swirling snow.

Grace wondered if she looked any less mercenary than the half hundred fur-wrapped warriors that traipsed ahead of her. Wrapping herself deeper into her coat she watched them march. Her breath steamed as it left her mouth and froze her face. She did not know what she was looking for.

She wished her father had returned from Orrush Khatak. She wished for it every morning and night when her mother insisted she pray to Kellos and Syraskil for the destruction of their enemies.

Thinking of her mother, she turned and looked down.

Grace was taller now, if only slightly, her mother consigned to the pony-drawn limber since the Uthuk Y'llan had forced them to abandon Castle Kellar. And any last hope for her father. Grace had watched the hero, Andira, draw her from her coma, but whatever magic she had wrought had failed to make her walk. Perhaps she had forgotten that part, or had intended to return and complete her healing after the battle. Her mother had added the hero's name to the long list of enemies against whom she planned vengeance, but her father, she knew, would have wanted her to look for the best possibility rather than the worst. It was exhausting, balancing them both in her mind. And it was a long road back to Kellar.

Mother was bundled up in skins and furs so that only her head and one arm were showing, the dirty whites and natural grays so distinct from the flamboyant hues of the Torue Albes. Her dark curls were tousled and knotty, her tanned face pinched, her lips blue, but refusing to bend to the cold and shiver. She was a princess though, whatever her trappings, and was herself dressed in mail and armed.

"Lutetia Dallia had less than this at her back when she set out to humble Lorim and become the first queen of the Torue Albes," she said.

"They are mercenaries," said Grace. "I don't trust any of them."

"Good. You should not. You are a baroness without a barony and surrounded by enemies. There is no one you can trust now but me."

"Not even Graf Thorne?"

"Trust that he would rather have an indebted girl in Castle Kellar than the son or niece of some other rival, but no further than that. Frostgate and Forthyn have problems of their own."

"I think… I think I'm a little scared of them."

Her mother smiled. It was neither reassuring nor kind. There had been little gentleness left in her since the hero had led her husband to war. It was as though something good in her was still asleep, paralyzed like her legs, waiting for the hero's return. It sounded like a story from one of the old myths. "That is good too."

"I just wish we could have waited a little longer."

"For what? For people to forget your claim, or to discover old claims of their own? No. Waiting is what your father would have done, and he was the first baron of Kell to lose Kellar since Penacor times. The time is now, while winter puts ambitions to bed and the coming of the Uthuk Y'llan occupies minds in Archaut."

Grace bit her tongue, her heart urging to stand up for her father's memory, but not wanting to argue with her mother.

It would do no good.

She was hurting. She needed Grace to be strong.

Grace sighed and nodded.

A misfit band of uncouths, sellswords, and motley adventurers, those miscreants too deep in their cups or too imbecilic to have departed Frostgate before winter closed the northern roads, and all led by an eleven year-old girl with nothing to offer but a lot of promises, and a bitter woman from beyond the Kingless Coast.

It did not sound like the opening to a propitious saga, not the ones with the happy endings that her father had always preferred to read.

But she hid it, and looked stern, and obeyed her mother.

She marched south.

To retake Kell.

CHAPTER FIFTY-FIVE
Kurt
Fort Rodric, Pelgate

Most of the refugees from Kell had stopped at Dhernas Keep. They had streamed through its narrow black gates, until the panicked officer at the watch had ordered them shut. After that they had pitched up outside, a new township of rough pavilions and tents spreading out along the broken rock of the Soulstone-era embankment that forcibly abutted the River of Sleep and had once marked the fuller extent of the old city. A hardy, wearier few had gone on. Of them, a fair few had taken the High Pass, never mind the enclosing winter and the warnings of dragon hybrids and undead in the Broken Crags. In the Free City of Forge there'd be sanctuary. And better, there'd be work. A future.

Kurt hadn't believed a word of it, and neither had Sarb. They had always been alike, he realized. Their last months apart had only made them more so. As world-weary and bitter as each other. Kurt was not sure he approved of the change, but he was alive. They were both alive and he would not tempt the gods now by asking any more of them than that.

Only a very few had carried on south and west into the

lowlands. They crossed, unremarked, into the occasionally contested border country sandwiched between Dhernas, Pelgate and Frest, funneled like many an eastern aggressor between the Mountains of Morshan and the Ashen Hills towards the great bastion at Fort Rodric. A world removed from the rich iron mines of the Broken Crags and Forge that landscape was, and many empty miles still ahead to the farmlands of Pelgate's Velvet Plains. It was just bleak grassland and scrub soil, as though Kell had extended its southern toe and added its own familial claim to the disputed border.

Rune-marked obelisks occasionally broke from the Ashen Hill to their right and stood watch, shepherding their westward trudge. Who had built them and who had marked them, no one knew. Dragons. Darklanders. Elves. No one gave it enough thought to care, except to shudder as they passed under their graven warnings.

At the last settlement before their destination, a walled village of a few dozen houses that one of the furtive locals they had passed earlier that day had called Koniston before fleeing into the hills, the path forked.

To the north was the baronial capital, and the mines that were its lifeblood, the village existing there solely to provision them with beef, tallow, and labor in exchange for Forge coin.

The other way went west.

The majority turned wearily at the fork and climbed upwards into the Ashen Hills.

They left just two men behind.

Sibhard stuck his spear into the ground. It had become less a weapon than a walking cane these past weeks on the road. "Is this far enough?" he said, the same question he'd been asking since Castle Kellar.

Kurt shook his head as he watched the others disappear into

the hills. In his bones he knew it would never be far enough. He could not envisage the day when he would be able to stop looking over his shoulder.

"Further west," he said.

"Until when?"

Kurt turned from the north road and looked up. Sibhard stood beside him silently. The inhabitants of Koniston stared sightlessly back from the tall stakes on which they had been impaled. Crows sat idly on their shoulders and cawed. Kurt set his jaw, resting his hand on the hilt of Hamma's sword.

He would not lose hope now.

"Until we run out of west."

CHAPTER FIFTY-SIX
Trenloe the Strong
Wildlands, South Forthyn

The hills of the far north were gray and cold, older and bitterer than those of southern Kell and the Barrowdales, bald-headed and freckled with white snow. Trenloe shivered, the thick muscles of his neck aching from hunching so deeply, and for so long, and drew his shawl of Uthuk rags and old coats in close. Winter was setting in hard. His impromptu shelter was a bit of drystone that must have been a thousand years old. Nobody had built in that forsaken corner of Terrinoth since the heyday of the Elder Kings. Trast had never felt so far away. Hunkering further out of the wind, he poked his fire with a spear. It was burning on splintered shields and scraps of cloth, gusting about in the east wind, hissing and snarling as snowflakes ran in to their deaths.

The woman laid out in the most sheltered corner of the wall moaned and stirred.

Trenloe ladled some broth that was cooking in the pot helmet he had set above the fire and poured some into a mug. He was no great cook, but at least it was hot. He turned towards the woman.

The man crouching over her growled protectively. His hand went straight to the hilt of his sword. There was a dead rune at its base and the metal had been scorched black. The jeweled cross hilt remained relatively unscathed however and bore a crest that Trenloe did not recognize but which was clearly noble. Tufts of beard sprang up like weeds between pale, glossy islands of burnt skin and his eyes roved wildly.

"Easy, said Trenloe, raising a hand, hoping the knight still understood the gesture for peace, and showed him the steaming mug. He gestured towards the injured woman.

The knight seemed to understand.

"Runehand."

His voice was a shiver, coming out on a huff of cloud. He was dressed in fine rags and a knight's armor, but would accept nothing to allay the obvious cold. The woman, the Runehand, seemed to be his only concern.

The knight shifted out of the way, hand hovering warily over his sword as Trenloe edged past him.

Propping the woman's head in the crook of one massive arm, he brought the wooden mug up to her lips. Most of the broth turned to steam or went down her chin, but the heat seemed to scald her more fully awake and the last half mouthful went down her throat.

She opened her eyes.

They were so startlingly blue that Trenloe almost flinched back and dropped her, afraid of what they might see in him. The blood witch Ne'Krul had dredged fears and desires out of him that even he had not consciously known were buried there. The thought of *these* eyes seeing the same or worse appalled him in a way he could not explain.

"It's all right if you're confused," he murmured as she continued to stare. "You were badly hurt when I found you. I thought there was some life still in you, but… I've never seen anyone heal themselves so fast without help. And I'm no healer."

"Then what are you, exactly?" she said, her voice as hard as her eyes, and as warm as the wind outside their little V-shape of wall.

"My name's Trenloe. In some parts they call me Trenloe the–"

"The Strong," she said. "I have heard of you."

He smiled grimly, almost laughing.

"What is it?" she asked.

"Nothing," said Trenloe. "It's not especially funny now I think about it. I suppose you had to be there."

"Be there …" the woman murmured. "Yes, I imagine that you did. I should not be so surprised that I was not the only one that destiny called."

"Since you know my name now, what would you say to sharing yours?"

"Andira. Andira Runehand."

Trenloe glanced towards the knight. His sword had been relaxed and he was now gazing contentedly into the fire, watching the snowflakes burn. "I'm afraid I've not heard of you."

"I have been longer out of Terrinoth than I have been in it. And I have never courted fame." The last sounded almost like a rebuke, and with a creak of filthy, gore-clagged armor, the woman sat herself up straight. Trenloe eased his arm out from behind her, half expecting her to fall back and yet not in the least surprised when she did not. "I suppose I have you to thank for saving my life."

Trenloe nodded to their company's third member. "And him."

Andira turned, regarding the knight with a searching look.

"Who is he?" Trenloe asked.

"I do not know yet. I think that he still has to find that out for himself."

Trenloe was too tired, cold and hungry to work too hard thinking about that. "I'm sure you're owed some thanks for my part too."

"You are modest for a man of renown."

"I'm not the one who killed the demon."

Andira looked down and frowned. "Baelziffar and those like him cannot be wholly destroyed. He will be raging now, plotting vengeance against me, you, him," a nod towards the brooding knight, "and those of his former allies who failed him so terribly. The war is not over. It is certainly not won. But the triumph will be sweet while it lasts."

Trenloe was silent a while, watching the fire dance. He drew himself some broth and slurped it straight from the ladle. It was utterly flavorless. But as he noted earlier, it was hot. "I saw the blood witch, Ne'Krul, slip out across the Gate at the same time as the demon king stepped in through it." He clenched his fist and looked at it. It was bigger than the head of a mace. He had never confronted a challenge that his strength had been unequal to. Until Baelziffar. He… did not know yet exactly how that made him feel. "I owe her. What, exactly, I don't know. But I owe her."

"Then why are you still here?"

"What?"

"Why are you not hunting for her even now?"

"She stepped through the rift. Or however it works. I wouldn't know where to start. And then…" He waved his hand around him. "I couldn't just leave you in the crater at the Gate. You two were the only survivors as far as I could tell, and devoted as he seems to be, he's in no good state to a wounded warrior. As quick as you've healed here with my fire, you'd have died in that valley if I hadn't found you first."

Andira looked down, searching.

Trenloe grinned. He did not know why. "Then I'm glad it was you that took the demon and not me. Never turn from one who's in need, that's what my father always told me."

"And what if there are two, both of them equally in need? What if there are three? A million? How do you begin to help them all without failing most?"

She sounded sincere in her question, as though she genuinely wished for an answer.

Trenloe shrugged. He had learned a thing or two about failure. "The real failure would be if I didn't try."

Andira smiled, and she was just a human woman again while it lasted. "I will go with you, Trenloe the Strong. We both will,' she said, indicating her silent companion. "I have need of a new purpose, and perhaps yours will serve. With my help you can find this Ne'Krul, and perhaps, together, we can frustrate Baelziffar once more."

Trenloe frowned as he considered. He was used to being the hero, the first amongst many, the one whose name was sung, and twice now he'd seen those who'd tried to follow him slain to the last. Perhaps it was about time he tried travelling with an equal. Assuming Andira Runehand was merely an equal.

What might they accomplish together?

But then, he wasn't entirely certain she had been asking his permission.

He offered out his hand. She took it.

His hand swallowed hers. The warm outline of the rune lightly burned his palm. But there was something else in her grip, something deeper than metal that said that one hand would come out worst from a contest of strength between them and it would not be hers.

Trenloe did not squeeze too tightly.

"Where do we start?"

ABOUT THE AUTHOR

DAVID GUYMER is a scientist and writer from England. His work includes many novels in the *New York Times*-bestselling *Warhammer* and *Warhammer 40,000* universes, notably *Headtaker* and *Gotrek & Felix: Slayer*, and the bestselling audio drama *Realmslayer*. He has also contributed to fantastical worlds in video games, tabletop RPGs, and board games.

bobinwood.wixsite.com/thirteenthbell
twitter.com/warlordguymer

DESCENT
JOURNEYS IN THE DARK™

Courageous heroes embark on quests across Terrinoth, exploring dungeon holds, battling monsters, claiming treasure, and preventing the evil overlord from carrying out his vile plot.

Explore the ultimate fantasy world with Fantasy Flight Games.
fantasyflightgames.com

THE EPIC QUEST CONTINUES...

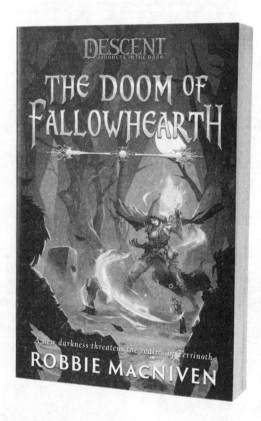

When the daughter of a baroness disappears, three legendary heroes are summoned to search for her. Their quest leads them into the sinister Blind Muir Forest, and between its boughs lurk treachery, a sorcerous ally turned to darkness, and a shocking infestation of giant, murderous monsters...

Venture into a land of duty and warfare, with Legend of the Five Rings

The discovery of a mythical city amid blizzard-swept peaks offers heroes an opportunity to prove their honor, but risks exposing the empire to demonic invasion.

When a charming slacker aristocrat is dragged away from a life of decadence, he discovers a talent for detection, uncovering a murderous web of conspiracies.

In an isolated Dragon Clan settlement beset by monsters who run riot at full moon, two rival clans must join forces to investigate the lethal supernatural mystery.

Defend the World from Eldritch Terrors in Arkham Horror

An international thief of esoteric artifacts stumbles onto a nightmarish cult in 1920s New England in this chilling tale of cosmic dread.

A mad surrealist's art threatens to rip open the fabric of reality, in this twisted tale of eldritch horror and conspiracy.

When a movie director shoots his silent horror masterpiece in eerie Arkham, moving pictures become crawling nightmares.

WORLD EXPANDING FICTION

A brave starship crew is drawn into the schemes of interplanetary powers competing for galactic domination, in this epic space opera from the best-selling strategic boardgame, TWILIGHT IMPERIUM.

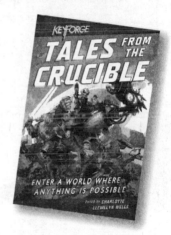

Explore the Crucible – a vast patchwork of countless worlds where anything is possible – from the hit game, KEYFORGE.

Alien detectives stumble across a mystery that could tear apart their patchwork planet, the Crucible, in the first KEYFORGE science fantasy novel.